THE
UNDYING
LEGION

THE
UNDYING
LEGION

Crown & Key
BOOK 2

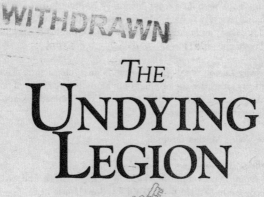

Clay Griffith
and Susan Griffith

DEL REY • NEW YORK

The Undying Legion is a work of fiction. Names, characters, places, and incidents either are the product of imagination or are used fictitiously. Any resemblance to actual persons, living or dead, events, or locales is entirely coincidental.

A Del Rey Mass Market Original

Copyright © 2015 by Penguin Random House LLC
Excerpt from *The Conquering Dark* by Clay Griffith and Susan Griffith copyright © 2015 by Penguin Random House LLC

Published in the United States by Del Rey, an imprint of Random House, a division of Penguin Random House LLC, New York.

DEL REY and the HOUSE colophon are registered trademarks of Penguin Random House LLC.

This book contains an excerpt from the forthcoming book *The Conquering Dark* by Clay Griffith and Susan Griffith. This excerpt has been set for this edition only and may not reflect the final content of the forthcoming edition.

ISBN 978-0-345-54048-5
eBook ISBN 978-0-345-54049-2

Printed in the United States of America

www.delreybooks.com

9 8 7 6 5 4 3 2 1

Del Rey mass market edition: July 2015

To sisters who love you
even when you are no longer
the same person you were.

THE
UNDYING
LEGION

Chapter 1

MALCOLM MACFARLANE LET THE FRIGID LONdon night swallow him. A cold hard rain had begun to fall. His thick, wool coat had soaked up so much water that it felt like he carried an additional load of ammunition on his broad shoulders. He wiped the excess water from his face, brushing it back over his coal-black hair, which was pulled and tied with a strap of leather. Tonight, he would do what he did best. Hunt. He had spent the last few months tracking down the stragglers from Gretta Aldfather's werewolf pack and putting silver bullets in their animal brains.

Malcolm had hunted the wild places of the Highlands and beyond all his life, studying the spoor of monsters until it was his art form. Here in this city, however, he found it was not so easy. The maze of filthy hovels and wash of humanity made such skills almost worthless.

Malcolm liked to believe it was the prospect of information and not the warm glow and promise of a dry place that led him to the soup kitchen in St. Giles. He was surprised to see it open since it was well past midnight. He had made a habit of haunting the poorhouses and soup kitchens because the people of the street heard and saw a great many things. They were the first to know when something was amiss, or a beast was stirring. This place would make the third one this evening. He stepped inside and the frigid cold lifted. Unlike the other hovels that made him despair over the condition of man, this one made him feel safe and contented.

His eyes found, at the far side of the dingy hall, a mouselike woman who was cleaning up after serving late supper to the unfortunates. Her bonneted head and her small hands focused on gathering dirty utensils and used plates. She was dressed in plain clothes and wore small, round spectacles. Her gaze lifted briefly to Malcolm, but then fell quickly toward the pile of dishes in front of her. Next to her were baskets of extra clothing, and odds and ends for those in need. The woman left her place behind the table and snatched a wool scarf from the basket. She held it out to Malcolm as she approached.

"We have finished serving for the evening," she said with a smile, "but I can find a bowl of soup for you if you'll wait."

"No, thank you. I'm not hungry." Malcolm dripped water from his sleeve to the floor. Drops glistened on his dark hair and thick eyelashes. "And I am not in need of your scarf."

"Please." Her voice had the timbre of a frightened rabbit. "I made it myself, and you will have need of it before this night is through. I can't have you falling into an ague from the damp."

He stared at her homely features. "I've seen worse weather in Scotland, and me in nothing but a kilt." She blushed but still she wrapped the soft grey wool around his neck.

She had seemed so unassuming that her sudden boldness took Malcolm aback. He wasn't one to accept charity, but he wouldn't offend the young woman. Perhaps he looked like a bedraggled vagrant after so many nights on the streets. He would give the scarf to someone more in need than he but let the woman think she had helped his poor soul.

"Tell me then, miss, have you seen anything strange about? Anything out of the ordinary?"

"Aside from yourself?" she asked, obviously judging his accent. "You are far from home, I hear."

"Aye, that's for sure." Malcolm let a little extra lonely brogue pepper his words to stir the tender heart of this woman. "But I'm here to do a job. And it would help me if you could say if you've heard talk of unusual events about."

The woman sized up Malcolm and took on a look of sadness that actually disturbed him a bit. She whispered, "I take your appearance as something of a sign then. Because some of the people here have been sorely frightened."

"Tell me."

"Tonight, a man said he saw figures robed in red with a young woman in white."

Malcolm exhaled in disappointment at the story. Clearly not a sign of Gretta's old pack. "Is that some local haint?"

"Not to my knowledge, sir. He seemed quite disturbed by it. If you're here indeed to help, you might look into it."

"Where was this weird visitation?"

"St. George's Bloomsbury, sir." The young woman swallowed hard as if gulping down her terror now that she had spoken it aloud.

"I thank you for your information."

"Bless you, sir."

Malcolm opened the frightened woman's hand and placed coins into her palm. "For the poor."

She grasped Malcolm's arm tightly and the gratitude in her eyes moved the hunter. "The Devil has great power."

"Well I know it. Perhaps after I take a look, I'll return for some of that soup."

She bowed her bonneted head shyly. "It will be waiting when you need it, along with a friendly word."

Malcolm smiled at her, thinking that her face could have been pleasing if not tightened in some permanent grimace of penance. "One can't have too many friends, eh?"

"No."

"Thank you for the scarf." With that, he went back out into the cold, miserable night, where he was more at home.

THE GREAT WHITE BLOCK OF ST. GEORGE'S Bloomsbury looked serene in the misty lamp glow. Malcolm could barely make out the odd, pyramid-like steeple around which the haunting dark shapes of lions and unicorns clambered while King George I looked down disdainfully in his pagan Roman attire. The church squatted between two tall neighboring edifices, enhancing its resemblance to a classical temple.

In its shadow, Malcolm saw two dim figures lurking under the massive colonnades by the south doors. Not too surprising. The spiritual presence of the church called vagrants and the poor to its doors whether they were open or not. But when Malcolm went round the side, he saw three more shapes in the narrow space between the buildings. There was a flare of a cigar end as well as a faint trace of spicy smoke. Malcolm came closer.

These were no vagrants. They were well fed and muscular, all with beefy shoulders and ham-sized fists. Guards of some sort, apparently meant to make sure no one disturbed whatever was happening inside the church.

That wouldn't do. Not werewolves, but suspicious enough for Malcolm to work off a bit of frustration. These men were probably paid off in a local pub for a couple hours' work. There was no need for the use of firearms. Malcolm stepped out of the shadows and strode up to the men. They started, as he was sure he looked like a wraith coming out of the mists in his black garb.

"Waiting for services?" he asked them in a friendly manner.

"None of yer business, Angus," snarled the man with the cigar, noting Malcolm's brogue. He was a big man with square shoulders with a noggin to match. "Best you head back where you come from."

"Nothing interesting happening there." Malcolm looked past him to the side door. "Seems like something interesting here though."

The second man pulled a bludgeon from his ragged wool coat. "Does this make you change your mind? You're no match for all of us."

"You're mistaken," Malcolm answered, flinging back his own black coat to show the twin Lancaster pistols.

"Hellfire!" said the man as he pointed at the weapons with his measly club. "What are you hunting? Lion?"

The big fellow laughed. "All's quiet here, Angus. Just move along."

"Is it?" Malcolm asked. "Or is there something going on inside that church you don't want me to see?"

"Folks need to stay out for a few hours. Why don't you come back at dawn?" A third man drew a thin, wicked blade.

"Step aside." Malcolm had to give them credit. Just the sight of his weapons was usually enough to cow most men, even a werewolf once or twice. These men were obviously paid very well for their bravado.

The two men who were armed came at Malcolm quickly, thinking they would catch him off guard before he could pull his weapon. They were wrong. The pistol rose in a blur and he shot one man, shattering his forearm, and the knife dropped with a scream. Twisting about, Malcolm slammed the gun across the face of the man who had raised his cudgel.

Malcolm rammed his shoulder into the big man's chest. So fast did the Scotsman move that the man could do little more than cry out in surprise. They went down in a tumble and he lost his grip on the pistol. Malcolm rolled away as a meaty fist drove into the ground where his neck would have been. He had to be quick and keep his opponents off balance. The big man was dangerous and needed to be disabled fast. Malcolm made it to his feet first.

Two new arrivals came running, and a red-bearded brute jumped into the fray. His chin lifted as he raised a wooden club. Malcolm swung a fast left jab into the man's jaw. Red Beard's head snapped around and Malcolm planted a right cross on the man's temple. He dropped.

As Malcolm whirled back to the big brute, Red Beard's partner grabbed him around the chest from behind. Malcolm used him as a brace and brought a boot into the brute's midsection. The man fell back with a grunt of pain. Then the Scotsman threw his head back and connected with the nose of the man holding him. Restraining arms dropped and Malcolm spun about with a wild look.

His opponent gave a wicked swipe with a razor, but it

caught in the folds of Malcolm's grey scarf instead of his jugular. Malcolm grabbed the man's arm and shoved his palm under the elbow and pushed up. The arm cracked, and the man flopped to the ground with shrieks of pain.

The big thug, shaking himself like a bear, rose from the ground. He plunged again with fists flailing, and the hunter let him come, slipping under to land a powerful blow of his own. It crushed the man's lips and sent teeth flying. Malcolm's fist darted out again, but this time it merely glanced off as his opponent shifted his head. Malcolm stumbled a step beyond the big man. The brute took advantage of the off-balance Scotsman and landed a hard blow on Malcolm's ribs. It took the breath out of him.

Malcolm ducked just in time to avoid the thug's next bone-crushing blow. He felt the wind as it passed over his head. He also heard the splintering of the wooden planks along the wall. Spinning on his heel, Malcolm locked both his hands together and brought them down onto the big man's unprotected back. The behemoth shuddered and fell to his hands and knees.

Malcolm turned to face the thug with the cudgel, who had gotten up finally. The man came in swinging madly. Malcolm dodged under the first two swings, then stood up quickly, smashing his elbow under the brute's chin. The man's jaw shut hard and his head jerked back. He staggered and allowed Malcolm to deliver a hard right cross. This time the man went down and didn't move.

Malcolm didn't turn around fast enough before the behemoth struck him hard in the side of the face. The sheer impact rattled his bones to the core. Malcolm fell into the dirt, a cloud of dust rising beneath him, his breath going with it. He struggled to stand and got a boot in his face for the effort. The world went black for a second, and when his vision returned, he found him-

self in the grip of the huge man. Iron arms were wrapped
around his chest so tightly that breathing was no longer
a possibility. Malcolm groaned with the agony that spread
across his ribs.

He struggled to shake off the darkness and get his feet
beneath him, but not before the big man whirled around,
slamming the hunter against a wall. His right shoulder
took the brunt of it and his arm erupted in agony. He
didn't have much time. There was a roar in his ears. His
numbing mind tried desperately to find a way out of the
bear hold.

Malcolm pulled a pistol from across his hip. He
couldn't lift the weapon up, but he could point it down.
Praying the leg he was shooting wasn't his, he fired. The
bullet blew through the big man's knee. The scream
that came almost brought a smile to Malcolm's lips except that he was too busy trying to breathe and stay
conscious.

The big man bellowed in agony and dropped Malcolm
to clutch his shattered knee. Slumping to the ground,
the Scotsman rolled to the side, sucking in a great lung-
ful of sweet air. Letting go of his bleeding leg, the man
came unsteadily at Malcolm once more. Malcolm slipped
under a clumsy blow and brought his hand up, and with
the heel of it caught the brute full in the face. Then a
series of strikes forced the man's head side to side. They
were short and quick, flicking in so fast they were just a
blur of movement. The man's big frame shuddered before momentum carried him past Malcolm, thudding to
his knees. He cried out in more agony, clutching his injured leg.

Malcolm's hand brushed across the blood dripping into
his eye. His strength was rapidly running out. Amazingly,
the lame man strained one more time to rise, fear in his
eyes as Malcolm took one step toward him. Using his
bloody left fist like a club now, and putting the weight of

his whole body behind it, he struck the man on the neck below and behind the ear. It made a sickening, dull sound and the big brute's eyes rolled white. He slumped into the dirt with a groan and did not move again.

The sudden relief of victory swept through Malcolm. He stared down at his lame and bloody attackers. Not one of them was conscious. The hunter was straight and deadly and utterly still yet every line of him was eager and alive.

"Done, are ya?" he spat out anyway. "Because I can keep going."

There was no answer so he limped back to the steps and shoved open the door of the church. Inside, a faint glow beckoned from the right. All else was cast into deep shadows. He stepped through the pews and saw, in a ring of light on the floor, a distant shape, as pale as the cold tile it lay upon. Malcolm's jaw tightened. The splayed figure was female. Her chest was a bloody mess. She had been flayed open to expose the organs inside.

Malcolm was too late.

Chapter 2

THE CARRIAGE SLOWED TO THE TUNE OF NEIGH-
ing steeds and the rough call of "whoa." Inside the vehicle, a nattily dressed tall man with dark-set eyes
reclined against the leather interior, his gleaming black
boot propped up on the doorjamb. His wool topcoat
was as dark in color as his raven hair. Simon Archer
stirred from his repose and opened the door, holding
out a hand behind him for Kate Anstruther. Tall and
regal, she accepted the offered hand and exited smartly.
Kate tugged her leather jacket down and strode toward
the church's thick-columned portico with Simon beside
her, his cane clicking sharply on the stone walkway.

They entered the dim interior of the church. Only a
few candles placed around the square nave lit the high
space. In the center of the church, they saw a figure. As
they approached, they realized it wasn't who they expected. A muscled workman wore plain twill and held
his hat respectfully in his hand.

"Good evening, sir. Miss." The sexton bobbed his
head. "Or good morning, I should say. I was told to
expect you by Mr. MacFarlane." He pointed to the east
apse.

Simon and Kate saw that the enclave was thick with a

collection of candles on the floor illuminating the macabre scene of a figure lying spread-eagle. Crimson blood was everywhere, staining everything. A sheet had been draped over the body, but even from a distance, the figure was unmistakably female.

The sexton whispered, "The poor thing was naked as a plucked bird. We covered her out of decency. What with the men about. You being the exception, miss." He nodded at Kate, but it didn't stop him from frowning at her unladylike attire.

"I made sure he left everything else as it was," came a thick Scottish voice from one of the pews. A figure rose in the shadows a few rows ahead. "You made good time."

"Malcolm!" Kate exclaimed. "Good God. What happened to you? Did you stumble on more werewolves?"

Malcolm's face was bruised, with dried blood caking his forehead. His normally tied-back hair was undone in spots. "Just a fracas with some fellows keeping watch outside to prevent me walking in on this deed. I . . . questioned them thoroughly, but they have no idea who paid them, nor what was being done."

Simon peered at Malcolm's forehead. "That looks deep."

"Go have a look at the poor lass. See what you can see."

Simon went to the draped body and drew the cloth back from the victim's face. She was a delicate blonde with near-porcelain features. Blood speckled her young face and there remained a look of odd pleasure still in the curve of her lips.

Simon glanced at Malcolm. "How did you stumble onto this?"

"Just look at her," the Scotsman retorted. "Don't worry about what I do."

Simon took a candle and bent to study the dead body. Kate leaned in close with him.

"Notice the lack of pox scars and the light dusting of powder on her cheeks," Simon said.

Kate noted one of the girl's hands. "And her nails are well cared for."

Simon gave the girl a silent apology before pulling the cloth completely off her naked body. Both he and Kate gave quiet gasps. The victim's chest was cut open. A flap had been sliced around her left breast and the flesh and muscle were peeled back to reveal ribs and organs beneath. Simon swallowed bile at the sight.

Malcolm stood behind them. "Knife wounds."

"Specifics would be nice."

"A bloody big knife," came the terse response.

"Better."

"Serrated knife," Malcolm added. "About twelve inches long. Four strikes encircling the heart."

Simon scowled. "My human anatomy is not strong. That is the heart, yes?"

"Yes." Malcolm pushed between Simon and Kate, pointing down at the girl's exposed insides. "Have a close look."

Simon gave the Scotsman a sour glance and leaned closer to the discolored heart. He saw what appeared to be dark marks on the mottled surface of the organ. "What is that? A burn?"

"Aye. Symbols have been branded onto her heart."

"I don't know that I would've even noticed that," Kate said. "How can you see it?"

"I've butchered plenty of animals," Malcolm replied. "And I've seen bodies butchered by animals."

"Can you draw what you see?" Simon offered a small pocket book along with a stub of a pencil that he always carried. The Scotsman knelt over the girl and began to draw. After a moment, he tossed the pad back to Simon, who studied the page along with Kate.

"Looks like Egyptian hieroglyphs," Kate said.

"Agreed," Simon replied. "Nothing I know. But I bow to your language skills."

Kate shook her head. "I can't make sense of it."

The sexton called out from the entrance. "Begging your pardon, but I'll need to summon the police now. If someone comes and finds you here, and I've not summoned a constable, it could mean my head."

"Go talk to him," Simon said to Malcolm. "Buy us another few minutes of solitude."

The Scotsman went toward the door, jingling coins in his pocket.

Kate turned away from the body. "Let's have a look around while we have time."

Kate and Simon, with candles in hand, began to comb the premises for anything odd. The church was in good order; certainly no sign of a struggle of any sort. No overturned chairs or broken objects. There was nothing unusual in the church at all except the mutilated body.

"Simon!" Kate's voice called out finally.

Simon spotted her in the northern end of the building, crouched on the floor by the altar. He walked across the church with his steps ringing in the silence. Her fingers were tracing something on the stone flooring. He looked past her long, curling, auburn hair to what she studied.

A word carved into the stone.

"What is this?" Kate asked.

"I don't know. I'm not familiar with that word either."

"*Luvah,*" Kate whispered, only to feel Simon squeeze her shoulder hard.

"Don't," he warned gently. "It's always best not to say strange words aloud. Speaking names gives them power."

"Right," Kate said. "Sorry, but this is probably the name of one of the mason's dogs."

"Perhaps. Still. Let's have a look at the other apses."

Kate went toward the west side and Simon returned to the murdered woman. He made his way around her and knelt. He felt a slight jolt of excitement to see a word carved in the stone floor. *Tharmas*.

Kate shouted from across the church, "There is one here!"

They met in the center and she wrote *Urizon* in the pocket book. Then they walked quickly to the door where Malcolm stood chatting with the sexton. The men were surprised to see the couple drop to their knees and begin to scour the floor.

"Here," Kate cried. "A fourth word."

Urthona.

"Yes, miss," the sexton said. "Those words have always been here. There are all sorts of odd words and symbols about. We prefer not to talk about it in case it has something to do with the black arts. Wouldn't do in a house of God."

"Why do you think there might be dark arts involved?" Simon asked.

"Hawksmoor, sir," the man replied cautiously. "The architect who built the church last century. He was always rumored to dabble in such things."

Simon and Kate exchanged glances, and she said with excited realization, "Of course. This is one of Nicholas Hawksmoor's churches. I'm so stupid. I should've known by the design. He was a master of sacred geometry."

The sexton looked disturbed. "That's the very thing we'd like to keep quiet. Pagan symbols and the like don't play well when you're asking the parish to contribute to the building fund. Naturally, we don't like to dwell on the elements that don't seem strictly Church of England, if you understand." He pointed toward the center of the ceiling. "Such as those strange marks up there that no one has ever figured out."

Simon turned but the center archway was lost in darkness. "What marks?"

"It's sort of a . . . line with a . . . cross. Here, let me see that." He reached for Simon's pad and pencil. He flipped it open and said, "Oh. You already saw it then, sir."

"What do you mean?"

"You drew it right here." The sexton held up the pad to the page with Malcolm's symbol from the dead girl's heart.

Malcolm looked into the dark rafters. "Those marks are on the archway above?"

"Oh, yes, sir. No one knows what they mean." The sexton handed the pad back to Simon. "But who knows what anything means when it comes down to it."

"Wise words." Simon slipped the pocket book into his coat. "One last thing, sir, then you may summon the police and let them do their duty for this poor woman." He walked back to the center of the church and knelt on the floor. He removed a piece of chalk from his pocket and began to write on the floor.

"What's he about?" Malcolm asked Kate.

"I'm not sure. I can't always tell what a scribe is doing."

Simon wrote a series of runes on the floor, then placed his hand over them and whispered. The runes glowed green. Simon stood and stared around looking for something. "Kate, would you join me?"

They walked together back to the east apse where the covered body lay. A faint green glow came from under the murdered woman. Simon dropped to one knee and slowly rolled the bloody form onto her side. Kate looked over his shoulder at a strange aura on the paving stone under the dead woman.

"What is it?" she asked.

"It is a scribe's mark. Every scribe has a unique rune to mark his spells. I have one as well."

"Do you recognize that mark?"

"Yes." Simon took a deep shuddering breath. "Byron Pendragon."

Kate gave a slight gasp. "The founder of the Order of the Oak?"

"One of the founders, yes, of that ancient guild of magicians. He was the greatest scribe in history, and my father's mentor. He's been dead nearly forty years now, but he clearly inscribed this church with a spell of some sort."

"Any idea what it could be?"

"No." Simon raised a nervous eyebrow at her and gently lowered the woman's body to the floor. He strode back to the center of the church where he scuffed his chalk runes with his boot, and then returned to the sexton. "Sir, I thank you for your generosity toward us, and your kindness to her." He handed the man a gold sovereign.

"Thank you, sir. I've got a terrible feeling this killing has some horrible devilish purpose, sir. It must be black magic, sir."

Simon nodded thoughtfully.

The sexton looked frightened. "Don't you wish to contradict me, sir?"

"By no means. Good morning to you." He led Kate and Malcolm out into the cold night where the carriage waited. Simon slid into the seat. "Horrifying ritual. Can't fathom a meaning though."

Malcolm stared at the pensive Simon. "Maybe there is none. It could be the work of a lunatic. Maybe you see magic where others don't."

"That murder was certainly the work of a disturbed mind. I don't want to trouble the police in their mission, but we will offer consultation. I'll make contact with my friend Sir Henry Clatterburgh at the Home Office."

The driver snapped the reins on the backs of the mounts and they were away as Kate said, "There were no ligature marks on the body, nor signs of a struggle. From the amount of blood, the killing obviously took place there."

"Drugged perhaps?" offered Simon.

Kate held up a small vial filled with blood. "I'll find out."

"I'm not as much concerned with the *how* as I am the *why*." Simon stirred from his contemplative pose and looked at Kate. "Didn't Hawksmoor design several churches around London?"

"Yes. Five or six. I'm not sure." Kate then posed the question, "If the killing is ritualistic, why not use the altar?"

"Who can say with occultists?" was Malcolm's response. "They're all a bit insane, aren't they?"

Simon offered the Scotsman a withering glance.

Kate took Simon's pad and pencil and wrote a few lines. "The names on the floor are peculiar. I'm shocked I don't recognize them at all."

"Let's have a look." Malcolm took the pad and regarded it curiously. Then he laughed and tossed it back. "Sorry, lass, you're on a wild-goose chase with those."

"What do you mean?" Kate exclaimed. "You recognize them?"

"I do."

"Well, who are they?" Simon urged.

"Don't get your cravat all bunched. They're the mad ravings of a lunatic poet."

"A poet?" Simon said.

"William Blake, ecstatic and rambler. Those names are from his works."

"How uncommonly fascinating"—Simon reclined and tapped his lips thoughtfully—"that you know something of poetry."

"Do you care to know what I know? Or would you rather be smug?"

"A difficult choice, but go ahead."

"These names are Blake's four *Zoas*. That's some sort of bloody spirit. In his unintelligible mythology, the great giant Albion, a first man of sorts, was rendered into these four elements in the ancient past."

"I see." Simon regarded the Scotsman with interest. "And then what?"

"And then nothing. Then the world happened as it did."

Kate asked, "Is this part of the legend that has the giants ruling Britain before Brutus and the Trojans arrived?"

Malcolm answered, "It's hard to say. Sometimes Albion seems more like Adam, sometimes like Jesus. Blake was prone to visions and he conjured an entire foundation myth for Britain that lacked the one thing a good mythology needs—coherence."

Simon said, "I've never heard these names before, so if he took them from some existing mythos or occult tradition, then it must be a very obscure one."

"They are from no existing tradition," the Scotsman scoffed. "He probably saw the names on the floor of that church, promptly forgot about it, then had some fit where he thought angels spoke the names to him."

"We need to know which poem in particular contains those—"

"*Jerusalem*," Malcolm stated. "*The Four Zoas*. And perhaps *Milton*."

Simon's lips twitched at the corners. "You seem very well versed on this matter."

"Why does it surprise you that I can read?"

"It doesn't. I just never took you for a poetry lover. Do you prefer the romances, or are the darker epics your cup of tea?"

Malcolm stifled a growl.

"I think it's splendid," Kate told the Scotsman with a warm smile. "The warrior poet."

Simon tried not to notice her enthusiasm and instead focused on Malcolm. "I had no idea, my good man. Do you write a bit of verse too?"

Malcolm angrily reached for the door of the carriage, but Kate seized his arm.

"Don't, Malcolm. We need to learn more about Blake and these four Zoas. Won't you return to Hartley Hall with us?"

The Scotsman narrowed his eyes at Simon. "Then you're going to pursue this matter as well? It isn't enough what you have dished out for us already?"

Simon shrugged helplessly. "Duty calls when it calls."

Malcolm exhaled and shook his head. He settled back against the side of the carriage. "You don't mind if I sleep on the ride back?"

"Not at all." Kate pulled out a coach blanket and draped it over the Scotsman. He must've been exhausted because he didn't even object to the mothering act. "By the way, there's been a development at Hartley Hall just in the last day or two."

Malcolm slitted one eye open in underplayed alarm.

"Do you remember that young werewolf who helped us at Bedlam? Charlotte?"

He merely waited in silence, continuing to stare at Kate.

"Well, she showed up at Hartley Hall," she said, "thinking she could find wulfsyl there."

Malcolm gave a savage smirk. "And you killed it?"

Kate tilted her head. "No. Actually we gave her a room and some warm milk laced with laudanum." She smiled and tightened the blanket around his shoulders with a hard dig of her hand. "There we are, all snug now."

Simon looked at Malcolm's eyes, which were wide with shock. "Enjoy your nap. We'll wake you when we arrive. I'm sure she'd like to meet you."

Chapter 3

CHARLOTTE SAT IN THE CENTER OF THE SIMPLE bed. She was a girl of around thirteen years old. Kate had provided her with one of Imogen's older dresses, a pretty frock with pastel flowers of pink and yellow, with only the barest hint of lace at the cuffs. Charlotte's left knee was up against her chest while her right leg was tucked beneath her, nearly hiding the blood-stained bandages that covered her leg. Around the young girl's slender left ankle was a heavy steel cuff linked to an iron chain bolted to the stone wall. Charlotte's blue eyes were wide and fearful. They darted between the imposing forms of Simon, who checked the heavy bracket in the wall to make sure the mortar around it was solid, and Malcolm, who leaned against the wall near the door, lost in shadow. Then the girl locked on Kate, who approached fearlessly with a tray of bandages.

Kate set the tray on a small table by the bedside. "My, you're a mess. Just look at your hair."

The child's hands pulled at the knotted, honey-shaded strands with embarrassment. "I lost my hairbrush." Her voice was a delicate thing, a pleasing sound with a hint of melody.

"Good thing I have an extra." Kate produced an ivory-handled brush from under a cloth on the tray.

"Are you going to kill me?" Charlotte asked with disturbing simplicity.

"Heavens no!" Kate gasped at such a question coming from the frightened child.

The girl's gaze slipped accusingly to Malcolm.

"Oh, don't mind him. He's just surly." Kate's voice was reassuring.

The girl's fingers touched the fine handle of the brush. "Are you going to help me?"

"We're going to try, but first, I want to look at that burn on your leg. May I see it?"

"It will hurt, won't it?" Charlotte slowly dragged her right leg out from under her with a small grunt of pain. A red gash showed along the calf and the skin was now yellowish purple and swollen, but it was no longer burned black. "It feels better." Though she cried out when Kate touched it.

Kate kept an eye fixed on Charlotte as she soothed. "It's a sight, all right. You're lucky. You grazed a magical ward. If you had caught it full on, it would've been much worse for you. The wound is healing. From the swelling, I gather it hurts a great deal now, but I expect you'll be running around in no time. You just need a few days' rest." With Simon's silent help, Kate cleaned and bandaged the leg.

Charlotte gave an occasional gasp and fought back sniffles. "I don't mean to hurt anyone. I just don't know where else to go."

"I'm glad you came to us," Kate assured the child.

The child shuddered and reached out desperately to Kate, her fingers digging so deep into her muscle that she grimaced. "I need wulfsyl."

"Get it from your master," snarled Malcolm.

Kate was admirably calm despite the girl's painful grip. "Why come to us, Charlotte?"

"You . . . you poisoned the wulfsyl at Bedlam. Dr. White said only an alchemist could do what you did. Do you have any wulfsyl?" There was desperate hope in the girl's voice.

"I'm afraid not at the moment." When Charlotte's face fell into despair, Kate patted her arm. "Not to worry, child. We'll get some. I don't suppose you know how to make it?"

Charlotte shook her head, a tremor in her voice. "Don't you?"

"Of course she does," Simon confided with a wink. "Miss Anstruther is wonderfully clever."

Charlotte's head turned to Simon and she slowly returned his warm smile.

"He's quite the charmer," Kate told Charlotte in a light whisper.

"He is also very handsome," the youngster admitted in kind.

"That's the laudanum talking I'm sure," muttered Malcolm from the back.

Charlotte once again became apprehensive, trying not to look toward the dark shadow against the wall. "I'll be good, I promise. I'll try as hard as I can not to change. I'm not a bad girl."

Kate took Charlotte's small hand in hers. "We know you'll be good."

Malcolm stepped into the candlelight and stared hard at Charlotte. "How did you avoid me in London? How many of you are left?"

The girl shrank back, almost burying herself in the blanket.

Simon said, "Easy, Malcolm. She did help us by attacking her own kind at Bedlam."

"Yes, and they should've killed it for what it did," Malcolm replied.

Charlotte whimpered and caught her trembling lower lip in her teeth. "There weren't many of us left, and we ran away from Bedlam when Gretta and Dr. White disappeared. We didn't have a leader and we didn't have wulfsyl. We were afraid."

Kate eased herself down onto the edge of the bed and held the girl. "Give her a chance to explain." She wiped a tear off Charlotte's cheek. "What about your parents, dear?"

The tangled head shook again. "There's no one."

Malcolm snapped, "It isn't some unfortunate waif. And it isn't a little doll to be played with. That is a murdering beast. It's deceiving you until you drop your guard."

"I'm not a killer!" Charlotte shrieked. She shrank back immediately, her eyes becoming frightfully large again. She was trembling. "Please don't hurt me."

Kate's voice never once broke in its even tone. "We won't harm you, Charlotte."

The girl shifted in the bed and the clang of the chain on her ankle made her start with a cry. She laid a small hand on the heavy iron shackle around her ankle and tugged. "Do I have to wear this chain like an animal?"

Malcolm said, "You are an animal."

Charlotte's trembling turned to horrific shaking. "Please . . . help . . . me! I don't . . . want to . . . kill!" The last word devolved into a mangled snarl. The child screamed and flung herself back.

"It's changing," shouted Malcolm, pushing past Simon with pistol drawn. "Get out of the way!"

Kate stood fast, blocking him. "She needs help!"

"I'm going to help," the Scotsman snarled. "I'm going to put it out of its misery."

Charlotte's grip tightened on the chain and her face twisted in sudden panic. Her muscles locked in a rictus. Long canines began to emerge from her once-pretty smile. Fingernails thickened from flat into curved talons, and they sank easily into the linen and the mattress beneath. She screamed in pain.

"Out now!" Simon slapped Malcolm's pistol aside as Kate leaned toward Charlotte, desperate to calm the frightened girl. He took Kate's shoulder and pulled her away. Simon dragged her out into the stone corridor even as she continued reaching toward the girl who lay quaking on the bed. Malcolm slammed the door shut. They heard the sound of terrible thrashing and howls from inside.

Malcolm shook his head. "I'd say the laudanum was a failure."

Simon gestured up the short hallway leading to the stairs. "That chain should hold her. And I've warded this door to be sure."

They all emerged from the staircase into the library and Simon opened wide the French windows. The sun was climbing in the sky and bright light streamed in. Simon poured wine for them all, trying to remove the tinge of worry from his face, but he was sure he failed miserably.

"She's just a child," Kate murmured. "We have to be able to help her. She has no one else. We can't leave her to nature. I won't have the world be that cruel."

"Your sentiments do you credit," Simon said. "But you must realize, everything we know about her kind tells us that in her heart she is a beast. Not a child. She would kill any of us simply because that is all she can do."

Malcolm nodded in vigorous agreement.

"I'm going to try." Kate looked intently at both Malcolm and Simon. "Neither of you need to help if you don't wish to. But I will make wulfsyl. I can help her."

Simon drained his glass of wine and set it down with an accepting shrug.

Kate was eager to begin when suddenly her face fell. She gave a weary laugh. "Well, in all this excitement, I almost forgot about Imogen. Excuse me." She touched Simon's shoulder with gratitude as she went out.

When the door shut, Malcolm started talking immediately, "Do you seriously intend to let her keep that beast?"

"How do you think I have the power to let or prevent her doing anything?"

Malcolm exhaled roughly and ran a hand over his sleek black widow's peak. "It's an idiotic risk."

"It is." Simon's face was indomitable. He sat at a disheveled desk and threw one leg over the corner. He removed a golden key from his pocket and stared at it. "The unknown can always be a risk but could be well worth it."

"Just to give Kate a new project? Just so she feels like she can help someone?"

"No."

"It would have been better if that thing upstairs had died," Malcolm muttered as he slumped on a bench near the glowing hearth.

"That *thing* is her sister." Simon shot the other man a fierce glare. "And she poses no threat."

"Except maybe to Kate's guilty conscience." Malcolm pressed his boot onto a glowing ember that had popped from the fire. "But that thing down there is the enemy. You're inviting a terrible nightmare."

"I'll take additional precautions beyond chains and locked doors." Simon smiled with an idea. "I'll send for Penny Carter and ask her to provide us with something for a bit of extra protection. I'm sure she has something useful lying about that shop of hers."

"You can manhandle that werewolf now because it's a juvenile! It's inexperienced or it would have been long gone already, leaving a trail of bodies in its wake. With time, though, it will develop its single skill: killing. It's as inevitable as death."

"I believe otherwise," Simon stated quietly.

"Why? Why take such a risk when there's a simple solution?"

"Because it's the right thing to do. This group has made a commitment to use our knowledge and power to help those who can't protect themselves."

Malcolm approached Simon. "Trust me, it can protect itself."

"Are we so callous and righteous as to simply say she is lost, and walk away?"

"Yes."

Simon's face was indomitable. "I won't. And neither will Kate."

Malcolm leaned heavily on the desk. "Just admit it. You love the idea of having a pet werewolf. I see that gleam in your eye."

Simon looked up quizzically. "Have you no science in you, Malcolm? Aren't you the least bit curious?"

"No."

"Let me ask you, as the resident expert on these things. If Kate can create wulfsyl, will it control Charlotte's transformations?"

"I kill them. I don't raise them." The Scotsman shook his head and shrugged. "I've heard different stories, but they all hint that wulfsyl makes the lycanthrope more aware during its transformation. Whether that's a good thing or bad, depends on your point of view. But I do know that once they take it, they can't stop, like opium eaters. And werewolves who are separated from it go mad with rage."

"We best make sure we don't run out of it."

"It may wear the skin of a child. It may act like a puppy now because it hasn't killed, but like any wild beast, there will come a tipping point. Think of a wolf. As a cub, it is all play and reaction, but once it learns to kill, it is never a cub again. All prey becomes food. All prey."

Simon's tone remained firm. "Even wolves can be domesticated."

Malcolm slammed his hand down on the table. "It's a monster, Simon! A monster!" He stared into Simon's unmoved gaze and dropped his head. "Maybe your friend, Barker, was right to leave. If he knew anything, it was you. Maybe he felt if he stayed, you'd get him killed."

Simon bristled, dropping his feet to the floor and templing his fingers in front of him in an effort to quiet the pain those words caused. He struggled to keep his voice even. "Would you be good enough to compile a list of William Blake's writings which use those four names that I might study?" He held Malcolm's dark gaze but then purposefully turned to the sheets of runes on the desk, taking up a pencil. "You know what we're about, Malcolm. If you don't agree with it, I won't hold you here. I didn't stop Nick. I won't stop you."

After a second, Simon heard angry mutterings about blood and stupidity, and the door shut as Malcolm went out. He threw down the pencil and slumped back in his chair.

DEEP SHADOWS PERMEATED THE ROOM IN THE east wing of Hartley Hall. What had once been a young woman's bedroom was now a murky cage that stank of despair and anger. A milky white figure crouched in a ball trying to jam its body into the dark corner between a tossed bed and an overturned night table. It was hairless and its skin almost translucent. Veins and pulsing organs could be seen even in the dim gaslight. One of the figure's arms was more machine than flesh and bristled with fierce filamentous quills from wrist to shoulder that rippled like a field of wheat. A dress that had been peach-colored was tattered and soiled.

An inhuman eye, guided by gears and wires, shifted every so often as if in fear. Its other eye, more human though utterly colorless, remained focused on what it held with long, boneless fingers. It clutched a nearly human skull, the skull of a monster, of a homunculus, half bone and half construct. The white object dripped with useless wires and in the empty cranium was an apparatus for recording and playing back sounds.

The figure's left hand was shaped normally but bleached white. Its fingers were shoved into a gap under the jaw of the skull and manipulated a small gear inside. The jaw moved up and down in an imitation of human speech while a tinny voice grated through the stale air, repeating the same words over and over: "*My sister has a gold key that our father made. It's what you want. My sister has a gold key that our father made. It's what you want.*"

Kate knelt beside the pale shade that was barely recognizable as her sister. She slipped a metal syringe into a brass case and snapped the lid shut. After more than a month of a regime that amounted to experimenting on poor Imogen, Kate no longer had any reason to expect a reaction to the injections. She had no idea if the alchemical concoctions she devised in her lab were playing any role in undoing the terrible damage wrought on Imogen.

The horrific figure of Kate's sister rested on top of a

tangle of ripped cloth, a nest of sorts that Imogen had created by shredding all of the exquisite clothing in her closets, dresses and gowns that the young woman had once treasured. Kate listened with a pained expression to the thin recorded voice that was fully recognizable as her sister's. She reached to take the horrible device that spoke only of betrayal. Imogen reacted wildly. Her mechanical arm grabbed Kate's wrist and shoved her to the floor. A man darted in to assist her.

Kate picked herself up. "It's all right, Simon. She just doesn't want me to take the skull." She moved slowly, careful not to make any sudden moves and to keep her emotions in check, despite the wild pounding of her heart.

Simon didn't look convinced but deferred to Kate's understanding of her sister's mental state. Kate believed her sister would never hurt her intentionally. The girl was lost inside her own head, unable to speak. She had been that way since they had brought her back from Bedlam in this condition, terrified of the dark but desperate to remain hidden in the shadows.

Kate knew she could reach her sister if she could get past the guilt that plagued them both. Imogen felt she had betrayed her sister to the madman, Dr. White. In fact, she had merely been a manipulated pawn, drugged and deceived into revealing secrets to White's homunculus spy, her traitorous words forever preserved in the skull's recording. Imogen was the victim.

Kate's own culpability tore at her insides. She had labored against Imogen's wishes to save her sister's life after Dr. White's horribly botched operation in that filthy chamber beneath Bedlam. White had known that Kate would never tell her secrets to save her own life, but to save Imogen's, that was another story. The damnable thing was, Kate didn't know the secret that Dr. White craved. The secret of the key. But White didn't believe her, and he mutilated Imogen, transforming her into a horrible homunculus. Or at least partly transforming her since Simon and the team arrived to interrupt the procedure before White could finish it. Kate had acted instinctively and saved Imogen's life by finishing the horrific transformation begun by the sinister White.

It was the nature of the transformation that Kate couldn't yet fathom. Something in White's alchemy changed Imogen's physical state—her muscles, her blood, her very being. He had hijacked her physiology. When Kate had attempted to remove the quills on Imogen's arm, they regenerated even though they weren't entirely organic. It was extremely powerful magic. Kate was nowhere near that level. At least not yet. She would never accept the fact that her sister was lost.

Kate couldn't tell if Imogen's playing of the recording in the skull over and over was a plea to absolve her of guilt, which Kate did wholeheartedly from the first, or merely a pathetic desire for Imogen to remember how her own voice sounded. Both reasons broke Kate's heart.

She heard Simon shift closer as she approached Imogen once more.

"Imogen, look at me," Kate told her sister softly. Imogen's mechanical eye darted, whirring and clicking to focus on Kate. The milky human eye remained fixed on the skull's moving jaw as Imogen continued to turn the crank, forcing it to reiterate its foul words. Kate squeezed her hands together so hard her knuckles turned white. "I'm going to help you or that poor girl at St. George's or Charlotte. By God. I'm going to help someone."

Simon sank slowly to one knee. "Imogen, a friend of yours wants to say hello to you."

His empty hands waved, trailing aether through the air, a green glow that cast them all in its enchanting aura. To Kate's joy, Imogen's head lifted to focus on what Simon was doing. Her hands stilled and the tinny voice from the skull stuttered to a halt for the first time in hours.

Simon's long fingers interlaced, forming a ball. Then he opened his hands to reveal a small, sleeping hedgehog cupped in them. The little animal ever so slowly unfurled and yawned. Imogen's throat convulsed silently with either delight or despair. Kate wanted to believe it was the former. Simon carefully drew Imogen's human hand away from the skull and set the tiny hedgehog in her palm. She watched the living creature curl placidly in her translucent hand.

Imogen released the skull and it rolled a few feet away, lolling on its side to stare with empty sockets. Ignoring it, Kate observed her sister touching the quills of the hedgehog, whose little nose twitched wildly as it explored its new perch. Spindly fingers caressed the little creature. Kate reached for Simon's arm and gripped it hard, her chest tight with barely restrained emotion. Imogen's head rose again to stare at Simon. Her human eye leaked tears.

Simon reached out to brush them gently away with a sad smile. "He needs someone to care for him. I'm rather occupied these days."

Imogen held out the hedgehog to him.

He didn't take it back. "He is safe with you, Imogen. I trust him with no one else."

It took a minute, but Imogen slowly brought the hedgehog close again and brushed her cheek against its prickly spines. The hedgehog crawled onto her shoulder and perched there with contentment.

Kate swallowed back her own tears and smiled at her sister. Her free hand found Imogen's biomechanical one and squeezed it reassuringly. To her amazement, Imogen squeezed back. Then Imogen pulled the hand free and picked up the skull once more. She reached into the jaw and started her ritual again: *"My sister has a gold key that our father made. It's what you want. My sister has a gold key that our father made. It's what you want."*

"Imogen," Kate began, but her voice faltered. She rose with Simon and he guided her heavy steps through the overturned furniture out into the corridor. Kate shook her head but gripped his arm in gratitude. "Months of work, and all I needed was your hedgehog trick."

"Kate, sometimes one hears a new voice clearer."

"That's why I wish my father were here. Imogen always heard his voice but never mine. I don't know why she would suddenly decide to pay attention to me now." Kate leaned against the wall and crossed her arms. Her massive wolfhound, Aethelred, looked up at her from his now-usual spot near Imogen's door. The dog thumped his tail twice and lowered his head again. "But there's no reason to assume my wayward father will return to help me, after all these years. Is there?"

Simon propped himself next to her. "No, there isn't. But you're not alone, Kate. And the only thing that hedgehog trick proves is that you shouldn't hesitate to ask for help. I'm not just here in Hartley Hall to drink your father's excellent wine."

She sighed and turned her head to regard him. "Thank you for that. Imogen does adore you."

"Who doesn't?" Simon quipped with a dashing smile.

Chapter 4

KATE LOVED THE STARRY NIGHT. IT WAS RARE for her to be out so late, especially recently since she was always locked away in her laboratory. Parties and social gatherings had never really been a part of her daily life past a certain age, but now they held even less of a place. A moonlight visit to a cemetery wasn't common for her either, but it was a great deal more invigorating than a party.

The glare from a bull's-eye lantern on the front of the steamcycle illuminated the narrow lane far ahead as the vehicle rumbled along. The fire roaring from the rear created a hellish glow as red cinders flew from the motor. Penny Carter sat straight astride the machine she had designed and built, grinning in the cold wind. Kate gripped tight to the rim of the small sidecarriage, not out of fear but anticipation of the evening's work and beyond. Her mind already raced with possibilities, going over alchemical formulas and additives in her head.

Kate pointed to a narrow turnoff. Penny maneuvered the bulky, two-wheeled vehicle down the path and under a wrought-iron gate above which were fashioned letters spelling out Primrose Gardens. Though there were no sweet flowers in this garden. Only dried husks placed at the base of small, stone monuments. The cemetery was overgrown with rampant ivy and desiccated stalks of grass. The deeper they drove, the more recent the stones appeared. Then the smell of newly turned earth reached their nostrils. Six plots, all fresh. Two large, four small. The ground was blanketed with a heavy mist that rolled slowly across the sorrowful sight.

Kate's heart tightened. She had heard of the tragedy on a nearby estate. One of the tenant families had perished in a fire, their house consumed in the dead of night before any could escape. The moonlight was bright enough to illuminate the grey stones gathered about them in the shadowy recesses, but they kept the lantern shining on the recent plots. In the beam, loamy white mushrooms covered the dark mounds of earth like small spirits dancing on the graves. Penny shut off the engine of the cycle and Kate climbed awkwardly from the small compartment.

Penny threw a leg over the padded saddle of the vehicle. She was covered in mud from head to toe. In her current state and with her heavy leather pants and jacket, it was easy to think she was a man. However, Penny was a lovely young woman in her early twenties. Never as striking as Kate but with a carefree attitude that Kate often envied. Penny's dirty blond hair had been tied down at the beginning of the trip but had escaped and run amok.

"We're in luck," Kate said, and instantly felt a sting of regret that she could even for a moment think of these fresh graves as a boon. But they were. She reached back for a hemp satchel to carry her harvest. She watched Penny draw her coat collar tighter about her in the chilled air. "Cold?"

"I work in front of a hot forge all day. It's a bit nippy."

Penny laughed and pointed at the odd fungi. "So we just pick them?"

"Yes. Exciting work, isn't it?"

"It could always be more exciting," the engineer replied with a grin.

"Simon wrote to you for silver armaments in case we have to . . ." Kate let her words trail off.

"Yes. A note from Simon Archer is usually the beginning of an adventure of some sort. Luckily I had a few things left over from our to-do with Gretta. I'll run up a few more tomorrow or the next day when I go back to London."

"Well, I'm glad you arrived at Hartley Hall today. Thank you for coming with me tonight. Simon was engrossed in his William Blake poetry, so I didn't want to disturb him. He has so many tasks to accomplish. Not only is he looking into this murder in London, but he is still trying to figure out the key."

"Yes," said Penny. "I've been looking at that too. Your father was an incredible engineer, I can tell you. That key he built with Simon's father is a beautiful piece of work."

"And you and Simon have no idea how it works?"

"Not a bit. But once we do, they claim we'll have a device that will transport someone anywhere in the world instantly. That's pretty keen."

Kate looked a bit crestfallen. "Then I'm sorry to drag you away from your work too."

"Oh please. You and I haven't gotten to spend much time together, so when you offered late-night botanizing in a graveyard"—Penny jerked a thumb at her chest—"I'm your girl!"

"You really enjoy all this, don't you?" Kate knelt on the ground at the first grave, placing a hand of respect on the dirt. Then she focused on cutting the stems of the fungi known as *ghostblooms*.

"Mushrooms?"

"The danger. The running and shooting."

Penny shrugged. "It's not boring. I love making things, but I do like seeing them used out in the field too. Nothing gives me more pleasure than the boom of a gun I built."

Kate chuckled at the young woman's enthusiasm. "I can understand that."

Penny took one of the cut mushrooms and studied it. "Will this help our little werewolf?"

"Yes. I hope. I'll have to experiment a bit on the potency and the method. But it should help her manage her transformations and be more true to herself. Charlotte has a kind heart, we just need to allow her to follow it."

"Without the hairy side getting in the way."

"Exactly. I can't seem to fix Imogen yet, but at least I know how to help Charlotte." Kate sliced roughly through a small mushroom, wielding her knife in mounting frustration.

Penny knelt next to her and laid a hand on Kate's shoulder. "You'll find a way to do both. But not if you lop off a finger."

Kate's frantic cutting stilled and she looked up, her gaze softening. "I wish I had your conviction. Every second Imogen is in that horrible form, the further she slips from me. She seems to hate me because I kept her alive on that table at Bedlam. All she does is sit and listen to that hellish recording of her voice hour after hour."

"It's only been a couple of months. I hate to tell you but you may have a long path ahead of you." Penny took a deep breath and added, "You haven't met my brother, Charles, have you? He looked the wrong way crossing Oxford Street. That was all it took, a second. A carriage hit him. He almost died. But it crippled his legs instead. He wanted to just quit, claimed he had nothing more to live for."

"I didn't know," Kate admitted quietly.

"It took all I had to convince him to keep going." Penny's blue eyes bore into Kate's, glistening with memory but not with tears. "I had a plan, you see. While Charles lay on his sickbed and Mama cried herself to sleep, I stayed awake at night in the attic, welding metal struts, running out into the alley for any parts I could salvage. I even purloined a few things, whatever I had to."

Penny's lips pressed tight together. She tucked a lock of her hair roughly into the strap of her goggles. "I made him an auto-motive chair so that he could move around like normal folks. Things changed for him then. He saw a future suddenly and he took it."

"He was lucky to have you as a sister."

"I'd say the same for you and Imogen. You'll make it happen, Kate. I mean, my God, you're bloody brilliant."

Kate gave a low snort. "If I'm so bloody brilliant, why can't I help her? Everyone seems to be helping her but me. Even Aethelred hardly leaves her side, sleeps outside her room as if he can sense she's so afraid of the dark he might be needed to comfort her at any second. Meanwhile, I flail in my laboratory. I'm able to make all sorts of potions, and I hardly think about them. I even made Greek fire one night when I hit a blind alley with Imogen, but I'd trade it all for even a small clue as to how to fix my sister."

"You will. Wait. Did you say Greek fire?" Penny tilted her head in astonishment. "Actual Greek fire? You seem rather blasé about it."

"Some form of it." Kate's expression turned hard as they moved to the next mound. "I find myself thinking more and more of weapons. Instead of elixirs to heal or potions to protect, I want to make fire that never stops burning."

"That should come in handy."

Kate stood. "When it's ready, it will burn the Devil himself."

Penny gave an admiring shake of her head. "So where did you learn your alchemy? Are there schools for that?"

"There are, of a sort, but they're all in dismal spots run by decrepit old alchemists half-mad from mercury poisoning."

"So Oxford then?"

Kate laughed. "Not quite. I'm self-taught mostly. You may not have noticed, but I'm not the most normal woman on the social register. Prior to Simon's wrenching me out of my laboratory, I was content to spend most of my time staring at beakers and studying plants."

"You taught yourself all those marvelous things you create?"

"Through trial and much error. And, honestly, my father had nearly unlimited resources so I don't pretend to be any sort of romance heroine who struggles to feed her children while studying to become a nurse. I started with many benefits." Kate's smile was warm and genuine. "What about you? Is your engineering self-taught?"

"I wish. I'm not like you. Ever hear of the Maddy Boys?"

Kate shook her head.

Penny arched a disappointed eyebrow. "They are a wild bunch of engineers and scientists at Cambridge. Britain's finest. Being a woman, I couldn't go to school, but our mother worked for a dear man named Professor Westgate, a scientist at Cambridge. He always thought Charles would rise in the world, but Charles had no scientific desires; he only wanted to help me because I had always been a tinkerer. Charles begged him to put me in touch with the Maddy Boys."

"So they accepted a woman?"

"Not officially, but there were a few women who

worked with them, in secret." Penny's chest puffed out in pride. "Just because we're not allowed doesn't mean we don't. Right?"

Kate grinned. "Right."

Penny returned the expression. "I stayed at Cambridge for near three years. Wrote home to Charles every day. At Christmas, I'd bring him some of the smaller things I made. That gave Charles the idea to start up our shop. His business sense was very astute. We were an instant success. Respectable gentlemen brought their family heirlooms for repair, and their equally respectable wives came to coo over adorable Charles and purchase his wonderful toys for their children."

"All made by you though."

Penny shrugged with humility. "We also got a reputation for crafting rare devices. And we acquired patrons of a unique nature such as Simon and Malcolm. If it weren't for that shop, we would have been on the streets. I haven't been able to make Charles walk, yet." Penny grinned with a maker's fire. "But he's never been more alive and determined because he has hope. It will be the same for Imogen. She'll find a way back to you." Penny held open the hemp bag for Kate.

For the first time in a long while, Kate felt rejuvenated. Her tread was lighter and her quick cuts at the ghostbloom stems weren't from anger but with promise. The last ones were placed in the bag and the two women rose, dusting the dirt from their clothes. That's when Kate noticed one of the surrounding shadows shift. Then another.

"We have company," she told Penny. Kate calmly undid one button on her jacket to reveal a military bandolier underneath that held an assortment of crystal vials. She plucked one out and held it tight in her hand. Penny quickly pulled a pistol.

Inhuman yellow eyes stared through the veil of night.

Six dark shapes rose on animal hind legs so that they stood over eight feet tall. Their fur was matted and filthy. The low rumble of angry snarls and discontented grunting permeated the graveyard. They twitched and shuddered like deprived addicts. Their features were wild with hunger and rage. They spread out around the two women.

The largest of them stalked forward, its fur as dark as the night. "Where is she?" it ground out in a barely intelligible growl.

Kate pulled another vial from her bandolier. "Where is who?"

"The little one who betrayed us." Bestial eyes darted left and right. "The one who fought against us."

Realization dawned on Kate. They were talking about Charlotte. This was a remnant of Gretta's old pack, or what was left of them after Malcolm's merciless hunting.

"I don't know who you mean."

"Give her to us." The great nostrils flared. "I can smell her on you."

"If that's the case, you should also smell my steadfast determination to oblige you nothing."

Penny stepped up behind Kate so their shoulders were near to touching, covering Kate's back, her weapon trained on the other hulking shapes lurching through the tombstones.

The black beast's whole body twitched with a violent spasm, either rage or a seizure. The others in the pack whined, fighting off their own muscular tremors, and the leader growled at them until their complaining ceased. Then the dark werewolf's molten gaze found Kate again.

"This is your death sentence," it snarled.

"Or yours." Kate flung a vial toward the leader. The glass shattered at its feet and it tried to run, but a gush of black liquid glued it to the ground. The black treacle held it fast, matting its fur with a glistening sheen.

Penny shot a werewolf that leapt at her over a crooked monument. It tumbled dead to the ground.

"Switch," Kate shouted.

Penny swapped places with her. Not needing to reload as her pistol was a small prototype of Malcolm's quad-barrel Lancasters, her second shot took another werewolf in midbound.

Kate tossed a vial at a werewolf on her left. The vial smashed against its chest, a gaseous cloud settled on the beast, and it fell gasping on the ground, where Penny shot it. The pack broke apart in the confusion of the onslaught.

Kate drew her other weapons. With a swift motion, a pistol swung to a werewolf rushing her and a lead ball struck it in the chest. It shuddered and swerved away, dropping to all fours in an effort to get past her. In her other hand flashed a steel blade and she stabbed deep with her sword, slipping it between the ribs straight to the heart. It collapsed atop a grave.

Penny's hand now held a small silver sphere about the size of a cricket ball and she threw it straight into another werewolf. The ball exploded and silver dust draped over the beast, who howled and flung itself backward, clawed hands slapping its burning flesh.

Penny stepped boldly forward and took aim at the crouching werewolf. The bullet shattered the tombstone beside its skull. Yellow eyes flashed in fear and it scrambled aside wildly before springing toward the young woman. It was twice her height. Wide claws extended, ready to rip into her. Penny didn't flinch; she stood steady as stone against the charge and fired directly into the animal's face. A shorn-off fang flew into the air, indicating a head shot. Penny tried to get out of the way as the beast fell to the ground and, carried by its momentum, rolled madly toward her. Kate grabbed Penny's arm and yanked her aside as the monster tumbled past. The engineer came up on one knee, already breaking her pistol at the breech to reload.

The leader, the last of the pack, wrenched free from the mire of tar and roared. Gathering itself, the werewolf barreled toward Kate. She turned with her bloody sword, tossing her spent pistol aside, auburn hair falling a bit over her face, eyes darting toward the beast. She threw a final vial. A hairy hand slapped the vial out of the air in an attempt to deflect it, but it smashed from the impact, spewing toxic gas. The monster held his breath and came on.

Kate dodged a swipe of his massive clawed hand and shoved her sword into his shaggy breast. This enraged the maddened creature. Penny suddenly stepped up beside Kate and emptied her pistol into the great beast. The werewolf shuddered just as it lunged one last time for Kate. Then it fell. Its great head flopped to the ground, its massive canines, each six inches long, drove into the dirt.

Kate stood, chest heaving, waiting for new attacks. There were none, merely dead and quivering beasts lying around them. She brushed the hair from her eyes and glanced at Penny, who was turning in a slow circle with her pistol extended.

Kate asked, "Are you loaded with silver shot?"

"Damn right. We found too many werewolves a few months ago for me to go about without some killing silver on me ever again."

Kate pointed at the small four-barreled pistol that Penny carried. "Perhaps we should all have those as well."

"No. They're temperamental. If you don't handle them just right, they'll blow up in your face. That's why Malcolm is always fiddling with his." Penny jammed the pistol in her holster. "However, when I get the chance, I can fix you up with cartridges so you don't have to worry about reloading with powder and ball. Faster and more reliable."

"Always prepared. Just like an engineer. Just like Father." Kate dropped to her knee and wiped a sleeve across her perspiring forehead. "What were you saying about how it could always be more exciting?"

Penny looked about at all the dead werewolves. "I need to keep my big trap shut."

Chapter 5

"HOW ARE THE ZOAS COMING?" KATE ASKED FROM her worktable in her laboratory at Hartley Hall.

"Oh, I've moved on from them." With the gold key in his hand, Simon indicated the several sets of William Blake folios on the table where he sat near the window. The library had a surprisingly complete collection of Blake's work, or perhaps not so surprising if the poet had some mystical nature. "I read the works Malcolm indicated, and despite his criticism, the language is quite lovely. However, it is difficult to pull much from them over the basic concept that this being Albion once existed and was rendered into four spirits, or Zoas. And I think those Zoas were, in turn, reflected by spirits called emanations. And perhaps, one day Albion will return. Resurrection myth. Every culture has one. Nothing terribly momentous."

"Do you think Blake was a practitioner?"

"A true magician? I've never heard tell of it. I think he may have been a sensitive, from what little I know. The poet had visions, but that's not terribly unique." Aethelred was trying to convince Simon to play, and the man distractedly complied by balancing the book in his lap while holding one end of a piece of rope so the jaws of the large wolfhound could wrestle the other end.

"What do his visions mean? And would they influence someone to kill?"

"That, I don't know." Simon held up the heavy tome that sat in his lap. "So I've moved on to hieroglyphics and your excellent source of spells from the *Egyptian Book of the Dead.*"

"And?"

"The symbols we saw appear to be Old Kingdom stuff, even Heliopolitan. I can make out a bit of it, but we may need to call in an expert on the texts."

"Egyptian hieroglyphics are difficult. I may know someone who can help us with the translation." Kate then indicated a pot that boiled on a flame and said with a voice hovering between fascination and horror, "Did you know you can hear the ghostbloom mushrooms?"

"Hear them?"

"The legend is that they have the voice of the person in the grave where they were growing. Come here. Listen to them." Kate's hair was swept back from her face into a knot that struggled to make order from the curling chaos. She was bent over the worktable, her clothes covered by a thick apron of tough leather.

Simon tucked the book under his arm, leaving the dog to exalt in triumph over the toy. The whitish mushrooms tumbled in boiling water. Kate lifted one of the fleshy objects from a tray of dirt and held it over the steaming pot. She released the mushroom into the water.

Simon thought he heard a faint scream. He straightened with a look of skepticism. "No. That must be steam escaping."

"If you say so."

He poked the mushrooms on the plate with his finger.

"So you just boil them and you get wulfsyl? That seems simple."

"Oh yes," Kate replied in exasperation. "That's all alchemy is, making weak soup. And is your scribing merely scribbling? No. I'm boiling them to release their essence, which I'll then filter and purify here." She gestured to a complex apparatus of a cucurbit connected to an alembic. "Afterward, I create the elixir through the difficult process of combining it with—"

"I concede the point." Simon put a mushroom to his ear. "You haven't told Charlotte that some of her old *colleagues* were looking for her?"

"No. And I don't intend to."

"Probably for the best. Could she just eat the mushrooms and get the same effect?"

"I suppose, though the result would be far weaker. No doubt that's what many werewolves do who don't have access to an alchemist." Kate pointed to a wooden rack where there were several glass tubes filled with green liquid. "Fortunately, Charlotte does."

She took one of the glass tubes and crooked a finger at Simon. Together, with Aethelred dragging his length of rope, they went to the Blue Parlor, where a table was laid for high tea. Several teapots rested in the center of elegant place settings for five. There was a tower of finger sandwiches and small cakes. Servants bowed and departed.

"Oh, tea!" Simon clapped his hands together and exclaimed, "I do so hope I'm invited!"

Kate slapped his chest. "You're an ass."

Without response, Simon went to the table and took a seat, all prim and proper. The door opened and Charlotte entered, with Hogarth close behind her. She was in a very fashionable dress with balloon sleeves. Her hair was done up in elegant buns with bouncing curls along the sides of her face. Kate stripped off the stained leather apron to reveal she was suitably attired in a flowing cotton dress of yellow. Simon felt inappropriate in simple black trousers, a white shirt, and a waistcoat, but no proper jacket or tie.

Kate put her hands on Charlotte's cheeks, inspecting the girl's demure appearance. "My goodness, Charlotte, how nice you look. Did Hogarth do your hair?"

Charlotte nodded, in silent awe of the hulking man-servant.

Kate smiled at the stoic Hogarth, who had taken up a position in the corner. "You're still in good practice after all these years."

"Thank you, Miss Kate. Her hair was more cooperative than yours, as I recall."

Then Charlotte saw the table setting and squealed with glee. "Oh! Tea! What fun!" She raced to the table and curtsied to Simon, who rose to seat her.

Then Malcolm entered cautiously with his typical dour black outfit and a confused look. "What the hell? I thought the—"

Kate raised a silencing finger.

"Malcolm!" Simon called out and patted the chair next to him. "I've saved you a seat."

The Scotsman wandered to the table, still quite puzzled as Kate assumed the hostess duties. "Everyone, please, sit."

Charlotte stared back at Hogarth, and she whispered to Kate, "Isn't he going to serve us?"

"No, dear," Kate said pleasantly. "Hogarth doesn't wait tables. We shall serve ourselves."

"How bohemian," Charlotte said with a smile. "It's like the French Revolution."

Malcolm sat and nodded to Simon. "Madame."

"Is Imogen joining us?" Simon inquired hopefully.

"I hoped she would." Kate's eyes betrayed her sadness at the last empty chair. "Perhaps another occasion."

"She's your sister, yes?" Charlotte's voice sounded a trifle disappointed.

"Yes. She's had a very hard time. She's been sick."

Though Kate had tried to state the matter politely, the young girl beside her bowed her head. "I know what happened. I wish I could help her. I'm sorry for what Gretta did. She helped Dr. White hunt your sister."

"Thank you, Charlotte, but you weren't to blame. That is reserved for those that did the deed itself. But enough of that. Today we concentrate on more important matters."

"Like tea and fancy dresses!" Charlotte beamed once more, her hands smoothing down the elegant silk material that bunched around her hips and legs.

"Yes." Kate poured tea and passed trays full of sandwiches. Charlotte began to pile her plate.

A shadow filled the door and there stood Imogen. She wore a dark gown that whisked the floor. Her hands were covered in black silk gloves although the right one fit poorly. Her face was draped in a black veil.

The gentlemen rose from the table, as did Kate, whose eyes were near to brimming, a hand flying up to her mouth to hold back an exclamation. Her throat was locked and she couldn't find the words to express her joy.

Imogen, suddenly fearful now that all eyes were on her, took a step backward. Thankfully, Simon knew just what to do. He quickly pulled out a chair for her between Charlotte and Kate.

"Here, Miss Imogen. This is a prime spot. Near the cakes."

Imogen hesitated and Kate was afraid she'd flee upstairs. But the young woman came forward with a slow deliberateness, as if uncertain how to even walk properly. There was only a slight bobble near the table, and she slumped into the seat as if weary with relief. Simon was quick to slide her forward while Kate poured tea and placed sandwiches on her plate.

Imogen didn't move. Her dark veil swayed up and back ever so slightly with her breathing. Then Charlotte stuck her face in front of her, and Imogen jumped.

"Hello. My name is Charlotte." Imogen sat mute, so the young girl continued. "This party is for me. I'm supposed to take some medicine. But then maybe you will play with me later? I think I'm wearing your dress!" Charlotte seemed pleased when Imogen turned to regard her.

Kate's first instinct was to say no, but she was so pleased to see Imogen react, any attempt at normalcy would be a step in the right direction. She smiled with encouragement.

Suddenly, Charlotte shouted loudly, which made everyone jump. From out of the folds of Imogen's dark veil poked a very wiggly nose.

"Oh, a hedgehog!" Charlotte cried. "I love them. I just love them! May I pet it?" Her index finger reached out toward the small bristly creature perched on Imogen's shoulder. Imogen didn't reply, of course, so Charlotte took it as a sign of acceptance and brushed her finger over the tiny animal.

Imogen froze, and because of the mourning clothes, Kate couldn't tell if she was frightened or curious.

Charlotte giggled. "I never had a pet. What does it eat? May I hold it?"

"Charlotte." Kate attempted to distract the child from her endless questions and held up the glass tube. "This is wulfsyl. I can't be sure it's correct."

The girl looked at Kate with excitement, then asked hopefully, "Will it stop me from eating someone?"

Kate looked uncomfortable. "We believe that if you take it now, you will never have to eat someone."

"But what if I do?"

"Eat Malcolm," Simon suggested.

Malcolm sat with a sour scowl on his face.

Charlotte pushed a sandwich in her mouth as she stared at the concoction. Then she attacked another sandwich, and mumbled, "What does it taste like?"

"Probably a bit strong. You should put it in your tea." Kate handed the glass tube to the girl.

She pulled the cork and sniffed. She threw her head back with a grimace. "That's horrible! It smells like dead people."

Simon could smell it too, and it did stink of death. Far worse than the rank earthiness of the mushrooms themselves. He snatched the sugar bowl and began to drop spoonfuls into Charlotte's tea. "Here. This should help."

"More," the girl instructed, and Simon tossed in two more spoons. "More."

"Try it first," he said. "Even I could eat a dead person if he had that much sugar poured on him."

Charlotte dribbled a few drops into the milky tea. "How much should I use?"

"Half the tube should do," Kate answered.

The girl poured with great deliberation. Then she stoppered the tube and gave it back to Kate. She took a spoon, turning it around in her hand to see her reflection. She realized it was plain dull pewter. "Miss Kate, are you not using silverware because I'm a werewolf?"

"No, dear." Kate selected a sandwich. "We're not using the silverware because we melted it all for weapons when Gretta attacked us. Drink."

Charlotte stirred her tea for a long time. "This won't make me change, will it?"

The rest of the company stiffened and exchanged worried glances.

"No," Kate said with some false authority. "No."

Charlotte lifted the cup to her lips, where she paused.

All eyes were on her. She let the liquid dab her upper lip and pulled the cup away. "Is that enough?"

Kate scolded, "Charlotte, drink it, please."

The girl sighed, brought the cup up in a quivering hand, and took a sip. She held it in her mouth, and then swallowed with much effort. Her eyes tightened. She let out a wet gasp and set down the cup with a loud clatter. Charlotte grasped her throat with palsied hands. She swayed in her seat and growled.

Chairs scraped back and clattered to the floor. Kate reached desperately for Imogen, who sat utterly still. The runic tattoos on Simon flared, while Malcolm drew his pistols and brought them to bear on the flailing girl. Alarmed shouts were cut by childish laughter.

Charlotte fell back in her chair and giggled uncontrollably. The adults stared in disbelief at the girl, who kicked her feet with delight.

"Did I scare you?" Charlotte laughed, looking at the stricken faces around her.

Malcolm angrily jammed his pistols back into the holsters with a look of incredulity.

Simon shook his head and joined in the girl's laughter. He righted his chair, finishing his sandwich between chuckles.

"Charlotte!" Kate stood with her mouth open and hands shaking. "That was horrible! Don't ever do that again."

The girl looked suddenly crestfallen. "I'm sorry, Miss Kate. I was just being funny."

"Funny gets you shot," Malcolm muttered.

"Spoken like a Scotsman." Simon turned to the girl and said with an even tone, "Finish the wulfsyl, Charlotte. And then we'll have dessert."

Charlotte took her cup and drank with a joyless slump. Kate watched her with a guilty face, and said, "I'm sorry

I snapped, dear. You must understand your condition is serious. You shouldn't joke about it."

"I think I know better than almost anyone how serious it is," Charlotte offered. Imogen shifted almost as if nodding.

Kate and Simon exchanged pained looks. Kate leaned over and kissed Charlotte's cheek. The girl gave a begrudging half smile.

Kate asked, "So how does it taste?"

Charlotte smacked her lips and pondered. "Needs more sugar."

Chapter 6

THE BRISK MORNING AIR REFUSED TO BE WARMED
by the sun overhead. Kate walked with Simon along one
of the many lanes that crisscrossed through the immense gardens around Hartley Hall. Despite the cold,
they were not heavily bundled, taking advantage of the
sunlight. The garden hosted no blooms this time of
the year but it didn't lack stark magnificence. Her father
had planted many species with winter color and ever-
greens, some brought back from his travels around the
world, plus he had laid intricate stonework and fascinating statues to make the stroll pleasant whatever the
season. Ahead of them, Imogen and Charlotte raced
after Aethelred. Charlotte laughed and turned to wave
on Imogen, who lagged behind because of her awkward
gait. Imogen still wore a veil over her face but was clad
in a lovely flowered dress, one of her old favorites. Kate
recognized it as one from Imogen's first debutante ball.
Their father had told Imogen it matched the blue in her
eyes. The fact that he had even noticed that she had
matured to a lovely young woman had meant so much to
her. Imogen hadn't fit into the dress for years now, but
her body shape had changed, withered a bit. Earlier this

morning, she had selected it from a box of her old clothes that had escaped her ferocious shredding.

Kate squeezed Simon's hand with a sudden rush of emotion. It was almost a normal morning, the first in a long time. In the days since the initial dose of wulfsyl, Charlotte had showed no signs of being anything other than an energetic thirteen-year-old girl. But more so, Kate was overjoyed at the simple sight of her sister enjoying a moment. Imogen outside the house in the sunshine for the first time in months, dressed in an old frock that reminded her of the sweeter days.

It was miraculous how Imogen had made remarkable progress thanks to Charlotte's joyous influence. The child's delightful nature was infectious, and Charlotte was instinctively welcoming. She never blinked or shirked when Imogen touched her. Imogen slowly showed signs of feeling safe around Charlotte despite knowing what she was, or maybe even because of what she was.

They ventured a little farther from the corner of the manor house to stay out of the growing shadow of the uncanny bulk of Hartley Hall. The great mansion was asymmetrically constructed in various architectural styles, deliberately chosen by Sir Roland. Still, Kate always acted as if it was any other home, feeling as if she had grown up in a quaint country cottage rather than a rambling palace with turrets and strange machines and the heads of monsters on the walls.

Kate cocked her head, hearing a familiar sound in the distance. A deep rumbling ripped through the serene morning. She could feel it in her chest. Birds poured from the trees and fled. Charlotte perked up and came back toward them, with Imogen following closely. Aethelred too returned and took up a position by Kate, barking with a deep booming voice. They all turned to the nearest corner of the house and waited. The din paused for a moment, then roared back into life, coming closer.

Within seconds, Penny's metal monster rolled into view through the wide lanes of the garden. Licks of flame were visible from the rear of the metal monster. The sidecarriage was empty. Penny bent low over the handles in front, her bright grin showing beneath goggles and above a heavy scarf. Charlotte squealed with frightened excitement and crowded behind Kate, with her face poking out to watch the machine belch its way across the gravel paths. Imogen's long fingers curled around Kate's hand comfortingly.

Penny braked a few yards from the group and kicked at a switch with her heavy boot. The beast continued to rumble, so she kicked harder. This time, the fiery motor coughed into silence. She waved.

"Aethelred, hush! It's Penny." Kate touched the dog on the snout and he went silent but remained vigilant.

"What is that thing?" Charlotte shouted, not quite used to the fact that the engine had stopped.

"Inside voice, dear," Kate said, then realized they were outside.

Penny leaned over to retrieve a heavy rucksack from the sidecarriage. She pushed the goggles up, clearly eyeing Charlotte, but she still smiled, betraying no fear around the girl.

"Charlotte," Kate said, extending an arm, "do you remember Penny Carter? She is an engineer. She builds things, as my father did. She made that machine she was riding like a horse from perdition."

"Oh my goodness!" Charlotte exclaimed. "You made that?"

"I did." Penny pulled off her gloves. "Nice to see you again. We didn't have much of an opportunity to talk last time." The engineer extended a hand and the girl seemed thrilled to shake it. Then Penny nodded casually to the hunched, veiled figure attached to Kate. "Imogen. Good to see you again."

Charlotte started toward the steamcycle. "Can I go for a ride?"

"Sure." Penny slapped her gloves against her thigh, raising a cloud of dust.

"No." Kate smoothly found a plausible excuse. "I'm sorry, dear, but not now. Penny is very tired from the ride out. She's been going back and forth a lot these days."

Penny looked a little embarrassed for overstepping. "Oh, I'm sorry, Kate."

Kate put a comforting hand on Penny. "Charlotte, you and Imogen keep exercising Aethelred. He hasn't had nearly enough activity today."

"All right." Charlotte stared at the steamcycle as she backed up, reaching out for Imogen's hand. "Come on."

The two ran off with the wolfhound in their wake. When they were a fair distance away, Penny said, "Good God, Imogen looks fantastic. I can't believe she's out."

"Yes," Kate said proudly. "This is her first time outside the house since we brought her back from Bedlam."

"She found that little bit of hope finally, I see."

Kate regarded her friend with a grateful smile. "She did."

"And that little darling is the werewolf that helped us?" Penny hefted the rucksack with a knowing glance at Simon.

"Yes." Kate laughed. "Needless to say, she's not always a little darling."

Simon added, "Thank you for coming back out, Penny. I know it's been difficult for you these last few days. And riding that monstrosity back and forth from London must be exhausting."

Penny waved a casual hand as she watched Charlotte pick up a heavy stick. "No troubles. It's proper exercise. I can crack a chestnut with my thighs now."

Kate couldn't cover her raucous laugh while Simon nodded with thoughtful consideration, saying, "Good to know."

Across the lawn, Aethelred splayed his front legs and stared openmouthed at the stick in Charlotte's hand. Charlotte handed it to Imogen and pointed into the distance. Imogen showed the stick to Aethelred once more, then reared back and threw it with amazing power. The dog roared off in a spray of dirt. The stick bounced near the service path and rolled under a wagon. The wolfhound loped toward the wagon and wedged his large body under it, reaching for the stick. The ancient horse hitched up front paid the dog no mind. Charlotte raced forward and crawled under the wagon too to help the hound while Imogen bent over and watched them as they wrestled for ownership.

Even more remarkably, Imogen paused to pull her veil up over her face. She raised her head to bask in the limited sunshine. Her bloodless lips stretched into a smile as she faced the warming rays. Kate's breath caught in her chest, watching her sister bask in the sun as if, for just a moment, she was a normal young woman again.

From around the back of the house came a figure carrying wicker baskets in his arms. Kate recognized him. He was the son of a tenant farmer who lived on the estate, likely delivering eggs. He was a young man, strikingly handsome, barely sixteen, and had a penchant for flirting with the pretty girls, even the higher-class Imogen in years past. He approached the two girls beaming broadly at their play, until Imogen turned her bared face toward him. She smiled back and waved at him, forgetting that her hand was nothing more than a bundle of tentacles.

At first he showed disgust, but then terror crossed his features as Imogen's mechanical eye rolled toward him and jutted in and out to focus. He screamed, his hand fumbling into his baskets. Imogen froze in place. The first egg he threw struck her in the chest, splattering her with its runny innards, yellow yolk soaking into the blue silk. The next ones coated the beautiful material even more and struck her in the head. Foul egg whites dripped off her chin and onto the delicate embroidery, covering it in a slimy film.

"No!" Kate shouted, breaking into a run. Her heart was in her throat as she stared at Imogen's face, watching it transform from the relaxed girl back into the hopeless creature of the last few months.

The lad staggered back and reached down beside the path to grab up several stones.

"Get away from my wagon!" He threw the rocks at Imogen.

Imogen cried out as one struck her cheek, covering her face and protecting her head. A moan of despair left her as she crouched in as small a ball as possible, too frightened to even run.

Kate ran with the rest in her wake, but she couldn't react fast enough to prevent what happened next. Charlotte let out a roar. She rushed the farm boy, her eyes flashing unnaturally. She was still human, but only just. She shoved him violently, and the young man flew backward to slide across the graveled road.

"How dare you!" Charlotte screamed at him. She picked up rocks of her own and threw them hard at the flabbergasted young man. Then she looked down at her arms, which had started to bulge with the transformation. She looked about wildly for help.

"I can't stop it!" She ran for the house.

Imogen stood up and started staggering after Charlotte. Kate threw her arms around her sister, trying to restrain her, unmindful of the quills that lay flat against her arm.

"Imogen! Stop! Calm down."

Imogen only moaned pitiably and used her good hand to tear at the sodden dress she wore, ripping the sleeves and the ruined bodice.

Penny grabbed the young farmer by the arm, yanking him to his feet. He pointed at Imogen and demanded, "What is that thing?"

Penny didn't answer except to kick him in the backside, nearly tumbling him to the ground again. The lad stared at the young woman in surprise, too shocked to ball his fists and fight back.

"On your way!" Penny slammed the heavy rucksack against the boy's shoulder. "Get on your wagon and begone before I do something terrible to you!"

Two figures appeared from the door into the kitchen. One was Mrs. Tolbert, the housekeeper of Hartley Hall, and the other a mature man in workman's twill who rushed toward the wagon when he saw the boy being manhandled by a young tough. He wrenched Penny aside, showing sudden surprise and shame when he realized she was a woman.

The grizzled man touched his beaten cap. "Begging your pardon, miss. I didn't realize . . . that is, I didn't know you were a . . ." He turned on the young man. "What's happening here, son?"

The lad stammered and pointed toward the house, where Kate could be seen struggling to calm the ragged and despondent Imogen.

Penny snapped, "The boy saw something that scared him."

"Oh." The man relaxed and gestured for his son to climb onto the wagon. "Is that all? Let's be on our way."

"But it was some sort of monster!" the boy shouted.

"Aye, no doubt." The farmer doffed his cap to Mrs. Tolbert, who had waddled up in alarm. "Sorry for the disturbance, Missus. It's the boy's first trip up to the

Hall." And then he gave Penny a slight bow. "And I humbly apologize for laying my hands on you, miss."

"No harm." Penny turned and legged it for the house.

The boy took the reins, still looking quite stricken as his father climbed up beside him. "But I saw it!"

"Drive on." The man shook his head ruefully. "The day you come to Hartley Hall and don't see something strange is the day you should worry."

The wagon was pulling off as Simon ran through the open French windows into the library. Charlotte was pulling open the door leading down to the cellar, trying desperately to reach the safety of her room. Suddenly, the young girl screamed and pressed against the door. Fingernails thickened into curved talons, and they sank easily into the paneled wood beneath. She wailed in pain as her glowing eyes locked on Simon as he froze in place.

"Charlotte, you handled that situation very well," he soothed, trying to keep her calm. "Try to relax."

If the girl heard his words, they were lost inside a raging beast. Gone was the beautiful youth. The thing that remained was over twice Charlotte's size, horrible and powerful. A human-shaped creature writhed on the floor, broad-chested, all knees and elbows. The horrific form was covered in grey fur. Its head was long with a doglike snout curling over savage teeth. Yellow eyes darted from side to side, squinted in pain or anger.

She was fast. Her muscled limbs propelled her forward. Long sinewy arms darted out. A deadly clawed hand slashed at Simon's face. He blocked the blow with a stiff arm, gritting his teeth at the impact. It bought him precious seconds as the werewolf staggered off balance. He drove himself at what once was Charlotte and shoved her against the wall, one arm across her neck, blocking her snapping jaws.

Her strength was far greater than before, now that she was recovered from the injury. He would not be able to hold her for long without doing serious damage or letting her harm him. He would, of course, act to protect those in this house, but he didn't want to kill Charlotte. She had tried to do the right thing. He didn't want Malcolm to be right.

With an explosion of power, Charlotte pushed Simon away so that he collided with the wall behind him and spun off it, crashing to the floor. She bounded high onto the floor-to-ceiling bookshelves overhead, ripping volumes into the air as she threw herself about like a trapped animal.

Charlotte landed with a thud behind Simon and the werewolf's jaws shut just shy of his back as he twisted aside. He slapped his hands together in front of the beast, shouting out a single odd word. A bright light flashed from his hand like a thunderclap. The creature reared back with her arms over her eyes, howling a dreadful shriek.

Simon darted out of the corner and moved behind her, but the beast anticipated his action and turned with him. Simon was forced to leap back. A hairy arm sliced the air in front of him. He seized her once again and used her own momentum to pull her off balance. With a single spell, the strength in his limbs once again rose and he slammed Charlotte into the wall.

"Simon! Get clear! I've got a shot!"

He recognized Malcolm's voice and knew the man had his weapon trained on the rampaging beast. The moment Simon stepped away, she was done for. He refused to move. Malcolm's loud curses sounded behind him.

A long, clawed arm lifted. For an instant, Simon stared into Charlotte's eyes. The molten irises widened, almost as if in recognition. She let out a mournful wail and her claws wavered above him for a split second, then they crashed downward. The wood shattered beneath the blow that landed next to him on the floor.

Charlotte purposely missed!

Simon backed away. The wulfsyl was working, just slowly, or perhaps she needed a stronger dose. Simon could not ponder that matter more as the werewolf stalked after him, though he couldn't be sure if it was to kill him or just instinct. Her lips curled over the long canines in a snarl and Simon realized he might be in trouble. The beast surged forward and Simon tried to twist aside but her shoulder clipped him on his hip and sent him sprawling.

The werewolf swiped as he tried to roll out of her range. Her claws sunk into his long jacket, just missing tender flesh. Furiously, she reached out with her other arm, catching him a glancing blow on the forearm, this time drawing blood.

Simon grunted at the sudden pain as he fell forward. Charlotte loomed over him. He punched her hard across the jaw. The amber eyes rolled up in her head. For a moment Simon enjoyed his success, but it didn't last. Charlotte roared in fury, spraying spittle through her bloody teeth. Behind her, he saw Malcolm stepping into place with pistol raised.

"Malcolm, don't!" he shouted.

"Just everyone drop to the floor!" It was Penny and she hefted a silver ball.

Simon covered his head. The round device struck Charlotte square in the chest. The ball exploded in a cloud of silver dust. Charlotte hacked violently, flinging herself away from Simon's prone figure. Clawed hands slapped wildly at her fur and face in a vain attempt to dislodge the fine silver powder. The werewolf's whole body shuddered and her muscles abruptly seized as the silver penetrated pores and nostrils. She hunched over, gasping for breath. Then the grey fur faded and long limbs shrunk as she transformed to human. Simon rolled under Charlotte and caught her before she struck the floor. As he cradled her still form, he feared that Penny had used too much silver. But Charlotte suddenly drew in a wheezing breath and coughed violently. Simon held her and gently rubbed her back. Penny knelt with a look of concern.

Simon said, "Well done, Penny."

The engineer hefted another silver ball in her hand. "Figured a little silver in the lungs would make breathing hard. Glad it didn't kill the child."

Malcolm holstered his pistol, glowering at the small, shuddering form surrounded by the unsuspecting.

Chapter 7

KATE WALKED UPSTAIRS. THE HOUSE HAD SET-
tled again into a quiet hum of subdued activity, but her
heart still pounded at how close they had come to disaster. Charlotte was chained safe in her room downstairs,
sniffling quietly. Kate would have to meet with the
farmer, Mr. Romley, to ensure that all was well and
that his son would remain quiet over the events.

But more important was Imogen.

Kate's stomach churned at the thought that all the
progress her sister had made was now undone. Imogen
had been so relaxed just moments before the Romley
boy had come upon her. She had been enjoying simple
pleasures like the sunshine and playing with friends.
How quickly those joyous highs had been replaced by
frightening lows.

Kate knocked on her sister's closed door. Only silence
greeted the action. She heard no movement beyond. She
prayed Imogen hadn't locked it but waited another minute before she laid her hand on the handle. It clicked
open and she entered.

The faint winter light barely penetrated the room
through drawn velvet drapes. Kate searched the gloom

for Imogen while her eyes adjusted. She knew better than to open the curtains to the outside world.

"Imogen," Kate called out softly.

A familiar tinny voice echoed from her left as the homunculus skull once again spoke its bitter words. Kate turned to see Imogen crouched on the floor in the corner, huddled over the meager flame of a candle to ward off the deepening shadows. The dark veil covered Imogen's porcelain face, but her once-pretty dress was shredded, revealing patches of pale skin beneath. Kate's heart fell, but she kept her despair from showing.

"There you are," Kate announced, coming closer and settling herself on the floor beside her sister, unmindful of the dirt and clutter. Imogen had made a new nest of blankets and clothes. Kate sat near enough that their shoulders were close without touching.

She didn't know where to start in reassuring Imogen, but she was desperate to silence the grating recording, which set her nerves on edge. "It was a good thing Mr. Romley was here today. You remember Mr. Romley? He is a good friend of Father's. He guarded all of our secrets."

The skull's voice faltered a bit.

Kate continued. "He'll set his son, William, straight. Of that I have no doubt. Remember when he caught us stealing apples from his orchard?" Kate laughed at the memory. "We got in so much trouble."

From the jacket of Imogen's torn coat, which she still wore, popped the little hedgehog, who proceeded to crawl onto her lap and wash himself. Now the talking skull quieted. Imogen brought up her fingers to stroke the hedgehog.

Kate took a deep breath. "I almost feel bad for poor William. It can be a bit of a shock to visit the Anstruther girls. You never know what you'll find." She laughed sadly.

Imogen raised a translucent hand and pointed down to the floor, which Kate instinctively understood was the direction of Charlotte's room in the cellar.

"Charlotte's fine," Kate said.

Imogen tilted her head questioningly.

"Truly," Kate replied. "She is well. We just have to find the proper dosage of wulfsyl. This time, she didn't hurt anyone. Much. I've already taken care of Simon's small scratch. He's weaving magic spells with his usual aplomb. Soon we'll have hedgehogs everywhere."

Imogen's chest quivered with what appeared to be gentle laughter.

Kate grinned at the hopeful sign from her sister. "Would you like to see Charlotte?"

Imogen shoved up the veil from her disfigured face so Kate could see her excitement at the prospect. The homunculus skull tumbled from her lap to the floor, forgotten for now.

Kate held out her hand and Imogen grasped it with long, tentacle fingers. "We should take her a new dress. Why don't you pick out one for her?"

Imogen hesitated but then shuffled to a closet and pulled a box from a high shelf. She slowly worked the lid from the box, with Kate watching but not helping. Imogen shuffled through the box, pausing to run her fingers over the luxurious fabrics. Kate stood beside her and laid a gentle hand on her shoulder. She could feel the small sobs shaking her sister. They stood quietly for a few moments until, finally, Imogen drew out a beautiful party dress, a lovely shade of lavender and embellished with delicate navy embroidery.

"She'll love that one," Kate agreed, finding a clean cotton chemise for Charlotte to wear tonight. Then together they went downstairs to the cellar.

Charlotte was curled in a tight ball under a blanket

on the disheveled bed. Her head rose meekly at the
sound of the door opening. She looked forlorn and
sounded miserable. "I'm in trouble, aren't I?"

Kate settled herself on the foot of the bed while Imo-
gen sat in a chair close to Charlotte's head. "No, dear.
You behaved admirably. We're all terribly proud of you.
Aren't we, Imogen?"

Imogen nodded and reached out to gently touch Charlotte's shoulder.

"Mr. Malcolm isn't," Charlotte whimpered. "He
hates me."

Kate shook her head. "Mr. Malcolm is concerned,
that's all. We are a family here and there is a risk to everyone's safety. He has been a hunter all his life and has
made a commitment to keep the innocent safe from
those who do not care about life. You two know more
than most that it is hard to change what you are."

"I don't want to hurt anyone!" Charlotte clutched Imogen's rubbery hand. "I think I recognized Mr. Simon! I
tried not to hurt him. I didn't, did I?"

"No, dear. He's fine." Kate rubbed the girl's chained
ankle beneath the blanket.

Charlotte flopped down into her pillow. "I tried so
hard not to change. But that boy was throwing rocks at
Imogen. He shouldn't have done that! It made me so
mad." She squeezed her face tight, trying not to cry.

Imogen held out the dress to her friend.

Charlotte opened her eyes and stared at it. But she
turned away. "Why should I bother? I'll just ruin it. I've
destroyed every dress you gave me."

Imogen sagged and brought the dress back to her lap,
and the two girls lapsed into silence.

Kate scowled and folded her arms. "Truly, the two of
you give up too easily. Charlotte, I can have more dresses
than an elephant can carry brought here from London.
Mrs. Tolbert will have them altered in no time."

"You mean I can stay?" Charlotte's eyes brimmed.

"Of course, but you must calm down and not cry."

"Not even tears of joy?"

Kate smiled. "Well, maybe just a few." She grabbed up the two girls and hugged them.

THAT NIGHT, MALCOLM UNLOCKED THE CELLAR door and swung it back. In the dim half-light from the short candle he carried, he saw the small shape curled on the bed. Heavy snoring came from the sleeping figure that appeared to be a little girl. He stepped inside and closed the door behind him, leaving his hand against the heavy wood and iron for a moment. He set the candle on a small shelf and continued to watch the figure.

Charlotte.

They used its name when they talked about it; when they talked to it. Like it was a dog. God help them, like it was a girl. That pathetic pantomime of a tea party Kate staged was ghastly proof of just how deluded she was. The wulfsyl had failed. The thing went berserk out in the garden and could have killed that innocent farm boy. And it could have killed others who would've been complicit in their own deaths.

Malcolm wouldn't stand by and watch them continue to make such a dreadful mistake. He would do what none of them could.

He pulled one of his Lancaster pistols, cracking the breech and checking to make sure it was loaded with silver cartridges although he knew it already. He had spent a long time in his room, loading and unloading, before he made the long walk through the silent house. Downstairs. Into the library. Through the door to the cellar. He had stood in front of the door to the cell with the key in his hand for nearly five minutes.

Malcolm carefully closed the pistol breech, but the snapping sound still echoed through the room. He froze. The werewolf grunted sleepily and kicked its feet. The chain jangled. The little creature rolled onto its back, dropping its blanket on the floor. It lay sprawled on the bed, arms outstretched, breathing through its wide-open mouth in the carefree slumber of youth.

The Lancaster hung heavy as if it weighed thirty pounds. Malcolm's finger worked its way around the steel edge of the trigger guard as his arm lifted. He could smell the gun oil. The thing on the bed snorted and moved its little mouth up and down. It sniffed the air unconsciously, then gave a sigh. He watched the gentle rise and fall of the thing's chest. It was clad in a soft nightgown embroidered with flowers. It pushed its head deep into the pillow and threw an arm over its forehead. The snoring commenced again.

Malcolm could no longer feel his fingers clutching the pistol. His heart pounded in his ears so loud he thought it would wake the sleeping creature. His arm lowered. He turned away from the bed, his jaw aching from clamping down so tight.

Imogen stood in the open door. The strange pale figure weaved on her feet. She wore a nightdress and had a bonnet tied tightly on her bald head. The common clothes against her inhuman, bleached skin made her even more disturbingly peculiar. The tendril-like fingers of her right hand dangled from her frilly lace sleeve and were paler than the skull that she clutched in the other. Imogen made no sound and her face had the stillness of rictus. Her glistening whitish eye gazed past him to the sleeping werewolf. The inhuman eye rolled downward to take in the massive pistol in Malcolm's hand before it whirred up to lock on Malcolm.

"Imogen." His voice was rough and hesitant. He held

the queer gaze for a long moment, unsure what she could even see with that false eye. "You shouldn't be down here."

She merely stood bobbing slightly back and forth. The mechanical eye remained stationary, independent of the small movements of her head.

Malcolm looked away. He walked quickly to the door, but when he reached it, Imogen didn't move aside. Her face was still turned forward as if the little werewolf snorting blissfully in the bed had her full attention. But the mechanical eye continued to make a soft whir as it tracked the Scotsman's every move.

Malcolm inched past Imogen with a lowered head, careful to avoid her touch, and he pushed into the corridor. He turned away, oddly embarrassed for her to see the pistol as he holstered it. Then he cleared his throat. "I must lock the door. It isn't safe to leave you here."

Imogen walked into the room. Malcolm tensed as she approached the bed. Imogen bent over and took hold of the blanket with her spindly fingers. She picked it up and laid it over Charlotte, slowly spreading it to cover the werewolf's bare feet. Then she returned to the door and joined Malcolm in the hall. He closed the door and locked it.

"Won't you come with me?" he asked.

She didn't move, but when he started off, she followed with shuffling steps. Once back in the library, she gave him a cold, lifeless stare with her mechanical eye as she glided out. Then he heard *My sister has a gold key that our father made. It's what you want. My sister has a gold key that our father made. It's what you want* from the whispering skull as Imogen went upstairs and drifted off toward her distant room.

Malcolm replaced the key to Charlotte's cell in the

small brass bowl where Kate kept it. He noticed with curious alarm that his hand was shaking. He clenched his fists. He didn't see anyone else moving about the house as he returned to his room, packed his meager possessions, and went out into the winter night.

Chapter 8

"NO ONE SAW HIM LEAVE?" SIMON ASKED.

"No. He's just gone." Kate shoved aside a heavy evergreen branch that then swept back along the side of the red stallion she led, eliciting a nicker from the horse.

"I'm sure he'll be back." Simon gave a despondent sigh, slapping leather reins against his thigh. His grey Arabian mare pulled with annoyance and snatched at greenery.

"He took all his things with him, which, granted, wasn't much." Kate nestled her head alongside her horse's powerful jaw. "Apparently he wasn't happy with our inclusion of Charlotte. So much so that he couldn't stay."

"I must say I didn't see it coming."

"He's wrong though. About Charlotte."

Simon hummed noncommittally as he ducked under a branch.

Kate looked at him. "Isn't he?"

Simon pulled a twig from his horse's mouth, causing the mare to toss her head. "What we're trying is unprecedented. The only way of judging right or wrong is whether we survive."

They continued silently. The winter forest around

them was cold and wet, and little sun penetrated to the spongy floor. There was no wind and the breath from humans and horses lay thick in the air. The brush was thick despite the season.

A nearby juniper bush rustled and burst open as a huge hairy shape roared into view. A massive beast bore down on Simon. He jerked up an arm to block the bounding Aethelred from trampling him and the wolf-hound crashed against him. The dog's tongue lolled wildly with canine enthusiasm. As he was toppled off balance, Simon caught a glimpse of a grey streak above him. He bobbed his head just in time to avoid the clamping teeth of the wild-eyed mare.

"Hah!" Simon scrambled to his feet, jerking the reins to snap the horse's head around. "I knew you were waiting for a chance to strike. Very cunning, this girl."

Kate calmly patted her own placid mount, who had barely twitched a muscle. "Yes, she's a firebrand. She nipped Hogarth quite badly last year."

"You might have warned me she's a biter."

Kate huffed and checked a saddle cinch. "You should assume every horse is a biter until you find otherwise."

"So now I need to be wary of *every* filly in the Anstruther stable?" Simon smirked, regarding her as he scratched the great wolfhound's head.

"I'm sure we could arrange a mule for you to mount if that's your riding preference." Kate offered a wise smile. "You might be hard-pressed to keep up."

He raised an eyebrow. "Mule or goat, the day you can outride me is a long ways off."

Kate's head snapped up. "I beg your pardon, Mr. Archer?"

"I was merely saying that I am a finer horseman than you."

She worked her jaw from side to side and took hold of her horse's bridle. "I'm sorry, give me a moment to adjust to the shock of hearing something so outlandish, will you?"

"Take all the time you need. Which is precisely what I would say to you should we race to the house."

The sound of leather creaking came from Kate tightening her gloved fists. Her green eyes flared with a light that was no longer quite a performance. "Are you trying to goad me, sir?"

Simon gave a grand laugh and set a foot in the stirrup. He patted the saddle. "Care to put your money where your shapely derriere is?"

Kate rose onto her horse with her expression set, her back straight and shoulders squared, sitting astride in blatant disregard for the proper fashion for a female rider. Her mount wheeled with his forelegs prancing and steam snorting from his nostrils. "Prepare to see as much of my shapely derriere as you ever shall, and from a great distance."

With that, she kicked her mount into action. The huge red blur roared past Simon just as he settled in the leather seat. His mare reared in surprise. He cursed and laughed and gathered the Arabian under control, spinning it around to gain her head. Then he shouted and the little horse exploded gamely in pursuit. The two horses weaved along the forest path, trees flashing by on both sides and branches slapping at them. Simon saw Kate break out of the forest and into the open ground.

She leaned low over the red stallion's withers. His glossy coat shone in the stark morning sun. His long legs ate up the terrain, flinging clods of dirt into the air behind them as they raced at breakneck speed over the rolling Surrey countryside. Beside them ran the long, graceful form of the Irish wolfhound, keeping even with the horse's ferocious pace.

As Simon cleared the tree line, the wind screamed

past his cheeks, making his eyes water. He could barely make out Kate and her stallion across the hills. She rode with wild abandon, her sure hands held tight to the reins. The ground was too uneven and too littered with obstacles for the animal to be given its head. A herd of fallow deer gazed at them in the distance over their up-turned noses before breaking into a run through the morning mist. The wolfhound swerved to give chase.

"Aethelred, heel!" Kate commanded so firmly that Simon heard it across the distance, and the hound fell back into stride alongside his master.

A hedgerow waited in front of them so Kate guided the horse to a high knob. The pounding muscles gathered, then they were flying over the obstacle with plenty of room to spare. Kate leaned forward, her hands and knees steady. They landed with a jolt but she never lost her seat. She slowed the stallion, waiting for Aethelred to find his way through the hedge. The horse reared and danced in annoyance. Then the broad-chested hound broke through, loping toward them, his pink tongue lolling.

Simon drove the Arabian now, sensing a chance to gain ground. Kate turned back and smiled. She waved her arm and gave the stallion his head. Like a thunderclap, he bolted down the open field, his giant strides swallowing up the miles until they were gone from Simon's view.

Moments later, as he approached the east wing of Hartley Hall, he saw Kate standing on the patio outside the library. She was pretending to be bored. She looked up at him approaching and began to tap her foot. Simon came in on a leisurely post, reining in before her with a gallant doff of his hat.

"Glad you could make it," Kate said quietly.

Simon patted his horse's glistening neck. "An uncommon combination in my steed. Savage and slow."

"Perhaps you don't know how to get your mount to respond properly."

"No." He swung out of the saddle. "That can't be it."

The wry smile on Kate's face was beautiful. Exertion had given her a reddish flush and the beating of her heart was visible in the pulsing of a small patch of bare skin at her collar. All doubt and fret were gone from her sharp-eyed gaze. She was capable and fearless in this moment. He needed that power from her almost like an element in a magic spell.

Simon handed the reins to a stable boy and before Kate could turn, he took her hand. "Sit with me, Kate." He was happy that she merely drew a breath as he led her to chairs on the edge of the grass. She gave him a quick glance to show that she was grateful to him for buying her a few more minutes away from her pressures. She leaned back, eyes closed, soaking in a bit of cold-morning sun on her face. They sat together quietly.

Coffee was brought and Hogarth came too, carrying a large envelope, which he handed to Simon. "This came for you while you were out, sir. Special courier."

"Malcolm?" Simon took the package, but when he didn't recognize the handwriting, he sat back, deflated.

"The courier said it was from Sir Henry Clatterburgh."

Simon unwrapped the string and lifted the flap of the envelope. There was a sheaf of papers inside. He pulled them out and saw notes relating to the murder at St. George's. There was a smaller envelope sealed with wax clipped to the first page. Simon cracked the seal and removed several sheets of paper.

He said, "It's dated yesterday. *Simon—Forgive the tardiness of my reply to your last note, as indeed I had no intention of replying—so forgive my stupidity as well. Here is information you may find useful. You perhaps know of the second slaying at Christ Church Spit-*

alfields three days ago." Simon looked up with alarm. "A second murder?"

"Christ Church is another of Hawksmoor's churches." Kate leaned in now to study the pages.

"That's clearly no coincidence." He continued reading. "*Or if the Metropolitan Police have their way, you do not. In any case, as you will see from the enclosed, two women have now been murdered in similar inexplicably brutal fashion at London churches. The police, when they speak of it at all, refer to these two as the Sacred Heart Murders. How clever of them. I know that you have certain particular interests, you and your friend, Mr. Barker—*"

"He knows you're a magician?" Kate exclaimed.

"If true, it's surprising. I never gave Henry much credit for noticing anything. I did mention the ritualistic nature of the murder in my letter to him. He likely thinks I'm some sort of cabalist or Rosicrucian. A poseur dilettante who toys with occultism, like the chaps at the Mercury Club."

"And you're not?" Kate asked with bland sarcasm.

Simon offered her a cool glance. "Perhaps you're forgetting I pulled a hedgehog from a hat."

"I had indeed forgotten that particular miracle. Forgive me."

"If I may? Where was I . . . *I know that you have particular interests, you and your friend, Mr. Barker, which may lend themselves to a unique angle on these blasphemous crimes. I fear there is little likelihood of a solution coming from official sources. There are no authorities currently looking for the author of these murders. I only have the enclosed documents because they were handed to me in a collection of refuse with instructions from superiors in the Home Office to destroy them.*"

Simon tapped a finger against his chin. "Well, good

for you, Henry. I see we won't be helping the authorities on this matter. We'll *be* the authorities."

When Kate didn't reply, he glanced at her to see she was distracted, surprisingly. She stared into the bright blue sky, half lifting from her seat. Simon followed her gaze, but only noticed a few wispy clouds and a single distant bird.

"Something wrong?" he asked.

"That bird." She stood and started for the library, keeping her attention skyward. After a minute, she returned with a brass spyglass. She put it to her eye and twisted the lens. "It doesn't look right."

"In what way?" He thought the small black shape seemed to be a normal bird wheeling in the air. It dropped and spiraled downward.

Hogarth returned to the patio carrying a long rifle. He put the butt to his shoulder and waited.

Simon laughed. "With everything you've seen here at Hartley Hall, this seems a bit extreme for a sparrow." The little creature rolled for another pass around Hartley Hall.

Kate continued to track it with the telescope until it vanished from sight beyond the roof. "It appears to be a common swift, but they're almost never here in winter. It's alone, and it isn't making any noise. Hogarth, stand ready. I don't like it."

The manservant put his cheek against the rifle and aimed where he expected the bird's path would reveal itself next. Simon didn't say anything else. He had little doubt the bird was a normal swift, but if it disturbed Kate, so be it. It was a little distressing, however, to see her so fixated on something so ordinary just when they had received such momentous news from Henry.

Simon reached for the spyglass and without seeming impatient, starting scanning for the offending avian intruder. A small shape flitted from behind the cover of a chimney at rooftop level. He brought the bird into clear sight through the glass. In an instant, Simon saw that Kate was right; it was not normal.

Simon swung the spyglass against the barrel of Hogarth's rifle just as it went off with a smoky boom. The lead bullet ripped through a line of shrubs and cracked off a dormant fountain in the garden.

"Simon!" Kate stared at him in shock, then looked back at the strange bird that glided toward them. The swift's eyes glowed unnatural blue. Kate also reached into her high boot for a thin dagger.

"Stop." Simon seized her arm. "It's from Penny. It's one of her mechanical creatures."

Kate still held the knife ready but hesitated as the little bird landed on the bricks and hopped a few paces. It stopped at Simon's feet, looking up with a turn of its head. The brass and metal of its body glinted in the sunlight, showing off miniscule gears and tight seams of segmented copper. One could hear the faint sounds of ratcheting and tight springs winding down. It hopped to the door of the library and began to peck on the glass. When its beak parted Penny's voice came out, "Simon Archer, please."

Simon stared at the bird with bemusement. "Um. This is Simon Archer."

The mechanical swift chirped and whistled, then twisted its head about. It fluttered into the air and landed nimbly on Simon's shoulder. He heard the faint whisper of Penny, "Simon, please come to my shop. Quickly. Don't bring Malcolm."

Kate watched in amazement. "Penny. What goes on in your mind?"

Simon handed Hogarth the spyglass with a sheepish smile of apology for spoiling his shot as the automatic swift sprang onto the ground. He took up the bundle of papers from Henry. "We need to go to London and visit Christ Church Spitalfields. But we'll stop by Penny's shop first. And we'll let her know she needs to study her ornithology a bit more or her birds may be blasted out of the skies."

Kate took a deep breath. "I don't know if Imogen and Charlotte are capable of being left alone."

Hogarth said, "I will tend Miss Imogen and Miss Charlotte. You go where you are needed."

"Thank you, Hogarth." Kate gave one last admiring glance at the strange bird and headed for the house.

WHEN THE ANSTRUTHER CARRIAGE PULLED UP outside the Wonderworks shop on Bond Street in London it was evening and the street was in deep shadow. Simon set down the dossier on the Sacred Heart Murders and peered out. He noted with concern that the shop was dark as if closed.

As he stepped out onto the sidewalk, Simon lifted his walking stick instinctively, fingering the handle, knowing there was a deadly short sword hidden inside the stick. The door had a shade pulled down to obscure the glass so he tried to peer in around the edges of the drapes pulled across the wide plate glass. He saw a sliver of the darkened front room with its familiar counter and chairs. The high shelves behind the counter were crowded with objects and packages awaiting pickup. He rapped the door with his stick.

The door handle rattled from inside. Penny's face appeared when the door pulled back. Her eyes were hooded with unusual distress and her face was drawn tight from strain.

"Simon, thank God." Penny took his arm, pulling him into the shop. Her hand was trembling. Then she noticed Kate and gave a gasp, sweeping the sidewalk with worried eyes.

"It's only Kate," Simon said softly. "Malcolm is not with us. As you requested. For some reason."

"Oh." Penny breathed out, and reached for Kate with an apologetic shake of her head. "I'm sorry. I'm glad you're here, Kate." She shut the door after they entered the shop. "This is something that Malcolm wouldn't . . . understand. I don't want him involved."

Kate put a comforting hand on Penny's arm. Simon caught another movement in the corner of his eye and spun around, twisting the handle of his stick. It was Charles, Penny's brother, and he rolled out of the shadows in his remarkable motorized wheeled chair. He sat tall and straight, his long fingers working the control levers with practiced facility. He was a handsome young man with sensitive eyes and long blond hair. His long legs were gathered uselessly before him and his knees pressed together to one side. Simon could see that Charles seemed even more stricken than his sister. He was pale and his jaw was set hard, with muscles bulging along his neck.

"Good evening, Charles." Simon lowered the stick. "I'm surprised to see you both sitting here in the darkened anteroom."

Charles nodded silently, seeming unable to speak. He glanced at Penny as if asking her to talk. Penny was holding Kate's hand, breathing nervously through thin lips. Kate tightened her grip to comfort the young engineer. Penny opened her mouth, then paused, trying to gather herself.

Simon found it disconcerting to see her so flustered. Of all his little band of adventurers, Penny always seemed the least affected by the strange events that cascaded around them. She saw everything as a problem to be solved or an opportunity requiring some clever device or gadget.

Finally Penny said in a faltering voice, "You may know that Charles and I were raised by our mother."

When she paused again, Simon inclined his head toward her, prompting her to continue.

Penny's eyes flicked to her brother and down to the floor. "We opened this shop five years ago, and she lived here with us. She took in sewing even though she didn't need to. The shop was successful and we told her she had done enough; she should relax. She wouldn't have it. She insisted on contributing. She would sit in her room upstairs and sew. Last year, she died."

"I'm sorry," Simon said.

Penny raised her gaze with a cold granite chill in her eyes. "Two nights ago, she came home."

Charles shuddered and sank back into his chair, glancing toward the rooms upstairs. Penny left Kate and went to her brother's side, putting an arm around his shoulders.

"I see." Simon watched the distraught siblings. "Can you think of any possible reason?"

Penny actually laughed. "Are there any normal reasons why people come back from the dead?"

"A few, but let's put that aside for now."

Kate asked, "Penny, where was your mother buried?"

"At St. George's Bloomsbury."

Simon and Kate exchanged knowing glances and Simon tapped his stick on the floor. "Well done, Kate. There's our answer then."

Penny looked up. "What?"

"The murder at St. George's has had a ritual effect."

"Someone is raising the dead?" Penny's voice was outraged in horror fueled by her personal connection. "How? Why?"

"We're not sure of either." Simon took a deep breath.

"Can you do something?" Penny asked simply.

He gave her a reassuring smile, knowing she referred only to her mother and not the ritual. "Where is she?"

Charles replied quickly, "Upstairs. Second room on the left. Her old room."

"You two wait here." Simon started for the stairs with Kate on his heels. "We'll have a look."

They went up and found themselves in a dim hallway. The carpet under their feet was worn. The wainscoting was dusty and chipped. Penny's focus was clearly not household duties, and they likely did not have domestics given the secretive and dangerous nature of the work she did. Simon lifted a guttering oil lamp from a sideboard.

Kate cleared her throat nervously. "Poor Penny. Can it really be possible that her mother is up here?"

"Yes. Or at least some other lost soul," Simon answered, as they stopped outside the second door on the left. Simon listened carefully and his heart beat faster when he thought he could hear faint shuffling from inside. He reached for the doorknob.

Kate touched his arm. "Why don't you just look in using your runes?"

"It's easier to open the door."

Kate took a deeper breath and grimaced. "Do you have any experience with the restless dead? Are we in danger?"

"It depends. Undead can range from quite polite to unfortunately ravenous."

"And if she's the latter?" Kate pressed anxiously.

"Likely she would have slaughtered someone by now, but stand back just in case." Simon opened the door.

A stench wafted out. Kate covered her nose. They stood in the doorway, and in the faint light they saw a shape moving. Someone was rocking in the dark.

Simon stepped inside and the sickly yellow light from the lamp crawled up a figure on the far side of the room. It had once been a woman. The bony shape was covered in moldering cloth, the remnants of graveclothes. As she rocked forward into the lamplight, Simon saw the toothy grin of a desiccated face still tied with a winding cloth. With her two grey hands, she manipulated a piece of cloth that rested in her lap. She worked bony fingers along the edge of the cloth while the other hand panto-mimed pushing a needle and thread. She pulled the imaginary needle up tight, then went back for another stitch along the hem. Sunken eyes followed each of her repetitive mock movements carefully.

Simon cleared his throat. "Mrs. Carter?"

The dead thing paused, but after a second, she began to finger the hem of the cloth again.

Simon glanced back at Kate, who stared in fascinated horror. He slowly crossed the room toward the rocking shape and set the lamp on a small table. The cadaver reached the end of her cloth and stopped, her imaginary needle paused in midair as if lost. Then she straightened out the filthy cloth and pushed the missing needle into the same edge, but now began her imaginary stitching back in the opposite direction.

"Mrs. Carter," Simon said more firmly, "can you hear me? Would you stop stitching, please?"

There was hesitation with her needle held aloft in her rotting hand. The dead thing seemed confused and un-sure of her next step.

Simon reached out and pinched the quivering cloth with two fingers. The cadaver growled wetly in her throat. She stopped rocking and pulled the fabric back. Simon held fast. "Ma'am, your children have asked me to tell you that your work here is done. You have com-pleted your task admirably."

The dead woman's brow knitted slightly.

"Yes, ma'am," Simon continued. "Your daughter would very much like you to return to your rest. She worries about you."

Dead fingers loosened the pressure on the fabric, leaving bits of flesh on the cloth as Simon slipped it from her grasp. He set it carefully on the table next to the lamp. The cadaver's hands dropped flat on her lap and she sat motionless.

"Will you come with me, ma'am? I will go with you back to your place."

The dead thing moaned. Simon tensed. He heard Kate shift behind him, most likely readying a vial. But the cadaver simply rose to her feet like an exhausted old woman. Simon extended his arm toward the door. The corpse gathered the tattered shroud around her and shuffled forward.

Kate backed out into the hallway ahead of the dead woman. The extent of the decay was clear now and the horrible stains on her graveclothes were obvious.

Simon said, "Kate, go down and warn Penny. She and Charles may not wish to see this."

A loud gasp from the top of the stairs showed that Penny was already a witness to her mother's corpse staggering into the hallway. The young woman's horrified gaze was locked on the thin figure of her mother. Penny's hands covered her mouth and tears began to stream down her face.

Simon called out, "It's all right, Penny. She's willing to go back. I'll ensure she reaches her rest safely."

Penny said in a strangled voice, "I'll go with you."

"You need not."

The cadaver shuffled to the top of the stairs and reached for the railing with a faltering hand. Penny didn't cringe; she instinctively took hold of the crumbling arm as the dead woman put an unsteady foot onto the first step.

"Careful, Mama," Penny whispered, taking the old woman's weight. The cadaver stopped and turned slightly toward her daughter. A grey hand lifted and the palm cupped Penny's cheek. The young woman didn't flinch and actually pressed her face tighter against the dead hand with closed eyes of comfort.

Simon smiled at the daughter who helped her mother slowly down the stairs. Kate put her hand to her mouth, her eyes glistening. When they all reached the bottom, a shocked gurgle came from Charles followed by racking sobs. Simon went to the man hunched in his chair with his eyes covered. "Charles, try not to think of her as you see her now. This is merely her earthly form reanimated by sorcery."

Charles groaned and pressed his forehead to his knees.

Penny said from her mother's side, "I'll be back shortly, Charles. Please don't worry. It's all right now."

Simon rejoined Kate a few steps behind Penny, who had an arm around her mother's waist. Penny opened the door and cold air washed in.

"Wait!" called Charles.

They turned to see the man sitting straight, his face locked in despair. But he lifted a trembling hand and pointed to the corner.

"It's so chilly out," Charles said. "Please give her a cloak."

"Good man." Simon nodded. Kate retrieved the heavy woolen cloak from a rack. She draped it over the frail shoulders of the corpse. Penny carefully adjusted the collar as she would when her elderly mother was alive.

With that, they were off into the night toward an empty grave.

Chapter 9

SPITALFIELDS WAS A DECAYING SECTION OF LON-
don. Crowded and ill-used, with no funds for repairs or
upkeep. It had once been home to families of wealth
and position, but few remained. Much of east London
was just like that now. Hawksmoor's Christ Church
was still a notable bastion of the parish though. The
church rose up with white columns and a pyramidal
steeple that nearly overwhelmed the façade beneath it.

Simon and Kate exited the carriage. They moved into
the church, through the antechamber, and into the main
sanctuary. It was a towering space full of straight lines
and even angles. Columns and arches marked time
along the sides to the altar at the far end. Galleries between the columns overlooked the floor and box pews.

The aging sexton, who was extinguishing candles at
the altar, looked up at the sound of visitors. He started
down the aisle. "There are no services this evening, if
you please."

"Oh yes, we know," Simon said with easy charm.
"My fiancée and I are planning on being married here
in the fall."

"The fall? You have ample time, sir. You should come
back tomorrow and speak to the vicar."

"Yes, well, tomorrow I leave for Portsmouth, where my ship is bound for West Africa." Simon took Kate's hand and pressed it affectionately to his chest.

Kate had been staring at Simon in surprise but now fell into character and slumped a wistful head against his shoulder. He patted her cheek, and she said to the sexton, "Would you mind terribly if we walked around for a moment and dreamed of that day when we will be wed?"

The old man looked annoyed but then relented to true romance. "Fine. I'll go tidy up somewhere. Please be as brief as you can. It is quite late and I've supper waiting and a wife of my own to get home to."

Simon slipped the man a few shillings as he passed them in the aisle. As soon as he trudged out of the sanctuary, Simon and Kate split up and headed for the east and west aisles. There were not true naves in this single massive gallery of a church.

Kate called, "What sort of flowers do you prefer for the ceremony?"

"I leave it to you. But I think hyacinth?"

She popped up from beside a pew. "How did you know I like hyacinth?"

"You mentioned it once. Here! Found it. It's partially hidden by a plaque that was added later, but one of the names is clearly here." Simon started for the altar.

Kate called out too. "One here as well." She walked back toward the door.

Soon it was clear all four of the mystical names were present, carved onto the floor or the walls. A quick inscription spell also told them that Pendragon's hieroglyphics were also present. It had been a short night after the affair at Penny's shop, and a long day of scouting the major churches of the London area. They had concentrated on those designed by Nicholas Hawksmoor, but they had stopped at other churches as well, including the important St. Mary-le-bow and St. Paul's Cathedral. The mystical names and symbols had been found only in four specific locations: St. George's Bloomsbury, of course, and here in Christ Church Spitalfields. Two other Hawksmoor churches hosted the names: St. George in the East and St. Mary Woolnoth. All others were devoid of those specific occult influences.

"Obviously not a coincidence," Simon said. "Two Hawksmoor churches with Pendragon runes. Two murders. And those four names."

"From what I've heard of Pendragon, it's surprising that he would delve into blood magic. He was the only one of the Great Trio who was sane and decent."

Simon ran a finger over a pillar where one of Pendragon's hidden runes was carved. "That's what I've heard too. He and Gaios and Ash created the Order of the Oak centuries ago. All of them so powerful in their magic that they lived through centuries. Gaios was the oldest, an earth elemental who went mad from power and perhaps just from the weight of living so long. Ash was a vivimancer who turned to necromancy to ensure her survival. Pendragon was a scribe, and he understood the balance of magic. And he understood the danger from those who practice the arts."

"That's why he designed the Bastille in Paris to act as a prison for sorcerers or monsters who were threats to mankind, like Dr. White and Gretta."

"He even imprisoned his old friend Gaios because the elemental was prone to uncontrollable rages, and Pendragon couldn't allow him to walk free any longer." Simon looked up to a dim, stained-glass face of Christ high above him. "Pendragon was a hard man, but I don't believe he would require blood magic to enact one of his spells. I'm convinced someone is trying to break his original spell, like a thief using a pry bar to force a lock for which he has no key."

"Do you have any idea what Pendragon's spell is?"

"No. I can't read his inscriptions. He uses scripts from many languages, including ancient Egyptian. It's incredibly complex, but I do get a sense of how powerful it must be." Simon glanced around the shadowy white space. "Hawksmoor built these edifices to be mystical dams, it seems. I notice the aether here, as I did at St. George's Bloomsbury."

"What do you mean you *notice aether*?"

Simon looked down at her thoughtfully. "I'd like to show you something. Will you step outside?"

"What is it? Can't you show me here?"

"I'd rather not. Not here where a murder has recently occurred. Outside?"

Kate tilted her head in acceptance and motioned for Simon to lead. He pulled a flickering candle from its ornate stand by the door and carried it out into the cold. She followed him into the burying ground beside Christ Church. The temperature had dropped and their breath misted into the air. Kate pulled up the collar of her coat.

Simon set his walking stick against a gravestone and blew out the candle. He crushed the black wick between thumb and forefinger. He held the blackened finger to her face and said, "May I?"

She nodded and he touched her forehead. He moved his callused fingertip along her face, studying his actions intensely. He finally stopped, considered whatever he had written on her forehead for a second, then placed his warm palm against her cheek. She heard him whisper and it sounded like the voices of a choir sweeping through a church. Her knees grew weak. Kate's vision flared. Her heart leapt with alarm as tendrils of green appeared between her and Simon.

He smiled from behind a weird, living swirl. "Don't be afraid. There's no danger. Look around you."

Kate turned and saw the once-dark cemetery aglow with aether. Emerald winds caressed every stone, sliding around trees, whispering across the serene facets of carved angels, slipping over the mournful faces of children in marble.

"Oh my God," Kate said. "What is this?"

"It's magic. It's aether."

"But it's everywhere. I've never seen anything like this."

"Few have."

She stepped away from him, turning, staring at the waves of mysticism whirling around them. "Have you?"

"This is how I see the world always." His voice was soft and low.

"You see aether everywhere? At all times?"

"Yes. I believe I'm actually seeing into the realm where aether exists before it's summoned into our world by magical spells. Apparently the boundaries between the spheres are thin and permeable. And it tends to haunt areas of magical potential, such as this church. It's so persistent that it's similar to the way you feel the wind or hear a noise in the background. Eventually you accommodate yourself to it unless it changes tone or pitch, then you notice it again." He looked around. "For example, I see it clearly now, more than normal. But that's likely because I'm attuned to it, showing it to you."

Kate looked at Simon as if for the first time. He stared at her, his gaze unwavering despite the wonder that was occurring around them. He lived in a different realm from others, from her. However, he looked ordinary. "I can't see aether coming off of you. With your power, it should be pouring through you."

"It doesn't work that way. I can't see it once it's in our world and in use."

Kate moved close and took Simon's hands. She turned from the visible magic swirling around her and looked into his eyes. "If this heavenly sight is common to you, how do you even pretend to be a normal man?"

"I'm not normal, Kate. Neither are you." Simon reached to cup her chin and leaned down to kiss her. Kate's lips were soft and she pressed into his. He could feel the warmth of her breath in his mouth.

She opened her eyes and let out a long sigh when they parted.

Simon ran a strong finger along the line of her jaw. "Perhaps a more romantic spot might have been arranged for a first kiss."

"No. This is lovely. I must no longer fear graveyards. I could feel that kiss down to my ankles." Kate's brow furrowed and she looked down at the hem of her gown, which touched the earth. The material was rustling. She grasped the fabric and lifted it slightly.

A hand protruded from the dirt and its fingers flailed at her petticoat.

"Jesus God!" Kate stamped her heel onto the grey hand.

She stepped back, but Simon noticed the top of a head beginning to breach free of the ground near his foot. Together, he and Kate ran toward the church, trying to avoid the crop of hands and fingers sprouting. The ground grew soft beneath Simon's shoes and he barely leapt aside as a sinkhole opened on a slowly widening morass full of struggling bone and hanging flesh and upturned, desperate eye sockets.

All around them gruesome marionettes rose awkwardly from the dirt before pausing to shake themselves and stare at their surroundings. One dead man stood and dusted off his tattered shroud, then immediately began to claw at the ground next to him, assisting a cadaverous woman to her own freedom. Some wandered in confusion, milling into corners of the walled cemetery. Others, rich with decay, moaned and flailed angrily.

A bony hand swiped at Simon's head. He ducked with a whisper and proceeded to grasp the moldering thing by the collarbone. With a quick pull, he used his runic strength to tear the rib cage loose. The cadaver fell apart like a broken toy, but its pieces continued to struggle.

Kate pulled a pistol from under her coat and fired, shattering the skull of the nearest corpse. There was no time to reload the heavy weapon so she used the blunt end to slam against approaching shamblers.

Simon spun and used his walking stick to crush the skull of an undead man reaching for them. He then swung both cane and rib cage to batter at the wandering dead. His coattails flew as he cleaved bodies into bits of bone and flying gobbets of meat. But that activity attracted the attention of more shamblers. The growing mob circled closer. Simon tossed the shattered rib cage aside.

Kate grasped her small handbag and pulled a small blue vial and threw it into the grinding mass. It shattered harmlessly, causing two creatures to pause with a look of confusion.

"What is that potion?" Simon asked.

Kate stared as the two undead things began to shuffle forward again. She glanced into her purse. "Damn it! That was my perfume."

"I hope you have something stronger."

"I have this." She was already filling her hand with another vial. She twisted the cap and immediately the vessel began to glow. She threw it across in front of her and a flowing sheet of bluish flame washed over a swathe of the undead. Though the corpses continued to come on, the weird fire quickly consumed their flesh and they fell into simmering piles of ash. Others that struck out across the field of fire were consumed, as the flame would not die. Still, there were more cadavers that moved around the blaze to take their place.

"Greek fire!" Simon shouted. "Do you have more?"

"One," she replied as bony fingers seized her flowing dress. She managed to tear a portion away. "I knew I should've ignored fashion and brought a sword."

"Take this." He pulled the sword from his stick with a whisper of blue. A quick word sent an electric glow coursing along the blade. Simon extended the stick sword to her, handle first. "Do not touch the blade or you will die."

"What will you use?" The moment she took the curved silver handle, the exhilarating surge of power registered in her face.

"I'll manage." He wrapped his arms around a large marble cross on top of a vault. With a grunt, he broke the huge ornament off and hefted it like a cricket batsman. As Kate worked the sword in a galvanic arc, slicing limbs and heads, Simon swung the heavy cross with thunderous effort. The wet sounds of impact filled the air.

Still there was no respite from the vacant faces with exposed teeth and sunken noses. Kate was swinging for her life, but the sword was losing speed and height. She didn't have the stamina that Simon's tattooed runes provided. If her arm faltered, she might fall under the ragged fingernails and clamping jaws of the dead.

"Kate," he roared over the squelching blows from his heavy cross, "I need thirty seconds."

"Of course," she rasped with faltering breath. "I have it under control." She drew her last vial of Greek fire, popped the cap, and sloshed it in a semicircle around them. Blue fire rose from the ground, consuming the wretched cadavers that approached without reason or fear. She turned to cover the other direction with the sparkling sword.

Simon lifted the cross over his head with both hands and hurled it with all his considerable power, mowing down the closest ranks of undead. He dropped to one knee and began to draw runes in the dirt with the end of his walking stick. This wasn't the perfect way to write a spell, but it was their best hope.

"Stay still," Kate warned Simon, and began a deft dance about him, the slight blade flashing as it crashed against the surrounding corpses, wreaking havoc more like a broadsword. She neatly worked her way around the focused Simon, leaving a ring of anatomical wreckage in a sheer ballet of viciousness.

He heard Kate moving around him and felt heat as the blade passed near his head. He tried not to see all the mud-crusted feet pressing ever closer. He smiled grimly, ready to make the last stroke on his rune, when the filthy hem of Kate's dress swept across his design and brushed it out of existence.

"Hurry please," she huffed.

"Yes, thank you." He set about redrawing the runes, keeping one arm out to block another gown disaster.

"It's been thirty seconds."

He didn't look up. The tumult grew louder. There was nothing but the sound of colliding bodies and Kate's desperate, hacking breath. He shoved it aside and continued to scribe in the dirt, focusing his concentration.

"Simon!" Kate's voice was a panicked shout. "Have you forgotten how to tell the bloody time?"

He traced one last line and hissed an ancient word. The rune glowed up into his face and an eldritch luster spread outward across the ground. He leapt to his feet. Kate's right arm was trapped by desiccated limbs. Clawed fingers grasped her hair and she was being dragged off her feet. Simon seized the arm holding her and snapped it in half. He kicked out at another cadaver while pulling the sword from her hand. He spun and sliced the wrist tangled in her hair.

With a whispered word for additional muscle, he grabbed Kate around the waist and leapt for a marble vault. Filthy hands reached out as his foot struck the edge of a tomb and he dropped hard to his knees. Dead figures surrounded the raised platform, reaching and clawing for the living pair. Fingers fell short of Simon and Kate, the cadavers slipping lower as if the vault were lifting into the air.

All around them the churchyard glowed with eerie smoke and the ground had turned near liquid. The flailing cadavers were sinking unwillingly back into the earth. Even the Greek fire was swallowed by the dark, cold ground.

The vault shifted to the side like a sinking ship. Kneeling quickly, Simon grabbed an edge to keep from slipping overboard into the quicksand of waiting undead. Kate did the same, her eyes wide in concern, but she said not a word.

Then the pitching stopped with a final burst of eldritch light as the ground hardened again. A few corpses around them still clawed up through the dirt, but found it less pliable than before. They were trapped. For now.

Kate leaned into Simon, taking solace in their survival. "For future reference, I now despise cemeteries." There were trails of blood on her face and neck but she wasn't badly injured.

Simon grinned and tenderly kissed her scratched forehead. He reached toward Kate as if to caress her, but instead fumbled with her hair, pulling painful tangles. He came away with a moving hand.

She grimaced in disgust.

"You had something in your hair," he quipped, tossing the living appendage away. He stretched out his legs and looked over the wriggling churchyard. "Now with a bit of time I should be able to fashion a spell to suppress these poor wretches and keep them in the earth."

"Good." Kate regarded him. "I'll have a first kiss story that will surely dominate the garden club."

Simon laughed as the bells began to chime in the frigid night air.

Chapter 10

IT WAS EARLY MORNING AND MALCOLM TRIED not to think about Hartley Hall and the creature sleeping there. He had been days dwelling on it while searching for any sign of lycanthropes remaining in London. He tried not to think of the blank expression on Imogen's face as he had turned from the slumbering little form with the pistol in his hand. Even though she had looked no more involved than staring at a tiresome painting, there was accusation in her strange eyes. Charlotte wasn't a little girl; it was a monster, Malcolm thought with a flare of anger. They would never understand that until it rose up and killed them. Malcolm had no intention of being one of them.

Amateurs.

Although he had to grudgingly admit Simon had done amazing things, led their frail little group against Gretta Aldfather and Dr. White, two of the most fearsome creatures that ever stormed from the darkness. Malcolm had started to believe that the man had promise even though he was a magician. But now the Scotsman started to think that Simon was typical of magicians after all, prone to absorb concepts of their own greatness the way they absorbed aether. The man was walking the path to destruction because he had begun to believe in his own power.

Well and good, Malcolm thought, except that Simon was taking Kate and Penny with him. Those two might stay with the scribe until it was too late. But it wasn't Malcolm's mission in life to exercise power over anyone else. Every man and woman was a free agent. He would no more tell anyone what to do than he would accept someone's telling him.

Malcolm found himself taking a cold, dark route that sent him past the St. Giles soup kitchen. It was nestled between a dilapidated storefront and an empty, crumbling building. He wasn't exactly sure why he went there. He fingered the thick woolen scarf around his neck. It felt ordinary, but his throat had been a hairsbreadth from being cut but for this scarf. He wanted to treat the woman who had made it to a fine meal. She had offered him warmth and a kind word in a city that teemed with opportunists and charlatans. For that alone he was willing to pay his respects and thank her.

There was a dim light in the window. The door was unlocked, as he suspected it would be, so he entered the deserted space filled with simple, long tables and benches.

Malcolm's knuckles rapped as he closed the front door behind him. "Hello."

There was a loud clanking as if someone was banging pots and pans about in the kitchen. He made his way to the back and opened the door. A rank smell wafted out that near brought the Scotsman to gagging. It was as if the week's garbage had been left to spoil in the bins.

Malcolm spied a figure beside the iron stove straight across from him. She had a wooden ladle in one hand and a pot in the other. This wasn't the woman he sought, however. This person was taller and heavier, and dressed in a ragged and filthy coat. He coughed as the over-whelming smell of rancid meat filled his throat again.

The figure shifted at the sound. A dead, rotting face, half-consumed in writhing maggots and with its jaw hanging askew, turned toward Malcolm. He took an involuntary step back and yanked out his Lancaster pistols, pointing them at the woman.

He hesitated, waiting for the walking corpse to make the first move, but it merely stood there, clutching the wooden spoon in a hand comprised of bone and sagging flesh. Malcolm flashed back on Old Mrs. MacIntyre, who had terrorized him as a young lad from her reclusive sod shack near Loch Lomond.

Suddenly, there was a sound behind him and he spun around, one pistol still on the dead woman and the other pointing at a new arrival. The young woman he was searching for entered, dressed in her familiar plain grey dress and white bonnet. The eyes behind the small glasses perched on her nose widened at the dark Scotsman. Then she caught a glimpse of the horrific creature by the stove and she screamed. The bundles in her arms tumbled to the floor.

The dead woman reacted wildly to the shriek, rushing Malcolm with its arms held high, grunting loudly. He pulled the trigger. The ball struck the corpse in the center of the chest and tore a huge hole in it, but then the thing was on him. Its strength was surprising and a flailing limb slapped the pistol, sending it clattering across the stone floor.

Fingers seized his throat, cutting off his air with a powerful grip that dug deep despite the folds of thick wool. Malcolm grabbed the arm, and putrid flesh dissolved in his hand until he held only cold bone. He blocked a wild swing from its other arm but he was unable to bring the second pistol to bear. It was all he could do to hold the thing at bay as the corpse jammed him into a corner.

Malcolm head-butted the undead woman. He heard a dull crack as its skull caved in with the shallow impression of his forehead. It staggered back. He planted a foot in its chest and kicked it farther away, with the sound of more bones snapping.

Gulping air into his desperate lungs, Malcolm brought his remaining Lancaster up and fired numerous booming shots in quick succession, the quad barrel spinning with a violent hiss of steam. Each ball slammed into the dead thing, forcing it back across the kitchen. When the gun clicked empty Malcolm drew a long savage dagger.

The young woman darted toward a row of hanging knives and mallets. Before she could reach the tools, the cadaver seized the woman by the hair and pert high collar. The woman twisted to face her rancid attacker and she was pulled close against it. As the horrid creature struggled with the woman, it turned its crumbling back to Malcolm.

He charged, grabbing the corpse around the neck to drag it away from the terrified woman, but it was like trying to move a rail of iron coated in grease. Bits of rotting clothes and desiccated flesh came away in his hands. He saw the young woman rearing back and pressing her small hands against the monster's emaciated chest.

A buzzing noise intensified in the room. Malcolm's skin started to tingle with electricity, his hair rising on his scalp and arms. He wasn't sure what was happening. He shook his head as a bluish aura enveloped the corpse. His first instinct was to get away, but he couldn't abandon the petite, bonneted woman. Then he saw multiple spidery arcs of electricity crawling over her slim hands.

It was the last thing Malcolm saw as the stunning

crash of Thor's hammer falling to Earth reverberated in the room. He found himself airborne and smashed against a wall before the world went dark.

MALCOLM CAME AROUND TO SOMEONE SHAKING him urgently. Everything hurt and his head was spinning. His eyes barely focused on the worried face of the young woman hovering over him.

"Oh, thank the Lord, you're alive," she exclaimed, clutching his rough hand.

He shoved himself up, dizzy, onto his elbow. "What the hell was that?"

The woman flinched. "I . . . I don't know."

"Are you hurt?" Malcolm asked groggily.

She looked amazed. "That, sir, seems a rather ridiculous statement when you are the one who was unconscious."

He rubbed his eyes. "Just being polite." He sat up straighter and felt none the worse for wear except for a sore back and the nagging heat of mild burns. He grinned wryly at her. "We have never been properly introduced. I'm Malcolm MacFarlane."

Her expression continued to hold a look of stunned shock, like a startled deer caught in the rush of Penny's infernal motorized contraption with its single blazing lamp.

"Jane." Her voice was barely above a whisper. "Jane Somerset."

"My pleasure, Miss Somerset." Malcolm examined the red scorches on his hands and forearms.

Jane's attention turned to the cadaver that was burned and blackened. It began to collapse into a shapeless pile. "That looked like Mrs. Higgensbottom, but that can't be." Jane stared back at him in confusion, and then offered, "She was the cook here for sixteen years till she died a year ago. That's when I volunteered to help." She clutched her hands together and wrung them fretfully. "But I recognized that dress. We buried her in it." She went dreadfully pale and whispered, "There were . . . were . . . maggots."

Malcolm was worried she'd faint. He tried to attract her gaze away from the sizzling thing on the floor. "Miss Somerset, that flash of light, it seemed almost like lightning."

Jane glanced at him quickly but remained silent.

"Did you see it?" he asked.

"No." Her retort was too quick and too quiet.

Malcolm took her hand firmly in his and examined it. She gasped at his boldness but didn't pull away. There wasn't a mark on her skin despite the fact that he had seen arcs of lightning envelop her hands completely. "It seemed to come from you."

"No!" She jerked her hand from his, and said in a desperate quivering voice, "I'll ask you please not to talk about it, Mr. MacFarlane, if you are a gentleman, sir. I beg of you."

Malcolm studied her plain face and her darting eyes. She gave off a sense of almost breathless desperation. He could see fear in her face, but not just fear. Near panic. However, there was something else in her too. It was shame, a terror of having some secret exposed.

He rose to his feet and helped Jane to hers. He moved across the kitchen, stepping over the smoldering corpse, and retrieved his pistol from the floor. He then went with Jane out into the dark dining room, where the stink of death and the acrid tang of electricity was a bit softer. He pulled a chair for her to sit. She perched on the edge of the seat with her hands clenched in her lap. Her head was down and her shoulders slumped under some unspoken burden.

Malcolm knelt in front of her, keeping several feet

between them to prevent her from feeling improperly crowded by a man. "Miss Somerset, whatever that lightning was, it's clearly nothing you need fear."

"I'm not afraid, Mr. MacFarlane." She didn't raise her head. "The Lord will guide me. Please, sir, I asked you not to speak of it further."

He began to reload his pistols out of habit. "I don't pretend to speak to your faith or beliefs, lass, but I spent many a long hour inside a good Presbyterian meeting house in my youth. I have a healthy fear of our Lord. And I can say without hesitation that your ability saved our lives."

Jane looked at him with a hint of gratitude and penitence shining in her eyes. "I would like to think so."

"I'd say it was a miracle." He snapped the Lancaster's breech shut.

"Most would think otherwise."

"Then they are damned idiots."

Her eyes widened with scandalous shock, but then she smiled ever so slightly as if bemused by his vulgar ways.

He slipped the pistol back into his holster. "There are names for such that wield lightning. They're called elementalists."

Jane stiffened. "Elementa . . . ?"

"Elementalists. Those who conjure fire, air, water, earth, or lightning."

"Only the Lord may command nature." She shuddered as if expecting a bolt of lightning to strike her from above. "Sorcery is an abomination before God."

"Well, I don't know about that, Miss Somerset, but I'll grant you it can be a great pain in the ass."

Jane edged farther away from him. "Are you an . . . elementalist?"

"Jesus no."

"Don't blaspheme. Why were you here tonight?" Jane

coughed to clear her throat against the disturbing odors in the room.

"I came to see you, I suppose." Malcolm stood and reached out to Jane. "Although I am surprised to see you here at this hour."

"I often can't sleep and come here to work." She stared at his hand. "Why did you want to see me?"

"Because last time I was here, you were generous to me for no reason other than you are a good person." He touched the woolen scarf around his neck. "You gave me this, and I credit it a great kindness."

Jane took his hand and rose, shaking her head. "I've had many say they feel a sense of spiritual warmth coming from my little tokens. I'm grateful to be able to do that for others."

He gathered her bundles of blankets and flour. "Let's go outside where the air is cleaner."

She walked with him out into the street, where she breathed deep of the relatively fresh London breeze, clearing her senses of the filth of the dead. The glow of the rising sun lightened the horizon. She started walking down the brick lane with the man quietly at her side.

After a moment, Jane regarded him. "I can't imagine what would have happened if you had not been there."

"I imagine everything would have happened exactly as it did. My guns did little."

Jane was quiet again, but then asked, "Why was she here?"

"Seeking someplace familiar most likely."

"No, I mean how." Her face held fear again. "The dead only rise at the end of time."

"Regardless of what the Bible says, the dead do rise, but they don't rise by themselves. It's black magic."

"Do you mean the Devil?"

"I mean a devil, sure. But likely not Ole Scratch.

There's plenty bad to worry about before we get to Lucifer himself. Where is she buried? Where was she buried?"

"St. George's Bloomsbury. She lived on the edge of that parish." Jane paled until she looked like a wraith herself under the stringent streetlamp's glow. She put a hand to her mouth in alarm. "That's where that murder was a few nights ago. The same night you came."

"Aye. I went there but couldn't prevent it."

Jane stopped walking, her face slack, her head filled with thoughts she obviously hadn't expected to contend with this night. She stood at an unimposing door on a street that was once fine but was now in decline.

"Is this home?" Malcolm asked.

"I live here with my father." Jane suddenly gave a dispirited groan and put a hand to her forehead. "What am I thinking? I have to go back. I must clean the place before the reverend comes in at noon. He mustn't see that."

She started to trudge back the way they had come, but Malcolm put a hand lightly on her arm. "Miss Somerset, I will go back and clean the kitchen."

"That's hardly a man's duty."

Malcolm laughed loudly, throwing his head back with guffaws. Dogs started barking in the distance.

Jane held up embarrassed hands. "Please, Mr. MacFarlane, lower your voice. I shouldn't be talking unaccompanied to a stranger at this hour. Or any hour."

He clamped a hand over his mouth and muttered through his fingers, "Sorry. I will make things right at the soup kitchen. Have no fears. I've been a bachelor long enough to have some homely skills. No one will know anything out of the ordinary happened."

"I was supposed to make the bread." It was such a trivial thing to worry about in light of what happened, and from her exasperated tone Jane knew it.

"Make it here at home," he told her. "You can find some excuse."

Jane paused nervously. She made ready to speak but thought better of it. Malcolm didn't question her.

Finally, she blurted out, "Won't you come inside? My father is awake. He rarely sleeps. I should like to give you breakfast, or at least something for your goodness."

"I don't want to disturb him."

She opened the door and turned back with an eager smile. "On the contrary, he would enjoy another man's company for a change, I'm sure."

Malcolm entered the trim little home, instantly feeling the weight of his guns in the domestic setting. The furnishings were sparse yet pristine and the interior was meticulously kept. An older woman of a rotund size hurried into view, flustered and harried, in a dressing gown wrapped around a nightdress. She looked surprised to see the mistress of the house, then flummoxed at the sight of the dark-haired man. "Miss Jane!"

"It's all right, Mrs. Cummings. A pot of tea, please. We'll have it here in the parlor."

"Yes, Miss." Mrs. Cummings curtsied. She stared at Malcolm with a glower of suspicion, then darted back where she had come from, most likely the kitchen.

Jane led Malcolm into a small room lined with bookcases. The tables were covered with lamps and vases and bric-a-brac. It was as if the pieces of a life once used to a larger home were now crammed into this little abode. She settled herself on the sofa and gestured Malcolm toward a high-backed chair that would suit his large frame. He mindfully pulled it near the open door to spare Jane any embarrassment of being alone in a room with a man.

Malcolm regarded her slender figure as he took his seat. She folded her hands in her lap, her long fingers interlacing. She looked weary. Beneath her steel-rimmed spectacles he could see dark circles under her eyes. He didn't see any other servants about so he wondered if Mrs. Cummings was the extent of the staff.

They sat in uncomfortable silence for a time until the tea arrived. Mrs. Cummings bustled about for a few minutes, pouring the beverage and distributing the cups until Jane thanked and dismissed her with, "Please tell Father we have a guest."

The two of them quietly sipped tea. Malcolm handled the dainty cup and saucer awkwardly. At first, Jane seemed to relish hers as if this were the first time she had had a moment of peace, but soon she placed the cup on the side table and regarded Malcolm a bit fretfully.

"Would you like me to leave?" Malcolm asked.

"No! I would never turn aside someone who is seeking something."

"What am I seeking?" His lips curved into a gentle grin. He drained his tea before it turned cold. "Salvation?"

"Do you mock me, sir?" Her eyes went wide as she stiffened with indignation.

Malcolm set his cup down a bit loudly. "My apologies, lass. My manners aren't parlor fit. Too many nights spent on the road, or off it."

Her voice spoke quietly, her affront passing like a sudden storm. "Do you believe your soul is in danger, Mr. MacFarlane?"

"I expect sometimes it is."

"I wish to know what it is you do exactly, Mr. MacFarlane, to hear it plain rather than couched in metaphors. I have had time to think on what occurred at the kitchen. As much as I would wish it wasn't real, I know it was. Men like you seem to face these things while I wear rose-colored glasses and take shelter here in this house."

Perceptive again, Malcolm noted, and smiled to ease

her fears. "Miss Somerset. Your glasses are not rosy, nor do you hide. There are many in need. You've placed yourself in the very heart of their battlefield. I admire and respect that."

She bowed her head gratefully. "Thank you."

"But you can do much more."

"How so, Mr. MacFarlane?"

"Because of your ability to wield lightning."

Color fled her cheeks. She glanced around nervously, afraid someone in the household would hear. Malcolm cursed himself for speaking so openly.

"My apologies again, lass. I should be more cautious."

Jane toyed with a loose thread. "Mrs. Cummings is hard of hearing. I doubt she could hear a storm outside her door."

"Your father then?"

She nodded.

"Is he a God-fearing man?"

"No, but he should be. However, it is too late for that now. He lives within a world of his own making. There are days he does not recognize even me. So it's best he not know certain things. He would not mean to do it, but I cannot be sure he wouldn't reveal something to the authorities."

"I'm sorry," Malcolm offered, "for your difficulties."

She fidgeted with her dress in silence.

"You do realize that you are extraordinary. You wield great power, lass, and there are people who will recognize this power and seek you out."

"As you are doing," she told him, lifting her chin to stare directly at him. "I will give them the same answer I give you."

"Some may not accept it. The risk that you will serve their rivals would be too dangerous for them to bear." Malcolm could see he was getting his point across.

She was trembling, but then she surprised him again.

"If I am that powerful, why should I fear them? Perhaps they should fear me."

He grinned at her spirit. "You could use your special abilities to help people."

Jane pursed her lips and shook her head with uncertainty. "I don't know if it's wise to use something so dark, even in a good cause."

"A wise man shouldn't refuse to help others in any way he can." Malcolm sat quietly as his own point struck home.

"I thank you for your concern, Mr. MacFarlane. I shall think on what you've said."

There was a sound behind him and Malcolm turned to see an elderly gentleman enter the room. He wore a suit of clothes, but his feet were shod in slippers and an ancient nightcap rested on his head. His eyes held confusion, knowing something was out of place in the house but unable to recognize it.

The old man asked Malcolm, "Are you a lamplighter or a bill collector? Who else would be about so early?"

"Good morning, sir." Malcolm bowed. "I'm neither."

Jane approached her father's side. "May I present Mr. MacFarlane. He is a gentleman and a servant of the needy."

Mr. Somerset relaxed and shook hands with Malcolm. "Then you are most welcome in this house."

"Thank you, sir," Malcolm replied. "Join us. We were just discussing"—Jane's eyes flashed fearfully—"the state of London's poetry scene."

She exhaled a sigh of relief and guided her father as he stepped toward a comfortable chair set between them.

The old man announced, "There was a poem about willow trees in last week's paper. I found it quite nice. I think a poem should be about something like a tree or a dog or a battle. Seems like so many new poems are just words laid across a page."

Jane sat down demurely and smiled at Malcolm, grateful for his tact.

Mr. Somerset's eyes clouded once more, uncertain of the memory, but then just nodded. "Ah, yes. Are you an author, sir?"

"I can't make that claim," answered Malcolm.

"I detect a burr. I'd say Glasgow, but there's some Edinburgh too."

"Raised not far from Glasgow. And I attended university in Edinburgh. Your ear is good."

"Scotsman." Mr. Somerset laced his fingers over his misbuttoned vest. "I don't hold that against you, son."

Malcolm found the comment amusing coming from the old man. "Thank you, sir."

"Are you gainfully employed?"

"I am my own man."

"Splendid. I think all enterprising young men should make their mark in the world." He patted Jane's hand, and told her, "John here is a wonderful choice for a husband."

"This isn't John, Father," Jane said with gentle patience. "John died at sea last year. Remember? This gentleman is named Malcolm. Malcolm MacFarlane."

"MacFarlane?" Mr. Somerset stared in confusion at Jane. "Surely Captain Perry should be home by now."

Malcolm glanced at Jane with admiration for her calm demeanor and kind disposition. Her worried expression regarded him, but then she nodded, slowly turning back to her father.

Her slim hand gestured to their guest. "But this is Mr. Malcolm MacFarlane. He walked me home from the kitchen and was visiting to discuss matters of faith and charity."

"Ahh, a pleasure to meet you, Mr. MacFarlane." Mr. Somerset rose unsteadily and shook hands with Malcolm again.

Malcolm nodded at the old man, not disrupted by the man's confusion. "Thank you for your kindness. Your daughter is a devoted humanitarian."

"Indeed," exclaimed Mr. Somerset before Jane could respond. "A toast! Jane, fetch the sherry!"

"Father, really. Your condition."

"Nonsense. A glass with you, Captain Perry."

Jane shook her head in exasperation, but then obeyed because protesting further would do no good. She poured the amber liquid into three small glasses and distributed them. Her father lifted his glass in a prost enthusiastically. Malcolm lifted his to Jane, whose cheeks were flushed with embarrassment.

Chapter 11

SIMON STOOD IN FRONT OF A MAP OF LONDON tacked over the ornithological wallpaper in the library at Hartley Hall. It was marked with four yellow spots corresponding to churches designed by Nicholas Hawksmoor. Two of the four yellow dots were marked with a black X.

"The Sacred Heart Murders," Simon announced, and tapped the two X's with his walking stick. "St. George's Bloomsbury and Christ Church Spitalfields. Both the sites of horrific sacrificial butchery." Then he pointed to the two yellow dots. "St. George in the East and St. Mary Woolnoth. Two other churches designed by Nicholas Hawksmoor where we found the same four names of the so-called *Zoas* from William Blake's poetry, as well as signs of Pendragon's inscriptions using Egyptian symbols."

Kate sat with Penny on a sofa across the room, where they studied a folder of information provided by Sir Henry Clatterburgh as well as various other slips of paper and correspondence associated with the murders. She spoke up. "Speaking of which, tomorrow we are scheduled to visit the British Museum. The records of the Office of Works are housed with the King's Library, and they contain many of Hawksmoor's papers. And we will speak with my friend, Thomas Clover, who is a curator of Egyptian materials, and ask him about the hieroglyphs."

"Right. Now, neither St. George in the East nor St. Mary Woolnoth have hosted a murder. And we are ruling out all other churches as having ritual importance. Correct?"

Kate raised her hand like a patient student. Simon looked at her in confusion, then gave her a lopsided sarcastic grin. He pointed at her.

She sat up straight like a schoolgirl. "Yes, Professor Archer, that is correct."

"Droll. And Henry is kindly providing watchmen for those two churches."

Penny said, "So we're operating under the assumption that the ritual links the four names and four churches."

"Yes, two victims who need justice." Simon drew his pipe from his mouth. "And two potential victims we need to prevent."

"I determined that the victim at St. George's, in any case, was not drugged so far as I could tell. However, it's impossible to assume she was a willing participant." Kate lifted a sheet of paper from the folder. "But there is so little on the two dead women except for what Henry gave us. The first victim, at St. George's, was named Madeleine Hawley. She was apparently a minor poet who had a few published works. The second, at Christ Church, was named Cecilia de Ronay. She was a courtesan of some note."

"De Ronay? Sounds familiar." Simon tapped his chin. "I believe I knew her."

Kate's face clouded, and Penny glanced away with a smirk. Then Kate shook her head. "Lord knows why that sort of thing still shocks me. Both victims were members of bohemian society. The interesting connection comes because Henry says both women's bodies were claimed by the same man."

"Were the two women related?"

"Not that he knows of. The bodies were claimed by a man calling himself Rowan Barnes."

"Rowan Barnes?" Simon tilted his head. "Why do I know that name?"

"A prominent Mayfair pimp perhaps?"

Simon laughed and went to a pile of newspapers on the table, where he began to paw through them, tossing papers over his head.

"Could you try not to use my house to re-create that bachelor sty of yours on Gaunt Lane?" Kate asked, then continued, "In any case, the police are not interested in solving these murders. Two dead women are considered disposable, clearly."

"In their miserable defense, the Metropolitan Police are barely formed and are more skilled at infiltrating reformist groups and pouncing on debtors. Fortunately, we have time to assist them." He held up a paper in triumph. "Ah! Here we are in the society notices. I remember now. Rowan Barnes oversees the Red Orchid salon."

"Salon?"

"Yes, he's an artist, apparently quite popular. And this Red Orchid salon is *the* place to be if you are artistic or intellectual or pretend to be either."

"So you've been there then?"

"No." Simon paused, looking at Kate for signs of sarcasm. He rubbed his thumb over the rune on the bowl of his pipe to fire the tobacco again. "But I should have gone. And now we shall."

Charlotte popped up suddenly from behind the sofa. "May I go?"

Penny leapt to her feet with a shout. "Good God!"

Kate started with surprise. "Charlotte! How did you

get in here? It's not appropriate for you to listen to this, dear."

"Why?"

"We're talking about very disturbing subjects. You should go to your room."

Charlotte pouted. "No. I want to stay. I don't like being in my room alone. I'm not upset by what you're saying. I've seen many dead people."

Simon gave Kate a grimace. "Yes, she's seen many dead people."

Charlotte nodded vigorously. "Oh yes! Don't worry, Mr. Simon. I'm very calm. I saw Gretta tear people to pieces and I could still go to sleep that night."

"Perhaps I should leave before I get upset." Kate took a deep breath. "Charlotte, I want you to go and find Imogen."

"But . . ." the girl began.

"No," Kate insisted. "Please, go. This isn't for you."

"But I want to help." Charlotte scuffed her shoe on the rug and moped around the sofa. "Because of me, you don't have anybody else."

Kate took the girl's hand. "What do you mean, dear?"

"Mr. Malcolm. He left because of me, didn't he?"

"No, Charlotte." Kate glanced quickly at Simon and Penny with concern, then gazed intently into the girl's eyes. "Mr. Malcolm had other affairs to attend to."

"He hates me because of what I am, so he left. He was your friend before me."

"Hush, dear. He just didn't understand." Kate pulled Charlotte close and embraced her.

The door to the library opened and Malcolm entered. He was covered in mud from riding hard. He dropped his rucksack on the floor and tossed his holsters onto a table. He looked with bemusement at the surprised stares from Penny, Kate, who was hugging Charlotte, and Simon, holding his pipe.

"Well," he said quietly, "this is a charming little family tableau. Father. Mother. Sister. Faithful hound." He paused before nodding toward Aethelred who lounged near the guttering fire, then turned his gaze on Charlotte.

"Ah, now the eccentric uncle." Simon tapped his pipe on the heel of his hand. "We're complete and cozy and ready for Christmas dinner."

Malcolm glanced curiously at the map on the wall on his way to pour a glass of whiskey. "You've got a new problem now with all that."

Simon motioned several worried servants who had trailed Malcolm into the house back out with a grateful nod, and closed the door again. "Have we?"

Charlotte grasped Kate's hand and anxiously watched Malcolm drain the glass, then pour another. He wiped his mouth with the back of his hand.

"Yes," the Scotsman said. "I encountered an undead in London. And she had been buried at St. George's Bloomsbury. I think this ritual murder is causing the dead to rise." Malcolm drank the second glass with a sense of dramatic satisfaction. He looked from Simon to Kate, and his brow furrowed, confused by their lack of shocked reaction to his announcement. Then he looked angry. "Did you hear me?"

Penny went quietly to the window and seemed to vanish in the shadows.

"Yes," Simon replied, with a concerned eye to the young engineer, "and you're right. How many undead did you see?"

"One." Malcolm looked annoyed. "How many undead do you need for it to be a problem?"

"Well, Kate and I encountered nearly one hundred of them at Christ Church two nights ago."

Malcolm set the glass down sharply and folded his arms.

"Don't be cross, Malcolm." Simon smiled as he slowly refilled his pipe. "I'm sure your one lonely undead was frightening. What did you do with it?"

"I destroyed it so it wouldn't harm anyone. A novel concept with monsters these days, I know."

Simon let the comment pass with only a glance at Penny. "Where did you encounter it?"

The Scotsman hesitated, then mumbled, "In a soup kitchen."

"Did you say a soup kitchen? Were you both in line for a meal?"

Penny chuckled.

Malcolm returned to the door and lifted his pack. "I see now there's nothing I can tell you that you don't already know. As usual. So I'll be on my way."

"Mr. Malcolm, wait!" Charlotte shouted. "Don't go!"

He spun around with a furious glare at the child. "What did you say?"

"Don't go." She straightened her shoulders. "I'll go."

"What?" Malcolm snapped. "What are you talking about?"

"I'll go." Charlotte looked at him with pleading eyes. "I'm better. As long as I can take some wulfsyl with me. I'm fine. We know how much I should take now. You can stay. I'll go." Kate reached out, but Charlotte slipped away from her hand. "It's fine, Miss Kate. He was here first. I just came for wulfsyl. If you'll let me take some, I can go."

Kate stared at Malcolm, her accusing eyes flashing between pity and fury.

"No, Miss Kate, don't be mad at him," the girl said. "I don't mind. I came here for help, and you helped me. See? I'm really very upset, but I'm not changing. See?" Charlotte rubbed her hands along her flowered frock and held them up. "Once I'm gone, you can all be a family again."

Malcolm watched the girl as tears began to drip down her face. He exhaled in resignation and dropped his pack on the floor again. "Stop your crying and sit down. Right then, what time is Christmas dinner?"

Simon put his pipe in his mouth and leaned on the hearth with a contented gaze about the room.

Chapter 12

THE BRITISH MUSEUM WAS A HIVE OF ACTIVITY, at least outside. Construction on the marvelous East Wing continued. The Greek Revival edifice was still obscured by scaffolding, with cables dangling, suspending heavy loads of stone and marble. Simon and Kate bypassed the old Montagu House, where the museum's collection had been displayed for many years, and still was. They made their way across the yard, walking along planks thrown down over the mud. Kate wore a midcalf-length skirt and heavy boots, suitable perhaps for riding but nearly scandalous here. Still, she trudged uncaring across the filthy boards, following Simon, who also wore high boots and rough tweed.

"A pleasant day." Simon's breath misted in the cold. "The museum and tonight a sociable salon. Almost like the old days when I was a bon vivant on the town."

Kate hummed. "I'd rather stay at the museum."

A shout alerted them to a man standing on a high porch underneath a network of scaffolding. The fellow waved to them so they hopped a few perpendicular timbers, listening to the squelching mud beneath. They both climbed the steps to a young, red-haired man.

Kate smiled as she took the man's hand cheerfully.

"Thomas, it's so good to see you. Thomas, this is Simon Archer. Simon, Thomas Clover, an assistant curator for Egyptian and Near Eastern collections. And an old friend of the family."

"Mr. Clover," Simon greeted warmly, "thank you so much for seeing us. I can't tell you how eager I am to see the new wing."

"Then let's do." Thomas escorted the two inside the East Wing, the new home to the King's Library. In the vast gallery, sunlight streamed from windows set high in the walls, highlighting the wood panels. They moved through the quiet maw with the unfinished plaster ceiling twenty feet above their heads and passed two columns into a completed section with walls crowded with display shelves. Row upon row of books and papers filled the gallery. Thomas extended his arm to a table in a shaft of light, where several heavy folios sat alongside a pile of thick, rolled papers.

"You asked to see the notes of Nicholas Hawksmoor, yes?" Thomas said to Kate, then with some doubt, "Just Hawksmoor, not Wren?"

"That's correct." She inspected the cracking labels on the spines of the folios and unrolled one of the heavy scrolls. "This is wonderful. Letterbooks and architectural drawings."

"That's all I could find from Hawksmoor. Architecture isn't, of course, my specialty, but I'm happy to help you, Kate, in any way possible."

"It's exactly what we need," she said, as Simon settled at the table and pulled one of the heavy books in front of him. "I do have another question that's a bit more to your specialty, which is why I contacted you." Kate pulled a sheet of paper from her pocket and handed it to Thomas. "Does this look familiar to you?"

He took the sheet with a gleam of excitement and looked at the hieroglyphics written there. Both Kate and Simon watched with anticipation. Finally, he said, "It does."

"What is it?" Kate asked quickly. "It's beyond me."

"I don't know." Thomas scrubbed a hand through his hair. "It seems familiar, but I can't remember why."

"Can you read it?"

"This symbol here is an Old Kingdom variation for the word *rise*. However, these other symbols are unknown to me, and they could alter how one reads *rise*. So it might not be *rise* after all; it might be a letter in a completely different word. It's a difficult language and script, as you know."

"Could you look into it for me?" Kate asked. "I would be grateful for any light you can shed on it."

"Of course." He concentrated on the paper. "I just wish I could remember where I thought I saw it. Most peculiar."

"I'm sure it will come to you." Kate sat across from Simon and reached for another folio.

"Well," Thomas said, backing away, "I'll leave you two to it. Oh, Kate, how is your sister?"

Kate bolted up straight and turned abruptly. "What do you mean?"

Thomas pulled back in surprise at the vigor of her reaction. "I . . . I just wondered. I haven't seen her in several years."

"Oh." Kate took a deep breath and gave an embarrassed laugh under Simon's steady gaze. "Oh, I see. Yes. I'm sorry. Imogen is well. She . . . she sends her best wishes."

"Does she?" The young man brightened. "If she is ever in London, I would be grateful to call on her for tea."

"I don't . . ." Kate began, then smiled. "Of course. I'll tell her. I fear she has little time for the city these days."

"I'm sure." Thomas sighed. "She's probably engaged to some handsome squire, eh?"

Kate struggled to laugh and made to turn back to the book. The curator coughed with embarrassment and walked away. When his steps vanished, Kate put her face in her hands.

"Oh God. I had forgotten how fond Thomas was of Imogen. I handled that terribly. He probably thinks I'm a lunatic or trying to keep him away from my sister."

"Don't worry, Kate." Simon tapped the book. "For now let's go to work. We'll handle that when it becomes an issue."

She sighed and nodded. Hours passed in near silence as they went through the material with only occasional questions or comments of interest. Endless letters about government approval and patronage. Notes about materials. Recommendations for craftsmen. Debates on designs, revisions, and more debates. Yet no mention of the four mysterious names. No discussion of Egyptian symbols.

Kate finally closed the last letterbook and pushed it aside. She rose with a groan of fatigue and took up the heavy rolls of plans. She flipped through them until she found long sheets with the drawings of St. George's Bloomsbury.

"The altar has moved," she said.

"What?"

"The altar. On the original drawings it's in the east nave where the body was found. They must have moved the altar later and realigned the church."

"Interesting. The killer knew that. Or simply knew to perform the killing at the point of greatest power." Simon stood and came around to her shoulder. He inspected all the marks on the plans, as well as those of the other three churches where the mysterious names were carved.

Kate said, "I haven't seen anything suspicious or il-luminating."

"Neither have I, but sometimes illumination is hidden." Simon went to another table and fetched a pen and ink. He rolled out the sketches of Christ Church and anchored the corners. Bending over close, he began to write a series of precise runes across the bottom of the sheet. Then he passed his hand over them and spoke a word. The runes flared.

Green light rose from the paper. Hidden runic symbols appeared. The four mysterious names showed brightly, with lines anchoring them to the four cardinal points of the church. A string of hieroglyphs wrote themselves across the top of the plans. Simon recognized several of the symbols as those branded into the victims' hearts.

Kate seized him by the shoulder with a cry of delight. "Is it what I think it is?"

Simon stared into the green aura. "Yes. This is Byron Pendragon's work. He warded those four churches with Egyptian magic. The spells of that land are some of the most powerful ever written. From what I know, most scribes, if they used Egyptian sources, only used versions diluted by later changes, particularly by the Gnostics or Hermetics. Look here, he's scrawled a note to Hawksmoor: *Strengthen the stone or they will not be held*. He was concerned about the ability of the construction materials to contain the magic. My God! And the fact that the note is mystically obscured shows that Hawksmoor was one of the craft."

"*Who* will not be held?" Kate asked.

"That he doesn't say." Simon gestured over the glowing symbols and he watched the notations written by the greatest scribe in the history of the world vanish into invisibility again.

Chapter 13

FROM THE HANSOM, SIMON STUDIED THE DINGY home that was the hive of the Red Orchid salon. It was a sprawling, wood frame two-story built in the era of the Restoration Stuarts. Sturdy to be sure, but hardly fresh, just like the decaying parish around it.

The Red Orchid was the shining light of London art. It had hardly been a year since Rowan Barnes rose from the faceless mezzotint mob to be the anointed new genius. His salon became the center for all those who sought to express themselves in paint or words or dance or song or declamation, or sought to have relationships with those who did.

"Not much to look at from the outside," Simon said. "I should have made an appearance long ago."

Malcolm snorted derisively.

"You, sir," Simon explained cheerfully, with a deliberate flourish of his wrist, "don't understand the burden of being a mysterious gentleman of leisure. I must *appear*."

"Why?" Malcolm asked.

Simon looked at him and at Kate, who was inspecting vials in her bag. "Let me ask you both. Had you heard my name before you met me?"

"Yes," they both answered.

"There you are. We weren't acquainted. I did nothing important so far as you knew. But you had heard of me. That's why I appear."

The Scotsman shook his head. "I thought secrecy was vital to you sorcerers."

"It is. No one knows I'm a sorcerer; they just know I'm a rich playboy with strange interests and a dark past. A *rich* playboy. Doors open. More importantly, mouths open."

"The only mouth open is usually yours." Malcolm swung out of the hansom. "Losh, let's go in before Barnes's art goes out of fashion."

"Well done, Malcolm." Simon laughed and handed Kate down. "Very snide. I'll make a London gentleman out of you yet."

"I'll kill myself, or more likely you, first. Where's Penny? Why doesn't she have to endure this?"

"She wanted to spend a bit of time with her brother, understandably," Simon replied.

Malcolm's gaze darkened, knowing now what Penny had been through recently. Simon added, "Besides, she said she wasn't really salon material."

Malcolm snorted. "And I am?"

"You're our poetry expert, Malcolm. Plus, you're tall and handsome and Scottish. Quite the showpiece." Simon led the way to the door and shoved it open. The warm damp of a crowd and the cloying scent of opium assaulted them. A few flushed faces turned their way, seeking familiarity or recognition, but then returned to their previous activities.

The dour Scotsman gazed over the crowd and leaned toward Simon. "I don't detect a ripple of awe at your appearance."

"They're all quite intoxicated." Simon helped Kate with her jacket and removed his own, along with his hat and gloves. No butler came forward, so he draped the coats over his arm.

"It's mainly women," Simon observed.

"What are they doing?" Malcolm's brows knit together.

Most of the people, who were gathered in small groups, visible in the flickering candlelight, in the large greeting room or through the wide doorway of a parlor, were young women. However, there was no idle female activity such as needlepoint or tea sipping as in country homes. They were animated in discussion, and many held books, reading from them or referencing passages for their friends. Several of them were smoking pipes, whether tobacco or opium was unclear, but either was unusual in a public place. Men sat with them, almost as afterthoughts, and hardly the centers of attention.

Kate replied dryly, "It looks as if they are thinking and speaking. I can see how that might come as a shock."

The Scotsman looked at her, surprised by her sarcasm.

She raised an eyebrow. "It is amazing to see how you are both surprised and confounded by the mere sight of women partaking equally in society." The two men started to object, but she continued, "Please don't. If these were men talking seriously, reading, smoking, ignoring you, it would have made no impression. But since they are women, you are nonplussed, as if you've walked into a room on Mars."

Simon chuckled. "It appears Kate has shot past Whiggish reform, pushed through July Terror, and is bound for Wollstonecraft utopianism. But," he admitted thoughtfully, "she is quite right. I think nothing of women laboring equally in *our* unique community, but I still fall back on old ways elsewhere. I'm ashamed before you, Kate. Again."

"Well, I'm not ashamed," Malcolm growled. "I've no idea what you're talking about."

Simon turned to the Scotsman. "You see, Mary Wollstonecraft is—"

"I know that bit, you pompous ass. You think I spent my time at university in the Grassmarket pubs?"

Simon looked contemplative, then saw an unusual sight across the crowded room. There were two people, obviously a couple. A large man and a small woman, at least small compared to him. Simon recognized the man. It was the ambassador from the United States, Mansfield by name. They had met briefly at various parties and balls. Ambassador Mansfield was a large man, not fat, but powerful, with a chest like a draft horse. He was a pleasant enough fellow.

The woman Simon had never met nor seen before. She must have been the fabled Mary Mansfield, the ambassador's wife. Little was known about her and she had become a bit of a legend in social circles since Mansfield presented his credentials to the Court of St. James last year. The fact that she rarely attended social events, which would seem a requirement for an ambassador's wife, was a topic of much speculation. And even more notable, when she did make the odd appearance, it was always an odd appearance indeed. And tonight was no exception.

Mrs. Mansfield was at least a foot shorter than her husband but hardly insubstantial or hidden in his shadow. She was dressed as if for a Turkish seraglio, with silken pantaloons and shoes that curled up at the toe. The odd clothing showed her figure to fine effect. She wore a long, colorful mantle that draped to the floor and her hands were covered in bright green gloves. Her face was lost in a silken veil that completely hid her features. To top it off, she wore a sizeable turban upon which perched a large, stuffed bird, wings spread.

Simon could barely pry his gaze from the peculiar bird, which seemed to stare at him so he hardly noticed the odd couple moving closer until he heard "Simon Archer!" blaring in an American voice. "I didn't know I'd see you here, but I'm damned glad I have. Now I have someone to talk to." Mansfield cast his eyes about him with unguarded disdain. "Mary likes to come out every so often. And I do run into a lot of important people here, so it's useful for me to attend. I've even seen Grace North out here. Now, there's a lovely women. You know, the prime minister's wife. Of course you know; he's your prime minister. But in general, the people here aren't my type of crowd though. Oh, you're not a regular, are you? Sorry if you are."

"Good evening, Your Excellency." Simon bowed, covering a smirk at the man's American bluntness. "No, this is my first time."

"Good, good. How are you, my boy, how are you?" Mansfield shook Simon's hand vigorously as he angled toward Kate, expecting an introduction.

"I am well, sir. Thank you. May I present—"

"Kate Anstruther." The ambassador flashed a grin and kissed Kate's hand. "I saw you at the Duke of Lincoln's summer regatta but never had the fortune to speak. It's a great honor, Miss Anstruther. Your father, Sir Roland, was an enormous hero of mine. I've read all about his travels and expeditions. He was a man among men. I was honored to meet him once in New Orleans many years ago. I'd welcome the chance to talk about him with you."

"Thank you, Your Excellency." Kate looked mildly confused. "I didn't know my father had been to New Orleans, but he did move around quite a bit."

"And this," Simon continued, "is Malcolm MacFarlane."

Mansfield, to his democratic credit, greeted Malcolm

with the same enthusiasm. "MacFarlane. Scotsman, eh? I enjoy your whiskey."

"Thank you," Malcolm said, his mouth a thin line. "I'll tell them."

The ambassador laughed and turned to the outrageous shape beside him. "I have the unique opportunity to introduce my wife, Mary."

Simon bowed deeply and reached for Mrs. Mansfield's hand, but she didn't move, like a statue from a harem. As he straightened, he smoothly raised the empty hand to his mouth to cover a slight cough. "Mrs. Mansfield, a great pleasure to meet you, and may I compliment you on the tasteful size of the taxidermied bird on your head?"

Her response was a bare whisper. "People have died for far less than this bird giving his life for fashion."

Ambassador Mansfield laughed. "Yes, yes. The poor thing's just returned from a long tour of the Continent and the Levant. Literally just off the boat a few days ago. But she wanted to come tonight. She's quite the warhorse."

"You must be exhausted." Simon smiled at her faceless lace visage. "I presume."

Mansfield crossed his arms and took up a position as if his wife was no longer present, as indeed she barely was. "Mary loves to travel. I hardly see her. I'd wager we haven't spent five months together since we met in Egypt, what was it, Mary, four years ago?"

The woman said, "It seems longer."

"You've traveled in Egypt, Your Excellency?" Kate asked the ambassador.

"Business, Miss Anstruther," he replied. "I'm in cotton. Know anything about cotton, Archer?"

"No more than any other plant."

"Well, they grow a lot of it in Egypt. Most people

think the place is a barren desert, but all along the Nile River is good farmland. Ever been to Egypt?"

"No."

"Damn place is full of old things. I bought a boatload of mummies for a few piasters and sold them to aristocrats all over Europe for a tidy profit."

"So you're interested in ancient Egyptian culture?"

"Not particularly. Most of the time, it's all a bunch of pictures of men standing sideways." Mansfield looked at his motionless wife, who cleared her throat. He stiffened, then gave the perfunctory smile to Simon that their conversation needed to end. "Well, all this diplomacy has made me thirsty."

Simon bowed again. "Thank you for your kindness, Your Excellency, Mrs. Mansfield. Will you excuse us?"

"Sure, Archer. Let's find time for a glass of champagne together later. Miss Anstruther, a great honor. I hope to see you again. Mr. MacFarlane, good to meet you."

Simon led his two companions past the unusual couple. When they were acceptably buffered by a noisy cocoon of surrounding conversations, Malcolm said, "What in hell is the situation with his wife?"

"Shh." Simon tried not to laugh. Kate did laugh and nudged the Scotsman as Simon said, "No one knows apparently. She has never shown her face in public. She remains a frustrating enigma to the society papers."

Kate said quietly, "You have to admit though, she sports a gigantic bird with great aplomb. That's very difficult for a petite woman."

Simon gestured to the crowd. "In any case, we are here to have a look at Rowan Barnes if we can find him through the smoke."

Kate held up a finger and strolled on into the parlor. The two men followed, as if she were their ticket of acceptable entry in this salon of women. There were a few glances of interest from the gathered but no attempt to engage the newcomers. Simon stepped over the sprawled legs of a few women and men who had indulged a bit much in opium and lay senseless in a corner. There were other women who sat together, holding hands, engaged in close intimacy that seemed a bit more than sisterly chatter. Nothing he hadn't seen before, but here at the Red Orchid it seemed more comfortable and natural, not hidden in shadows.

Kate paused to chat with several young women who were huddled over small volumes of poetry. They smiled in welcome and pointed up.

Kate returned. "Rowan Barnes is upstairs."

Malcolm leaned close to his partners. "What's our play?"

Simon said, "We're here to talk and observe."

"Right enough." Malcolm adjusted his pistol under his coat. "You two should be able to handle a painter. I'll nose about down here."

"Let's not have a riot," Simon cautioned, and started up the stairs with Kate.

As they made their way up, they saw paintings hanging as well as stacked against the wall. Landscapes. Scenes of heroic figures and biblical images. Most of the figures were nude. Simon stopped to peruse.

"Common," Kate observed. "He doesn't reach very far, does he?"

"You think not? This *Brutus at the Temple of Diana* is vigorous and powerful, yet touching and with pathos. There is skill in perspective and color. It has the common immediacy of watercolor but with a foundation of excellent draftsmanship."

"Please. All heavenly light and muscles. I wouldn't hang it in my stables."

Simon suddenly wondered with alarm if his tastes were more plebian than he had thought. He took Kate's arm and went on. The upstairs was more open than the ground floor thanks to a peaked roof. The hallway was still crowded and hazy, and all space seemed occupied by small groups deep in discussion or busy sketching. It seemed questionable that the old wooden floor could hold up under the strain of so many feet. Kate led the way to a large doorway that opened onto a vast chamber, likely once a ballroom. A throng of fifty people, overwhelmingly women, stood shoulder to shoulder inside. Beyond the multitude of heads, in the center of the room, was a man and an easel. The fellow had his back to the door. He was tall and well built, clad in black pants and a blousy white shirt. His red hair was tied in a long queue.

Beyond the easel, Simon saw a nude woman leaning on a marble pedestal. The blatant exhibition of her nakedness in the center of so many clothed people struck Simon as decadent and shocking. But he realized there was no sense of licentiousness or judgment in the room. The model herself displayed no embarrassment and her attitude was as normal as if she had been chatting with a friend in Hyde Park on a Sunday.

Rowan Barnes moved around the easel with odd, palsied motions. He was silent, pausing to study the nude woman, then making swift definitive strikes against the canvas as if it were an enemy. Seemingly random marks combined over time to form an extraordinary rendition of the model's body. The artist left the easel to prowl around the naked woman. He gave off a sense of fascination without lewdness. He admired and studied her anatomy as one would a fine home or a wild glen.

There was no restless shuffling or whispered conversations in the crowd. They watched Barnes as if he would soon pronounce some great discovery.

The artist had been bent over making a close inspection of the model's lower back when his face rose over her shoulder, and he froze. His eyes peered toward the door, two shining caramel-brown lights. The crowd began to look at one another, slowly turning around to find the object of the great man's attention.

"I was hoping to stay more unobtrusive," Simon whispered. "This is embarrassing for me."

"More embarrassing than you know," Kate responded quietly, "because they're looking at me."

Simon reevaluated Barnes's fierce gaze. The object was indeed Kate. Not surprising, Simon realized. Kate was quite the most fascinating woman in London.

"That's what I meant," he said.

"Of course it is."

Barnes ran his hand along the model's bare shoulders and whispered something to her, never shifting his stare away from Kate. The blond nude looked briefly at Kate too. The artist parted the crowd, slowly striding toward the door. He stopped a few feet from Kate, regarding her as if she didn't have a male companion with his arm looped through hers. Barnes extended his hand with its long, supple fingers.

"I am Rowan Barnes."

"Enchanted." Kate took his hand with a bemused half curtsy. "I am—"

"Kate Anstruther." He turned her hand as if studying her knuckles and tendons in slightly different light. "I know you."

"Do you?"

"May I say you have remarkable proportions?"

Kate smiled uncomfortably. Barnes tilted his head, peering at Kate's face like an object. He had yet to slide his gaze over her sensuous figure. That was admirable restraint, Simon thought with mild annoyance at the man's boldness because even he found it impossible to keep himself from staring as she left a room.

Kate sighed. "May I present my companion, Mr. Simon Archer."

Barnes didn't even glance at him. "Archer? I've heard your name."

"Have you now?" Simon gave Kate a smug, knowing look.

Kate extracted her hand from the artist's grip. "Would you be so good, Mr. Barnes, as to cease staring at me?"

"I'm truly sorry. You're hypnotic. Your face is . . . mathematically perfect."

Simon briefly thought that was an excellent line.

"I must paint you," Barnes exclaimed.

"Must you really?" Kate exhaled, growing annoyed.

"Yes." Barnes was sincere, or at least a remarkable facsimile of it. There was no hint of the trolling lascivious artist tempting an eager model. He was only tempting a savage beating as he continued to stare into Kate's face. "You are the protofemale. You are the emanation of the primeval woman."

"I am impressed by your boldness, sir," she replied, "if confused by your words. However, you seem to travel with an ample supply of women who would pose for you."

"I see none of them with you here. I see my Jerusalem in you. Would that I could worship you with burnt offerings and pungent oils." Barnes pressed his hands together in obvious passion. "You must pose for me. I would make yours the most famous visage in England . . . in the world. Armies of men would go forth with your face in their hearts."

"No doubt you feel it is the dream of all women to be the object of men going forth," Kate replied sarcastically. "But some of us serve in lesser ways."

"There can be no lesser way for a woman such as

you." Barnes's eyes were wide with fervor. "If you do not allow me to paint you, I will burn this place to the ground! For there will no longer be a purpose here. I swear by all the gods I will!"

Simon laughed. "I've heard the arts are not for those with a sense of compromise."

Barnes continued to stare at Kate, but said, "I am not sure why you choose to accompany this man. Surely not for his wit."

"You'd be surprised," Simon said. "We cackle like hyenas from morning till night."

The painter was done with the diffident playboy now. He gave no sign of hearing Simon and only gazed at Kate with ferocious desire. She met his eyes with admirable concentration. The two of them stood like that, the faces of desire and intellect, in confrontation for a minute. The crowd watched with breathless anticipation.

Simon finally cleared his throat softly and leaned to Kate's ear. "Are you actually considering this offer?"

"No, I'm not considering it. I'm doing it," Kate said firmly. She gave Simon a quick smile of confidence and nodded to the artist. "I have made a decision. I will pose for you, Mr. Barnes."

The artist clenched his hands together and dropped to both knees in a religious swoon. He swept his arms around Kate's knees and embraced her.

Simon and Kate glanced down at the top of the man's head while he clutched her legs in supplication.

"Well," Simon said, "this shouldn't go wrong."

Chapter 14

KATE TAPPED THE ENRAPTURED BARNES ON THE shoulder. "When shall we begin? How long until you finish your current painting?"

"Finish?" Barnes rose suddenly. "That is a mere exercise. Eleanor, go! Clear this room!"

Everyone immediately began to file out. Kate watched the exodus in surprise. They seemed excited by being ejected, chattering to one another about Kate and the new painting that was about to begin. When Rowan Barnes was operating in the pure fire of creation, the entire salon vibrated with joy.

Simon stood to one side of the door, nodding politely to those who departed. He glanced up to see Barnes glaring at him.

"You!" the painter cried. "Out!"

"Me? Surely you can't expect me to leave Miss Anstruther unchaperoned."

Barnes was walking back toward his easel. "Take your bourgeois foolishness and be gone. There can be no audience."

Kate took a step toward Simon and nodded confidently. He adopted the outraged face of the scorned man, but his whisper to her was calm. "I'll be watching." Then he stormed out with much display of anger.

Kate called, "Don't worry, darling. I'll make sure he uses enough green in my eyes." She laughed and said to a passing woman who looked at her with awe, "He's just upset that Barnes isn't painting him."

The blond nude who had been Barnes's model stared at Kate for a long moment before leaving her spot by the pedestal. She strode to the door with her bare feet slapping the wood floor, weaving through the other departing salonistes. Finally the room was empty and the door closed.

Barnes paused in his gathering of paints. "You may disrobe."

"Oh, may I?" Kate snorted. "I prefer not."

His disappointment was plain for an instant. Then with a wave of a color-filled hand, he brushed it away. "Remember, you are the primordial female. You are Jerusalem."

"Isn't that a city in Palestine?"

"Jerusalem is everything." Barnes placed a fresh white canvas on the easel and led Kate some yards away to a short pillar surrounded by large, potted ferns. He took her arm and extended it with a caress of his fingers. "Here is where you will ponder your nature. Jerusalem is the emanation of Albion. She is the first woman to his first man, but it is even more than that because they are the same. Together, they are one, all humanity. You are she. You are the creative spark of the world. The lush forest of birth. The warm haven of life. You must embrace that power and that freedom. Before you was nothing but God."

Kate hid her reaction to the mention of Albion. Barnes was certainly conversant in the elements of William Blake's mythology. Though, as Malcolm had pointed out, many people had read his poetry.

Barnes touched her hair gently, breathing in her scent.

"You are my masterpiece, the envy of every woman and the desire of every man." He arranged her again, touching and prodding her into position. He studied her face with the disturbing intensity of a scientist staring through a microscope, no longer seeing her, but minute parts of her. His hands lingered a bit long on her hips, taking slight liberties in arranging the folds of her dress. Finally, he took her hand and kissed it, his eyes boring into hers.

Inwardly, Kate shuddered at the caress of his soft wet lips.

Barnes returned to the canvas and took up his brush and palette with the vigor of a hunter snatching up his gun. He enfolded her in a heated gaze that penetrated her in a threatening way. He frantically began to paint without taking his manic attention from her. There was a compelling power in his manner, but Kate felt nothing but revulsion. She almost bolted for the door. She wasn't sure if it was her determination or his that kept her leaning against the cold marble amidst the forest of ferns.

"You are familiar with the works of William Blake?" she asked a little breathlessly, thinking that *obsessed* was a more appropriate word.

Barnes stopped in midstroke and stared at her. "How can one answer that? The entire cosmos is in that statement. I knew the great man. He was my guide, and I am his chosen successor. What was hidden, he saw. He saw the past. He saw the future. He laid out the path." Barnes rested the brush against the canvas. "I now stand where the master did. My mission is to bring a light that will free this world from a shadow of oppression that hovers over it."

He walked to a table in the corner and poured a glass of wine. He didn't offer anything to Kate. He drank and studied her from this new angle, swirling the wine in the goblet. After another moment, he returned to the easel and took up his brush, still holding the wine in the other hand.

"That sounds radical"—Kate tried not to sound too dismissive—"for a man who so openly welcomes the approval of aristocrats."

"I use those people for my own purposes," Barnes said smugly. "The Red Orchid has created a steady stream of upper-class ants plowing through the dim refuse of this parish to reach my shining light of London art." He held the brush just off the canvas. "Your own father was a man who made his bold way in the world. And for his efforts, they castrated him."

"I beg your pardon?" Kate's eyes narrowed to slits.

"They made him one of them—*Sir* Roland—and attached him to their failed world so he would stop striving against them. It wasn't a reward; it was a bribe. He forgot his obligations to those who helped him."

Kate glared with a balled fist on her hip. "How do you deign to speak of my father?"

"I know him. I have known countless men who feared to be as great as they should. And women too. I have invited you to join us so you will not succumb to those fears. Britain will need you and every ounce of bravery you can muster." Barnes stared at her with hunger. "Would you please resume your pose?"

Kate considered storming out. The door was only a few steps away. No one would blame her for leaving, certainly not Simon. Still, she hadn't learned anything useful except that Barnes was a coffeehouse Jacobin who despised the rich while becoming one. She owed it to those two poor women slaughtered and left exposed on church floors to swallow her disdain and stay until she found what she needed. Proof he murdered them.

She placed her hand lightly on the column and turned her head back to face the window.

Chapter 15

IT HAD BEEN OVER AN HOUR SINCE MALCOLM watched Kate and Simon venture upstairs in search of Rowan Barnes. Everything remained quiet. Malcolm heard fascinating snippets of readings and mentions of Shakespeare, Milton, Shelley, and most often, Blake. He had spent time with writers and poets in Edinburgh as a university student, and these people here had that same hungry contemplation of the world. In fact, the only picture in the house, so far as Malcolm could tell, that was not a Barnes was a small watercolor by Blake. It was a naked young man with arms spread wide and blossoming colors behind him.

"Beautiful, isn't it?" came a voice.

Malcolm noticed a young woman standing next to him peering at the painting, and then at him. She was blond and voluptuous, amply shown by the simple dress and full blouse scandalously unbuttoned to display her cleavage. She seemed oddly unaware of her state of dress. Even odder, she was barefoot.

Malcolm felt his strict upbringing welling up and fought the urge to scowl in Presbyterian judgment. He shrugged wordlessly at her art appraisal, preferring that to contradicting her.

She stared at him incredulously. "You don't like it?"

"It's dramatic," he said begrudgingly. "And there's color."

"It's glorious. Don't you perceive that?"

He found her tone annoying with its implication that he was incapable of deep thought if he didn't appreciate the picture. He dug in his artistic heels. "It's mediocre."

Her mouth fell open as if he had just denied that the Earth was round or fire was hot. Then she grew suspicious and challenging. "Clearly you have no artistic training."

"As much as he." Malcolm tried not to smile proudly at his off-the-cuff jab. He would remember to tell it to Simon later.

The blonde ran a ferocious hand through her hair and practically growled. "Perhaps you found your way here by accident, sir. Did you mean to stop into a country house so you could admire the oils of heifers and farm maids?"

Malcolm snorted in amusement. "Perhaps you're correct, miss. I am no artist. I am more moved to poetry."

She brightened with excitement. "As am I! Surely then you appreciate Master Blake's brilliance in verse." As he turned his sour expression to her, she gasped in shocked disbelief. "No! You cannot possibly call yourself a poet and find disfavor with the Master. Have you truly read him?"

"I truly have. And then I truly reread him because I couldn't credit the rubbish I was reading the first time."

The woman couldn't find words to reply. Her eyes wavered between pity, horror, and fury.

"You realize"—Malcolm pointed at her as if lecturing—"there is room in the vast universe for different views."

"Perhaps over minor issues such as the existence of God, but Master Blake's words are the music of the spheres made solid. He is the soul of mankind."

Malcolm rolled his eyes. She seized his arm and for a second, he feared she was going to attempt to throw him out. Instead, she tugged him down the corridor to a room that had likely been servants' quarters. It was small, but with a serviceable grate where glowing coals threw off a fine heat. Four women sat on the floor, with a brass tray between them and long-stemmed opium pipes resting there. They all looked up blearily at the frantic blonde and confused man. They were older than the young woman towing Malcolm, and they regarded her with the comforting welcome of older sisters.

"Eleanor?" one of the reclining women, a grim-eyed redhead, exclaimed. "What have you there?"

"A Scotsman," Eleanor replied. "He claims to be a poet yet he disdains the Master."

Malcolm prepared to bolt for freedom from the clutch of frenzied cultists, but the blonde shoved down on his shoulders. "Sit." One of the others reached back and dragged a heavy folio into the circle.

Malcolm lowered himself awkwardly because the pistols under his coat were digging into his waist and thighs. Once he was settled with young true-believer Eleanor at his side, the redhead opened the book and pronounced, "From *Jerusalem*."

Malcolm exhaled with annoyance. "Please, we're all Christians here, have mercy."

"Quiet!" Eleanor barked. "Proceed, Lilith."

The redheaded Lilith cleared her throat and intoned:

> " 'And the Four Zoa's clouded rage East & West &
>   North & South
> They change their situations, in the Universal Man.
> Albion groans, he sees the Elements divide before
>   his face.
> And England who is Brittannia divided into Jerusa-
>   lem and Vala

> And Urizen assumes the East, Luvah assumes the
>   South
> In his dark Spectre ravening from his open Sepul-
>   cher.' "

Malcolm buried his face in his hand and wished for an opium pipe to blunt the blows of those banal words. "Blake is a bloody disturbance."

"He was a visionary," Eleanor explained. "He didn't experience the world as we do."

"That's plain." Malcolm stared at the blank euphoric faces around him and felt frustration rising. He practically shouted, "You can't tell me you understood a syllable of that!"

"Of course we did," Eleanor said with a sly wink at her fellows. "And bellowing is the refuge of a man with no reason. Shall we enlighten you on the Master's meaning?"

"Pray do," Malcolm replied in a whisper.

Eleanor now leafed through the book, cleared her throat, and began:

> " 'Her voice pierc'd Albions clay cold ear. he moved
>   upon the Rock
> The Breath Divine went forth upon the morning
>   hills, Albion mov'd
> Upon the Rock, he opened his eyelids in pain; in
>   pain he mov'd
> His stony members, he saw England. Ah! shall the
>   Dead live again
> The Breath Divine went forth over the morning hills
>   Albion rose
> In anger: the wrath of God breaking bright flaming
>   on all sides around
> His awful limbs: into the Heavens he walked clothed
>   in flames' "

She stopped and breathed in, letting the words soak into her. "That was one of Cecilia's favorite passages. She used it when she ascended."

The dead live again, Malcolm noted to himself. Cecilia's favorite passage indeed. However, he remained visibly unimpressed. "Is *ascended* a Blakesian term for going round the shop?"

"No, you would call it dying, but that isn't correct at all. She is waiting in Jerusalem." Eleanor turned to Lilith with disappointment. "Where I thought I would be soon."

"You will," the other woman said.

"Perhaps not." Eleanor gave a tragic sigh. "He has a new one."

"No, dear. You will be one. He chose you. He doesn't lie."

Lilith now stared at Malcolm as if suddenly remembering he was present. He tried to keep his manner unconcerned, studying the five passionate faces shining around him. These women could have been nothing more than intense but harmless enthusiasts; however, he felt an odd sense of unease spreading.

He tensed to move quickly if necessary. "Two women from your salon were murdered recently. Cecilia de Ronay and Madeleine Hawley. You knew this, yes? And their bodies were claimed by Rowan Barnes? Do you know why?"

"Because that's what you do for family," Lilith replied serenely. "What would you have him do, let their bodies go to some nameless parish plot? No, sir. They are our sisters. We brought them home."

"Can you tell me where they're buried?"

"You needn't worry about Cecilia or Madeleine," Eleanor said. "Perhaps you knew them before they came to the Red Orchid, but they are no longer those people.

None of us are. They are emanations waiting. In Jerusalem. For Albion."

Lilith hissed, "Eleanor, shh."

The young blonde smiled innocently. "I don't see a problem, Lilith. He's probably looking for an old friend. He surely didn't come here because of his knowledge of poetry or art because he has none." She touched Malcolm on the arm. "I'm sorry, but neither Cecilia nor Madeleine is here any longer. And when they rise, you will not know them."

Lilith motioned Malcolm toward the door with her pipe. "Will you leave us now?"

Eleanor looked embarrassed, as if this was poor etiquette. "But we are discussing the Master."

"Eleanor, please." Lilith narrowed her eyes at the younger woman. The rest of the women exchanged glances and instantly adjusted their postures to become withdrawn.

Lilith regarded the Scotsman. "Sir, if you will, leave us, please."

Malcolm rose, keeping track of all the women, watching for any sudden movements. He bowed and backed to the door. Before he went out, Eleanor scampered to him.

"I hope you will come back," she said. "I would enjoy teaching you about poetry. Wait!" She leaned back into the dim room and shuffled through books and pamphlets on a side table. She handed Malcolm a small, cheaply printed volume with a yellow cover. "These are my poems. I wrote them before I came to the Red Orchid, but they're all I've had published. I'm afraid they're not very good."

Malcolm glanced at the book. It was truly a published volume of poems by a reputable, if small, London printer. He nodded in appreciation. "I'm sure they're very good. Thank you, Eleanor."

"And do reread *Jerusalem*."

"If you wish it."

The pretty young blonde smiled at him and disappeared back into the room, closing the door.

Malcolm slipped the small book into his coat pocket and continued down the corridor. There was a sense of ecstatic dedication in those women. Their lack of concern about their two friends who died disturbed him. They knew what had happened; they just didn't care. And their use of the word *ascending* to diminish the idea they were murdered was ritualistic and unnerving.

Malcolm noticed another door, narrower and shorter than the rest, which had odd runic symbols painted on it. He checked around him before opening it. Behind the door were dark steps to a cellar. He found a lit candle on a side table and took it down creaking stairs. At the bottom, his foot stepped into soft dirt. The musty smell of damp earth rose around him. The ceiling was only five feet so Malcolm had to crouch. The faint candlelight hinted at heavy beams and rough brick walls. Spiderwebs crinkled across his face. He saw a shelf with jars of preserves and another with bottles of wine. Next to those shelves, Malcolm noted something square about five feet high, covered with a tarp and leaning against the wall.

Malcolm dripped wax on a shelf and fixed the candle. He then began to work with the tarp. Beneath it, he found a portrait of a beautiful nude woman. Olive skin and black hair. She stared back openly at the viewer. One hand extended out and the other lay on her stomach. She was serene, even beatific. She wasn't oversexualized, nor idealized. The setting of the painting appeared to be the interior of a church. The juxtaposition of the nude woman with the holy setting seemed purposefully indecent. Then Malcolm noticed at the bottom of the painting was a symbol. It was a series of Egyptian hieroglyphs, the same as those in the Pendragon/Hawksmoor churches.

There was a second portrait and he felt a shock seeing it. The woman in the painting was the living portrayal of the lovely young blonde whom he had seen lying naked and vulnerable in a pool of blood at St. George's Blooms-bury with her chest cut open and her heart branded. Madeleine Hawley. The poet.

"Here, what are you doing?"

Malcolm spun around with his hand slipping inside his coat for the butt of his pistol. He saw a burly man in a tweed jacket hunched on the bottom step. His face was wide and his nose flattened from numerous break-ages. His massive hands had fingers like iron bars. His ratlike eyes squinted ominously at the Scotsman's hand buried in his coat.

Malcolm thought he saw a glimpse of red hair as the door closed upstairs. "Lilith asked me to bring up a bottle of wine."

"The wine is over here. What're you doing muddling with those pictures?"

"Caught my eye."

"What do you have under your coat, mate?"

"A bottle."

"You're a liar. You've got a knife or a pistol."

Malcolm drew back his coat to expose the heavy weapon in its holster. "Fine. It's a large pistol. Step aside and I'll be on my way."

The man shook his head. There was a strange cold-ness in his beefy features, a certain simplicity that trou-bled Malcolm because this type of man often had to be killed.

Malcolm said, "This is a Lancaster pistol. It was de-signed in India for hunting tigers from the back of an elephant. The ball will tear a hole in you large enough to insert your own freakishly huge head. Do you understand?"

The man replied, "I understand, but I'm going to kill you."

"Just for looking at pictures?"

The man proved fast and nimble in the cramped space. Malcolm felt an incredibly strong arm lock around his neck. The brute had him in a headlock. Very smoothly done, an excellent wrestling maneuver. Malcolm saw sparkles of light even as he tried to bow his neck and shoulders.

He preferred not to kill the brute so his fingers rubbed along the nearby shelf until they touched a smooth, narrow cylinder of glass. He pulled a wine bottle and smashed it back into the man's head. He felt liquid and glass shards splash onto his hair. The man shook his head and tightened the vise.

Malcolm had done a bit of grappling in his day. He tried to take out the man's ankles but it was like kicking the legs of a Clydesdale. So Malcolm braced his own feet and, with a twist, slammed the brute against the brick wall without effect. He surged up and bashed the man's head against a heavy beam.

The brute fell slightly off balance so Malcolm began to push toward faint slivers of light he saw on one wall. They picked up speed and Malcolm turned so the other man took the brunt of the impact when they hit what proved to be a fragile door. The two tumbled into a cold alley amidst splinters of wood, slamming against the brick wall on the far side.

Malcolm tried to pull away, but there was still no give in the murderous, choking grip. He heard his blood drumming in his ears. He couldn't draw breath. His vision was dimming. He desperately gouged the jagged neck of the bottle into the man's wide face, grinding the glass shards deep. The brute gave a shout of pain.

With tingling fingers, Malcolm fumbled for the hilt of the dagger that hung next to his rib cage. The stinking dark alley was spinning around him, but he concentrated on the feel of the bone handle in his hand and the rough slide of steel past leather as he pulled the knife. Malcolm pressed the blade into the man's thick white shirt. He hoped the prodding would've convinced the brute to release him. But no.

With eyesight going red and misty, Malcolm jammed the blade between the man's ribs. His opponent made a gurgling gasp and Malcolm was thrown aside by the neck. He first assumed the man had twisted his head off and he was experiencing the weird effect that chickens feel after they are beheaded.

Malcolm crashed against the wall and slid to the ground. The brute collapsed with him, his massive arm still draped on Malcolm's shoulder. He could see his torso and legs from the proper perspective so his head hadn't been torn off after all, much to his relief. The alley wafted into focus. The dagger was hilt-deep in the dead man's rib cage.

He pulled it out and struggled to his feet with his ears humming. He staggered down the alley, pushing past confused onlookers. He paused to take several deep breaths and to rotate his head to ensure his neck wasn't broken. Then he sheathed the knife and buttoned his coat. His eyesight was clearing and his hearing was returning over the faint ringing.

He thought of nothing but those dead women on canvas and Kate upstairs with that creature Barnes.

Chapter 16

KATE STOOD VERY STILL, DOING HER BEST TO study her surroundings and coax Barnes into useful conversation. She had succeeded in swallowing her anger at his barbs toward her father, and to her relief, he had lapsed into silence while he painted. Finally, she dropped her arm and stepped toward him. "May I see?"

"No." Barnes ceased work and rushed to her, positioning her once again.

"You perform in front of your . . . students."

"They're not students. And I don't perform before anyone with a great work like this. This is a private . . . a solemn . . . matter."

Kate arched back purposefully against him, her neck poised near his mouth. She wasn't sure what might trigger a reaction in the man, but it was time to experiment. Barnes was all too ready to respond. His hand lifted to pull her waves of thick hair away from her ivory flesh, his fingertips trailing along her skin. She let out an exaggerated shuddering sigh as he lifted her arm out in front of her. He was well built and muscular. He brought his hand back and brushed it languidly across her chest, boldly caressing a breast. Kate's eyes flashed open and she took a hard swallow.

"Tell me your secret," she breathed in her best licentious voice.

"Secret?"

"You have mesmerized everyone with your art and your mere presence. Even me. I have never been so wanton. You must have a secret."

Barnes laughed deep in his throat. "The secret is to know what one desires in her heart. You desire to be free of your burdens. I can help you."

"Can you?"

"I will remake you." He turned her face to his. "Will you allow me?"

"Yes," she whispered. This was what she was waiting for. *For pity's sake just hurry it along so I don't get ill.*

"I knew you were perfect. You have the fire of the new world in you. You can sense my purpose, can't you?"

Kate grasped the pedestal for support. "Tell me what you want."

Barnes nearly purred as he lifted her chin just as Simon did and kissed her. "You asked what power I have. Are you ready to know?"

"God, yes," Kate murmured. Where Simon evoked a blinding want in her, Barnes was foul and brought on only nausea.

"I have the power to remake the world, and I want you to be part of it."

"How can I do that?"

"I can give you freedom. Freedom from the burdens of your family. Freedom from the shadow of your father. Freedom to become something more than you ever imagined. And it will be you who accomplishes it. Not your father's daughter. You. Your mind, your heart, the very blood in your veins will become pieces of a god. You will become a stone to build Jerusalem. You will become a limb of a giant. Your blood is the sword that will cut down hatred and defend the innocent. You will know things no other human has ever, or will ever, know. Do you believe me?"

He continued kissing her and, even with her senses acute, she didn't see or hear a door open. Suddenly two women stood near her.

Kate's gaze flicked to them. Both were young, with shapely figures, clad in the barest silk shift so all the nuances of their anatomies were on display. Their skin, however, was slightly gray and looked oddly thick. Both women had a gruesome scar that ran down the center of their chest and across the top of their left breast. It was a horrific welt, crudely stitched and poorly healed. One of the girls looked familiar.

Barnes reached out to touch the first woman's shoulder. "Ah, my dears, you shouldn't be here. I haven't yet called for you, but no matter."

The woman he touched stirred and turned her face toward the artist. Her expression was quietly expectant. She put her own hand over his. Then she slowly turned her eyes to Kate and stared without expression. Her features finally stirred Kate's memory. She had seen that face lying still and pale on the floor of St. George's Bloomsbury. Kate felt cold seeping through her own limbs and her gaze was drawn to the long, puckered line on their chests. She realized there was no rise and fall to their breasts.

Kate tried to pull back from Barnes, who was staring at her like a cat tracking a wounded bird. He gripped her tightly. Her hand tried to reach for a vial in her pocket, but Barnes yanked her arms forward.

"Don't be frightened of them," he said. "Madeleine and Cecilia are harmless. If I wish it."

There was a crash of glass behind her followed by a crack of thunder. A concussive blast swept them all off their feet. Barnes's grip was lost. Kate scrambled up and ran toward Simon, who crouched in front of a broken window.

Barnes came up onto his elbows, sweeping broken glass off himself. He eyed Simon with amazement as he gained his feet and ran his fingers through tousled red hair.

Simon's expression showed nothing but contempt. He stepped in front of Kate. "You'll not harm another woman, especially her."

"I haven't harmed anyone yet. Your perception is so small," the artist remarked, "for a scribe."

"You killed and mutilated those women in an unspeakable ritual," Simon said icily. "And you've reanimated them as trophies. You are something even worse than I suspected. Something inhuman."

Barnes went to a pitcher and basin on a dresser along one wall. He began to wash his hands. The two dead women rose off the floor and continued to stare at their master. "They're not trophies. They are Jerusalem. They are Albion."

Simon whispered and clapped his hands together. Another shock wave rolled over Barnes. The artist slammed against the heavy dresser and toppled to the floor. He glared up at Simon, for the first time showing anger and concern. Barnes reached out toward Simon and spread his fingers wide. There was a faint glow of yellowish-green aether crackling in the air around Simon. The artist grunted with effort.

Simon clutched his chest with a grimace. Kate grabbed him. Simon leaned on her, cursing through the sudden agony.

Barnes struggled back to his feet with his hand still outstretched, his fingers closing as if around Simon's heart. Simon doubled over screaming.

"Archer, I don't know who or what you are," Barnes

hissed through gritted teeth, "but I'll find out from your corpse once I wither your heart."

"Stop it!" Kate shouted. Her hand pulled a vial of amber from her pocket and threw it at Barnes. The dead women stepped purposefully into its arc and the vial broke against their waxy skin. The amber swelled to encase them.

Barnes exclaimed in surprise at the vision of his re-animated disciples trapped in an ocher resin.

Despite the agony that had brought Simon to the point of collapse, he staggered over to the easel where the figure of Kate was taking form, nude despite Barnes's assurances. The oils were still wet and Simon slapped a desperate hand on the canvas. With sharp strokes, his finger traced a dark rune across her breasts. His other hand grabbed the real Kate's forearm, drawing her close against him. With a shuddering exhale, he whispered a word in her ear and the aether responded to him, spreading over them. Kate supported him as he sank to the ground with a rush of relief from the fierce pain in his chest.

Barnes tilted his head in confusion, tightening his grip in the air without result. He smiled angrily. "An aether shield. Impressive. But you can't sustain it for long. I can wait."

Kate was formulating a plan in her head when there was a faint noise behind them. There was a shuddering crash and the door shook on its hinges. Barnes leapt back with alarm as a second vibrating boom smashed in the door, spraying splinters of wood. The artist scurried for another door on the far side of the room. He pulled it open and darted away just as what was left of the other door exploded in thunder.

Familiar dark boots paused at Simon and Kate. The magician muttered a word with stiff lips and the shimmering shield fell away like water.

"Are you alive?" Malcolm crouched next to them, his pistol aimed at the far door, his hand resting on Simon's shoulder.

Simon could only nod.

When Malcolm started to give chase, Kate cautioned, "Stop! Barnes is dangerous. He's a necromancer. We're not ready to face him here. We must withdraw."

Malcolm grunted in disappointment but reached down to pull Simon to his unsteady feet with Kate's help. The Scotsman locked eyes on the two women covered in amber. He shivered in recognition. "God help us. Is that Madeleine Hawley?"

"Yes," Kate said. "And Cecilia de Ronay."

"And both of their portraits are in the cellar," Malcolm said.

Simon grinned in a strange vicious way. "So he paints them, kills them, stitches them up, and reanimates them?"

"I'm going to be sick," Kate muttered.

They went to the window and Kate was relieved when Simon was able to throw a leg over the sill. Heavy footsteps were heard in the hallway and he began to clamber back in, intent on a fight.

"Don't you dare!" she told him.

Malcolm forced Simon out the window, holding him by the arm. "Is there a fish wagon still below?"

Before Kate could answer, Malcolm released him. Simon dropped onto a mound of shining fish and toppled to the street in a landslide of herring. Kate jumped down after him, scowling at the smell and the slime. Malcolm landed just behind and vaulted off the wagon.

Simon took Kate's shoulder for balance with a hand smeared in paint that mimicked Kate's skin tone.

"Come on," insisted Malcolm. "We need to leave. Now."

A large man filled the window above and glared at the three figures below, who were surrounded by fish.

Malcolm raised the pistol and fired. The ball struck the man in the chest and smashed him back inside the room.

"Malcolm!" Simon gasped, grabbing his gun arm. "You've killed that man! He might be an innocent in this."

Malcolm began to pull Simon down the street as the fishmonger screamed at them. "He's not innocent. And I didn't kill him."

"How can you know that?"

"Because I already killed him in the alley earlier."

Chapter 17

KATE GAVE A QUICK RAP ON SIMON'S BEDROOM door at Gaunt Lane and entered. Simon stood in a shaft of morning sun. He reached for a shirt as he saw Kate's form appear. His tattoos were dark shadows against his pale skin. They entwined along his muscled back and across his broad shoulders, reaching down to his strong forearms. She stopped, bemused, as he slipped into a shirt.

"Sorry," she said without conviction and with a touch of suspicion. "Did you actually throw on a shirt out of modesty?"

"There is such a thing as decorum." The shirttail hung below his waistband, with his braces dangling lower. He was in his stocking feet still.

"Think of me as a physician." She smirked as he ran a hasty hand through his pleasantly disheveled sleek raven hair. "However, I could fetch a chaperone."

"A man's bedroom is sacred. You may see things you'd rather not."

"How terrifying." Kate picked up his razor from the marble-top basin. It was still warm and damp from shaving. She found the worn heft of the ivory handle comforting.

"You have been warned." Simon wiped his face with a small towel. "I'm sorry if I leapt in too soon at the Red Orchid. I suspect you were close to securing information from Barnes, but when I saw those two women, I had to act."

"I understand. I don't know how much Barnes would have actually told me." Kate set down the razor. "I assumed you were lurking in the hall. How exactly were you outside the window? Can you fly?"

Simon smiled.

Kate waited, but he said no more about it. She idly took the towel from him and folded it onto the rack next to the basin. "God help me, but I keep thinking we should just go to the Red Orchid today and level the place."

"I do as well, but Barnes is no fool, in addition to being a powerful magician. He surrounds himself with innocents so any enemies with a moral compass, such as ourselves, must hesitate before launching an attack."

"I know." Kate handed Simon his hairbrush with a slight smile, enjoying the brief moment of domesticity. Watching a man prepare himself was a rare glimpse into a secret world, and she found it oddly appealing. He proceeded to brush his hair with slow, measured strokes. Then he slowly tucked his shirt into his waistband and struggled to lift the braces over his shoulders with a painful breath.

Kate came forward and adjusted the braces for him. "Perhaps I should examine you."

"It's nothing. Would you hand my waistcoat to me, please?"

A bit concerned by his dismissal, she lifted the garment from the bed and held it out so he could slip his arms into it. When he turned back to her, Kate peered at the upper edge of the tattoos visible above the open collar of his shirt. She ran a finger along one of the lines, feeling his skin and the light hairs. His muscles twitched beneath her touch. She looked up into piercing eyes as dark as any numinous forest.

"That is most improper, miss," he breathed.

"Is it?" Her voice was surprisingly deep and her hand slid down along his chest.

Simon flinched, his mood changing immediately. He stepped away.

"I . . . I'm sorry, Simon." Kate was surprised and embarrassed. "I didn't mean to . . . I don't know, but I didn't mean to."

"No, Kate. It isn't you."

She almost laughed as he began the oldest speech in the manual.

He took her hand in a quick reassuring gesture. "It's merely that I have a bit of a souvenir from the Red Orchid."

"It is more than just the fall from the window, isn't it?"

Simon looked down into Kate's green eyes and gave a glib wink. He was going to make light of the situation. Her heart raced with trepidation.

"Yes. I survived, but I didn't quite escape." He unbuttoned his shirt and drew it down from his neck. On his chest, where his heart would be, was a horrible reddish patch. The skin was inflamed, almost blistered.

"Oh Simon." Kate started to touch it, but he backed away again. "No wonder you're in pain. I have something to alleviate the burn."

"It isn't a burn." He covered the wound. "It's a necromancer's curse."

"Oh my God," she blurted out, but then worked to make her voice steady and analytical. "What will happen to you?"

Simon let out the breath he had been holding. "I can't be sure, but the most traditional result is pain."

"How bad?"

"It's a bit annoying at the moment. I suspect it'll get considerably worse until I can't do much useful because of the pain. That's usually how these things go."

Kate couldn't believe what she was going to say. "Are you going to die . . . again?"

"No. Well, not unless I kill myself, which is difficult with a necromancer involved. Damned inconvenient. They simply bring you back."

"We'll find a cure."

"Possible, but not likely. Even for your considerable skills. I've never heard of a necromancer's curse being cured except by complementary magic. Usually, it's the necromancers themselves who remove it. Traditionally, that's how necromancers get wealthy. Curse. Ransom. Cure. And so on for years until a mob with torches finally has enough and burns them or throws them off a cliff."

Kate pulled out a chair, urging Simon to sit as if he were an invalid. He gently pushed the chair in again.

"Why are you so stubborn?" she exclaimed.

Simon held up a cautionary hand. "Don't worry."

"Don't worry? Are you insane? You have a scar over your heart that will send you into madness from the pain, and I can't help you! But I shouldn't worry? Well, fine then. As long as everything is perfect. What shall we have for breakfast?" Kate glared, her chest rising and falling with gulping breaths of rage and terror. She grabbed the chair and slammed it on the floor. "You can't just smirk and say something oh so charming and make it go away. This isn't a joke, Simon."

"I'm not laughing, but I'm not dying either." Simon crossed his arms. "I told you this because we have no secrets from each other, but we have to deal with it reasonably. We'll have Barnes eventually. And I'm sure we can impress upon him the necessity of removing this curse." He gave a wan smile and straightened his shirt.

Kate started to embrace him, but hesitated. Not about to decline her tender mercies again, he leaned forward and took her in his arms without reservation and with no sign of pain. His lips brushed hers. She put her head against his shoulder.

There was a hesitant knock and they turned to see Malcolm in the open doorway. The Scotsman looked embarrassed to interrupt, staring at the floor.

"Sorry." Malcolm held out an envelope. "I took the liberty of retrieving your mail from the Devil's Loom. I thought you should see this."

Simon noted the feel of heavy-weave stationery and saw a crest on the envelope. He laughed. "It's from the prime minister's office."

Kate looked over his shoulder. "Prime Minister North is writing to you?"

"Shocking, I know." Simon broke the wax seal, slid out a thick note card, and read it. "It isn't signed, but I'm requested for a meeting. Well done, Henry. I'm astounded by his success. Care to join me, Kate?"

"I'm not invited."

"You're an Anstruther." He handed the card to her. "Invitations are redundant for you lot."

"These directions are unusual, and detailed. Far south of London. It isn't even a town." Kate tapped the note card against her chin. "Why not meet at the prime minister's residence? Or at Whitehall?"

"These murders are a delicate matter. They have a desire for discretion."

Kate tossed the card on the table. "I'll change."

AN HOUR LATER, A FOUR-HORSE CARRIAGE ROLLED south out of London along Kent Road, and through nu-

merous crossroad villages surrounded by rolling brown
fields. Simon watched the grey rows of homes grow more
scarce and give way to a winter landscape.

Another hour passed, and he went to check the surroundings again. He felt a painful tug at his chest, re-
minding him of Barnes's curse. He was careful to cover
the discomfort, but Kate's quick glance showed he was
unsuccessful.

The carriage wheeled off the poor road onto an even
poorer cart path. Heavy brush slapped at the sides of
the coach. Simon and Kate both watched out the windows as the carriage rocked like a ship in heavy seas.
The wheels slammed through ragged holes. The path
made a steep decline and they hung onto the seat while
they listened to the voice of Malcolm roaring from the
driver's bench, cursing and coaxing the team of four
Friesians by turns.

They tore out of the high scrub into a wild stream
valley. The land had not been tilled or grazed for gen-
erations. A ramshackle little cottage stood near the
water, strangled by vines and nestled in the shadow of a
twisted grove of ancient oaks. However, smoke drifted
from the chimney. Simon noticed an area near the
house where the brush was thinner, and he saw the jagged stones of a forgotten graveyard hidden in the high
grass.

"Charming," Kate said, as the carriage thrashed down
brambles and rocked to a stop yards from the oaks, which
seemed frozen in a moment of terrible writhing.

"It was probably someone's honeymoon cottage once,"
Simon said.

"I'd say the marriage didn't thrive." Kate took a long
dagger and slid it into a sheath under her coat. Then she
looped her bandolier of vials over one shoulder.

Simon gave her an appreciative look. "Very striking,

but hardly an appropriate accessory for meeting the prime minister."

"I'm an Anstruther. They expect the unusual from us."

"At least you're not resorting to wearing gigantic ravens on your head."

Kate's door opened and Malcolm stood outside with pistol in hand. He didn't speak but was clearly suspicious of the setting. She gave him a pat on the shoulder as she stepped out.

Simon leapt out the opposite side. "Nicely done, Malcolm. I'd say you have a career in transport should you tire of hunting monsters."

Malcolm stalked around the carriage. "I'll wait out here so there are no rude interruptions for you."

Kate kicked thorns with heavy boots. "Glad I didn't dress for tea."

She and Simon stomped through brambles, clearing a path to the door. The cottage was worn stone with a long-neglected thatch roof. The smell of mold and wet grass nearly overwhelmed the scent of woodsmoke.

"Ready?" Simon asked.

Kate put her hand on her bandolier. She nodded.

He pushed the thick door. It squealed back to reveal a fire crackling in the hearth on the far wall. A table sat in the middle of the cottage with several indistinguishable objects on it. A shape moved in front of the fire.

Simon whispered a word and felt aether surge in him. He noted how the pain of the curse eased slightly. He prepared to slam his hands together to create a shock wave.

"Come in, Mr. Archer," a female voice said from the darkness.

Simon and Kate both looked to their right to see a long, pale gown shimmering in the firelight. As their eyes grew more accustomed to the interior, they saw a woman with a pale face and blond hair cascading about her shoulders. She sat in the corner in a plain chair.

Simon recognized the voice, and now the face, as did Kate, as would nearly anyone in the realm. Grace North, the prime minister's wife. Beloved and beautiful, the people's queen. It was jarring to see her here in the middle of the wild in a filthy cottage.

"No one means you harm." She indicated the man standing in the shadows. He was tall and dressed in a long coat with a scarf wrapped about his face, revealing only his eyes. "He is merely my bodyguard. There is no danger."

"Mrs. North." Simon lowered his hands. He eyed the shadowy man by the fire. "This is unexpected. Is your husband with you?"

"He is not. I am the one who sent for you, Mr. Archer." Grace North's voice was calm, almost drowsy. She nodded to Kate. "Miss Anstruther, I didn't expect you, but I suppose I should have given that I'd heard you and Mr. Archer were attached now."

Kate replied, "I hope you don't mind my presence, ma'am."

Grace clutched a shawl around her shoulders. "Mind? I applaud it. Would you please come in and close the door. I abhor the cold."

Simon nodded to Malcolm, who stood by the coach, and shut the door behind them. Grace slowly raised her hand a few inches toward several simple wooden chairs against the far wall. "There are no great comforts here, but we'll be brief. Tea? Something stronger?"

"No, thank you." Simon remained standing near the door with Kate. "We're eager to get to it. So I assume the government is aware of the dangerous situation in London?"

From Grace North's demeanor, she could have been meeting with the Kensington Garden Improvement

League, until she leveled a shockingly hard stare at Simon. "The dangerous situation in London is entirely created by *you*, Mr. Archer."

"I beg your pardon?"

"The difficulty with amateurs is that they don't appreciate the full ramifications of a situation. They don't have all the information to make a rational decision, and so they form a course of action, derived from self-interest only, like a child. Because they have no broader frame of reference from which to judge."

"I fear you've lost me, ma'am."

"I refer to you, Mr. Archer. And you, Miss Anstruther. You are the danger, and I brought you here to see that it ceases." Grace shifted slightly in her seat. A sheen of perspiration showed on her forehead. "Rowan Barnes is fighting to save Britain. If he does not succeed, the consequences will be apocalyptic. I am asking you, if you love this realm, to allow him to do his good work."

"Ma'am," Simon said, "you have been cruelly deluded. Rowan Barnes may be many things, but patriot is not among them. He has murdered two women. And he will attempt the murder of two more if he isn't stopped."

"There have been no murders, Mr. Archer. Those two women willingly sacrificed themselves for the good of Britain. If Barnes does not complete the ritual, millions will die. Do you understand? Those women understood that. Millions of innocent men, women, and children. Weigh those against four lives. Any reasonable person would know which choice to make."

Simon stared at her in complete confusion. He was beginning to sense a hint of the Red Orchid acolyte in her. She had the scent of one of Barnes's people. Frightening. Barnes had access to the wife of the most powerful man in the government.

"I disagree," Simon said firmly.

"That's because you don't understand. I know what you are, Mr. Archer. I know you are a magician, so let me explain in terms that will persuade you. Many years ago, a great magician, perhaps the greatest of all time, named Byron Pendragon, put a spell in place to protect Britain from a terrible threat he feared would one day occur. He was right, but unfortunately he was killed by that terrible threat. Britain needs Pendragon's magic to save it. Rowan Barnes will do that, and he is the only one who can."

Simon's lips were a thin line. "So Barnes is using blood magic to pervert Pendragon's intentions. He is slaughtering innocents to break the lock on the spell."

"What we are witnessing," Grace North said, "is the end of a tragedy set in motion centuries ago. There is, loose in the world, a madman named Gaios. No doubt you've heard the name, and perhaps thought it a myth. He is very real and he is one of the most powerful magicians in the history of mankind. He is an earth elemental and, in his long time on earth, he has killed millions. Most recently, he caused the eruption of Tambora in the East Indies in 1815, of which you no doubt read. Thousands dead. The volcanic debris thrown into the air blocked the sun even here. There was no summer that year. That is how obscenely powerful his magic can be. That is how low his regard for human life is. We believe he has already set foot in Britain, and he is bringing the end of the world. Only the sacrifice of four women can stop him."

"How could you possibly know any of that?" Simon asked brusquely. "Are these more of Barnes's fantasies? Are you in line to be one of his innocent sacrifices?"

"I know far more than you can possibly understand, Mr. Archer," she said with a snide edge in her voice. "The rulers of this land have long had relations with many great magicians, including Byron Pendragon, and I am privy to stores of hidden information about this secret history."

Simon started toward Grace, but the shrouded man came up to her shoulder in a threatening posture. Wary of a fight when he had no idea what he was facing, Simon stepped back. "Ma'am, you may know then that I'm a scribe, like Pendragon. I can study his spells and find another way to break them. There's no need for Barnes's lunacy. There's no need for further blood."

She gave him a smug smile. "Please, Mr. Archer. It would take years for you even to comprehend Pendragon's magic, and another lifetime to overcome it, if you ever could. I know you are a carver. You tattoo your body with runic spells so you can engage in physical combat. Pendragon would never have stooped to such vulgar magic. He was elegant and his power was incomparable. No, Mr. Archer, Gaios is at our doorstep. We don't have time for you to grow up."

Simon breathed through clenched teeth. His eyes darted around the cottage, catching a glimpse of something before focusing again on Grace North. He stared at her, letting his silence testify to the degree of cooperation she could expect.

Grace North's voice was growing ragged and strained as if she was inexplicably fatigued. "We can make you a very rich man."

"I'm already a rich man."

"Well, there's rich, and there's acceptable. There's that troubling element of your parentage, isn't there? You may be wealthy and one of the popular faces about town, but that's all very transitory. Wealth can be lost. Popularity fades. But class transcends. We can make you a man of consequence. Would you care for a baronetcy? Sir Simon Archer. Higher? Viscount Archer. Higher still? Lord Warden. There is little we couldn't give you. Surely your mother would be proud to see the family brought into the House of Lords. And when Gaios is dealt with, there will be a place for a talented scribe in the new order."

Simon could hear Kate breathing. He knew she was watching him. The fire crackled low.

Grace pursed her lips at his silence. "No? Then what about power? True power. I have connections that could provide you with knowledge of mystic arts beyond what you can discover on your own. Whatever your goal may be, I can arrange for you to become more than you ever imagined."

Her shadowy footman nodded in agreement.

"No," Simon replied quickly.

"Mr. Archer, you cannot survive this contest."

Simon took Kate's arm. "Come, there's no more to hear. Mrs. North, thank you for your time." Simon pulled open the door and bowed back out of the cottage. Then he slammed the door shut and virtually dragged the nonplussed Kate through the brush to the carriage.

Malcolm came around, pistol ready, with a look of confusion at the hasty exit.

"Let's be on our way," Simon said in a quiet tone that betrayed great urgency. "Hartley Hall is closer than London." He and Kate were barely settled inside when the coach started off over rough ground.

They rode on for a long time in tense silence, watching through the windows, expecting an attack. They cleared the heavy forest and returned to the road. The carriage clipped on at a fast pace toward the northwest and Hartley Hall.

Finally Kate said, "Care to tell me why we left so quickly?"

He wiped beads of sweat from his brow and whispered a word that triggered a runic tattoo. The pain subsided. "I had a terrible sense in that cottage. I noticed runes inscribed along the beams."

"I didn't see them."

"They were well hidden, but I recognized them. They were written by Byron Pendragon." Simon glanced out the window, relieved that the little cottage was well behind them. "I can't be sure that some evil entity such as Barnes hasn't gained access to Pendragon's magic. In any case, I'm tired of fighting battles on the ground of the enemy's choosing."

"What next then?" Kate asked.

Simon tapped his walking stick, deep in thought. "That's what we need to determine. We'll go to Hartley Hall. Imogen and Charlotte have both been too long out of our view. I don't mind telling you, I'm worried. Did you see Grace North? She was almost entranced when she spoke of Rowan Barnes. If the man has the influence to turn Grace North into his messenger, how far up does his influence go? Prime Minister North? The Crown itself?"

Kate looked out at the rolling hills. "What if she's correct about Barnes's purpose? Or about the women being willing sacrifices? Simon, if four sacrifices will save millions from the wrath of Gaios, do we have the right to stop him?"

"She's talking rot. She's a Red Orchid acolyte. We know nothing about Gaios setting off a volcano in the East Indies. She'd say anything for Barnes. We don't just have the right to stop his ritual; we have the obligation."

The carriage suddenly keeled hard over with a jaw-snapping crack.

Chapter 18

SIMON SLID INTO THE DOOR, WITH KATE CA-
reening against him. Malcolm cursed over the sound of
the whip and the team of horses screeching in alarm.
The vehicle nearly toppled over on the other side before
smashing down on all four wheels again and rolling to
a stop.

With cane in hand, Simon was out the door, hissing at
the pain in his chest but summoning runic strength. He
turned in every direction, seeking some enemy but all
he saw was a disheveled Malcolm tying off the reins.

"It's nothing." The Scotsman spun around and held
up a cautioning hand. "Just the bloody road."

Behind the coach, worn tracks extended into the
darkness. Several yards back a deep furrow cut across
the path. Malcolm's feet hit the ground and he swept his
coat back to reveal his pistols. He walked back toward
the trench as Kate climbed from the carriage. The Scotsman kicked loose dirt and stared into the distance down
both sides of the channel. Simon continued to study the
silent grassy hillocks around them. A light snow was
falling over the landscape.

"A washout?" he asked when Malcolm returned and
knelt to look under the carriage, checking the wheels.

"Maybe," he muttered. "It looks freshly dug. There's another gully ahead of the coach too."

Kate glanced around. "We're not far from the estate now. We can walk if need be."

Malcolm pounded on one of the wooden wheels. He rose and went forward to where the four admirably trained black Friesians huffed breath into the air. He ran his hands along glistening flanks and down their legs, checking for injuries. He inspected the tack next, pulling harnesses and testing braces. "Looks sound enough. We should be able to ease over the gulley and move on."

"No worse for wear then," Simon said.

"Simon." Kate had walked a few steps away, staring over the downs. "Have a look at this."

He joined her, sheltering his eyes from blowing snow, and followed her pointing finger. He shook his head. "I don't see—"

"There."

At the base of a hillock, something moved. At first he thought it was simply high grass in the wind. But no. There was motion along the ground.

"What the hell?" Malcolm said from behind them, staring out over their shoulders.

In the distance, the heavy grass parted and dirt shifted beneath it. A hump of soil rose and moved. A furrow nearly three feet high slid along the ground as if a large, burrowing animal was tunneling. The mound shifted direction and vanished into the side of a hill.

"You have enormous voles in Surrey," Simon quipped.

"I think we should go." Kate tugged on the men's coats. "I'd feel safer closer to home inside the wards."

When they all turned, they saw the figure of a woman walking across the dark field, moving closer, coming toward the front of the carriage. Some twenty yards away, she stopped and stood quietly in the high grass. She was short and appeared to be naked, except for a necklace with a heavy stone between her small breasts. Even more distracting, her skin was blue. There was an odd shimmer about her; something small and bright slipped over her in random movements. She looked otherwise normal, with an opulent figure. Her hair was straight black and cut short. Her eyes were bright, set off by broad dark liner in an ancient Egyptian style.

Malcolm raised his gun. Kate's hand went to her vials.

"Good evening." Simon leaned on his cane and eyed the nude woman through the snow, trying to sound casual in the face of her peculiar appearance. "A chilly night for a walk."

She smiled and her teeth were sharpened. "I'm glad I found the three of you together. It saves me time."

"Are we acquainted? I think I would recall meeting you."

"You may call me Nephthys."

"Nephthys," Simon repeated and his stomach dropped in despair. "The Egyptian demon queen, and another of the infamous Bastille Bastards. England seems overrun with you vermin lately."

"We go where we please, Mr. Archer." Nephthys grinned. "Once we were bound, but Pendragon is dead. There is no one who can hold us now. The old days when we hid in shadows and let humans rule us are coming to a close. A new age of magic draws near."

"What a shame then that your old cellmates, Gretta Aldfather and Dr. White, won't be here to enjoy it," Simon said. "We killed them a few months ago."

"They must have been terribly stupid," the woman replied. "No matter. I never liked them, and now there's more for the rest of us."

Kate glanced at Simon, her features creased in shock. But when she looked back toward the nude woman, her expression was resolute. "Are you here to plead the case of Rowan Barnes too?"

"I don't plead, Miss Anstruther." Nephthys raised her bare arms, and her hands traced iridescent streaks of aether through the air. "I bring horror."

"Now, Malcolm, if you please," Simon began, but before he finished, the Lancaster pistol roared twice.

The glowing patch that swirled over Nephthys's body moved at the speed of thought. It appeared at her shoulder where the first ball struck it, then seemed to instantly appear at her hip, where the second shot hit. Nephthys was staggered from the force of the balls, but the only effect was to elicit an angry grimace from her. Two shots from the Lancaster could have dropped an elephant. She continued to weave her spell.

Malcolm raised the gun again and took aim. He fired and the bright patch appeared on her forehead, where the ball struck it with a spark. Her head snapped back violently, but then lowered again. She snarled from pain but didn't cease conjuring.

Simon pressed Malcolm's arm down. "She's wearing a dragonscale necklace. Don't waste your ammunition. We need to stop her summoning spell."

"I'll stop her." Kate lobbed a vial at Nephthys.

The ground in front of the sorceress erupted and a huge, horrid shape rose into the snowy night. The creature swept its huge claw and batted the vial. The glass shattered, filling the air with an amber cloud. The snake-thing roared and thrashed within the mist. Nephthys backed away as amber hardened over the creature's arms and shoulders.

Pinned as it was, Simon and the others got a clear view of the thing. Its horrible worm-like body was covered in strange, undulating scales. The torso and arms were those of a strong human male. A large head with two staring eyes was surrounded by a mane of thick, fleshy tendrils. The gaping mouth bit angrily at the amber that trapped it.

"It's a chnoubis. A Coptic earth demon." Simon drew the sword from his walking stick. The blade flashed blue.

"Simon!" Malcolm shouted. "There are more coming in. We have to go!"

The chnoubis opened its mouth and drooled a viscous liquid over the amber trapping its arms. The crystal began to sizzle and melt away. As the creature tore itself free of the amber, Simon ran to the coach. Malcolm climbed onto the driver's bench and started reloading his pistol. Simon had his hand on the door, but Kate followed Malcolm up.

She took the reins. "I'll drive. You two keep those things off us."

Simon slammed the door and hopped onto the side step like a footman. From this vantage point, he saw three new furrows moving in from the darkness behind Nephthys, who continued to gesture with aether through the driving snow. Malcolm pulled his second pistol.

"Walk on!" Kate called. The horses started off, pulling slowly. The coach creaked forward over the last of the large furrows. They couldn't afford a busted wheel now. She clucked at the team, urging the Friesians to strain against their collars.

The first snake-creature shook off the remnants of the amber and started crawling for the lumbering carriage. It was well ahead of its brethren. Malcolm aimed forward and fired. The heavy ball slammed the thing back onto the ground, but it immediately started to rise. The coach gathered headway with aching slowness. Malcolm shot again, smashing the creature down once more as the carriage rolled past it. When it tried to rise again, another shot smashed it into the dirt.

"Get up!" Kate shouted at the horses. "Get up now!"

The creature ceased its pursuit and slithered back toward its master. Simon almost cheered until he saw the other raised mounds shifting direction in pursuit. They tore through the grass, throwing up dirty snow like a wave crashing on the shore. Kate snapped the reins and the coach rocked back and settled into a bone-rattling pace. She gripped the heavy leather straps with her bare hands, staring forward, studying the ground as best she could through the blinding snow. The trail ahead was barely visible beneath the thickening white blanket on the ground.

Malcolm slipped a pistol back into the holster so he could hold on to the bouncing carriage for safety. He gazed forward, then looked back at the pursuing wakes with an expert eye. He tapped Simon on the shoulder and pointed. "We'll be shifting south soon and those three have no chance to catch up. If we can keep our pace." He indicated another furrow coming from the south. "That one could catch us."

"Can we go off the path?"

"Too dangerous. A horse stumbles or we hit a stone, and we crash. We dare not be afoot." Malcolm quickly leaned over to help Kate see the trail, indicating the timing and angle of turn. She wheeled the galloping horses southward admirably, keeping the carriage rolling along the flat path avoiding the worst of the ruts in the road. He patted her arm with an encouraging nod and turned back to their pursuers.

Simon could see three mounds falling back, just as Malcolm had said. But the other one was pushing forward of the coach, angling for the road far ahead. Kate saw it too. Her head shifted back and forth from the wave of flying grass and snow to the wagon path. She cracked the whip, trying to coax another ounce of effort from the team. The horses were laboring, with foam flecking their mouths and a coat of lather on the rippling flanks.

One of the lead horses stumbled. Kate shouted and let the reins slip slightly in hopes it could recover. The animal gathered itself well but swerved over into its mate. The back pair threw their heads in confusion. The coach skated to the side and the wheels bogged into the thick snow and grass. They rocked and lost headway. Amidst loud shouts and creaking wood, Kate wrestled the laboring team back onto the trail.

The furrow roared ahead of the carriage and darted into the road. Earth erupted up into the air and a terrible snake-creature, seven feet tall, blocked the path in front of the spooked horses. Kate cracked the whip. The horses obeyed and drove straight onto the creature. It bounced off the broad chest of the lead stallion and disappeared beneath pitiless hooves.

The coach rocked, causing Simon's boots to slip from their purchase, and his legs flew out wildly. He kept his one-handed grip on the rail and Malcolm gave up his own hold to lock onto Simon's wrist.

The carriage bolted violently into the air. Simon caught a glimpse of one of the wheels bouncing over a long, thick snake tail. Then he rose high into the air and slammed onto the roof. Malcolm kept his hold with gritted teeth, but he nearly went over the side at the same time. The coach crashed down onto all four wheels.

Kate looked over her shoulder. "Everyone alive back—Simon!"

At her wide eyes, he looked back to see massive hands crawling over the rear of the carriage. Then a flesh-maned head peered up at them. The creature dragged itself up with claws sinking into the roof. Malcolm pointed his pistol and fired while off balance. Simon felt the discharge and heat on his back. The ball clipped the creature's shoulder. It growled and pushed itself up on powerful arms. As the fleshy beast drew its massive tail up behind it, the coach sank back.

Simon braced himself with one hand and started to stand. His stick sword was still in his hand and once again he triggered the runic glow. The carriage rolled heavily and he braced himself like a man on a ship's tossing deck. The snow whipped in eddies around them. He swung the blade with a hissing arc. The beast reared away, then instantly clawed at the man. Simon dodged, but his knee buckled under the rocking carriage and he toppled backward.

"Careful there." Malcolm's hand pressed into the small of his back.

Simon could've sworn the Scotsman gave him a shove forward as you would a mate in a pub brawl. The blue blade struck home in the creature's stomach, biting deep. The thing screamed. Simon drew close and began to work the blade in the thick flesh. The hide parted with a sizzle of reddish ooze. Scaly arms closed tight around him. The skin of the creature was sandy and rubbed Simon's face raw. The stench was unbelievable. He felt as if his ribs would shatter until he uttered the spell that turned him into stone. His breath stopped and his eyes were locked on the chest of the brute trying to crush him. The creature continued to try, but there was nothing it could do to hurt him. Then Simon actually felt warmth spreading across his head and shoulders; he had never felt anything while in a stone form before. The snake thing must have been drooling its corrosive spit on him.

The carriage jolted. Simon sensed that he and the creature were airborne. The world flipped around him. He felt steady bumps and jostling but no pain. The thing's skin was replaced in his line of vision with the snowy ground. He expelled the last bit of breath as the simple spell and the stone skin relented. Simon gasped for air, fighting to move and get his bearings. He stretched to crack the hard slough covering him. The crumbling skin flaked away and he struggled to stand. A residue of acidic heat scorched his neck before he reached up and tore away the sizzling stone skin resting there.

The coach had continued down the path, where it entered the outskirts of a forest. Kate brought it to a clattering halt. Malcolm was already leaping off the rear. Kate was soon visible too as she jumped from the box and started running back.

Simon lurched toward then, still fighting the aftereffects of his spell. His chest burned from the curse, threatening to drop him. He focused on Kate's face as he lumbered through the pain.

As he ran, he took a quick glance back and saw the snake-creature rising from the snow. It angrily pulled the sword from its stomach and flung it aside. Then it glared at the fleeing Simon. It vomited onto the ground and plunged headfirst, diving into the dirt as if it were water. Then a great mound rose and chased after Simon down the rutted trail. Malcolm's pistols thundered but merely sent balls flying into rumbling earth.

"Stop!" Simon shouted, raising his hand at the Scotsman and Kate, who were still twenty yards away. "Come no farther!"

Malcolm instantly grabbed Kate's arm as she started to run on. She struggled to break free, but he held her fast. Simon turned to face the onrushing thing in the dirt. He dropped to one knee, head lolling forward with exhaustion, hand pressed against the frozen terrain. The mound roared forward, plowing within ten yards.

Suddenly there was a tremendous muffled boom. The ground around the head of the furrow blossomed in a dome of loose earth, blown upward from below. The torn beast was partially visible amidst the debris until pieces of the chnoubis slapped into the deep crater in a dusty cloud.

Simon staggered to his feet, watching for any sign of movement in the ground. Footsteps rushed from behind and Malcolm stepped ahead, pistol ready. Kate took Simon's arm and handed him a vial of *elixir vitae,* but her eyes remained focused on the smoking hole ahead.

"What did you do?" Kate asked.

"Nothing. We're inside the wards." Simon laughed and drank the elixir.

She looked around with surprise. "How can you tell? At night? In the snow?"

"That tree." He indicated an ash tree standing amidst other ash trees.

"It looks like a thousand other trees."

"No, it looks like you." Simon took a shallow, pained breath, but smiled. "It's my marker."

Both Kate and Malcolm stared at the tree. Kate cocked her hip. "It looks like me? A tree? That's flattering."

"Yes. See how the curves—" Simon worked his hands in an hourglass shape. "It looks like you."

"Oh." Malcolm grunted. "I see."

Kate glared at the men. "Let's get to the house."

Simon and Malcolm watched her walk ahead of them through the wind-driven snow. The magician clapped a hand on the Scotsman's shoulder, leaning heavily against him. Malcolm cast him a wry glance, and nodded.

KATE WALKED PAST DARK WOODEN WALLS AND busy wallpapers in Hartley Hall toward the Blue Parlor, where breakfast was typically laid. She would normally be buoyed by the smell of coffee and bread and bacon, but she hadn't slept much thanks to terrible dreams about snakes. It was a bitter cold morning and her heavy woolen clothes couldn't keep the gooseflesh from creeping up her arms and legs.

As she entered the Blue Parlor, Kate looked past the

elegant coffee urn on the table to see Simon and Malcolm sitting across from each other near the window. They were huddled close, their faces intense, engaged in some desperate plotting, which had her nervous. She noticed that both men were unshaved and in the same rumpled clothes they had arrived in the night before. There were half-filled glasses of whiskey near their hands. Both men looked fatigued and pensive; Simon even more so.

"Good morning," Kate announced loudly.

They turned in surprise and Simon glanced to the window, where the morning sun streamed in, brightened by the thin coat of snow outside. "So it is. Good morning, Kate. Surely you could use a bit more sleep." His voice was gravel and his movements lacked their usual spark.

"Have you two been up all night drinking whiskey?"

Simon seemingly noticed breakfast for the first time. "The whiskey was a minor part of the evening, unfortunately." He took a cup of coffee that Kate brought to him. "Thank you, but I must finish the night before starting the day." He drained the whiskey glass and only then sipped the coffee.

Kate rolled her eyes in exasperation and signaled the newly arrived maid to prepare plates and bring them to the two men. Simon thanked the girl and held his breakfast without interest. Malcolm set the plate on his lap and started to eat like a starving man.

Simon said wearily, "Kate, there has been a slight change. I need to journey to my home at Warden Abbey in Bedfordshire. Would you care to accompany me?"

Kate looked confused by yet another shift in the agenda. "When are you planning to leave?"

Simon checked his watch. "Now."

"Are you mad?" Kate slammed her coffee cup onto the saucer. "Look at yourself! Warden Abbey is at the very least a hard day away, perhaps two. Not to mention that Nephthys may be watching the roads."

Simon reached into his unbuttoned waistcoat and removed a folded slip of paper. He handed it to Kate. "This arrived for me. Apparently a copy came here, and another to London. They were eager to find me."

The severe look on Simon's face cast a cold sheen over Kate. She opened the paper and saw a brief note: *Sir. There has been some disturbance at Warden Abbey. I grieve to inform you that it appears as if your mother's grave has been vandalized in some fashion. Please advise as to a proper course of action. Winston.*

She looked up at him. "Simon, I'm . . . I don't understand. What could this mean?"

"I don't know. But Barnes is a necromancer." Simon paused, unable to continue for a moment. "I must go up."

The horror of what Barnes might have done to his mother's body with dark magic clawed into Kate's mind until she forced it out again. She could only imagine what Simon was thinking.

Malcolm, who clearly knew about the situation already, set down his coffee cup and laid a hand briefly on Simon's stooped shoulders. "If there's anything you require."

"Thank you, Malcolm."

The Scotsman nodded and wandered to the breakfast table to search for more food. His sudden public concern for Simon made Kate even more ill at ease.

She settled beside Simon and draped an arm over his shoulders. "Of course I'll go with you."

"Good."

"What about Nephthys?" Kate asked.

"Well, her appearance was a shocker, I'll grant you. I wasn't prepared for yet another of the Bastille Bastards. And while she does alter the power balance considerably out of our favor—"

"Was it in our favor before?" Malcolm asked sarcastically as he scouted for sausages.

"No, but it's worse now that she's involved. I find it hard to believe that a relative unknown like Rowan Barnes could be ordering about someone of her advanced magical pedigree. Still, she doesn't seem to have any trace of righteous vengeance for our defeat of her Bastille friends. And since she is intent on killing us, I can only assume it's to keep us from mucking about with Barnes. Therefore, Nephthys or no Nephthys, the Sacred Heart Murders and the ritual to break Pendragon's spell are under Barnes's control and our central question remains: What shall we do about Rowan Barnes?"

"Kill him." Malcolm stabbed a sausage with a knife. He looked at Simon from under downturned eyebrows. "Now. Today."

Kate objected, "We can't just kill him."

"Why?" Malcolm asked coldly. "Is there any policeman who could arrest him? Any gallows that could hang him? We don't live in that world."

"How can we dare face him in the Red Orchid?" Kate retorted. "Barnes is forewarned and terribly powerful. And the home is always full of innocents."

"I don't need to face him," Malcolm replied. "I'll wait across the street. He will come out or pass before a window. All I need is the proper weapon, which Penny has at her shop. Magicians, for all their godlike powers, are just people. Right, Simon?"

Simon gave a wan grin. "Indeed we are. Provided we don't know it's coming, a lead ball will end our days as surely as it would a grouse's."

"Simon! We can't kill Rowan Barnes." Kate stared at Simon expectantly, but he stayed silent. "Tell him, or I will."

Simon raised his eyebrows. "Secrets are meant to be such."

"Tell him," Kate repeated.

Malcolm looked at Simon.

"Very well." Simon took a breath and held up his hands helplessly. "In my skirmish with Barnes, he cursed me."

The Scotsman looked blank, obviously unsure of the implications of Simon's statement.

Kate exhaled. "He struck Simon with a black spell. Now Simon will find himself in greater and greater pain over time until he is in excruciating agony at all times. The only person who can lift the curse is Barnes himself. If we kill him, we are condemning Simon to a life of unspeakable pain."

Kate sat gripping the arms of the chair, her face a mask of barely controlled anguish. Simon took one of her hands. She leaned toward him, beseeching him to understand her fears.

"Kate, I'm so sorry for the suffering this causes you." Simon kissed her hand and pressed it to his cheek. Then he turned. "Malcolm, kill Barnes."

Chapter 19

FADING SUNLIGHT TURNED THE RIBS OF A RU-
ined church into a grim shadow against the sky. The remnants of a medieval gatehouse hunched beside the road.
The carriage rocked along a rough country lane as it
approached the distant abbey on a piece of open ground
amidst bare, wintry trees.

"Welcome to Warden Abbey," Simon announced. "My
childhood home."

"How long ago was your childhood?" Kate asked, as
the skeletal abbey grew nearer. A flock of night birds
rose in a carpet and blotted out the sky briefly before
settling into the scabrous forest.

Simon laughed a bit stiffly. "Don't judge by the abbey
church. It has been a ruin since the Tudors."

The thought of Simon's boyhood home being some
crumbling wreck was too sad for Kate to contemplate.
Then they rolled past the dead old church and came upon
a large country home with lights blazing in the many
windows. It was a heartening oasis in the darkening
landscape. Warden Abbey retained the character of its
medieval ecclesiastical past, with spires and even turrets on both ends of the front façade.

Simon had his hand on the carriage door for a long

while as the vehicle rolled past low, untrimmed shrubbery and clattered up to the portico in the center of the house. A footman scurried out to meet the carriage.

"Good evening, Mr. Archer, sir. Welcome home."

"Thank you, Nickerson." Simon exited and handed out Kate. "How is your good wife, and your son?"

"Well, sir. Thank you." The young footman grinned at the attention.

"Gratified to hear it." Simon turned to meet the butler and housekeeper, who waited on the steps but were obviously so eager they would have come out if it had been proper. They were both fit and likely in their early forties.

"Good evening, sir." The butler bowed. "Good to have you back."

"Winston!" Simon grabbed the man's hand and shook it so that the exertion created a slight wince of pain. "And Mrs. Winston. Thank you both for your efforts. The place looks splendid."

The butler bowed and the housekeeper curtsied. The woman's eyes were on Simon and she put a handkerchief to her face, suppressing tears. Winston turned to his wife kindly, and said, "Perhaps you should see to dinner."

"Very well," she muttered and hurried away.

"I'm sorry, sir." Winston said. "She's very upset about the incident with Mrs. Archer."

Simon shook his head graciously and led Kate through the grand door. He stared around at the stone-walled entryway, open to the vaulted ceiling. A heavy iron chandelier glowed with a covey of lit candles. The vast foyer was dim and only slightly warmer than outside. The flagstones were rough and uneven.

"It seems rather spartan for a magician's lair," Kate said, as servants collected coats and hats. "Where are the skulls and jars of herbs and tomes of runic spells?"

"Warden Abbey was the home of the Archers. My mother's family was distinctly unmagical, in all ways. I thought it sociable to confine my mystical activities to a room in the turret. Otherwise, this is a normal country home that used to be a medieval monastery. So if you've ever admired the comfortable way of life of the Cistercian monk, prepare to be disappointed." Simon turned to the butler, standing a few steps away. "Winston, after Miss Anstruther settles in, we shall reconvene for dinner if that's convenient?"

"Indeed it is, sir. We've laid a fire in the great hearth and it's warmed up nicely."

Kate followed a maid toward a set of narrow stairs winding upward and on to her private accommodations along a dim corridor. She freshened up in the chilled room, lit by a single oil lamp. The view from the frosted window was of a dark, foreboding forest creeping so close that spindly branches nearly tapped the thick glass. Neither the house nor the grounds had the vivacity and strange luster of Hartley Hall. Craving Simon's company and a warm fire, Kate went downstairs.

She found Simon in a large room that once must have been a great hall. A long table was set for a small dinner and Simon stood with Winston next to a blazing stone fireplace along one wall. The two men were in close conversation, which Simon broke off to seat Kate before taking the chair at the head of the table. "Please, have a bite to eat. It's been a long day, and it may be a long night. Winston, tell Miss Anstruther what you were just telling me."

Kate's appetite had vanished in the coldness of her room, but now that there was food in front of her, she began to eat. It had been a day of hard travel.

The butler stood next to Simon's chair, hands behind his back, and said, "I was relating our discovery of the dreadful event. It came to my attention through one of the groundskeepers, a fellow named Greene, relatively new here. He was inspecting the grounds and noticed something odd about Mrs. Archer's grave, which he brought to my attention."

Kate noted the respect in the man's voice, and his use of "missus" even though Simon's mother was never married and was an Archer by birth. Simon was frozen in contemplation, staring at the untouched food in front of him.

Winston continued, "Her grave appeared to have been disturbed. The earth was unsettled."

"Was her casket disinterred?" There was a cold distance in Simon's voice that made Kate's heart ache.

"Not when we saw it, sir."

Kate asked, "Could it have been dogs digging?"

"No, miss. It appeared to me that the grave had been exhumed, then refilled."

"Are you sure her body is still present?" Simon asked with odd directness.

The butler's glance flicked uncomfortably to his master. "We dug deep enough to find the coffin. However, we were unwilling to open it without your presence. I hope you understand, sir."

"Of course, Winston." Simon ran a hand through his hair. "I appreciate your efforts. I'll want to see this Greene."

"Of course, sir. Shall I have a lantern and your coat ready? Will you go down to the grave later?"

Simon sat with his eyes down on the tabletop. Kate had never seen him frozen by indecision before. It was stunning, even frightening. He remained motionless for several minutes. Finally, he nodded.

"Very good, sir." Winston walked away.

Simon sat back, tapping his fingers on the table. The fire crackled behind him, the light wavering in the un-sipped wine. Kate ate quietly, but Simon showed no interest in his food. She allowed him to sit silently, lost in thought. And so he remained until after Winston had removed the last course and laid a plate of cheese along with two glasses of port.

"Simon," Kate said softly, "tell me about your mother."

He looked up at her with almost grateful eyes. He stood, reaching out his hand.

SIMON LED KATE DOWN A LONG HALLWAY THAT grew darker and colder. Plaster and wood gave way to ancient stone. They entered a turret door and started up a narrow spiral staircase. It was virtually pitch-black but for the starlight coming through occasional embrasures. Kate let her fingertips trace the wall to guide her upward as she placed her feet on the well-worn steps.

Simon suddenly halted before a door. He ran his hands over the rough wood and whispered. A light flared under his fingertips, then faded. He grunted and turned a heavy iron handle.

He pushed the door in and pressed into the room beyond. It was a round chamber atop the turret. Simon spoke and light appeared from ghostly spiderwebs draped in the rafters of the peaked roof. Three embrasures were closed by wooden panels. There were many bookcases and tables covered in tomes and scrolls. Several heavy trunks rested about the floor. He began to inspect the room, glancing over the books on shelves and the papers on desks. Finally, he leaned against a table with a breath of relief. "No one has been here. My wards are still active."

Kate stood in the middle of the cold room. "This was your boyhood room? I won't come across old love letters, will I?"

His smile was pleasant but she saw the strain there. His thoughts were not on romantic banter—neither were hers—but she felt a burden to offer him some distraction.

Even so, Kate could hardly contain her excitement at the many journals and few published books in the room. "Are these books yours, or were they your father's?"

"Most of them were his. All I have of his is here, or at Gaunt Lane. A large number of his papers were destroyed or taken the night he was murdered."

"In Scotland?"

"Yes." Simon walked around the room, glancing at everything but not touching. He seemed fearful of disturbing the books and papers, as if they had gone from useful objects to artifacts. The mere arrangement of the chamber represented something he didn't wish to alter. "It's sad when I think of the treasures he had that are lost to me now, including materials from Byron Pendragon himself. My father was Pendragon's last student."

Simon shook his head and went to a window, pulling back the oaken shutter. He leaned against the stone and stared out the narrow gap in the thick wall. "My mother didn't deserve this."

"What do you think happened?"

"I think she has been disturbed."

"Perhaps body snatchers?"

"No. Her spirit has been disturbed. I think someone came here, found her body, and forced her dead spirit to speak to them. A necromancer. Rowan Barnes."

Kate watched the side of his face as he continued to gaze out into the night. A deadly rage was building in his eyes despite his emotionless visage. Her own outrage flared. "If that is so, what could he have learned from her?"

Simon's breath misted in the frozen air. "I don't know. Very little. Barnes already knows I'm a scribe, but my mother had little concept of my magical skills. I kept the details from her. I was afraid it would remind her of my father."

"She might have liked that."

Simon smiled sadly with fresh realization. "You're right. There's another small joy I might have provided her but didn't. I locked it away from her." He gave a sharp laugh that had nothing to do with humor. "I don't see anything useful Barnes could acquire from her. It was purely an exercise in cruelty. Her life was a struggle, and now she has no peace in death either. Because of me."

"You don't know that," Kate said quietly. "You don't know that her spirit was attacked."

"Of course I do. She was involved in the world of magic, first through my father, then through me. But she was not part of it. All she did was love one man, then love their son." He turned to her, his eyes haunted. "I'm going to her grave now. Please come with me."

Kate slipped her hand over his and held it tight. "Of course."

MALCOLM LIFTED THE RIFLE. THE WEAPON STILL looked remarkably normal despite having come from Penny's tinker shop. It was the size of a standard-issue Baker, but with a lighter heft that felt odd in his hands. Rather than the usual ball and powder, it used a special shell similar to those Penny made for his Lancaster pistols, ten of which could be stored at the ready in a chamber near the breech. Attached along the top of the weapon was another of Penny's gadgets. Just ahead of the breech, a small magnifying loupe was fixed, aligned with a series of concave and convex lenses, each one capable of being moved in line with the others down the length of the barrel.

Malcolm brought the stock to his shoulder and pointed the rifle at the French window in the library of Hartley Hall. He took aim at the head of a strange monstrous statue on the far edge of the garden over one hundred yards away. With deft fingers, he flipped the small round lenses of glass up and down in several combinations until the distant head grew close but it was still lost in the dark. He lowered another yellow lens into the row and suddenly the statue lit as if in a bright sun. Its teeth were bared and its eyes stared straight back at him. It looked as if he were standing right upon the creature.

He let out a low whistle of amazement. Penny's modification was incredible. As a hunter, he knew the value of such a telescopic advancement. He could take out any number of beasts from a great distance without the danger of getting close enough to be shredded by claws. This was the perfect weapon for killing.

The perfect weapon for murder.

Malcolm didn't flinch at the thought because it wasn't murder if the beast was slaughtering innocents. Rowan Barnes was a beast, no doubt.

"What are you doing?"

Malcolm started and the rifle fired with a suppressed whoosh. The glass of the French window shattered and the head of the statue exploded into dust in nearly the same instant. He glared down at Charlotte. He hadn't even heard her approach.

She covered her mouth and stared wide-eyed. "Oh. You're in trouble."

He breathed out angrily, trying to ignore the child, and started packing.

"Is that the gun Miss Penny modified to shoot Barnes?"

Bloody hell! Penny was a chatterbox at the worst of times.

"May I come with you to the Red Orchid?" Charlotte

rocked back and forth on her heels, making her pastel frock sway about her ankles. "I'm terribly bored here."

"Go away."

"I could help."

"I don't see how."

"I can hold on to your stuff." She grabbed for a box of ammunition on the table, but tipped it over so the specially designed bullets scattered across the teak surface.

"Stop it!" Malcolm rebuked crossly. "These are delicate."

She held up one of the bullets to the light. It was long and made with a shiny brass casing. "Oh, how pretty! What do they do?"

"They kill things." The hunter snatched the bullet from her hand.

"Miss Penny made these also?" Charlotte pointed at the stylized gear cog on the box that was Penny's brand. "She's terribly clever."

Malcolm took the ammunition box from her. He could still barely stand to look at her despite the evidence of her improved demeanor. As a werewolf, she was a threat he knew how to deal with; as a girl, she was an annoyance with which he was unfamiliar. "Go outside and play with the dog."

"I want to go with you."

"No."

"Why not?"

"No. You need to stay here with Imogen."

"Imogen is grumpy." Charlotte scuffed a foot on the rug. "Just for a little? I'm bored."

"Ask Hogarth for something to do."

She quieted. "He scares me."

"Aye, he scares me too," Malcolm admitted. "But you're still staying."

"Please! I'll be very quiet. I promise. You won't even

know I'm there. I'll be so careful. I haven't changed in forever. I've been so good they moved me out of the cellar. I have a room upstairs like everyone else. I'm so calm all the time I'm practically asleep."

Malcolm's exasperation with the child was fast coming to a head. He threw on his heavy greatcoat, patting his pockets to ensure Eleanor's poetry book was there. He grabbed the box of ammunition and his satchel of supplies before he strode from the library. Charlotte remained on his heels as he made his way down the corridor and into the kitchen. When he passed through the door outside, she stopped at the threshold.

"What happens if you need me?" she called out after him into the growing twilight.

"I won't." Malcolm didn't turn around so he wouldn't see her pout. He continued to the stables. She was Hogarth's problem now. He had more pressing concerns to deal with. Finally, there was a monster he was allowed to kill.

Chapter 20

WHITE SLIVERS OF CLOUDS PASSED ACROSS THE stars. Kate followed the yellow glow of Simon's lantern through the towering ribs of the skeleton church. Simon stepped around blocks of heavy stone long fallen in the collapse of the old chapel. Swathed in his long frock coat, he seemed no more than a grim shade in the night. Winston walked behind them, followed by another servant carrying shovels and picks. Ahead, a high, wrought-iron gate was hanging from a single hinge, tall spikes askew. Inside the fence were gravestones, some tilted and broken and colored black with age. Simon tugged the gate back with a horrid screech of old iron and strode into the field of tombs.

He stopped before a sizeable cenotaph. It consisted of a broad granite base about four feet high, topped by a beseeching angelic figure. The base proclaimed *Elizabeth Archer 1781–1822*. Simon laid a hand on the monument and stared down at the sunken mound of dirt. There was clearly space for a plot next to her.

Kate whispered, "Is your father here?"

"No, but she wanted a place for him." Simon knelt next to the grave and set the lantern on the ground. The wind tossed his hair and shadows increased the intensity of his face.

"Must you exhume her?" Kate asked.

"Yes."

"If Barnes took her, there's nothing to be done. We're going after him in any case. Why put yourself through this?"

"I must know." He stood and reached out toward Winston.

"No sir." The butler flinched, pulling the pick he carried tight against his chest. "That isn't a fit job for you."

"It's my honor, Winston." Simon's voice was firm but pained. When the servant begrudgingly handed him the pick, he slid out of his heavy coat and motioned everyone back. Then Simon hefted the tool high over his shoulder and drove the iron point into his mother's grave. Loose chunks of cold earth rolled back. He slammed the pick down over and over, grunting in pain from the curse, but pausing only to kick dirt clods aside. He was silent but for sharp exhalations with each swing. Sweat began to drip off his face and coils of steam rose from his head into the freezing air.

"What the hell are you doing?" came a shout from behind.

Simon had hoisted the pick up and was nearly toppled by the momentum as he spun around. Winston turned and exclaimed in shock as a figure ran toward them from the abbey.

"It's Greene, sir. The man who discovered the trouble."

"What is he about?" Simon growled.

The new groundskeeper, Greene, was young, perhaps twenty years old, and thin. He was wearing old tweed and had a scarf looped around his neck and partially around his face. He pushed past Winston and actually pulled the pick out of Simon's hands. The servants were shocked by the lad's inexplicable temerity. Even Simon just watched the young man with surprise. Winston stepped forward quickly and grabbed the groundskeeper by his collar, pulling him away.

Kate exclaimed, "I'll be God damned."

Her voice was so incredulous that Simon looked at her. She was staring at Greene, but her expression was not shock at his odd behavior; it was complete disbelief.

Greene snapped at Simon, "I didn't send for you so you could dig up your mother, you idiot."

"Quiet!" Winston shook the man. "I'm sorry, sir. I'll have this wretch dealt with immediately. I—" Now he looked down at the figure in his grip who was no longer the young groundskeeper, but was rather an older man, broad-faced and worn with years, eyes that were dark and bottomless. The butler released the man and stepped back. He looked from the stranger to Simon, with alarm. "I'm sorry, sir. I thought it was Greene. I could have sworn." He looked at the other manservant for support, but that chap was nonplussed and clutching shovels in defense.

Simon felt his own incredulity. Before him stood his old friend, Nick Barker.

Nick straightened his jacket and smiled snidely at Winston. "I'm surprised you don't remember me, Winston. I was up here a few years ago. I'm Mr. Archer's particular friend."

"Mr. Barker, sir? I'm terribly sorry. I could have sworn it was . . . I could have sworn."

Simon went to his butler, without taking his surprised gaze off Nick. "It's all right, Winston. Both of you go back to the house. Don't worry."

Winston turned without speaking and started off into the dark, stooped. He was followed quickly by the other servant.

"Leave the tools," Simon called. The servant dropped the shovels and practically ran away.

Nick started laughing and threw his arm over Simon's shoulder like two pals out for a night on the town. Simon tossed the arm aside roughly and rounded on his old friend.

"What is wrong with you?" Simon shouted. "Why are you here? You said you were leaving England months ago."

"Easy, old boy." Nick held up his hands in defense. "I'll explain everything. But you have to admit, that was funny."

Simon couldn't speak. He shook his head with angry sputtering and went back to Kate, who was staring at Nick as if he had just flown in on a winged horse.

"Miss Anstruther." Nick nodded to her. "You saw through me. How did you do that?"

Kate breathed out cynically. "Mr. Barker. You're not all that hard to see through."

He grinned, a bit harshly. "You think so, do you?"

"Nick!" Simon roared. "Shut up and tell me why you're here!"

Nick grew serious and stiff. "Easy, Simon. You're overwrought. I don't blame you, mind." He used the toe of his shoe to kick up the shaft of the pick and lift the tool. "But you've no call to shout at me. Look at yourself. Look at what you were about to do. What could have driven you to that? I've only been away from you for a few months. You best take stock of your path if this is where you are."

"You don't know," Simon ground out.

"I do know. I'm the only one who does. I'm the one who found out what happened to your poor mother and had Winston contact you. There are things you don't know, but you need to."

"Why are you here?" Simon repeated.

"I've been here for months. Almost since I left you sitting in the Devil's Loom." Nick tossed the pick into the pile with the shovels. He blew on his hands. "I warned you then. I warned you that if you made too much noise, you'd attract attention from people you don't want noticing you. And you have. And now so has your poor mother."

"What do you mean?"

"Simon, a terrible thing is coming. When the Order got shattered, the magical world was like a capsized ship that pitched its crew into the water. Pendragon was murdered, and Gaios and Ash were the two biggest sharks in the sea. And eventually they'll start ripping into each other. Any magician with any sense is scared to death to be floating in the open. But not you. You had to pick now to make a big splash, didn't you? I begged you to keep your bloody head down, but you just couldn't because you're a show-off at heart. Look at me, I'm Simon Archer, the last of the scribes. The new Pendragon." Nick spat on the ground. "Well, now very bad people know your name."

"I heard rumors that Gaios is planning something monstrous, but I haven't heard anything about Ash."

"You haven't kept your ears open then. What have you been doing these last few months?" He jerked his thumb at Kate. "Sitting with her and trying to make your magic key work? Have you even left Hartley Hall?" Nick shook his head in disgust, and eyed Kate with bitterness. "Ash has been managing what's left of the Order of the Oak. Not doing a good job of it, mind, but trying. Gaios hates her from way back. And he's coming to kill her."

Kate's eyes blazed back at Nick. "If there's such a storm on the horizon, why are you up here at Warden Abbey? Why aren't you hiding in Mandalay as you said? Did you make up the story about Simon's mother's grave to bring him home?"

Nick gave her a cold glare, then turned to Simon with an admirable shift to regret. "No. The bit about someone disturbing your mother's grave is true. That's the whole reason I came here—to protect you. Your mother is the only possible source of information about you and your father, Edward Cavendish, and his connection to Pendragon. There's a good reason you kept the secret of your father for so long, even from me. Pendragon and your father had a lot of enemies, and they could be your enemies too. I was afraid a necromancer might try to rip information out of her, information about you." He crooked a finger at Simon and directed him to the back of Elizabeth Archer's monument. He clawed away some dirt at the base to reveal a symbol etched into the marble.

Simon knelt and ran his finger over the rune. "Someone has inscribed her tombstone."

Nick nodded. "I did it. I know a bit of scribing. I thought it might protect her, protect you. But I was wrong. I wasn't near strong enough to stop whoever came for her."

Simon looked up at his old friend, and the shocked anger had faded. He saw the friendly face of the man who had taught him so much about magic over the last few years, the man with whom he had shared so many long evenings of laughter. He took a remorseful breath.

"I'm sorry, Nick. Thank you for trying." Simon stood and extended his hand. Nick hesitated, then shook. "We are, in fact, facing a very powerful necromancer named Rowan Barnes."

Nick shrugged. "Never heard of him."

"Nor had I until recently, at least not as a necromancer. I thought he was an artist."

"An artist?" Nick smirked. "Like a painter, you mean?"

"It isn't a joke," Kate said testily. "Barnes is dangerous, and he's mastered blood magic to unravel one of Pendragon's containment spells."

"You're daft," Nick cried. "That's impossible."

Simon shook his head. "Barnes is undertaking a blood ritual in London to break the bonds of one of Pendragon's wards. We don't yet know what will emerge from the broken bonds, but the magical power involved is extraordinary. Pendragon's inscription was pure Heliopolitan."

Nick whistled. "Yeah, I heard he went in for that old Egyptian stuff. Never thought much of it myself. Too complicated. There's always an easier way to get a job done."

Simon leaned down and lifted a shovel. "Will you help me? I must determine whether my mother's body is still present. If Barnes took it for some ritual reason, it will alter my approach to him."

Nick continued to stare at Simon's hard countenance. "Put that shovel down and stop acting like a bleeding laborer. I can commune with her."

"No, Nick. I don't want that. It's necromancy."

"I don't care what you want. I won't stand here while you dig up your own mother's body when I can do my bit and touch her essence." He started toward her grave.

"Nick, no."

"Why not, Simon?" Kate asked. "If he can do it, let him." Nick pointed to the tip of his nose and then at her as if telling Simon to listen to her. "And perhaps he can determine what information was given up, if any."

Nick stood at the turned earth of the grave. "I can already tell you that she's been deeply injured. She can't move away." He glanced over his shoulder and tapped the dirt with his foot. "I can help her."

"But," Simon argued, "communing with the dead is dark magic. I don't want you to endure it. You said that saving me after the fight with Gretta made you mortal. Necromancy drains life, and if you have no way to restore it . . . I won't be the cause of your moving closer to death."

"Come off it. I've seen about all I care to see of this world anyhow." Nick gave a crooked grin. "Look, she's your mother. I won't do it if you forbid it. But she's down there alone and scared."

Simon's expression suddenly broke and his voice was a hard whisper of agony. "Do it."

Nick took several deep breaths, staring down at the plot. He slowly dropped to his knees on the cold earth. He pressed the palms of his hands on top of the grave and closed his eyes. The dirt strangely gave way and Nick pushed until his forearms were buried.

Silent minutes passed. Simon waited on one knee, dark eyes locked on Nick. Kate stood near with a hand cupping the back of Simon's head. The icy wind continued to howl, rippling his shirt. Kate draped his coat over his shoulders, but he didn't respond.

The older magician blinked his eyes rapidly and moved his mouth as if his teeth were chattering from the cold, but that wasn't the reason. His breathing altered from slow and steady to harsh. Nick grunted, causing Simon to tense, ready to come to his aid. Then Nick whimpered.

Simon started to rise, but then froze in place, watching his friend drop forward until his forehead touched the dirt. Tortured groans escaped the man. Nick's back stiffened, muscles rigid. Simon straddled the grave and seized Nick's arms.

Suddenly it was a spring afternoon and Simon was surrounded by warmth. He smelled the pear trees that were blooming in the west garden as well as the hint of wet soil from a gentle rain. A soft breeze ruffled his hair. He felt the stones of the back walk under his shoes and the hard pommel of a fencing foil in his right hand. His knees betrayed the telltale soreness that came from hours of drills. Alone, without an opponent. Simon always preferred to practice alone, to master himself rather than compete with others. He turned from the green expanse of the garden toward the terrace.

There, his mother stood watching him. She was young and beautiful. She was slim, yet strong, with long dark hair that waved in the spring air. Her eyes shone with protective pride and a slight tinge of worry that was always present. She had never appeared carefree for a moment of her life, and Simon used to think she was waiting for him to trip, to fumble with each step. When he was young, he had found her expectations insulting, but only later did he realize she was merely worried that he had been born into a difficult situation that might come back to haunt them both. He came to feel sad for her and her inescapable pall. Simon lowered the foil. He desperately wanted to speak to her, but his throat locked with waves of emotion. He simply stared.

She reached up to her neck and pulled on a gold chain. The key appeared from her bodice and she held it up.

His mother said something that sounded like, "Mor-thul."

The sound of her voice struck him like an epiphany. It had been so long since he had heard it, and had thought never to hear it again. All the years of her washed over him.

Then she smiled. It was a wide, exhausted smile of relief that showed in her eyes as well as her mouth. Simon had never seen her look so tranquil. She regarded him with a gratifying expression of hard-won confidence.

She turned and went back inside the house.

Simon wanted to stop her, to call out and run to her side. He craved to embrace her once more. But he couldn't.

He felt something rough under his hands and frigid air scraped over his face. He saw Nick's back. His friend's head was slumped in the dirt that covered the body of Simon's mother who had just a moment ago been stand-

ing in the spring air smiling at him. He pulled Nick
away from the grave and the other man's arms slid from
the dirt. Nick gasped in shock as if roused from a deep
sleep. Simon dropped roughly to one knee and shook
the disoriented man.

"Nick!" he shouted. "Nick, can you hear me?"

Nick's eyes were wide for a second, then they focused
on Simon. His facial muscles relaxed with the realization of the place. He exhaled with shock, and muttered,
"Jesus. Jesus."

Simon took Nick by the jaw and turned his head from
side to side, inspecting his eyes, looking for a normal
reaction. When he saw enough to let him know that
Nick had come back intact, he gave his friend a light
slap and fell back onto the ground beside the grave.

Simon felt his own face being turned. Kate looked at
him, her expression full of more shock than his own, he
felt sure. Her lips pressed tightly together in dismay or
confusion.

"I'm fine, Kate," Simon breathed out in relief. "I saw
her."

"Are you sure you're well?" Kate insisted.

"Of course." Simon laughed raggedly. "I feel quite
fine, thank you. No pain at all at the moment. Why are
you so worried?"

She wiped her hand over his cheek and it came away
wet. "You're weeping."

Simon suddenly felt tears running down his face in a
torrent and dripping from his chin. He was crying uncontrollably. He buried his face in Kate's arms.

Chapter 21

NICK TOOK A WHISKEY FROM SIMON AND DRAINED it without pause, gasping with wet desperation. He handed the glass up for another. Simon merely gave him the bottle, leaving his friend to guzzle.

"Nick," Simon said as he sat on the bench on the far side of the hearth and took Kate's hand, "are you sure she was targeted by a necromancer? She seemed content."

Nick wiped his mouth. He stared at the half-empty bottle. "She loved your father."

"I know." Simon stretched out his legs, feeling a sense of ease he hadn't known in a long time.

"Whatever bastard came after her," Nick said, his face still pale, "did damage to her, all right. I could sense how they tried to wrench information out of her, but she fought back. I've never known a normal human being who could resist necromancy. She kept all your secrets. Damned incredible." He drank deep gulps without pause.

"Easy, old man," Simon cautioned gently.

Kate asked Simon, "She seemed content to you?"

"She did. She looked wonderful. Younger. Stronger.

As I remember her from my youth. Not as she was when she died."

"Perhaps seeing you helped heal her. It's a great gift."

Simon nodded. "Communing with the dead is a strange business."

"Hear hear," Nick cracked sarcastically, holding up the bottle.

"But," Simon continued with a broad smile, "I'm grateful for a moment with her. She seemed pleased enough with what I've made of myself."

"Did she say anything to you?" Kate asked.

"Good God!" Simon sat up quickly. He pulled the key out of his waistcoat pocket. "She did. She was holding the key and she said a word."

Kate leaned close with excitement. "What word?"

"What does *morthul* mean to you?"

She looked up to the ceiling, shuffling through the extensive glossary of languages in her head. "Is it a proper name?"

"I don't know."

"It means hammer," Nick muttered, staring into the fire.

"Hammer?" Simon mused.

"Hammer. In Cornish." Nick hung his head, fighting fatigue. "Your accent's atrocious. Maybe hers was too unless she was Cornish."

"Simon," Kate said, "fetch a copy of Munro's *Britannica Cornish Grammar*."

Simon laughed. "Sorry, Kate, I don't have a copy. The closest thing was a stable boy from Truro who once worked here."

She gave him a frown of scholarly disappointment. "Well, my Cornish isn't strong. In Welsh, hammer is *morthwyl*. Similar. But what could she mean?"

Nick looked inebriated, his head in his hands. The whiskey bottle had only a few swallows left. "She didn't mean anything. You can't trust what you hear from the dead. Most of it you bring yourself. It might've been in your head."

Simon walked over to Nick's slumped figure. "Go to bed. You need sleep."

"I'll sleep when I'm ready. I'm going for a walk." Nick stood and stumbled against the hearth. He caught himself and shook Simon off.

"Nick, please. It's a miracle you can stand." Simon froze as a hauntingly familiar feeling crept over him. Nick started to argue and Simon snapped, "Quiet! Quiet!" He struggled to make coherent sense out of his swirling thoughts.

Kate rose to her feet, watching him.

Simon stared at the key and, without speaking, turned and walked from the room, down the darkened corridor with increasingly long strides. Kate's footsteps sounded behind him. Then he nearly sprinted up the circular stone steps. He reached the door to his tower sanctum and entered. A quick word raised the soft luminance. He went to his desk and began to pore over a stack of journals.

Breathless, Kate stood in the doorway. "Simon? What is it? Can I help you?"

Simon shook his head without answering. He slammed one book shut and seized another, frantically rifling pages. Leaf after leaf of runic symbols flashed across his vision. Finally, he pressed his finger against a page with a shout of triumph. "Ha! I knew it!"

"What is it?" Kate joined him at the desk.

"Do you read druidic script?" Simon asked.

"I've seen some, but very little survives."

"That's because my father had it all. He received it from Pendragon. And now I have much of it." Simon flipped the book toward Kate. It made little difference for most of the script was unfamiliar to her. He pointed to a symbol. In his other hand, he held the key in a tight grip.

"I'm sorry," she said. "I don't know it."

"It's druidic runes writing an ancient Celtic language. I think I misheard my mother. I think she was saying *marthsyl*."

The key glowed green.

Simon leapt to his feet, holding the key out as if he had received an electric shock. It felt warm in his hand, and sharp pinpoints of otherwordly light wrote hidden runes across the gold surface.

The wavering emerald haze colored Kate's amazed face. "Oh my God, Simon. Oh my God. What's it doing?"

"I don't know." He stared at the key.

"What did you say? Does *marthsyl* mean hammer?"

"No. It means miracle or wonder." He glanced up at Kate to see her staring past him with eyes wide in shock. Simon turned and saw a strange glowing spot on the wall. He stepped closer.

"It's the symbol from the key," Kate said. "The same one that's on the wall in my father's study at Hartley Hall."

Indeed it was the stylized compass icon forged into the top of the key, and it was burning bright green against the rough white plaster. Then suddenly, between Simon and the glowing sigil on the wall, a strange wavering patch appeared in the air. He blinked hard at first, suspecting his vision was blurred. But the weaving distortion was the air itself, swimming before him, just above his eye level.

"Simon, step back," Kate called.

The weird quavering space began to coalesce into a recognizable vision. It became a pulsating oval and in its center was a map of the world. Simon looked at Kate in wonder, and she was already coming around the desk to join him. There were marks on the map in various places, many of them overlapping and crowded atop one another. There was one on London, and several more around Britain, including one that was likely Warden Abbey where they stood. Some were clearly recognizable just from their geography. London. Paris. Cairo. Calcutta. New Orleans. Java.

"I know what many of those are." Kate pointed at the glistening world suspended in midair. "They're my father's travels. Those must be all the places he went using the key. He was in New Orleans, just as Ambassador Mansfield said. And he was also in Cairo." She reached out toward the map and where her hand came near, the scene suddenly reoriented itself to her touch, zooming in. The view drew tight on the eastern Mediterranean and new dots became visible including Alexandria and Jerusalem. She pulled her arm back, shaking it. "It tingles."

Simon raised a finger to the dot over Cairo. The entire map shimmered and vanished in a swirl of energy. Both Simon and Kate stepped back as the aether whirlpooled before them. Out of the disorienting lines of power swimming in endless circles, recognizable shapes coalesced into a scene. A sandy street bathed in thin morning light. Walls rising up around it. Awnings. And the telltale enclosed wooden balconies that Simon had seen in drawings of Cairo streets.

"It's Egypt," Kate breathed. "It's right in front of us. I can feel the heat. Look! There's someone moving. We're looking at Cairo!"

"It's not real," came Nick's slurred comment from the door. "It's a glamour or an illusion."

Simon reached into his pocket and brought out a shilling. He thumbed it toward the portal. The coin flipped through the air and created ripples across the scene like a pebble striking the surface of a pond. The distortion quickly stilled and the shilling appeared midair in the Egyptian dawn and fell to the street with a puff of dust.

Kate laughed wildly.

"It's real." Simon gazed down at the small coin lying on the ground. It had traveled a few feet and now rested thousands of miles away. "It's a portal through space. That is Cairo, even as we speak, within arm's reach, as we stand here in Bedfordshire. Our fathers made a miracle."

Kate grabbed his arm. "Let's go through! Let's step into Cairo. We could see the pyramids. The pyramids, Simon!"

"No, Kate," Simon said without conviction. "We have other pressing business before the pyramids. Plus, we don't truly know how to operate it."

"My father obviously used it many times. Probably your father too. There is a mark here at Warden Abbey."

"Yes, but we must be cautious. If we were trapped in Cairo, at best it would be months getting back."

"Why do you want to come back?" Nick's voice broke his reverie. "There's your great mystery solved. You've mastered the key left to you by your father. Let's use that thing to go somewhere far away. It's a sign. You spoke to your mother tonight. And now here's your father saying the same thing. He never meant for you to stay in one place. He gave you the power to go anywhere in the blink of an eye. Think of the magic you can learn. No one could find us."

Simon continued to gaze at the common Cairene alley as if it was the most exotic place in the world. He was tempted to lift the sole of his foot off the freezing floor of Warden Abbey and set it down in the sands of Egypt.

He quickly waved his hand over the shimmering portal, and the scene vanished, replaced by the world map. He then touched the dot that corresponded to Hartley

Hall and the portal swirled. Soon they were staring through the threshold into Sir Roland's study in Surrey. "Here is a location we can test, I think. Let me just tell Winston that we're on our way, so he doesn't wonder where we've gotten to."

Kate grinned with excitement.

Simon left her the key and went off to make arrangements. After he had a quick word with his trusted butler, he returned to find Kate staring with wonder at the room where she had been countless times. Nick slumped in a corner with his chin propped in his hand.

"Right," Simon said, "are we ready?"

Kate took his hand. "Always."

Simon and Kate stood squarely before the strange window to another place. They looked at each other with expectant nods. He squeezed her hand and stepped forward. It felt like submerging in warm water. Immediately he was bombarded with sight and sound, bright and loud, and odd smells as well. The magic of aether burned his nostrils and the thick mist swirled around him as if alive. It pulled at him. For a moment, Simon was terrified he was becoming lost, but he could still feel Kate's hand, and he realized the aether was towing him in a specific direction. He stopped fighting against it.

He felt solid ground beneath his feet though he didn't remember not having it under him before. His knees nearly buckled and he reached out to steady himself. His hand struck a bookcase and he leaned against it, breathing hard. He could smell cold musty air and the mildewed scent of old books.

Kate stood next to him, wavering on her feet. "Are we really in Hartley Hall?"

Simon laughed and kissed her cheek. "You feel real enough." He looked back at the portal. He could see his private sanctuary at Warden Abbey. And he saw Nick standing on the other side. Simon waved him forward with a jovial grin.

Nick shook his head and held his hand up in a fare-well gesture. He turned for the door.

"Nick!" Simon shouted as the door closed. "I'll go back for him. He's still confused from the necromancy. I knew I shouldn't have allowed it."

"Simon." Kate grabbed him. "Let him go. He isn't disoriented. He doesn't want to be here. Give him time. He said he was leaving before, then he came back. Nick obviously loves you. He'll come around again."

Simon let out a disappointed sigh, watching the empty room through rippling air.

Kate handed him the key. "Why didn't you tell him about the curse? He might have been able to help you."

"He can't."

"He might have tried."

"That's why I didn't tell him." Simon held up the key and said, "Marthsyl."

The window on his boyhood shrank to a pinpoint in an instant and was gone.

Chapter 22

THE RED ORCHID SALON STOOD IN THE PALE
light of the winter moon. The house itself was finally
quiet although the neighborhood was still active with
tradesmen and costermongers and laborers trudging
into another night. Wagons full of tomorrow's catch of
fish teetered past.

In the shadow of chimney pots, Malcolm blew on his
chapped hands while crouching beneath his black greatcoat. From his rooftop post, he could see the front door,
the window of Barnes's private bedroom, and the cellar
exit into the alley. He had a vantage point on the three
lanes that led away from the house. Malcolm had been
waiting like a soot-blackened stone for three days. Every
limb was cramped. It reminded him of how long it had
been since he had hunted from ambush.

The modified rifle lay across the peak of the roof with
its metal wrapped in dark cloth to suppress glints. His
stiff, cold fingers flipped two of the magnifying glass
lenses down, adjusting the range once more. He leaned
over to squint into the scope and peered at a small crack
on the door. He positioned the rifle to train it on Barnes's
bedroom, which appeared to be empty.

A sound behind him brought him onto one knee. His

heavy dagger flashed up, blade tip between his thumb and forefinger, raised above his shoulder. He spotted a dark figure below him at the eaves of the roof.

"Don't!" Penny fell against the tiles. "It's me!"

Malcolm lowered the knife and said matter-of-factly, "Careful. You're on a rooftop."

"I know that!" The engineer spat angrily. She rose nervously to her feet, glancing back over the edge to the street thirty feet below. She pulled strange metal discs with small spikes off her hands with a scowl. "Don't stab me. I brought you a present."

Malcolm indicated the metal discs that she slipped in her pocket. "Did you climb up here?"

"Yes, for the pleasure of you trying to kill me." Penny picked up a leather satchel she had dropped. "Didn't you climb? How did you get up?"

"I walked up the stairs and stepped out an attic window." He slid down and helped her up with him.

"I guess some people are just born to take the easy road." She settled just below the peak. "How is the starlight telescope working?"

"Excellent. I can see all the places where he hasn't shown himself very clearly and very brightly."

Penny pulled a small piece of oilcloth from inside her bag. She unfolded the cloth to reveal two long cartridges. They didn't look appreciably different than the ordnance he was already using.

"More shells?" Malcolm asked.

The engineer held one up. She shook it slightly and small wings popped out of the casing. Malcolm leaned in for a closer look and Penny took obvious pride in his intense stare.

"These shells," she said, "will increase your accuracy tenfold at least. I've only had time to make two, so don't miss. At least not twice." She folded the wings tight against the brass casing and handed both shells to Malcolm.

He quickly took up the rifle and snapped it open. He fished out the shell and replaced it with the new winged cartridge. Closing the breech, he said, "I'll only need one. But I'll keep the other. Thank you."

"So, no sign of him?"

"Brief glimpses. No chance of a shot."

The wind changed and black coal smoke descended over them. Penny began a hacking cough and clamped the inside of her elbow over her mouth and nose. "Even I can't breathe up here. How do you manage?"

"I stopped breathing yesterday." Malcolm took the rifle and replaced it in its perch just as the front door of the Red Orchid opened.

A crowd of people emerged onto the street below. They were all clad in red-and-white robes. Malcolm recognized a broad-shouldered shape in the center as the behemoth corpse he had fought in the cellar. Rowan Barnes was in the center of the crowd. Malcolm dropped flat on the roof, the rifle pressed close to his shoulder, and he laid the sights on Barnes. He heard Penny speaking, but her voice was a soft buzz as he focused only on the target. He slipped a lens into place and the dim nightscape burned yellow like sunlight. Barnes was surrounded by a group of fifteen women who were distressingly active with giddy frolics, leaping about, holding hands, dancing together around the great man. Barnes smiled with not a care in the world. The necromancer's head appeared in the center of the scope. Suddenly Eleanor's face drifted in front of him.

Damnation.

Barnes stopped. The hunter again brought the target clearly into sharp focus, settling his breath for the shot. The necromancer was as good as dead.

Malcolm didn't pull the trigger. He saw the face of Kate, quietly distraught at the idea that killing Barnes meant endless agony for Simon. The scribe wouldn't care; he understood. But Kate cared for Simon, and Malcolm was about to drive an aching pain into those beautiful green eyes.

Barnes vanished from the scope when he bent over but then popped up again. Another shape wavered into view. It was a young girl, no older than Charlotte. Barnes lifted the waif onto his shoulders as if he were a loving father. Then it caught Malcolm by surprise when the necromancer looked up to stare at him directly with a smile twisted with diabolical glee. Barnes actually winked at him. Malcolm clenched his teeth and his finger tightened against the trigger.

Barnes and his acolytes started off down the street. Malcolm was sure he could place a shell in the man's head without hitting the little girl. *Relatively* sure. So he didn't. Barnes and his group turned a corner and vanished.

"Damn it!" Malcolm pushed the rifle away. "He knew I was here the whole time. Idiot! Idiot!"

"Where he's going?" Penny asked.

"He's about to kill one of those women." Malcolm slapped a furious hand against the bricks. "We don't know which church."

"We'll split up," Penny said. "I'll go to St. Mary Woolnoth. You go to St. George."

"All right. Be careful. You're armed, I take it?"

Penny grinned and slid down the roof to the eaves. She affixed her climbing gizmos to her hands. "Worry about yourself, Malcolm."

He waved her gone and headed for the window.

MALCOLM MANAGED TO FIND A HANSOM. THE rifle was hidden in the folds of his coat and the driver

paid him little mind, grateful for the coin on such a cold
night. The cab moved onto the Ratcliffe Highway. Malcolm gripped the rifle tightly, all the while hoping Penny
didn't do something foolish if she did encounter Barnes.

The hansom made good time to St. George and Malcolm stepped from the cab. He entered the creaking
gate and blended in with the dark shadows that permeated the grounds. The air was heavy with moisture, and
if the temperature dropped any further, there would be
snow. He tripped over something on the ground and
stumbled against a gravestone. It was a body, a man in
a long coat and cheap hat. His face had frozen in a grimace of pain, and his hands had locked on his chest,
clutching at his heart. A lantern lay extinguished on the
ground nearby. The watchman, no doubt, paid by Simon's friend Henry to keep an eye on the church. He
had had no time to raise an alarm. He had been no
match.

Everything else seemed serene. The church squatted
in the thin moonlight, with an imposing, medieval-style
steeple and pepper-pot turrets. Malcolm pulled the rifle
from his coat and slipped toward the church.

The altar lay at the eastern end, so he went to a door
on the northern side, the gospel side. It was locked. He
drew out a long silver pin and proceeded to unlock it.
He quietly entered the darkness and closed the door behind him. There were voices and the dimmest of light.
He actually breathed a sigh of relief since Penny would
not face the danger.

Creeping behind a column, he peered toward the altar,
where white-and-red-robed figures milled about. On top
of the dais was a naked woman. Eleanor. She seemed
unafraid and, in fact, almost excited as she stared out at
the Barnes cultists. Barnes himself was behind the altar,
so he was only visible from the waist up. His red hood

was thrown back and he talked calmly to Eleanor, but was still intent and fierce. She listened to him and nodded peacefully. Then she lay back on the cold stone. She couldn't possibly be so naïve that she wasn't aware of what was happening, Malcolm thought furiously, urging her to run. The Scotsman put the rifle to his shoulder and adjusted the sight, bringing Barnes into sharp focus in the dim candlelight. The necromancer suddenly smiled at Eleanor with such rancid joy that Malcolm switched his attention back to the woman.

Eleanor reached down beside her and lifted a knife with both hands. She poised the blade at her chest. Her face was placid, as if she were going to sleep. Then Eleanor plunged the knife deep into herself.

Malcolm shouted with horror and disbelief. All heads save Eleanor's turned toward him. He fired. The shot was hurried and the bullet struck Barnes high in the shoulder, spinning him to the stone floor out of sight. Some of Barnes's consorts screamed, and some rushed to his side. The robed women surrounded him, placing themselves in harm's way to protect their master. Shockingly, Barnes struggled to his feet, glaring at Malcolm but keeping a low profile to prevent a clean shot. The bullet had put a hole in the necromancer's shoulder large enough to shove a croquet ball into, but he was still standing.

Two robed figures separated themselves from the mob and faced Malcolm. He recognized the faces under the cowls as the necromancer's *brides*: Madeleine and Cecilia. The rest of the acolytes who hovered around Barnes appeared to be living women. Like Eleanor, they were ensnared not by undeath but by Barnes's sickly words. Malcolm recognized some of them from the poetry circle about William Blake.

Gritting his teeth, the Scotsman fired into Cecilia. The bullet tore through her, but she barely flinched. He took a step back with the rifle ready at his hip, glancing around the church, trying to plan a path of attack. "Come out from behind their skirts, Barnes. Have you not an ounce of man in you?"

The necromancer seemed to be experiencing surprisingly little pain despite his massive wound. He moved behind Lilith for cover and fished out a thin chain around his neck. A small object dangled on the end of the chain; it was a ring.

Malcolm took another step back when the two brides inched closer. He raised the rifle to his chest. "All of you clear away from him. This must stop tonight."

None of the women, living or dead, moved. If anything, their faces grew harder at the threat. Several joined hands.

Malcolm stared in disbelief at the enraptured women. "What is wrong with you? You saw what he did to Eleanor. You see these two things here?"

"No," Lilith cried out. "He didn't do anything to Eleanor. She chose. Any of us would have done the same. We must save Britain from villains such as you. We are Jerusalem."

Barnes nodded placidly and slid the ring on the middle finger of his left hand. "Well said, Lilith. Would you hand Eleanor's knife to me, please."

The hard-eyed Lilith smiled with pride and yanked the bloody dagger from her friend's cooling body. Barnes took it and moved closer to the altar.

"It should be clear by now," Barnes called out, "that you and Archer are on the wrong side of history. We are saving this land. Our great enemies will be vanquished. But you won't live to see it because you don't deserve to do so."

Barnes lowered his head and took several deep breaths. From nearby, off to the side of the altar, a door slammed open. The brawny tough from the salon emerged through the dark rectangle. A group of ten or so walking cadavers followed him. They moved purposefully toward Malcolm, dragging their damp shrouds behind them.

Barnes placed the knife over Eleanor's chest, preparing to carve. "My dears, please tear him into pieces."

The two brides charged Malcolm with dead hands upraised, mouths agape. He fired. Both undead women were hit, jerking with the impacts, but kept coming with remarkable speed. Madeleine grabbed him, and threw him. Malcolm slammed hard into the wooden pews, his grip on the rifle lost as his arm went numb. He heard a crack and hoped he hadn't broken a bone. He pulled himself up onto the back of the pew. He yanked his coat out of the grip of one of the ghouls only to slam into the other on the opposite side. Ungodly strong hands were on him, and proceeded to throttle him. He pulled a pistol and fired, blowing a large hole in Cecilia's chest. The walking corpse staggered back, more disconcerted than in pain. Madeleine dragged him into her arms.

He struggled, twisting the barrel behind him, and fired. Flesh and fluids covered him. He felt the grip ease so he pulled away and scrambled under the pews. The two silent things started climbing over the wooden benches in pursuit. As soon as they passed over top of him, Malcolm stood and ran down an aisle. He stopped suddenly as a gang of cadavers staggered in front of him, reaching out with clawlike fingers. He battered at the moldering things with his heavy pistol.

The Scotsman holstered one of his guns and drew a long blade. The undead thug from the cellar rushed him, and Malcolm ducked under a heavy swipe of the man's solid fist. Malcolm maneuvered behind and clamped his arm around the man's forehead, tilting the head backward. The dagger made short work of the exposed throat, cutting to the bone. With a jagged wrench, Malcolm pulled back hard. The brute's head tilted toward the right shoulder. Malcolm released the man and kicked him square in the back into the reaching cadavers. The force was too much for the decaying tendons, and the head snapped off and rolled under a pew. The large body fell heavily to the floor.

A corpse without lips grabbed hold of Malcolm's left arm and he shot it. Another quickly grabbed his right. More hands reached for his throat. One clamped onto his shoulder with its teeth, snarling like some animal. They dragged Malcolm down to the flagstones. He couldn't feel his arms or legs, only the dead pressed on top of his chest and around his throat. He felt cold, clammy hands squeezing the breath from him.

An echoing howl erupted, rattling the church. It raised the hairs on the back of Malcolm's neck. Even the undead paused now. A massive hairy figure stalked from the shadows with pounding steps, her narrowing canine eyes sweeping from side to side.

"Charlotte!" Malcolm gasped.

The werewolf leapt. Clawed hands seized and tore at the undead that held Malcolm. Where once the sight of such a beast would have chilled him, now it filled him with elation. He was jerked back and forth as the cadavers were plucked off him like ticks. The smell of blood and gore crowded his nostrils. Bodies flew all about him. He heard growling and recognized a furry face that pushed into his blurry view.

The frightening wolfish countenance appeared to be grinning, and Charlotte actually licked him in her exuberance. Her massive hairy hand pulled him upright so fast, his head spun. Then she whirled back to the fight. Her great long limbs took hold of a gentleman who looked quite respectable but for his exposed rib cage. She threw him into a faltering group of undead, tumbling them over. Malcolm shook his head to clear it, rubbing at the growing goose egg on the back of his skull. His throat convulsed when he tried to talk, and he swallowed painfully.

Malcolm glanced at Barnes, who was pressing his left fist into Eleanor's exposed chest cavity. Even while doing so, the necromancer was looking up in shock at the terrifying lycanthrope stomping through the remains of the undead. His robed acolytes around the altar were grasping one another in horror, but they crowded closer around Barnes. He pulled his hand away and the ring on his finger glowed and smoked.

The two brides had moved between Malcolm and the altar. He took the chance to shoot them, staggering them. Charlotte pounced. The brides fought silently, taking hammerblows from the werewolf while swarming her, tearing and biting the huge beast. Charlotte cried out in pain, twisting her gigantic frame, trying to pull Madeleine off her back and shake Cecilia from her arm.

Suddenly a sickly green light filled the cavernous church. It convulsed within the confines of the walls and fell like a blanket to cover the floor, hovering like a dead fog before the tendrils seeped into the earth and out under the cracks in the door. Whatever magic Barnes was conjuring, he had succeeded.

Malcolm staggered forward as Charlotte took a firm grip on Madeleine, her huge hand covering the undead face. She lifted the cadaver high over her head and slammed it down onto its sister, driving them both off their feet. The werewolf snarled and stamped onto the writhing pair, crushing them hard to the floor.

"Charlotte, hold still." Malcolm struggled to keep his pistol leveled at the head of one of the undead. Madeleine's eyes swiveled toward the open bore of the barrel. He pulled the trigger four times, emptying the weapon into her.

Charlotte reached down and grabbed the second bride by the shoulder. Without taking her foot off the thing's abdomen, the werewolf pulled up with all her unnatural might. There was a moment when Charlotte growled with effort, and then Cecilia's frame tore neatly in two, leaving the beast holding the upper torso over her head. She then threw it across the church. The remnants of the two brides stopped writhing although they were likely not yet truly dead. They simply had run out of reason to fight.

Even though Malcolm was watching a large werewolf, he couldn't help but see the little girl with blood on her hands and a decapitated corpse under her foot. He took involuntary steps back.

Charlotte looked up, regarding him with curious eyes. Her nearly unintelligible voice ground out, "Don't be scared."

"I'm not scared." Malcolm spun around, remembering the point of the entire bloody event and intent on dealing with Barnes. However, the necromancer was gone, departed with his living followers. Only Eleanor remained behind, dead on the altar.

"Damn it." He limped up the aisle where he saw the familiar desecration wrought on the young poet. He found an altar cloth on the floor and draped it over her naked body.

"Chase?" Charlotte prowled about the altar on all fours, sniffing the air.

"No. Barnes is done for tonight and I don't want to invite him to wreak any further damage on his followers or on innocent bystanders." Malcolm leaned on the altar for support and shook his head at how much that sounded like Simon. "I had a shot and didn't take it. I could have prevented all this."

The beast pressed her head against Malcolm's shoulder affectionately. He patted her gently, then froze in horror, realizing what he was doing. He couldn't tell if she was smiling or snarling at him the way her lips curled back.

Her chest chuffed deeply, almost like a laugh. She squatted on the ground and stared up at him. "Are you happy to see me?"

Malcolm let out an exasperated breath, not wanting to tell her the truth. The child would insist on coming with him everywhere on every assignment. He shook his head in frustration, but then replied quietly, "Yes, lass. I'm happy to see you."

She giggled though it sounded nothing like the little girl he knew.

"We'd best go," Malcolm said, staggering slightly.

Charlotte grabbed Malcolm and threw him over her muscled shoulder.

"Blast it, girl! I can walk." Malcolm pushed himself out of the werewolf's disturbingly gentle grasp back onto the floor. He brushed himself off. Then he slowly made for the heavy wooden doors on the west end and shoved them open, allowing the brisk air to sweep inside the church. It revived him.

Charlotte could have easily outdistanced him but instead she bounded around him on all fours like Kate's overexcited wolfhound. Across the cemetery, dark shadows dotted the ground covered with a light dusting of snow. At first Malcolm thought more dead were rising now that Barnes had completed his ritual, but they were only the lonely shapes of the numerous tombstones.

"I told you not to follow me," Malcolm scolded in a less-than-convincing voice.

Charlotte's massive head tilted and she laughed, or at least he hoped the sound she was making was laughter. It was hard to tell.

Chapter 23

THE NEXT MORNING, JUST AFTER SUNRISE, THERE was a great uproar at the front of Hartley Hall. The front door was open and several footmen either escorted or fought Malcolm inside. The servants seemed to want to support the Scotsman, but he cursed and tried his best to shove them away. Simon and Kate rushed from the Blue Parlor, where coffee had been served.

"Malcolm!" Simon exclaimed. "What's happened? Is it Barnes?"

Malcolm shrugged off the final young footman and strode forward. There was a noticeable limp in his gait. His shirt was covered in blood and mud. He carried his holsters in his hand. Penny came after him with her gigantic rucksack over her shoulder. She was not injured or dirty.

"Malcolm, what happened to you?" Kate still held a letter she had been reading when the tumult began. Then the servants moved aside and she saw Charlotte coming in the door, draped in Malcolm's greatcoat, which trailed behind her like a queen's mantle. Her feet were bare and her hair a tangled horror. Hogarth brought up the rear, with a comforting hand on the girl's shoulder. "Charlotte!"

Kate ran forward as if to put herself between the girl and the hunter. She took Charlotte by the shoulders and looked intensely at her. "What happened, dear? Did you change? Are you all right? Imogen told me you were asleep in your room. When did you leave the house?"

"I'm fine, Miss Kate." Charlotte was smiling as if she was returning from a picnic. "I changed but I remember everything. The wulfsyl works."

Kate turned to Malcolm. Her voice was growing frantic. "Explain this. Were you tracking her? What happened?"

"Calm yourself," Malcolm retorted irritably. "She went to London."

"What!" Kate shouted, now rounding angrily on Charlotte. "You went to London? I told you to stay in the house at all times unless I was with you."

"But I wanted—" the girl began.

"She was with me," Malcolm interrupted. He tossed his holsters over his shoulder, staring Kate in the eye. "I took her to London with me."

"You did what?" Kate hissed. "Don't you know how dangerous that could be?"

"More than anyone," the Scotsman retorted. "It's done now. She's saved my life. We're back." He dropped his eyes from Kate's strong glare and walked toward the stairs.

Simon asked as he passed, "Did you get Barnes?"

Malcolm shook his head. "No. I failed at the church."

"Did he murder a third woman?"

"Her name was Eleanor." The Scotsman continued to the stairs and started up, one foot dragging slightly.

Kate stared silently at the retreating Malcolm for a long moment, then she put a hand to Charlotte's back, and said quietly, "Come, dear. Let's get you cleaned up and some breakfast in you. You must be exhausted."

"No," Charlotte said cheerfully.

Kate smiled and pushed her on. "Up to your room now. I'll be along."

The girl skipped past Simon. "Good morning, Mr. Simon."

"Good morning, Charlotte. Lovely frock."

"It's heavy. And smells like Mr. Malcolm." Charlotte giggled and ran for the stairs, catching up with Malcolm, and the two of them trudged off together.

Kate joined Simon as Hogarth urged the servants to go about their business. She said, "Do you think Malcolm took Charlotte to London with him?"

"No, of course not. I think she followed him there against everyone's wishes."

"So he lied for her?"

"Yes."

"You don't seem very worried about that."

"I'm not." Simon began to twirl the key on its chain. "Oddly enough, I'm rather pleased by it."

Kate handed him the letter she carried. "Here's a bit of good news. It came yesterday. Thomas Clover claims to have information for us about the hieroglyphs."

"Ah. Excellent." Simon read the simple note requesting Kate to call on Mr. Clover at her convenience, and sending his best wishes to Imogen. "We'll talk to Malcolm about the killing, then go to London."

Penny looked up eagerly from where she had stopped to rearrange her rucksack. "I've got the steamcycle right outside. We can leave anytime."

Simon and Kate exchanged worried glances, and he quickly held up the gold key. "Thank you, Penny, but you'll be excited to hear we now have a faster, and safer, means to London. I'll want to stop at the church to inscribe it to hopefully prevent or delay undead from rising before seeing Mr. Clover."

Kate took the note back from Simon. "Barnes requires only one more sacrifice to complete his ritual.

And he will summon whatever thing he's trying to raise in the center of London."

"I know." Simon gripped the key. "I know all too well."

THE PORTAL OPENED IN AN UNUSED CELLAR IN what turned out to be the sprawling magnificence of Somerset House. Kate noted that it was the home of the Royal Society, of which her father had been a powerful member. It made perfect sense that he would maintain an entry spot there. After Simon and Kate recovered their senses, a quick cab ride to St. George in the East allowed Simon to inscribe temporary runes around the burying ground and in the doorways to the crypt. Simon's bribe to a groundskeeper got them inside despite the still-obvious damage from what must have been a terrible fight with Barnes's forces.

Once that was done, he and Kate set out for the British Museum. It was late afternoon and darkness was already descending. A few lights shone in the windows of Montagu House, the Jacobean mansion where the bulk of the collection resided and where Thomas Clover had bade them come. Kate's letter from the curator was sufficient for a watchman to unlock the door and go upstairs to fetch their host. Simon and Kate waited in the foyer amidst stuffed beasts.

After a moment, Thomas appeared on the landing, smiling down at the pair. "Kate! Marvelous to see you. I have exciting news." He padded down to meet them, sending the watchman back to his frigid rounds outside.

Simon noted that the young curator hesitated before greeting him. He knew the curse was taking its toll, and no matter how much he might wish it wasn't so, his appearance was beginning to show the ragged edges of constant pain.

Thomas beckoned him and Kate down a corridor

toward the rear of the house. "I finally recalled where I had seen those symbols."

Thomas led them into a back salon that was cramped with desks and tables. There were items of antiquity scattered about: vases, small statues, pottery, and piles of coins. Papers with careful sketches and descriptions littered the room too. He went to a small desk in a dark corner and lit a lamp with a sudden look of embarrassment.

"This is my area. Not terribly large, I know, but it should improve with the new spaces. We're abominably cramped here. Only a miniscule portion of the collection is capable of being displayed."

"Long overdue," Kate placated while looking over pages of hieroglyphics. "So, are our symbols here?"

"Oh yes. Somewhere." Thomas shuffled through large sheets of Egyptian script and drawings. He laughed at the disorganization. "Scholarship, eh? Ah! Here we are." He laid a huge roll of drafting paper on top of the pile and spread it open to a length of five feet by three feet. There were ten lines of hand-copied hieroglyphics written across the sheet.

"What is this?" Kate asked.

Thomas said, "It's a hymn to the god Ra. It . . . um . . . calls on him to come forth, to *rise*"—he pointed at the symbol he had identified earlier—"and protect his servants. The usual sort of things you ask a god in a hymn."

Kate and Simon saw that the symbols branded on the heart of Madeleine Hawley, and supposedly the other sacrifices as well, were at the beginning and the end of the long string of hieroglyphs.

"Can you read this?" Simon asked Kate.

"A bit of it, but it's quite old. It's Heliopolitan to be sure. It summons Ra, then beseeches him to trample his enemies." She ran her finger along the symbols to the end of the long string. "And here it appears to be calling him to return, to *set* like the evening sun." Kate looked confused. "Why would Pendragon inscribe English churches with a spell for summoning an Egyptian sun god?"

"I don't think he did exactly," Simon replied. "I think he used the functional construct of this spell. The binding and summoning elements. It's like taking a song written for violin and adapting it for pianoforte."

"I'm sorry." Thomas laughed nervously. "Are you two still talking to me?"

Kate said, "Yes, Thomas, of course. From what did you transcribe this text?"

"A linen. A mummy linen."

"This spell is written on a mummy?" Simon regarded the curator.

"No, just a linen. Part of a consignment we received years ago, I believe it came to us from a private collection. Nothing terribly exciting. Just a box with a very long strip of linen. This text was written on it. That's the reason we never displayed it; it's just a length of cloth in a box. Not very dramatic."

Simon felt a surge of excitement going through him. He looked at Kate and her eyes were wide too. He smiled despite the fear that always accompanied the possibility that an artifact of unimaginable power was bubbling to the surface of the rational world. "Kate, are you thinking—"

"I am." She studied the hieroglyphs on the paper again. "The Skin of Ra."

Thomas looked between the two of them. "The Skin of Ra? I've never heard of such a thing."

Simon joined Kate, staring at the symbols. "It's a unique object, usually thought to be mythical. Like the Holy Grail or Excalibur."

"Ah. What is it?"

"It is a linen used to wrap a mummy," Kate said. "In ancient Heliopolis, where the priesthood of Ra was centered, it was used to re-create their god here on Earth, in a physical form. Once summoned, Ra would lead the armies of Heliopolis against enemy cities, destroying their god and leaving the city weak and helpless before the invading forces. In this way, the priesthood made Ra the dominant god in ancient Egypt, destroying or absorbing all rivals. The pharaohs were all subject to the will of the priests of Ra for their power on Earth. The Skin of Ra allowed the followers of the sun god to rule Egypt for thousands of years."

"What happened to it?" Thomas asked.

"No one knows, of course. It was lost or stolen or destroyed, depending on the story one believes."

"But, of course, it's just a story. Yes?"

Kate and Simon exchanged knowing glances, and she said, "May we see it?"

"Well, yes, I suppose so." Thomas looked confused and nervous.

They followed Thomas and his oil lamp out of the common workroom and along the corridor. The curator stopped at a door and fumbled with a key ring. Finally, he unlocked the door.

"Do be careful on the steps," he said.

They descended into the dark, cold cellar on stone steps. The musty smell of damp earth surrounded them. There were a few thin windows set deep in the stone walls near the ceiling, but they were black from the night. The oil lamp threw a faint yellow glow on the surrounding mob of stone faces and frozen, snarling, animal snouts and rows of pottery and towers of wooden crates. There was barely room to walk between the detritus of cultures. A faint thumping noise came from the darkness.

"Rats," Thomas suggested weakly. "They've eaten half of the world's history down here."

The three came to a stone wall lined with shelves covered with pots and urns. Thomas studied labels on the shelves. The bumping noise came again to their right. He looked warily in that direction.

"That way." Thomas tried to urge lamplight into the distant black corner.

The thumping continued in the dark. Thomas froze.

"That's a very insistent rat." Simon saw Kate reaching into her bag to have a defensive elixir ready at hand. The sound was not rhythmic like a loose object swinging freely. It was an irregular scrabbling like fingers scraping rapidly with energy, then slowing as if tired. It resembled the sound of an animal testing the limits of a cage.

Simon clasped his hands behind his back. "You don't keep living specimens down here, do you? A parrot or a jaguar?"

"No."

"Well, carry on then. No doubt the rat will scurry at your approach."

"No doubt," Thomas said timidly.

They squeezed between crates and shelves, moving toward the sound. Simon followed close behind Thomas. The curator stopped short and he bumped into the man's back.

"There." Thomas pointed. On a shelf at the edge of the lamplight was a wooden box. It was pitch-black, made of rich, ebony wood, perhaps a foot in width and length and height. Delicate gold highlights accentuated the corners. Around the sides were carved hieroglyphs.

The thumping sound was coming from inside the box. Thomas gasped, watching the wooden container move. The corners lifted a few inches off the shelf, up and down as if something inside wanted to get out. Simon pushed past Thomas.

"Simon, don't be stupid," Kate warned. "For once."

He stood in front of the jumping container. Slowly, his hand went toward the lid. The thumping sound stopped and the box dropped motionless to the shelf. He raised an amused eyebrow.

Just as his fingers brushed the cool ebony, he heard a clicking noise. Regular. Rhythmic. It came from the direction of the stairs. Footsteps. He looked at Kate. She turned around, listening as well.

Thomas pressed against the wall, unnerved by another unexpected sound. He whispered, "I shouldn't have brought you down here."

The steps continued to approach, stopping occasionally to avoid an obstacle in the path. A small figure could soon be seen against the grey background. It turned and moved slowly toward them along the same narrow path they had taken. Finally the shape stopped a few feet from Kate.

The figure was female, draped in a long gown, with her head completely veiled.

"Mrs. Mansfield?" Thomas asked with surprise. "Did we have an appointment? I'm so sorry to have inconvenienced you. I hope the watchman didn't give you a problem getting inside."

"No," Mrs. Mansfield whispered. Then she raised both hands and held them out in front of her in a peculiar pose. She spoke with a familiar voice that sounded like a rusting gate. "He's dead."

"I'm sorry?" Thomas inclined his head politely.

Simon felt the box thump from the inside. His stomach twisted at the sound of Mrs. Mansfield's voice. "Kate, you might wish to have Mr. Clover step back."

"You will all be dead soon," Mrs. Mansfield croaked in a low voice. "I have been searching this city, waiting for his call. He can sense the rise of the new god and he longs for blood." She moved one hand slowly toward her veil and lifted it up over her head. Her face was blue.

Nephthys. The demon queen lowered her head and took a step back.

Earth exploded and filled the air around Simon. Huge shapes rose up so close they slammed against him with their scaly bodies. Before he could speak, clawed hands slashed. He was pummeled one way and another, feeling battered as if he had fallen between two galloping horses. He crashed into the stone wall. The high columns of crates and boxes began to collapse and split open. White marble heads tumbled over him, cracking against his skull. Simon saw stars and felt nausea rising. His vision was lost under a collapse of antiquities and his ears rang with thundering vibrations.

Simon gathered his wits and spoke his runic strength into life. He pushed himself up. The crushing weight on his back held him down. He took a deep breath and shoved again, slowly creaking up through crates and planks and marble. He felt the cool air wash over him and wreckage fell away from his shoulders.

He struggled over the uneven landscape, slipping and falling, toward the corner where he had last seen Kate and Thomas. The shelves were still against the wall but crates and display cases leaned against them. Simon started pulling objects away, throwing them back into the center of the cellar. He seized what appeared to be a mummy case and lifted it.

Kate's face looked up from beneath it. She blinked against the dust that drifted down into her eyes and stared up at Simon holding the massive sarcophagus over his head.

"Thank God." He breathed and set the mummy case aside. "Are you badly injured? Anything broken?"

"I don't think so." She turned her head slightly. "Thomas, you?"

The curator's dirty face appeared under her shoulder. "I think I'm alive. What about Mrs. Mansfield?"

Blood dripped from jagged scratches across Simon's body. He lifted Kate and set her on her feet. He then reached down and pulled Thomas up. He patted the curator on the shoulder, then glanced toward the shelf where the ebony box had been. It was clear of wreckage. Most of the objects that had been there were still present, except for the container.

Kate reached into her satchel, scrabbling for vials and kicking debris out of the way. She looked around the dark cellar, searching for attackers, and handed an *elixir vitae* to Simon.

"She's gone. She didn't want to kill us this time. She just wanted the Skin. Mind where you step, the chnoubis have left a mess." Simon stared down into one of the many large holes dug out of the cellar floor. "God help us. Nephthys has the Skin of Ra."

Thomas sat on the overturned marble head of a Roman emperor with his own head in his hands. "What do I tell my directors? I might lose my position."

"We might all lose our positions, Mr. Clover." Simon drained the elixir and slumped to the floor with a hand pressed to his chest.

Chapter 24

MALCOLM SCRATCHED IN IRRITATION AT HIS hands. It wasn't that they itched, but the thought of the magic under his flesh unnerved him. Things he had sworn he would never allow were now commonplace since he had joined Simon's band of magic knights in shining armor. From letting a werewolf live to taking alchemical elixirs to allowing Simon to inscribe him. He swore he could feel the aether moving around under his skin. Simon had inscribed everyone's hands with temporary marks that allowed a simple signal to be sent to the entire group warning them that the final event was about to occur at St. Mary Woolnoth and for everyone to converge on the church.

Penny didn't seem fazed by it. Her hands played nonchalantly with the elaborate equipment on her head as she crouched with Malcolm behind a hedge. They were inside the wall surrounding the mansion leased by Ambassador Mansfield. It was on a park-sized bit of land east of London proper. The spying pair was distant enough from the house not to be noticed among the foliage, but close enough to keep an eye on arrivals and departures. It wasn't a particularly imposing manor, but there was a huge greenhouse at the rear as high as the mansion itself constructed of darkened glass that reflected the fading sun.

The petite engineer was dressed in pants and a worn leather jacket that covered a white linen shirt. Her hair was pulled back and braided. She wore a pair of goggles she had modified just like the telescopic sight on Malcolm's now-defunct rifle. She scanned the windows of the sprawling home for movement, of which there hadn't been any for hours. Bored, she absently reached for another sandwich only to find that they were gone. Shoving the goggles up on her brow, Penny glanced down and then up at Malcolm.

"I thought you weren't hungry," she said.

Malcolm brushed the last crumbs of the crusty bread from his dark lapels. "That was six hours ago. It's hungry work watching for an Egyptian demon queen."

With a halfhearted huff, Penny dug into her satchel and produced two apples, tossing him one of them. "Here."

"How much stuff do you lug around in that bottom-less bag of yours?" He crunched into the crisp fruit. "And how do you have fresh apples in winter?"

"I have whatever I think I might need."

"Like Kate's entire larder."

"Ha, that's funny from the man who just wolfed down three sandwiches without even a single thank-you," Penny scolded. "And stop scratching at your hands."

"I can't stand this damned magic. It's like having Simon with me every second."

"Oh, you can't even feel it. You just know it's there." She then said with her voice tinged in wonder, "It was very exciting that they managed to trigger the key. The fact that I can watch it work now means I can likely create more."

Malcolm bit a worm out of the apple and spit it away. "I suppose."

"You're not impressed by the ability to travel across the globe in an instant?"

"I can travel fast enough now, thank you. What good did it do for the men who built it? Simon's father is dead. Sir Roland is gone, likely dead. All of us were almost killed by creatures searching for that key. I don't see much evidence of good coming from it."

"Well, Simon was awfully excited about it."

"He was, true enough. I hope it took his mind off the pain he's in for a moment. Maybe that's value enough, but here he is with his magic key and he looked like hell. He could barely walk." Malcolm tossed the apple core away. "And I'm sure he's right now sitting in St. Mary Woolnoth watching for Barnes if he can get enough of Kate's elixir to keep him upright."

"Kate loves him," Penny said quietly.

"Aye. And he'll break her heart one day."

"Why?" She looked surprised. "You think Simon doesn't love her?"

"Oh no. He does. But that's not enough. He doesn't appreciate how lucky he is to have her. And I don't think he knows just how far she'll go for him. That's the problem. She's a remarkable woman."

Penny crunched the apple and chewed loudly in the silence. "So, you fancy Kate?"

"No." Malcolm looked into the distance, pretending he was studying the house. "I admire her. Her strength. The fight that's in her, I've never seen the like. All she's been through. First her sister. Then Charlotte. She had to fight like hell for those two, and she did. And she was right. If there's ever a time when I could choose one person to walk into Hell with me, it would be Kate Anstruther."

"Oh." Penny threw the half-eaten apple away with all her force. "I'd choose my brother, Charles, because he knows the way out."

Malcolm looked at her. Her usual jovial expression had fallen as she studied the Mansfield residence. The way she had said the last line tugged at him. He was silent, unsure of how to approach her because, for the first time, he was worried about Penny Carter. She hadn't come out clean this venture. And while Penny seemed all right on the exterior, he knew that deep inside the damage could be festering. He knew because he was just like that. Penny was only a bit more polite about the matter.

It couldn't have been easy to face what she had faced. Malcolm wasn't sure just how well he would have taken it if his own Da had come back. Though most likely his father would have tried to smack him around, and Malcolm would have retaliated.

"I heard about your mother." Malcolm gave her a questioning glance, as if that explained everything he was thinking. "That couldn't have been easy."

Penny's expression suddenly softened. "No, but I'm fine with it. I got to see my mother one more time. She wasn't suffering anymore. She only wanted to see how Charles and I were getting on. And we got a chance to say good-bye. Proper-like." There were no tears in her eyes, only a gentle memory.

A blush came over Malcolm's pale cheeks as he realized suddenly why Penny had reached out to Simon instead of him. He could never have seen her mother's walking corpse as anything but a walking corpse. He would have dealt with it as he dealt with any monster, without thinking, without caring. His gaze fell away from her. To all appearances, he remained still only a brute in her eyes. What did he expect after his behavior with Charlotte? He couldn't blame Penny, but suddenly he felt like a lout talking about Kate. In truth, he knew who always had his back.

"I'd walk into Hell with you, Penny Carter," Malcolm admitted quietly.

Penny's eyes widened at the remark and her cheeks grew even rosier in the brisk air. She glanced away toward the house, parting the bush with her hands, changing the subject. "Are we going to wait out here all day?"

"Yes. We're only here to observe and follow them if they leave the house."

"Bugger that."

"Impatient?" he asked.

"Hungry." Penny rubbed her eyes. "Someone ate all the sandwiches. The best I can hope for is a buttered roll in the house." A steam horn blared from a boat on the Thames, which flowed nearby along one edge of the property. Penny clamped her hands over her ears. When the noise abated, she suggested, "Let's just sneak in and snatch the box."

"Demon queen," he reminded her.

"I'm not afraid of an Egyptian snake charmer."

"I am."

"You said yourself, magicians are merely humans. One good shot and it's all over."

"She has a dragon scale."

"I'll nick it and you shoot her."

Malcolm scowled at her, but he was just as antsy. He hated sitting, doing nothing.

"Without that mummy box, the Mansfields would be out of the game," she pointed out. "One less villain to deal with. We can go focus on Barnes and curing Simon."

Malcolm's jaw worked incessantly as he considered the option. "Maybe we could go in and just look around for it."

"That's the spirit!" Penny stood up. But Malcolm didn't. "What are we waiting for then?"

"Waiting for dusk."

She squinted pointedly toward the west, where the sun was a mere fan of light on the horizon.

He continued scowling. Her agitation was causing his own to stir.

She scoped out the manor with her goggles. "Which entrance are we going to use?"

Malcolm indicated a cellar door that lay on the left side of the house, barely fifty yards from the river sparkling through the trees. "With luck there will be no one down there."

"There will also be no sandwiches."

Malcolm let out a harsh sigh. "I'll buy you a bloody sandwich after."

"Done." Penny dug deep into her pack and produced a small pistol. The little weapon had a thick iron tuning fork where the hammer should've been.

Malcolm eyed it warily, knowing the engineer's penchant for contraptions. "What does that do?"

"It produces a harmonic wave."

"So it hums?"

"You'll see. I heard your guns weren't getting the job done so we should try something else."

When he raised an eyebrow in her direction, Penny indicated the heavy cartridges he carried for his Lancaster pistols. She gave her little weapon a pat and shoved it in her belt. Then dug into a pocket to produce a handful of dice. "Will we need to blind anyone?"

Malcolm couldn't help but smirk at her enthusiasm, and looked at the little cubes. "Keep them handy." With that, he rose and moved low toward the cellar door. Penny shouldered her heavy pack and chased after him. No groundskeepers challenged their approach. The estate was oddly silent as Malcolm grabbed hold of one-half of the dual cellar doors. He glanced over to Penny, who pointed her wee pistol. She gave him an excited nod as she took aim at what might lie inside. Malcolm flung them open.

A stale darkness greeted them, silent and still. The loamy smell of earth welled up into their noses. Mal-

THE UNDYING LEGION   243

colm paused to light a lantern and went first, his Lancaster pistol in his other hand. The light revealed only a hard-packed dirt floor and damp stone walls.

The light also flashed on a pile of bones, white shapes against the blackness of the earth.

Penny gasped. "Please tell me they aren't human."

"They're not." Malcolm knelt beside the heap. He lifted a bone near as long as his arm.

"What is that? A cow?"

"Or a horse."

"Horse? They were butchering a horse down here?" Her face crinkled in disgust. "Or do they have very hungry dogs?"

None of the bones had cleaver marks on them. And they weren't very old. They were clean as if they had been boiled and stripped of flesh.

"Well, there's one good thing," Penny remarked.

"What's that?"

"I've lost my appetite."

Malcolm noticed something else nearby; a hole in the ground about four feet across. He shone the light down its gullet. It went straight down about ten feet before curving horizontally. "Snake-demons. Very nasty. Let's hope we don't meet up with them."

He motioned Penny forward with him, heading deeper into the basement, looking for a way up into the house. They passed a brick slab in the corner, raised a foot off the dirt, littered with oaken casks, many holed, empty, and shoved to the side. The stone walls glistened with dampness. They were below the waterline of the nearby Thames. He wouldn't be surprised if the damn place flooded easily during heavy rains.

Penny touched his shoulder and pointed at stairs. Malcolm moved toward them, anxious to be out of the dirt-floored cellar. She stayed close on his heels as they went up. There was a closed door on the second landing. He listened for several minutes while Penny kept an eye behind them with the lantern. He tried the handle and found it was unlocked. Dim light spilled in as he opened it a crack. The hallway was empty so they darted in and quickly closed the door behind them. The corridor was simple and unadorned, likely the servants' quarters. There was no sound of activity or any smells of cooking.

They weaved their way through the maze of halls, but still no one challenged them. Malcolm almost saw disappointment on Penny's face. Anxiety rose in the Scotsman. Something wasn't right.

A staircase curved up around a corner. The engineer indicated that Malcolm should lead on. He crept up the stairs. They had no real idea where to look for the box containing the Skin of Ra. It was unlikely it would just be sitting out. No doubt it was secured somewhere safe from prying eyes. They came up on the ground level in an alcove just off the dining room. The table was set elegantly for eight, but the dishes actually had dust on them.

"Their guests are really late," Penny jested.

They quickly surveyed the room, which produced nothing, then moved to the room adjacent. It was a study with an oaken desk that was covered with immense maps. Penny pored over them, studying the locations marked.

"Cairo. Calcutta. Java," hissed Penny in amazement. "They certainly have been traveling a lot."

"Find the box." Malcolm was already rooting through the desk drawers.

Penny's tongue clucked curiously as she regarded the objects on the bookshelves. Malcolm could hear her thrilled gasp all the way across the room.

She whispered, "Do you know what this is?"

"I know it's not a box."

"It's a sextant." There was wonder in her voice.

Malcolm glanced at her curiously. "Perhaps I over-estimated your scientific knowledge."

"It's not a normal sextant. Look here." Penny pointed to a mechanism attached to the brass, boasting intricate gears and a green vial of swirling gas. "This is aether inside a compression chamber. And the aether is guiding this pointer."

"Can it find a box?"

"Blast it, you daft man! This was made by a damn fine mystical engineer."

"Better than you?"

"Let's not get irrational. This is their symbol. I've never heard of 'em." There was a small design etched into the base.

"Put the blasted thing down and help me find the box."

"All right, all right." Penny checked her pack for room, but then returned the device to its place and continued rummaging to no avail. The box was not here.

It was the same for the next four rooms, so they moved to the east wing. However, when the door opened, they stared in amazement.

"Holy," breathed Penny as she stepped inside. The vast room was empty and silent so even the barest of whispers still echoed across the chamber. "Are we still in London?"

A gigantic Egyptian temple, one to rival any true shrine nestled on the banks of the Nile, occupied the huge greenhouse. Mighty columns held up the ceiling thirty feet above their heads. The walls were lined with obelisks covered with ancient script and Egyptian carvings. Colors were rich enough to be breathtaking, with yellows that glittered like gold and blues that could match any desert sky.

A dais, like an altar, occupied the middle of the chamber. It was raised ten feet off the floor. Candles and urns surrounded it, all lit and smoldering as if someone had just left or was about to arrive.

"I'm going for a closer look." Malcolm stepped forward but had to stop Penny with a strong hand as she moved with him. "Stay here." His foot sank into sand. The Mansfields had re-created the Egyptian desert inside this greenhouse. He felt exposed in the open chamber. The eyes of the paintings on the wall seemed to follow him as he walked toward the altar. He told himself the room was empty. He climbed onto the platform around the dais. The altar's top was hollowed out slightly.

He was about to wave Penny forward when a door opened on the far side of the temple chamber. Malcolm leapt from the dais and sprinted back to Penny. He slid the last six feet back to her as she crouched anxiously behind a great lotus pillar. She made to exclaim something, but Malcolm motioned her to silence. Penny bit her lower lip tight and pulled him in close beside her.

Far across the sandy floor, Mr. Mansfield and Nephthys entered. The ambassador held a whiskey decanter in his hands along with a glass filled to the brim. The decanter was less than half-full, suggesting he was well into an inebriated state. Nephthys wore a long black cloak that swept the floor. She looked very much like a goddess painted onto an ancient tomb. Nephthys clutched the ebony box tightly against her chest. The box shuddered violently. Whatever was inside was trying to get out.

The demon queen marched purposefully to the dais and climbed up two steps. She set the box on the altar, and her lips moved, whispering to the agitated thing within. Her bluish hand opened and closed in an odd motion, almost as if she were signaling. The sand floor of the chamber suddenly undulated and a mound like a burrowing animal came at extraordinary speed straight at her. A second mound appeared and roared toward the altar from another direction. They both stopped at the base of the dais. She held out her hand, palm downward. The mounds shivered and two large shapes rose, with sand pouring off them.

Penny nearly gasped at the sight of the huge snake-creatures. Malcolm placed a calming hand on her arm with a confidence he did not feel.

Chapter 25

NEPHTHYS GATHERED HER DARK CLOAK CLOSER
about her like a shroud and spoke to her husband without looking at him. "Do try not to drink yourself into
oblivion just yet. Too much depends on our success."

Mr. Mansfield drained the glass of whiskey in his
hand, but he dutifully placed the glass and decanter on
a bust of Hathor. Nephthys scowled at his irreverence.

"Eternity beckons me." Nephthys gazed out over the
temple. "I am the lynchpin of his endeavor."

Mansfield's face boiled red. "Without me, my dear,
you wouldn't be able to accomplish your work. Or his."

"Yes, yes. You've been a valuable commodity, like a
wagon or a coal scuttle. You must be so proud."

Mansfield sneered drunkenly and his drawl grew ever
more rustic. "Don't forget, I'm the one who spent years
with him traveling out in the wilds of the Louisiana Ter-
ritory. I stood around while he dug in the dirt and
picked up rocks and talked to every damn Indian he
could find. Now, I've always been interested in the ar-
cane. I saw root doctors down South do some mysterious things. But I saw Gaios do things that even New
Orleans witches said only God could do."

From behind their column, Penny gaped at Malcolm

with wide eyes and mouthed the word "Gaios." The hunter tried to look unshaken, but lifted his pistol and took comfort in its weight.

Nephthys regarded Ambassador Mansfield with surprise. "So, tool, do you know what Gaios is planning?"

"Honey, I got no idea what he's planning. Just like you don't know. He doesn't tell anyone what he's thinking. We all have jobs and he puts it all together. We're just the pawns that run around helping him gather his precious artifacts like"—he jabbed an accusatory finger at the simple box—"that damn thing."

"Which I found for him." Nephthys stroked the ebony box.

"Well, most of what he has now, I bought for him. He owes me."

She waved dismissively. "If that's all you care about, you'll get what you're owed. Once he settles his score here in Britain, we'll all get what we're owed. Now be quiet. Your sniping pains my head. I must prepare. I need utter silence to meditate."

The ambassador laughed with contempt before falling against an elaborately carved column. "I could use some entertainment about now. Please proceed with whatever production you are going to undertake."

Nephthys glared at him, joined by the snake-creatures, whose narrow eyes bored into Mansfield. "Careful, Ambassador. My chnoubis don't care for you. Perhaps less than I."

"I'm not afraid of your pets. I've dealt with snakes my whole life. Get on with it."

The black shape of Nephthys drifted around the dais almost as if she floated. "This magic is only revealed to the high priests of Ra."

"So you're a high priest of Ra now?" Mr. Mansfield threw his head back and guffawed. "You're a miserable conjurer who got famous because Pendragon threw you in prison. And the only reason you act so important is because you're the only one willing to risk using the Skin of Ra. Not even Gaios himself would do it. That either makes you the most stalwart or the most foolish."

"It is my birthright. I am of the ancient sands of Egypt."

"You were born in 1713. Now, I admit, you've got a fine figure for a woman of your age, but I know you're the fifth *Nephthys*. So stop acting like some kind of old pharaoh come to life."

Nephthys ignored him. She took a position at the altar and dropped the cloak from her shoulders. The woman stood naked. She was well formed, a bit plump, with disconcerting azure flesh. Mansfield looked at her without interest as she lifted the lid of the ebony chest. "You witness the birth of Ra at your own peril."

Malcolm studied her naked form but only to confirm there was no glowing dragonscale flitting over her. She was not wearing her protective necklace. The time had come.

Mansfield staggered drunkenly across the sandy floor and clambered up onto the dais with heavy grunts. Nephthys kept her head held high with worshipful poise, facing the altar. The chnoubis shivered ominously. Nephthys nodded at them and the snake-creatures settled.

A pistol shot rang loud in the chamber and Nephthys gasped as a bullet struck her in the chest. Blood sprayed over Mansfield's white shirt. He spun about, showing a long dagger in his hand and a look of surprise on his face.

Nephthys didn't scream; she groaned, almost in pleasure. Blood dribbled down over her stomach. Her legs quivered. She leaned forward to let a stream of blood trickle from the tip of her breast into the wooden box.

Malcolm stepped from hiding, and the chamber echoed

with roaring pistols and filled with clouds of smoke. The chnoubis' bodies jerked wildly in the hail of bullets. Mansfield leapt for the floor.

Malcolm then heard a strange guttural tongue reverberate through the room. Nephthys's mouth was moving, but the voice seemed to be emanating from the ebony chest. The air in the chamber became suddenly arid and hot like a true Egyptian desert. Something appeared at the rim of the box.

A small white snake.

No, he realized. It was a ragged strip of linen curling out of the box, up into the air, as if alive. Both sides of the yellowish cloth were covered in hieroglyphs that seemed to glow with a dim light. It rose on its own power several feet over the waiting Nephthys. It quivered, then it started to pour over her naked body like a stream of water from a fountain. It slithered along her arms and legs, fluttering as if caught in a desert whirlwind.

Malcolm continued his barrage. Penny stood beside him, firing with her smaller four-barreled pistol. Lead balls seemed to pass around the swirling aura, smashing the temple walls and columns behind Nephthys. The flashing linen tightened around the woman's body, wrapping each thigh, her stomach, and chest. The hieroglyphs on the linen grew brighter. As it climbed along her shoulders, Nephthys's expression changed from intense pleasure to discomfort, then terror. She started to scream, but the cloth filled her mouth. Energy seemed to boil out of her and feed the Skin of Ra as it slid over her wide, panicked eyes. And then she was totally encased.

The air turned desiccated. Malcolm's throat was bone dry and his skin felt like it was ready to crack. Penny slid her empty gun into her belt, coughing against the dryness, and pulled out the small pistol with the tuning fork.

The room was deathly silent. Then the mummy moved. An arm. A leg. Even though her eyes were no longer visible, the thing's head turned slowly to stare at the pair of intruders.

"What do we do?" Penny shifted nervously under the mummy's gaze.

"Kill it if we can." He holstered one pistol and drew a dagger.

The hieroglyphs on the linen flared and the mummy lifted her arms. Cloth shot out from her fingers and seized Malcolm and Penny around their chests. Malcolm sliced at the linen, but with no effect. He roared as his hands seared with pain. Penny cried out as well. The mummy lifted them off the ground and flung them at the chnoubis.

The snake-creatures seized the Scotsman and the engineer, claws digging into the soft flesh of their shoulders. Mansfield strode beneath the bizarre figure of Nephthys.

He pointed at Malcolm. "I've seen you with Simon Archer at the Red Orchid. So you're with Barnes? A toady of Ash? Well, too bad for you. Your master's scheme is at an end."

"Ash?" Penny said in renewed confusion. "How did Ash get involved in this? And we're not with Barnes; we thought *you* were."

"Stupid girl. You've got no idea what's happening."

"If you don't serve Barnes," Malcolm snarled, "why did Nephthys try to kill us?"

"We want the idiot to succeed in his ritual." Mansfield laughed at them. He climbed back onto the dais, eyeing the motionless mummy. He took the ebony box and put it under his arm. Then he hopped back down. "My dear, let's be off. Mr. Barnes will soon take action to complete his summoning, and we don't want to miss the party."

"Wait!" Penny called desperately. "We can tell you how to defeat Barnes."

Mansfield laughed again. The mummified Nephthys started toward a door that led outside, walking stiffly as if the wrapping drove the body inside like a puppet. Through the heavy glass of the vast greenhouse that enclosed the temple, a carriage was visible waiting outside. The ambassador pointed at the shambling mummy. "Thank you, but I already have the means to defeat Mr. Barnes. Now that I have her, there's nothing he can make that I can't unmake."

"Goddamned blood magic," Malcolm growled. "I finally get to shoot someone and it actually helps them."

"What are you going to do with us?" Penny demanded as the ambassador walked away.

Mansfield looked back from the doorway, then smiled malevolently at the chnoubis. "Devour them." He slammed the door shut and in an instant their carriage rattled away.

The chnoubis holding Malcolm opened its jaw wide. Penny twisted, raising her clenched fist. "Close your eyes!" She crushed the two dice together in her hand and threw them.

Even with his eyes shut, Malcolm sensed the bright flare. Clawed hands released him and he lurched forward a few steps. He opened his eyes to see the chnoubis grasping their faces. Malcolm and Penny ducked past the blinded snake-creatures and raced for the door where they had entered. Malcolm paused to scoop up his Lancaster and dagger. He kicked open the door and they left the Egyptian temple for the mundane hallway of a London mansion. Behind them, the chnoubis surged unsteadily forward.

Penny whirled and brought up her little gun. It began

to vibrate. Within seconds, the hum built to a crescendo and she pulled the trigger. The staggering discharge plowed a swathe through the temple columns as wide as a London lane and propelled Penny back against Malcolm. The vibration filled the corridor, making Malcolm grab his ears in pain. Suddenly the deafening crash of breaking glass washed over them and a wave of yellow dust poured out the door as the temple collapsed and debris sealed the chamber.

Malcolm grabbed the coughing Penny and dragged her with him down the hallway. They passed countless empty rooms, working their way to the front of the house. He heard scratching sounds coming from behind the walls.

"Look out!" He shouted as timber and plaster exploded in front of them.

From the rubble rose one of the chnoubis. The beast attacked, tossing wreckage aside. Malcolm charged it and stabbed directly into its throat with his knife. He buried the blade to the hilt. With a cry of rage, Malcolm drove the blade downward, slicing through the flesh and tearing a gash in the thing's abdomen.

"Come on!" Penny lifted a chair and threw it through a dark window. She then kicked out the remnants of the sharp glass. However, a shape slithered outside and a chnoubis reached for her. She ducked the swipe.

Malcolm leapt between them, blasting with his Lancaster, each shell forcing the beast back. "Go down!" he commanded.

They pounded down the stairs to the servants' quarters, where more empty halls greeted them. There was a crash ahead of them and one of the chnoubis smashed through the ceiling and dropped to the floor in a shower of wood. It rose up in front of Malcolm, towering over the man, with its oily skin twitching. Its body swayed like a cobra.

Malcolm backed up, taking Penny with him. She screamed when the other creature came slithering down the stairwell after them. Its rubbery body thudded down each step. Despite the trail of blood it left, it looked spry as ever.

Penny ran for the one exit left to them: the cellar. Malcolm tried to stop her, but it was too late. The chnoubis charged and he had no choice but to chase the engineer down into the darkness. On the final stone step, he whirled around to aim up at their monstrous pursuers but none came.

"Why didn't they come after us?" Penny asked in a breathless voice.

Malcolm suspected but didn't tell her. They were deeper in the earth now, and the creatures could be all around them. They could strike from nearly any direction although hopefully the stone walls would give some protection. He knew now what the bones were from. They were the regurgitated meals of these monstrosities. The disgusting things had herded Malcolm and Penny right to their feeding grounds.

They ran across the cellar, heading for the outside door. Behind them, explosions of earth sent the lower half of the wooden stairs crumbling in a shower of dust, leaving the upper floors now out of reach.

Malcolm and Penny kept charging for the exit. The ground rocked beneath them. The stone steps ahead cracked and shifted. Then the wall itself split into pieces and tumbled in a roar, burying the cellar door. Penny slid to a halt, staring at the pile of rubble that had been their last escape route. The moving mounds in the dirt burrowed across the cellar floor until they touched, then arms burst into the air followed by horrible heads and torsos.

"Cover your ears!" Penny aimed her pistol. She fired

and a rippling wave of pressure rolled across the ground like a swell on the ocean and broke against the snake-things. One of them shook its thick-maned head, disoriented. Penny fired again. The second breaching chnoubis slammed against the ground, screeching in pain.

She cheered and ran forward. However, the first creature recovered and lunged. Penny flung herself back, falling to the ground to stare up in terror at the chnoubis looming over her. The monster stooped and clamped a clawlike hand on the girl's stomach.

Malcolm hurtled against the chnoubis. The beast was thick and strong but felt boneless. It shuddered from the impact and brought its arms up to seize him. He had to drop the dagger, grabbing the thing's wrists to keep the claws away from his head. He felt pressure around his legs and a quick glance showed a fleshy tail wrapping around his calves. The sickly weight tightened. His legs were squeezed together with a crushing pressure. The chnoubis snapped at him; its teeth came inches short of Malcolm's head.

A slim piece of metal protruded out of the creature's stomach. The monster reacted with surprise, briefly looking down at it. Then the chnoubis screamed and thrashed. Malcolm fell back onto the ground. His Lancaster was in his hand and he emptied the weapon into the exposed wound. The gun glowed hot orange in the darkness of the cellar. The thing screeched and slumped over, warm liquid gushing onto the ground.

Penny stood behind it, Malcolm's dripping knife in her hand.

"Hellfire, that's disgusting!" Penny declared, inspecting her own spattered clothes.

"I thought I told you to stay put," Malcolm growled.

She thought for a moment, then shook her head. "No. You didn't."

"I meant to."

Malcolm drew his second pistol, searching for the other chnoubis. From out of the darkness, he felt a thunderous clout to his shoulder. He rolled to his feet, spitting dirt. The creature raked at him again. Malcolm dodged the blow, slipped in, and placed the barrel of his weapon against its abdomen, pulling the trigger and opening a fusillade that echoed through the cellar.

The chnoubis flung itself back, then flopped facedown onto the ground, vomiting up the corrosive acid. Then it quickly brought its arms forward in a flurry of powerful activity. It opened a hole beneath it and the massive thing began to undulate into the earth, slapping at Malcolm with the blunt end of its tail before disappearing with a slurping sound. The Scotsman turned to see that the other creature had burrowed away as well.

"Malcolm," Penny shouted, and ran for the raised brick platform in the corner. She climbed over barrels and jammed her back to the wall.

Malcolm staggered up and dropped next to her. His ragged breathing was the only echoing sound in the vast chamber. He felt better with something solid under and behind him.

Two mounds started to rise on either side of the room. The chnoubis broke the surface in a spray of dirt and stared quietly at the two humans huddled on the brick island.

Malcolm reloaded one of his pistols, but then cracked the breech of the second weapon and patted his pockets. "I don't suppose you have any ammunition in your bottomless bag."

Penny pulled the satchel off her back and dug out more cartridges. "I knew you'd run out. You waste bullets."

Malcolm grumbled as he slipped the shells in. "Monsters are hard to kill."

One of the chnoubis dove under the earth. In a second, they felt a bump from under the bricks.

Penny stared intently at the walls. She pressed her hand against the stone and asked, "Can you swim?"

He regarded her curiously. "Aye."

Her face held a wild, reckless grin. She gestured with her little pistol with the tuning fork atop. "The river is just that way and we're below the water level." She held up her damp fingers.

"What good does that do us? We can't get to the river." He cursed as the brick slab shifted slightly and the mortar started to crack.

"I'm going to bring the river to us. Brace me." Penny pointed her pistol at the damp wall and pulled the trigger.

Malcolm sat against the satchel strapped to her back and pressed his feet against the bricks. Vibrations ran through him like an earthquake. His ears rang and his head swam. A glance over his shoulder showed that Penny's incredible weapon was blasting the stone wall to pieces, throwing chips of rock into the air. Finally it tore through the stone and started pounding dark earth. Wet soil flew. The wave of sound smashed deeper into the ground and smoke boiled out of the tunnel Penny was creating. The wee pistol was as effective as a heavy mining drill.

Penny's outstretched arms quaked. Her teeth were clamped together as if her jaw would shatter. Malcolm could imagine the beating she was taking because he could hardly stand the violent vibrations he felt coming through her. His foot slipped, kicking out shards of red brick. The platform was shattering beneath them.

The vibrations ceased and smoke no longer roiled out of the shallow cave. Penny dropped her arms. She gasped for breath and a trickle of blood ran from one ear. She fiddled awkwardly with the tuning fork. She shouted,

"Out of range," but he barely heard her through the throbbing in his head.

Bricks rattled from beneath and popped up into the air. Malcolm leapt to his feet and took Penny by the arm. They pushed past the jagged remnants of the foundation wall and crowded into the dark cave she had just created. The ground was muddy with trickling rivulets of water seeping around their shoes. They reached the end of the cave, only twenty feet from the cellar. Penny took a deep breath and raised the pistol again. When she pulled the trigger, nothing happened.

"No!" she shouted and began to manipulate the gun.

The dirt wall erupted and two arms jutted into the tunnel. Clawed hands seized Penny. She screamed, trying to pull away. Malcolm fired as a monstrous torso emerged.

Clods of muddy earth smacked into him from behind and he knew the second chnoubis was coming. Penny's arm and shoulder had nearly been swallowed in the muddy wall. Malcolm grabbed hold of the fleshy mane on the fearsome head and pulled it to him with all his strength. He laid the muzzle of his Lancaster against the skull and held the trigger down. The barrel spun and fired ball after ball into the creature's cranium. The shells penetrated into pulpy flesh but did not seem to do it damage.

"Die, you miserable soddin' beast!" he screamed.

Penny punched frantically with her free hand, but the thing would not let go. Then claws clamped on Malcolm's shoulders from behind, dragging him away from Penny. The hot breath from the monster's gaping wide mouth washed over him. Penny's dire scream cut through him. He wished he could spare her from such a horrible death, but he couldn't do that for either of them.

Abruptly the earth groaned and a jet of hard water slammed Malcolm. Then another shot out and another.

Mud cascaded and the earth yawned open with a torrent of water. He scrambled for Penny, but couldn't feel her as he was swept back into the cellar. He fought through the icy flood, kicking to the frothy surface. The roof of the cellar was only a few feet overhead. He whipped around wildly searching again for Penny, but she was gone. Then he remembered that bloody great satchel on her back.

The chnoubis were in full panic, flailing about violently, their meal forgotten in a desperate scramble to stay afloat and breathe. Malcolm ignored the terrified demons, got his bearings, took a deep breath, and dove down into the murk in search of Penny. He desperately flung about trying to find her. There was no visibility, and his coat weighed him down. His lungs screamed and his body grew thick in the frigid embrace of the river. Then a hand grabbed his.

Penny.

Countless objects in the dark water struck Malcolm. He wanted to draw a breath; he couldn't hold it. Only the faint touch of Penny reminded him to kick harder and bear down for another second. And then another.

The color of the water lightened and together they struggled for the brightness. They surged into the air and gasped loudly, sucking in breath for long minutes. He could see the lights of boats bobbing on the Thames.

Malcolm looked back and took fierce satisfaction watching the water of the river lapping at the nearest corner of the great house. Then the mansion started to sink into the marshy ground. He couldn't hear the sound of the collapse over the roar of the river and the pounding of his own ears, but he saw the chimneys begin to topple in sprays of bricks and dust. He contemplated a rude gesture to the vanishing house. Instead, he turned his complete attention to swimming for his life.

"I had to dump my pack." Penny was sputtering and furious. "All I managed to save was my gun."

"That little beauty saved our lives. I'll display it on a bloody shelf."

When they finally heaved themselves up into the reeds, they collapsed, shivering and exhausted. They felt weighed down with numb limbs and sodden clothes. Malcolm lifted his hand, but he no longer felt the aether beneath his skin. He rubbed at it.

Penny saw what he was about and tried to activate the rune on her hands. She regarded Malcolm with a stunned face. "The magic is gone."

"Mine too." Malcolm helped Penny to her feet and they started limping away. "We need to warn Simon. He's going to be apoplectic when he finds out there's another monster to fight. Hard to see how this will end well."

Chapter 26

SIMON AND KATE STOOD ACROSS LOMBARD Street from St. Mary Woolnoth, studying the crowd for any sign of Rowan Barnes. A slow stream of coats and bonnets and walking sticks entered the church, which was aglow with lamplight.

Simon's vision swam so he took another swallow of *elixir vitae*. Pain still knifed in his chest so he sent a surge of aether through his body, which drowned out the fire for a short time.

"Do you think Barnes would attempt something during a service?" Kate shifted the leather bandolier draped over her shoulder under her coat. She also adjusted the short sword she had strapped tight along her thigh.

"There's something stirring the aether. Something large."

Suddenly she stiffened and seized Simon's arm. "That man just by the front column on our side."

Simon stared into the black morass of churchgoers. As shapes shifted, he caught a glimpse of a face beneath the wide brim of a hat. It was a slight profile, but the cut of the chin and the line of the nose suggested the figure of Rowan Barnes.

"You're right." They angled for him but the man disappeared among the crowd. Simon pressed his hands together, which sparked a quick flash of aether. "That should bring everyone. Come, the north gallery will give us a better view of the church."

Simon began to push as they passed the doors and went up the stairs. They filed out onto the gallery overlooking the main floor. They found two places on the front row. The sanctuary was dim despite the many glowing candles and the massive chandeliers. The proper occupants filed into the box pews, greeting those around them.

St. Mary Woolnoth was a cube, without much of the traditional cross shape of most churches. It was larger than it seemed from the outside, but still not a huge church by any stretch. The corners of the space were dominated by groups of white Corinthian columns. The altar at the eastern end was covered in a purple cloth, with its candles still unlit. On the wall behind it was the noticeable reredos, a huge replica of the Ten Commandment tablets. The central ceiling was raised into another cube, with windows on all four sides.

Simon and Kate sat together, viewing the crowd below them. The church filled with parishioners and hushed chatter reverberated around their ears. Simon checked his watch as time passed with agonizing slowness.

Kate pointed across the church at Hogarth and Charlotte, who filed into the opposite gallery. Charlotte was smiling with excitement. Hogarth watched her carefully. He sat in the front row and Charlotte went to the rail and leaned over, staring down into the crowd. They were both dressed in somewhat proper fashion, but they had obviously come hurriedly from the rooms Simon had let nearby, where they had intended to stage their shifts watching St. Mary Woolnoth.

Kate waved her arm to the disdain of two maiden aunts sitting nearby. Charlotte's face lit up and she waved back eagerly. Hogarth noticed too and a look of relief washed over him at the sight of Kate and Simon.

Hogarth pulled Charlotte back to the pew. They whispered to each other. Simon and Kate continued to scan the congregation, searching for a sign of Barnes or any of his women. It was difficult to see faces in the gloom below.

"I hope Malcolm and Penny can get here," Kate said.

Simon grunted quietly. "They're a long distance away."

The organ roared to life and a procession emerged from a door beside the altar and began to circle the church. A curate with a smoking censer led the way, followed by young robed boys with massive candles. A churchman carried a tall silver cross and another a large Bible. And finally the rector came in his white cassock with purple surplice. His hands were clasped before him. They made their way around the church, then moved back up the center aisle. The incense wafted up and filled the air. The boys lit the candles on the altar. Then the rector kissed the Bible and placed it open on the purple frontal. The other churchmen withdrew as the reverend stood with his back to the congregation, arms outstretched, robe draping like wings.

"You, Christ, are the king of glory, the eternal son of the Father. When you took our flesh to set us free, you humbly chose the virgin's womb. You overcame the sting of death and opened the kingdom of Heaven to all believers. You are seated at God's right hand in glory. Let us pray."

All heads bowed.

Simon's line of sight was invaded by a small figure on the floor beneath him. A tall woman in a long cloak with a prim bonnet emerged from underneath the gallery where he sat. She walked quickly toward the altar and shrugged off her mantle to reveal her nude body. She tossed her bonnet to one side, revealing long red hair cascading down her back. In her right hand was a glinting serrated dagger.

The congregation stirred in shock and surprise.

Simon leapt from the gallery. He landed lightly onto the back of a pew amidst a crowd who were already rising and jostling one another. Far ahead of him, the woman shoved the unprepared rector aside and began to climb onto the altar. The congregation flooded into the aisles in confusion, streaming for the main door in a crush.

Simon jumped into the air, rising above the growing sea of chaos. Several struggling parishioners knocked him aside as he came down again onto another pew. He tried to keep his feet, watching the woman on the altar lie flat on her back. Her knife caught the candlelight.

As Simon began to spring forward again, he was held fast. The wound over his heart roared like he'd been shot with a musket ball. The spell on Simon's lips faltered and he fell hard onto the wooden bench. Pain racked his body, causing his vision to blur. Doubling over, through the haze he saw Rowan Barnes grasping his ankle.

"I am sick to death of you!" Barnes snarled. "Britain is depending on me. Albion must rise."

Simon tasted bile and fought to push himself up. He tried in vain to focus. If Barnes was close enough to touch him, he could be struck. If only Simon could fight through the pain. His limbs grew numb and empty noise roared in his ears.

Then the pain vanished, leaving him sweating and facedown on the wooden pew. A slight turn of his head revealed Barnes reeling above him. Simon caught a glimpse of Kate behind the necromancer with an expression set in ferocious anger and her left fist cocked back for a finishing blow.

Simon whispered a spell and reached to where Barnes

still held his ankle. He wrenched the fingers free and proceeded to crush the man's hand. The snapping bones sounded like dry twigs.

Simon looked at the altar. The woman held a serrated dagger above her chest, blade pointed down. She paused, as if waiting for an order from Barnes. Simon searched for Charlotte, who was crawling along the edge of the gallery with her shoes kicked off. "Charlotte! Stop her!"

The girl smiled and threw her head back. She loped down the gallery rail passing through patches of light and dark until the flashes of shadow on her body were permanent because of sprouting fur. Her arms and back tore free of her dress. Her face grew dark and savage, no longer human. Screams pierced the melee of the fleeing crowd, pointing up at the creature that leapt for the altar in a long lunge through empty space, suspended in midair, stretched out like an animal going for the kill. Girlish fingers turned long and gnarled and clawed.

The great beast landed hard on the altar, crouching atop the nude woman. Charlotte's massive hand slapped the dagger aside, sending it spiraling against the Ten Commandments. The woman lying beneath the were-wolf was undisturbed by the slavering thing over her. She was nearly catatonic, her eyelids quivering. Hogarth dropped from the gallery and fought to Charlotte's side at the altar.

Simon heard Kate cry out. Barnes had driven an elbow into her face and she toppled out of sight. Simon's strength was still with him and he landed the handle of his walking stick against the side of the necromancer's head. The man went spinning to the ground, dark blood spurting from his nose and mouth. The necromancer turned back to Simon and cursed. The word delivered a burst of searing pain, which slammed Simon against the seat.

Kate brought her sword up into the light, but Barnes

knocked it aside, and called out a word in a strained voice. She fell back, screaming as if engulfed in flames.

Simon was on him, brutal fingers around the man's throat, digging in so hard that Barnes's face began to turn purple. "Release her! Remove your influence from her, or I'll tear your head off!"

Barnes stared fearfully at Simon and waved a quivering hand at Kate. She gasped with relief and shook her head to clear it. Simon yanked Barnes to his feet. The necromancer was surprisingly spry. Barnes was no doubt struggling to use his powers to hold back the damage and pain.

Charlotte and Hogarth stood before the altar, preparing to come to Simon and Kate's defense. The prospective bride dropped off the back of the altar and crawled toward the reredos to retrieve her knife. The manservant spun and seized the hopeful sacrifice by the wrist. The naked woman struggled and screamed. Hogarth wrenched the dagger away and held her tight around the waist.

"No! No! Don't stop me! It's not fair!" She looked up at Hogarth with a tear-streaked face and mewled like a child begging for a toy. "Give me my knife. Give it to me!" She dissolved into a shuddering wreck, with fingers outstretched to her dagger. As Hogarth started to slip off his coat to cover the woman, she cried, "Please don't take this from me."

"Hogarth! Get her out!" Simon called. "Charlotte! Close the doors, please, and block them. No one comes back inside."

The beast dashed down the aisle and the last few stragglers screamed and thrashed their way outside as she came toward them. Charlotte waited for Hogarth to carry the woman to the main door. He set her on her feet and spoke to a panicked elderly woman trying to get out. The matron listened and looked at the shocked young woman in a disarrayed state of dress. The well-dressed older woman put an arm around the stunned victim and led her out, whispering sympathetic words as they went. The booming sound of Charlotte and the manservant shutting the great doors silenced the commotion outside.

Simon shook Barnes like a hound with a rabbit. "After all the horrors you've perpetrated, nothing I could do to you is too much."

"You've done all you can now, you idiot. If you don't allow that woman to sacrifice herself, you are damning every man, woman, and child in Britain."

Simon snarled sarcastically, "I'm not disposed to allow murder."

"It isn't murder, as you can see. It's sacrifice in its purest form. A soldier for their crown. A parent for their child. A love true enough to give your life for the life of others. Something you will never understand."

Kate rounded on the smug necromancer. "If your goal is so noble, why aren't you man enough to take part? If you need a final sacrifice to finish your ritual, why not kill yourself? It's easier to slaughter helpless young women? You're a coward."

"Shut up!" Barnes screeched with surprising venom. "I won't have you above all questioning me. Your father knew what Gaios was all about. He even tried to uncover Gaios's scheme himself. He sacrificed enough of his comrades hunting down allies of Gaios. He had the knowledge and ability, and I begged him to help me, but he was too good to sully himself with me. And you notice he isn't here in Britain now that that madman is coming back to destroy us all. The great Sir Roland!" Barnes gave a wet, derisive cackle, blood bubbling in his mouth. "If he had done his duty, none of this would have been necessary."

Kate felt her rage building. "How do you have the temerity to speak of my father, you murderous troll?"

"I knew your father long before you were born. He was vain and selfish, but you're worse. You live among his greatness, and you can manage nothing but to stand in his shadow." He nodded toward Simon. "Or in *his*."

Kate saw the necromancer's eyes flick toward her with a bitter coldness. It wasn't just that Barnes was a murderer or that he was mad; Kate saw now that he was truly a monster. There was an odd hesitation in his movements, not in the general actions of his limbs, but she noted a peculiarity in the way his features altered with emotion. When he spoke angrily, his mouth moved with an odd sluggishness, as if he was laboring. His skin was slightly waxy. But more, Kate felt a flitting consciousness looking out from his eyes that was not part of him. She got an overwhelming sense of watching a puppet. She whispered in a sharp breath. "You aren't Rowan Barnes. You're Ash."

Barnes sneered. "I may have underestimated you. You're right, Miss Anstruther. Rowan Barnes has been dead for nearly three months. It has been getting more difficult to preserve the illusion of life, even for me. I've had to keep him just this side of death with some breath and some pulse. Fortunately, I won't need him after tonight." Barnes, or Ash, turned slightly in Simon's death grip. "I implore you, Archer. The need for this ritual is greater than you could imagine, and the risks of its failure are apocalyptic. Grace North told you this. I am doing the work of Byron Pendragon."

Simon stared into the dead eyes of the necromancer. "What power is hidden here?"

"Four ancients: Luvah, Tharmas, Urizon, Urthona. They are the shattered life force of the great god Albion from a time before. Pendragon called them from their banishment and bound them here, to wait his call. Their power is so great, Blake sensed it although he didn't fully understand it." Ash's eyes were ablaze with righteous surety. "Still, even that doddering old poet knew that Albion was the savior of this land, of the world. This ritual must be completed. You understand the way of things. The path of magic is not always black-and-white. This is no longer an issue for mortals. I am dicing with the power of gods because that is what is needed to stop Gaios. You have no idea what that fiend might do."

Simon could barely speak due to his rage. "Your game comes to an end tonight."

"You are destroying your own world!" the necromancer screamed.

"Pity."

Ash dropped her head in apparent defeat, but Simon felt a sudden lance of pain. His chest flared with agony and he doubled over, hearing himself scream. Kate shouted something as he was slammed over the low wooden barrier into the pews. He saw Ash racing for the front of the church.

The necromancer jumped onto the altar in full stride, sank her puppet to its knees, and grasped the sacrificial dagger lying there. She fell back against the altar and plunged the blade into Barnes's chest, driving it in up to the hilt. She curled over the wound and gave a final deep push of the knife. Barnes's body then sank flat as his last breath finally escaped.

Simon and Kate reached the altar. Thick blood welled around the knife's guard, spreading out over Barnes's unmoving torso. The necromancer's eyes were frozen wide. Simon carefully placed a hand on the chest of Barnes's body, then the throat. He probed with his fingers. "If he wasn't before, he's dead now."

A drop of black blood dripped onto the altar. A geyser of white erupted and Simon found himself skidding across the floor to smash against the pews. Papers and candles were tossed everywhere. The church filled with the sound of glass from shattered windows dropping to the floor.

Simon felt strong hands under his arms and flinched in shock at the hairy, clawed fingers he saw. Charlotte lifted him to his feet like a doll. He pulled himself from the unnerving grip of the werewolf. "Thank you, Charlotte."

The altar was surrounded in light like a waterfall flowing up. Simon tried to approach, but he felt enormous pressure pushing him back. His head ached from the sheer force of it. Kate was crouched where she had been tossed, her arm thrown before her face as if weathering a gale. Hogarth fought his way up beside his mistress to protect her from the deluge.

In addition to the strange eldritch power flowing out of the altar, Simon could see the aether gathering in the air. The greenish wisps were thickening into streams. The mystical event was pulling aether across space to this spot in London.

On top of the altar, Ash stirred with palsied wildness like a marionette. Eyes seemed unfocused, but the body still looked around at the torrent of power. "Blood enough at least."

Ash seized the hilt of the dagger and pulled it from her own chest. Barnes's body sloughed off a tattered jacket and tore open the shirt, baring the muscular torso. She shoved aside a thin chain around her neck and plunged the dagger into her side, betraying no pain or feeling. With both hands working the knife, she sliced through the heavy muscle of the chest, cutting a long incision from the side of the rib cage to the breastbone. With almost disinterested precision, she began to cut up between pectoral muscles.

Simon spoke a word and a rune glowed on his arm. Bracing against the solid form of Charlotte behind him, he slapped his palm to the floor and unleashed a colossal shock wave up the aisle. It smashed tiles into the air along its path until it reached the roaring altar, where as he watched in disbelief, it dissipated into nothing.

Simon rose with another whispered word, sending runic strength into his limbs. He tried to force his way toward the white flood covering the altar. Charlotte was at his side, on all fours, gripping the flagstones with her claws, dragging her powerful frame along with him. Her head twisted from side to side, growling. The ancient wind blasting into them felt like a Harmattan from the desert, driving sharp pricks of unseen sand into both man and monster. Slowly they inched into the maelstrom.

Ash dug fingers into the gash in the body's flesh and began to pull open the chest. Pinkish muscles and yellowish connective tissue showed clearly under the separating skin. There were hints of white bone from the ribs. In the midst of the exposed gore, the knot of Barnes's heart was visible, but still as the grave.

Ash struggled to get some view of her unprotected heart. She ripped the chain free of her neck and took the gold signet ring in her hand. She pressed it into the heart. There was a small curl of smoke. With a faint wet voice, she said, "Rise."

Ash looked toward Simon. A pleased smile forced itself onto the slack face. The necromancer pulled the ring away from the dead heart and the rush of power around the altar instantly vanished. Simon and Charlotte both toppled forward onto the floor as if a wall had disappeared.

Simon gained his feet and he heard Kate's voice shout in the sudden silence. Behind the altar, a ghostly figure stood in the darkness.

Simon saw another specter pass through the south wall behind Kate. Then a third walked shimmering between the columns on the north side. Charlotte touched Simon's arm and he saw the wolf girl staring toward their rear. A final spirit passed through the main doors and began to drift up the aisle. All four specters then converged toward the altar, where Ash sat with Barnes's chest cut open and branded heart exposed. The necromancer waited.

Chapter 27

THERE WAS SOMETHING OMINOUS ABOUT THE four specters that told one to step aside. Simon, Kate, Hogarth, and Charlotte gathered at the corner of the front pew box. They watched in curious awe as the uncanny figures walked purposefully toward the altar.

There was nothing clearly male or female about the four spirits. One second they were old and wise, the next young and fierce. The hard features of a man or the soft curves of a woman. They were all things at all times. The spirits glowed as if the light that glimmered around them was a slit into Heaven.

"Who are they?" Hogarth asked in a hushed whisper.

"They are pieces of the god Albion," Kate replied.

Charlotte asked, "Are they good or bad?"

"Good or bad doesn't enter into it. They are beyond such frivolities." Simon grimaced from the pain thudding in his chest. "That's why it's unwise to summon such things."

Kate asked, "What should we do?"

All faces turned to Simon. He stared at the fiery godlings, now only yards from the altar, where Ash sat motionless, with Barnes's face blank and dead. Simon's jaw was set. "We stop them."

The specter on the main aisle looked at him without turning its head. One of Simon's tattoos flared and he found himself frozen in his stone form. His own spell had activated at the figure's glance. The shallow breath in his lungs was hardly enough to hold on to consciousness.

Kate went for a vial when suddenly another of the specters glanced her way and a glass container shattered in its place on her bandolier. She saw orange mist swirl around her and tried to back away, but her feet grew heavy. She took one hard step and found her legs trapped in her own amber.

Charlotte roared and bounded onto the glowing spirit. And then she was gone.

"Charlotte!" Kate screamed.

A solid thump alerted them to the large form of the werewolf hitting the floor near the main doors as if dropped from a great height. Dust bloomed around her and flagstones cracked. The hairy body bounced once and lay still.

Hogarth vaulted the pew box and raced to the moaning werewolf as she was blindly trying to rise. Blood dripped from her toothy mouth. Charlotte pushed briefly, but then collapsed again in a gasping pile.

"Stay down," Hogarth whispered close to the girl's large ear. "Wait until Mr. Archer has a plan. Then you can fight." He stroked Charlotte's panting snout, watching her canine eyes flick about in terror and pain.

The four illuminated Zoas came to the sides of the altar. Ash dragged herself out of their circle and collapsed against the Ten Commandments. The four heavenly figures stretched out their hands, intertwining their fingers. Light began to pulse from one godling to the next, slowly at first, then increasing in pace until a growing constant flare swirled between them.

The air in the church shimmered, caught in the birth

of a new beginning or a new end. Every column and all stonework, Simon included, shuddered as the energy inside the fragile building filled it to its capacity. The simple stone walls didn't seem capable of holding such an act of creation.

The light surrounding the four turned to white fire. It enveloped the figures and spread out to fill the four corners of the church, sweeping over all. Simon heard gasps of fear and surprise around him. One of them would have been his own if he could've drawn breath. But the fire didn't burn, just like the Sinai bush that appeared to Moses. The energy that had spread throughout the church was sucked back to the altar and swirled tightly about the four figures, pulling them all into the center of the engulfing vortex. An even more brilliant light emerged from the four, a new, singular, beating heart. Simon couldn't look away. His lungs burned with starvation. He felt his consciousness slipping.

A new figure coalesced above the altar in the center of the whirling galaxy. It ripped the particles of the four emanations into the air, pulling them apart and absorbing their essences until finally they were no more. The vast ocean of aether that had coalesced in the church began to pour into the thing that was rising now. It was a giant of human shape, devoid of gender, beyond perception, clothed in fire. This being was no mortal. It was a thing outside this world. Its gaze drifted about the church, taking in all present.

Ash struggled awkwardly to her feet and looked up at the magnificent creature even though they were the same height, and announced in slurred speech, "Great Albion, I have called you. You are bound to me."

Albion lowered its gaze to Ash.

"You are my sword." The necromancer raised Barnes's arms to the glowing god. "You have been brought here to find the one called Gaios and destroy him."

Albion's face grew full of sublime resolution.

Simon felt no fear, only a sense of awe. His hardened skin started to crack and fall away. He managed a deep gasping breath to ward off unconsciousness. Pain stabbed at every joint and lanced his heart. His knees buckled, but he immediately whispered his strength into being and stumbled to Kate's side. His still-shaky hands began to pry the amber from around her hips.

A cackling laugh came from the main door. Two people entered the church. The first was Ambassador Mansfield, staring at Albion as an engineer studies a new bridge. He carried the ebony box in his arms. Just behind him came a second figure, hardly five feet tall, swathed in a long cloak with a full hood. Then it threw back the hood and slipped off the cloak to reveal a woman mummified in linen. The hieroglyphs on the linen illuminated in a random chaotic pattern, creating a weird, syncopated vision as the mummy walked forward.

"Holy God." Simon's shoulders dropped momentarily and he looked at the faint tattoo on the back of his hand. "Nephthys used the Skin of Ra. If she's here, what's happened to Malcolm and Penny?"

Charlotte and Hogarth were blocking the main aisle. Despite Hogarth's efforts to quiet her, the werewolf rose, snarling at the mummified Nephthys. The mummy raised a hand and her hieroglyphs blinked faster. Tendrils of linen shot from the bandaged fingers. They latched onto Charlotte and the beast thrashed with agony as aether snakes twisted about her, binding and constricting. Charlotte's furious howl became a feverish scream as she began to shift back to the form of a little girl. With a flick of her hand, the mummy sent her flying over the pew box to crash into the back corner.

Hogarth raced to her, skidding to a halt beside her.

He did a quick expert check for broken bones and serious wounds. Satisfied she was merely battered, he took his waistcoat and covered the naked girl.

The mummy now looked at Simon and Kate, daring them to make the same foolish mistake. Simon took a deep breath and clenched his fists. At the same time, Albion raised a hand and pure light lanced the mummy. She staggered. Simon squinted at the spectacle through painful tears. The hieroglyphs flared on the mummy and she regained her stance, straightening. The gods stared at each other in silent reflection. Simon could see an aether storm swirling around Nephthys. She was gathering power.

Albion raised both arms and twin bolts of radiant energy struck the Skin of Ra. This time the massive power didn't stagger Albion's opponent. The swirl of linen cascaded around the swathed figure, moving so fast the naked eye could barely keep up, sucking up the excess energy like a sponge, glowing ever brighter.

"Archer!" Ash stumbled away from the altar.

Simon drew his sword and spoke it into a blue glow. He handed it to Kate. "If Ash escapes me again, cut her down."

"My pleasure." Kate brandished the sizzling blade, her tangled hair a wild halo around her.

Then Simon launched himself at Ash, seizing the cadaver by the throat and shoulders. The lolling head turned to him and Simon felt a strange burst of cold inside his chest. The knife-edge of the necromancer's curse vanished. The sudden absence of pain was almost euphoric.

"What did you do?" Simon whispered.

"I've cured you," Ash slurred through flaccid lips. "I need you."

"Simon, you owe her nothing," Kate called out.

Ash said, "I am an idiot, Archer. I never saw this

coming. Gaios knew I would activate Pendragon's spell and raise Albion. He was just waiting for it. I was so focused on you; I thought you were his agent, trying to stop me."

"Damn it. Nephthys is working with Gaios." Simon pulled Ash close. "That's her inside the Skin of Ra."

"Yes!" Ash's voice was growing weaker in the husk of Barnes. "That creature carries the power of the god-killer. The Skin of Ra is a magic eater. If we don't stop her, she will strangle Albion in his cradle. The reign of Gaios will begin here tonight. The bloodbath will start. Choose a side, Archer: me or Gaios."

"Jesus! Enough!" came a booming voice.

All heads turned to see Malcolm and Penny standing behind Ambassador Mansfield. Malcolm had the barrel of his pistol to the American's head. He shouted, "Stop whatever the hell you're all doing or he dies."

The mummy didn't alter her attention. Her hiero-glyphs pulsed intermittently as the pure white power of Albion continued to pour over her.

Malcolm waited with an annoyed squint on his face. When he realized the two gods weren't listening to him, he bashed the heavy pistol against Mansfield's temple. The ambassador toppled to the floor with an insensible grunt. Then the massive Lancasters came up and start-ing thundering. The heavy balls struck the mummy in the back and knocked her to the floor in a tangle of writhing linen. The pistol barrels smoked and ro-tated, shot after shot. Eight .577 caliber balls slammed into the small, linen-wrapped body. The mummified figure jerked grotesquely from the pounding impacts that pushed her along the stone floor. Then she lay still.

Malcolm strode up the aisle, stepping over the crum-pled mummy, reloading his pistols as he went. He raised his guns at Albion. Before anyone could speak, the Lan-casters roared again.

Bullets flew in impossible directions, everywhere except at the shimmering specter. Plaster chipped near Simon's head. Wooden splinters flew from a shattered pew. He ducked, releasing Ash. He and Kate dropped to the floor. Hogarth went prone, covering Charlotte. Penny dove for cover near the door.

Malcolm stood in the aisle, staring at his pistols in surprise.

"Malcolm," Simon shouted. "Stop shooting at gods and come over here."

The Scotsman backed away from the unmoving Albion, his disloyal weapons still aimed. The radiant figure paid him no mind. Malcolm joined Simon and glared at Ash, who stood with chest cut open and heart exposed.

"Barnes looks terrible." Malcolm reloaded his pistols.

"Long story." Simon brushed plaster and wood from Kate's hair and turned to Malcolm. "Glad to see you and Penny are all right."

"Who's that then?" Malcolm jerked a thumb toward the immobile god.

"That's Albion."

The Scotsman huffed in dismay. "Good thing Blake is dead or we'd never hear the end of this."

Strange tendrils rose out of the center aisle. Strips of linen quivered in the air, touching the pews and grasping the edges of the high gallery overhead. The mummified Nephthys rose off the floor into the air, suspended by her wrappings, which twisted and reached like incredible appendages. The hieroglyphs sparked furiously. She turned toward the small group, expressionless, but full of intent nonetheless.

Simon whispered and dropped to his knee, slamming his hands flat against the floor. A shock wave rolled out from him, cracking pews and sending them erupting into the air. Nephthys took the brunt of the savage attack and the linen surrounding her flew away from her body briefly, revealing the blue skin beneath. The linen quickly swirled back into place.

Malcolm's fingers tightened on the triggers. "Right. Her, at least, I can hit."

A flashing strip of linen reached for the Scotsman in an arc of jade light. The cloth wrapped his hand and squeezed. Malcolm roared in pain as fingers were crushed against his weapon.

Simon leapt for him, grasping the linen. Several tendrils swarmed him at the same time. Suddenly, beyond his control, all of his tattoos flared at once and aether roared from Simon's body in an explosion so great it was visible to all. The room swam around him and glowed green, then red. He could barely draw a breath. The ever-brighter linen strips withdrew, leaving Malcolm clutching his hand, but he forgot it when he saw Simon collapse to the floor in a silent scream.

Kate was first to the stricken magician, taking him by the shoulders. "Simon! Simon! Say something."

Simon's eyes lowered from where they had been rolled up in his head. "My God. Such power."

Kate searched him for injuries. She gasped. "Simon, your tattoos."

"What of them?"

"They're gone."

Simon looked down where his shirt was torn over his chest. Indeed, the dark greenish runes that had once covered his torso had disappeared. And he could feel no magic around him. He tossed his head back and forth, staring around like a man suddenly struck blind. He saw no aether. Panic surged at the thought of the horrible mystic cataclysm that must have occurred to rip all the aether from the air. But then, with a terrible, seeping, cold realization, he knew that the aether was not gone. He simply couldn't see it. Simon was cut adrift from the world he had known. He felt a deep ache. He was alone in a way he never had experienced before. He felt mortal. Simon closed his eyes to shut out the world.

Malcolm leapt to his feet and cracked his heavy pistol across Ash's face. The corpse's head spun with a sharp crack, and the body collapsed to the floor.

Ash lay quivering on the tiles, with her head turned sideways. The cadaver brought arms up slowly and adjusted the head with grinding sounds of bone. The voice was slurred. "What did that gain you?"

"Not for me." Malcolm turned and went toward the front to check on Charlotte. Penny followed him, regarding the dark hunter gratefully.

Simon opened his eyes again, fighting the hopelessness. He felt Kate's hands on him and concentrated on that. He had to keep working; too many people depended on him. Then a rush of blunt heat pounded into him. Everyone was shoved back by the wave of energy from the two gods facing each other.

Albion seemed to have grown to incredible size. The god was strong and beautiful, with the crystalline music of spheres coming from its every motion. The light of Heaven bathed it.

The mummy, on the other hand, had become a chaotic thing. She was a swirling mass of linen tendrils. The body of Nephthys was carried in the center of the mire like an insect wrapped in the middle of a nightmarish spider's web. Her tentacles struck out in all directions, slithering along the ground at Albion's feet, striking at the titan's well-formed trunk like adders.

Albion's halo of white furiously deterred the probing tendrils as the linen caromed off the god's light and smashed against walls, cracking the plaster and sending showers of dust and debris flying. As the fingers of linen were thrown around the church, the intensity of the colors and lights flowing along the hieroglyphs increased.

Then finally a strand of linen slipped through and struck Albion. Its eyes widened, but its expression remained staid. Another strip of cloth snapped onto Albion's arm.

"No, no," Ash howled frantically. Barnes's body was bent with one of its arms twisted in a horrific angle. "Do something! Albion won't survive her!"

Simon struggled back to his feet, intent on trying something, anything, to stop the warring gods. Several tendrils tore up the heavy wooden pews near him. The massive benches crashed around them. He bore Kate to the ground and it felt as if half a hundredweight of bricks had dropped onto him. His head pounded and his ears roared from the pain.

"Kate?" he called out roughly.

Her green eyes blinked up at him. "Still alive. We're nothing more than an afterthought to them."

Simon tried to lift the pew off, but it was immovable. His whispered commands failed to bring any strength. The enormous flood of aether cascading around ignored him. It was infuriating, like a phantom limb that seemed to respond but didn't move. He could do nothing as blow after blow of power rolled across them, pounding their mere human senses into stunned complaisance.

The insane weaving mass that had been Nephthys filled the church, smashing columns, breaking galleries, bringing down showers of stone. A portion of the roof gave way and a huge avalanche of slate and timber crashed to the floor.

Albion raged against the increasing barrage of linen. Countless strands of cloth struck, caressed, and bound the god's arms and legs, then its chest and neck. Albion braced with a roar that shook the crumbling structure. The glowing giant seized the linen in powerful hands and drew the horrifying mass that had been a mummy toward the altar. Albion's divine face was furrowed with pain and effort. Bare feet gouged furrows in the floor as the god dragged the Skin of Ra ever closer.

Albion was soon barely visible because of the horrendous linen crawling over it. The light emanating from the god was suffused by the chaos. Albion wrenched a mighty arm out and plunged it into the center of the roiling mass. Light flared from the darkness in the core of the mummified thing. Albion seized the physical heart of Ra, the body of Nephthys. The massive hand of light, fighting against the steel-strong linen that pulled at its fingers, strained to close around the human shape amidst the terror. Albion's glowing eyes narrowed in triumph, and its mouth tightened in righteous fury.

Then the divine expression changed. Eyes widened with alarm. A blinding burst of light roared from its strong back. Linen strips had sliced deep along Albion's spine, releasing a raw explosion of power that shattered the stone commandments behind the altar. Multitudes of tendrils suddenly shifted in their attacks and descended on Albion's back, fighting and crowding for the chance to burrow into the god. Albion looked frightened now, fearing the approach of the void. The glowing white power was being eaten by the ancient cloth.

Countless tendrils clutched Albion. They tightened and tensed. Every hieroglyph flared at once. The god screamed as it was ripped into four pieces. The raw quarters of Albion's body bled pure light and an exquisite song. For a brief moment, the four Zoas re-formed. They appeared panicked and agonized in the grasp of Ra before the tendrils hurled them into the abyss. Darkness fell in the church.

The heavy wood of the pew suddenly shifted and Ash's dead face peered in. Decaying fingers seized the edges of the bench, and Simon found enough strength to push, sending the wreckage clattering off him and Kate.

Across the church, the hideous tangle of linen drew back into itself, re-forming around the female body at its core. The victorious god stood in the center of the aisle.

"Albion is destroyed." Ash's voice was the flat wheeze of the dead. "Everything Pendragon prepared has been wasted. All is lost."

"That's rather fatalistic," Simon said. "I'd always heard there was more steel to you, Ash."

"There is no sense denying millennia of reality, Archer. I healed you hoping you were more than I suspected, but you are not. The Skin of Ra was crafted to destroy gods and prepare their followers for conquest. Gaios has won. There is no reasonable path now but to hide and pray we survive his wrath."

Simon grimaced in anger as he used Kate's shoulder to stand. "I'll be goddamned if that's so."

Chapter 28

"HOW ARE WE GOING TO FIGHT THAT THING?" Kate asked breathlessly.

"Since we're in a church, we might want to pray," Malcolm offered, climbing to them over a large piece of marble. The few stained-glass faces still intact on the walls watched with silent empathy.

Simon stared in wonder at the destructive machine of Ra. The mummy was motionless, as if unsure of its next move now that the primary mission was accomplished. Clearly, it felt no threat from Simon and his team. It was immensely old magic that held Ra together, but Simon knew that any magic could be undone. They only needed the proper spell and the time to enact it. At the moment, they had neither of those things. His tattered group formed around him, looking expectantly for answers. "We have to break its anchor to our world."

"Nephthys," Kate said.

"Right." Simon knelt in the midst of his people. "If we can deprive it of the human being inside, we can weaken it, perhaps even sever the spell."

"That's impossible," Ash slurred. "You can't get through the Skin of Ra."

Simon frowned at the dead body. "How did you live so long? If you can't help, shut up."

Penny climbed next to Simon. "I saw her eyes when the thing was wrapping her up; it wasn't what she wanted or expected. It was horrible. It looked like it was tearing her apart."

Malcolm said, "I shot her; hit her square. Unless it's keeping her alive somehow."

"Alive may not matter. It's the connection to the human form that allows the Skin of Ra to function completely in our reality." Simon looked up at the cracking ceiling, racking his brain. "How can we separate the linen from Nephthys? My shock wave disrupted it, but I've lost that power."

"I may have it." Penny held up the small gun with the tuning fork. "I can rig this to overload. It will explode and create a disturbance similar to your shock wave. I hope."

Simon raised a thoughtful eyebrow. "We'll try it. But we need to distract it so that Penny has a clean shot." He glanced up. "Malcolm?"

The Scotsman huffed and raised a pistol. "Fine. It's what I do best around here. Distract monsters with my vulnerability."

"Right you are. Keep that thing's attention on you for as long as you can. Penny, prepare your weapon. Kate, I'm praying you have your Greek fire."

Kate looked shocked and began to run her hands over her depleted bandolier. She checked the few glass vials remaining and finally breathed out in relief. "One."

"One is all you'll need or have the chance to use." Simon stood, eyeing the writhing creature in the aisle. "Hogarth, I need you up top in case we need to pin it down. Malcolm, Hogarth, off you go. Good luck, gentlemen."

"What about me?" Charlotte now wore Hogarth's waistcoat, which came down to her thighs.

"You stand against the wall and try to stay alive," Kate commanded.

Malcolm vaulted a chunk of wreckage to maneuver toward the far side of the crumbling church. Hogarth nodded without question and climbed the pulpit into the shattered gallery over their heads.

Penny activated the tuning fork on her bizarre pistol. A rumble began to build. Her teeth chattered as the weapon vibrated into a high-pitched whine. She held it until her entire body shook wildly.

Malcolm leapt onto a pyramid of smashed pews and opened fire. The Lancaster boomed and hissed, throwing heavy balls into the mummy. The creature staggered slightly and the whipping strands of linen that had been reaching and stretching around it began to aim toward Malcolm. The Scotsman jumped down and ran, raising his second pistol and firing as he moved quickly along the wall. The mummy was punched to one knee, staggered but unharmed. More tendrils slithered out toward the fleeing Malcolm.

Simon waved his hand in front of the nearly insensible Penny, catching her attention, and signaled her to throw. With great effort, she lifted the vibrating gun, her feet slipping, and she heaved it toward the mummy. It bounced to the bandaged legs. The mummy seemed to pause in its pursuit of the Scotsman and bent slightly toward the little quivering object that was causing the stones around it to vibrate off the floor.

Then the small pistol exploded and the air rippled. The soundless impact blossomed. The Skin of Ra cracked as if it were a picture painted on glass and the mass of linen blew outward. Nephthys was visible suspended in the center of the tangle of cloth. Her body was no longer that of a nubile woman; it was a withered husk, drained of life and energy, but the linen refused to release what gave it form.

Simon shouted, "Kate, go! Destroy the body!"

Kate rushed forward, heedless of the linen writhing on the floor. She made a sweep with an open vial toward the swirling morass before it could close back around the corpse. The liquid stream burst into Greek fire as it coated the figure. Nephthys's body erupted into molten lava. Oily flames spread over top of the tangled cloth too, engulfing it in blue fire. Blackening skin peeled off Nephthys as the linen tightened back around its host. It wasn't able to secure itself about the flaming corpse, leaving gaps between the encircling cloth. A cerulean fire burned from within as if the mummy had a heart of flame.

The glowing mummy lurched toward Kate, leaving a wake of burning cinders. The stench of boiling flesh overpowered all. Kate raised her sword, knowing that it would likely do little against the enraged creature. The mummy raised an arm to strike her down, and she stabbed into the flaming heart of a god. Her sword glowed hot but lost its magic aura.

"Hogarth," Simon shouted.

The big manservant suddenly appeared overhead as he flung himself from the gallery, latching onto a great chandelier suspended over the Skin of Ra. The heavy fixture shuddered at the extra weight and the chain snapped. Hogarth managed to leap aside, bouncing roughly off flowing linen and slamming to the ground. The stumbling mummy was battered to one side under the bulk of the crashing chandelier. Linen sloughed off the crumbling body beneath. Panicked and desperate, the mummy struck out around it.

Kate swung the sword, striking away strands of cloth

that reached for her. She ducked and kicked through the churning chaos. She reached down to grab Hogarth's arm. The manservant fought to regain his feet, trying to protect Kate even as she pulled him up.

Simon dove toward them, bowling them both aside just as the center of the roof fell on the mummy, driving the god to the floor under an avalanche of stone. The creature stirred, shoving the wreckage aside. It barely maintained a human shape, glowing with a furious blue fire from inside.

Simon glanced back at the floundering Ra and seized Kate's arm. "Look!"

The linen shuddered as the flaming corpse of Nephthys suddenly imploded in a shower of sooty ash and rolling black smoke, finally consumed in its entirety by the Greek fire. The Skin of Ra fell to the floor in a tangle of twisting linen.

"About bloody time!" Kate shouted, victory creasing her face with a sharp grin.

Penny and Charlotte let out joyful whoops on the far side of the church. Malcolm appeared over the edge of a barricade of wood and stone, reloading his pistols.

"Is it over?" Kate leaned against a capsized pew.

Her answer was the sound of rocks clattering to the side. Long thin tendrils of linen lifted into the smoky air. First one, then another, then many more. The ends of the cloth pressed against the floor like spindly legs and the linen lashed out to lift its now-shapeless form from the ground like a spidery tangle. It swayed, still smoldering blue in spots, sending feelers out in various directions.

"Damn." Simon retreated, pulling Kate and Hogarth with him. "There must be a way to incapacitate it. The priests of Ra couldn't have used this thing as a weapon if they couldn't control it."

"The box." Kate wiped her soot-covered face. "It must be a containment vessel. There must be a spell on it."

"It's our only hope," Simon said, then shouted, "Where's the ebony box? Where's Mansfield?"

Malcolm scoured the area. The spot where he had left the insensible ambassador in the main aisle was empty, except for wreckage.

Charlotte yelled out, "I saw that man run out with the box a few minutes ago."

"I'll find him." Malcolm sprinted for the main door, which was now ajar.

"I'll help you," Charlotte shouted as she raced to the hunter's side. When he paused, she stared up defiantly at Malcolm, expecting a rebuke. He just gave a curt nod and left. She followed in his wake.

"The Skin will look for a new host," Simon warned. "But it wants someone with magic. And none of us do . . . now." As it was, only one remained in the church that suited its purpose.

The linen made a sudden lunge toward Ash. She back-pedaled awkwardly from its spiraling grasp and shouted in surprise.

Simon ran to get between the necromancer and the tendrils of the Skin of Ra. He grabbed hold of strips of the linen and pulled them away. It reacted violently, coiling around him like a python and for a moment he thought the Skin might choose him instead. Perhaps there was still a trace of magic left in him. It tightened around him, wrapping his chest and arms, crushing the breath out of him. Then abruptly it loosened and flung him aside. He tumbled across the floor and collided with one of the columns surrounding the altar.

The Skin whipped like a snake, pursuing the staggering Ash down the side aisle. A small vial sailed over the slithering linen and smashed in front of it. A black wash of Kate's treacle elixir covered the floor like a patch of tar. The rolling wave of linen tumbled right into it and it slowed as the black concoction coated every filament. Wild tendrils flashed out and strained to reach to the corners of the once-beautiful church, wrapping itself around the galleries, roof beams, and columns. It began to pull itself free of the sticky mire.

Simon glanced up as fine bits of stone drifted over him and he saw a massive crack in the column next to him. He struggled to his feet and ran around the other side. He began to push at the crumbling buttress. "Penny! Hogarth! Help me!" Simon cursed the lack of aether. He could have toppled the damn thing easily if he still had his tattoos. Hogarth smashed a shoulder next to him and the great column shuddered. "Keep pushing!"

Penny grabbed hold of a tall brass candlestick and jammed an end of it into the widest section of the crack. Then she put all her weight against the makeshift lever. Simon saw her and put his strength on it also.

The Skin of Ra coiled, preparing to pull free of the treacle, when the column snapped loudly and suddenly shifted its weight like a great tree falling. The pillar creaked to the front and slowly toppled onto the frantic tangle of linen. The disembodied god struggled to escape as it was smashed beneath the thunderous collapse. The vibration of the tumbling column rocked the chamber. The sudden quake cracked the other weakened columns at their bases. Their huge forms slid unstoppably forward, crashing into each other, toppling in a divine cataclysm of deafening power. The Skin of Ra disappeared into the inescapable rain of stone, obscuring it in dust and tons of pure wreckage.

Simon heard nothing but crushing noise as the thunderous crash seemed to tear him apart. A choking wave of dust rolled over him, turning his world grey and thick. He covered his face, gagging on grit rushing down his throat and blinking against slivers of stone stabbing his eyes.

"Kate!" he called out, fearful that she might have gotten caught in the collapse.

"Here! I'm over here," she answered, standing near the prone body of Barnes, whose legs were crushed under a large piece of the broken column.

Hogarth and Penny helped each other to their feet as Simon stood and started to climb over the debris to get to Kate. He saw the mountain of stone shift. Among the twisted rubble, he saw something move. A burnt scrap of linen slithered out.

Simon's heart sank.

The wreckage moved again, loosing another tide of stone and wood. More horrible pale tendrils appeared and pulled themselves loose from the tomb of the ruined church. The nearest tendril grasped angrily at Simon.

He tried to move, but slipped. Something grabbed him and pulled him back. The tendril slapped down where he had just been. Noise roared in his ears. He stumbled over loose detritus as Hogarth steadied him.

A wall started to collapse along with a massive portion of the ceiling. One of the huge bells from the shattered tower above crashed down. He barely moved in time for it to thunder past him. Then a huge chunk of the gallery fell toward Penny. The strength spell was already past Simon's lips before he realized how useless it was. He shouted in alarm at Penny to jump. She gave a valiant try, but timbers fell on her and she was buried under a cloud of debris.

Hogarth was the first to Penny and he struggled to pull her limp body free. Kate also made a move to help her when the linen slapped her aside. Simon felt heavy shards of stone still falling onto his back. The church was coming down around them.

The Skin of Ra began to pull itself out of the tar. Dripping black, it crawled across the wreckage. Long tendrils of still-sparking linen lashed Ash's arm, swiftly wrapping its way from wrist to elbow. Ash screamed in terror.

"Don't let it take you!" Simon shouted at the necromancer, kicking free of rubble.

A tendril tossed aside the stone that pinned Ash. The linen quickly undulated over Barnes's body and closed over the dead features of the necromancer.

MALCOLM AND CHARLOTTE PUSHED THEIR WAY through the crowd outside. Everyone was looking at St. Mary Woolnoth, pointing and shouting or crying. Surely the militia would arrive soon; the Lord Mayor's residence wasn't far from the sounds and sights of destruction. Charlotte glanced back at the sound of another section of wall collapsing. Malcolm held her hand tight. He wasn't sure what she could accomplish in her human form, but they had few options left.

"We need the box. That's the only thing that will stop that monster."

Charlotte swallowed hard and nodded.

"We have to find that bastard Mansfield." Malcolm searched in every direction but saw no trace of the ambassador. A huge piece of the roof had slid into the road heading south, leaving Lombard Street the most likely escape route. He looked east and west and decided a man of Mansfield's limited bravery would move west so as not to pass the danger of the church. Malcolm pulled Charlotte along, searching the crowd for the familiar face.

Suddenly Charlotte tugged on his hand and dragged

him into an alley. She was moving faster, pulling him along. Her vigor was returning with every second they pushed farther away from the church and the dampening effect of the Skin of Ra. Charlotte grasped Malcolm's hand tight enough to hurt. He looked down to reassure her, but instead noticed that Charlotte was in the midst of changing. Long, clawed fingers curled around his. The waistcoat she wore ripped at the seams as she grew larger. Malcolm wanted to scream and jerk his hand away, but he did not let go. She looked up at him with amber eyes that glowed and gave a triumphant growl.

"Follow," she snarled. With a toothy grin, she sniffed the air. She had found a scent. Letting out a bark of triumph, she started running, dropping to all fours. Malcolm ran hard to keep sight of her as she loped down the alley and turned a corner.

As soon as he came around, he saw Charlotte crash against a heavy door with no effect and fall back weakly. Malcolm ran up to her as she whined in frustration. He tried the latch, but it was locked, bolted from the inside.

"Stand back." He drew a pistol and fired two rounds into the lock. A solid shove by the two of them and the door broke open. Charlotte was about to rush in, but Malcolm laid a hand on her shoulder as a warning. The young werewolf looked up at him, her muscles twitching in expectation. He leaned in and peered around the corner of the door frame. He caught a glimpse of Ambassador Mansfield before a pistol shot rang out and the wall next to his ear exploded from the impact of a bullet. Jerking his head back, he looked at Charlotte, lifting his Lancaster.

"When I make him dive for cover, in you go."

She nodded her shaggy head.

"Just disarm him."

Charlotte exhaled a disappointed growl and crouched at the ready. Malcolm extended his arm through the door. His Lancaster roared twice and Mansfield ducked behind a long table heaped with ironworks. The lithe werewolf leapt to the far side of the room and bounded toward the table. Mansfield saw her coming and raised another pistol. A bullet slammed into Charlotte. It sent her tumbling into wooden crates.

Malcolm shouted and ran inside, firing his second weapon empty before he had to duck down behind some barrels and reload. "Charlotte! Can you hear me, girl?" A sliver of fear lanced Malcolm.

Mansfield chuckled. "Your little dog is dead."

The Scotsman didn't deem to reply but scuttled forward for a better position.

"Ra will wipe this place clean of interference," Mansfield continued, "so Gaios can work his wonders."

Malcolm let him prattle on as he lifted his head to spy on his target's position. "Aren't you afraid your mummy bride will run loose without you?"

"She'll come when I call. But first she needs to deal with your friends."

"She'll have to take down all of London to do it," Malcolm snarled back.

"I doubt that. You're like bugs to her."

The bellow of a Lancaster firing rhythmically drowned out Mansfield's words. A dark shape streaked toward the ambassador, and a scream ripped through the room. Malcolm stood up and aimed both smoking pistols. Mansfield dangled from Charlotte's outstretched arm, her claws wrapped around the man's throat. Her other arm was raised, ready to strike.

"Charlotte!" Malcolm shouted.

The werewolf hesitated. Her eyes turned toward him, reflecting oddly in the limited light. There was a wildness in them, an angry resistance. On instinct, he almost pointed his weapon at her instead of Mansfield.

She growled at Malcolm, long white canines flashing, but slowly her arm lowered. Her snarl ended in a shriek of pain as she dropped Mansfield, holding her side. Mansfield scrambled away clutching a bloody knife, trying to rise to strike again. Malcolm vaulted the table, swinging his pistol like a club against Mansfield's shoulder. The man rolled to the floor, but swept up with the knife, narrowly missing gutting the Scotsman. Malcolm shot Mansfield in the knee. He then kicked the knife out of the screaming man's hand and jerked a pistol from Mansfield's belt. It was empty.

The Scotsman turned to Charlotte. She lay panting, holding a bloody gash in her side. There was a black crease along her shoulder. He dropped to one knee beside her. "Let me see."

She growled at him like any wounded animal, but did not strike. When he pulled her huge clawed hand away, it wrapped around his and she whined. He wadded up his scarf and placed it on the wound.

"Just a scratch," he told her.

"Hurts," she moaned thickly. Her voice sounded masculine. He didn't think she could say anything without the low rumble in her chest. Even with the wulfsyl, her speech was rough and broken.

"You're very delicate for a werewolf."

"I am not! That knife was as long as my claw."

"Hardly." He lifted the cloth. The wound had bled profusely, but the blood was already drying and crusting around the hole. "It's practically healed already. So is your shoulder."

That made her smile, baring her sharp teeth.

Malcolm turned back to Mansfield. "Where's the box?" The ambassador clutched his shattered leg, crying and moaning. Malcolm strode over and stepped on the man's bloody knee, eliciting a horrific scream. "Where is the box?"

Mansfield snarled through his twisted, bloodless lips. "I smashed it."

"I smell ashes on him," Charlotte offered. Malcolm caught Mansfield's frenzied glance toward the empty hearth.

"Watch him," he told Charlotte.

"Can I eat him?" Charlotte growled, and licked her lips. Mansfield went silent and pale.

"Not yet." Malcolm went to investigate the hearth. There was nothing but cold ashes in the stone maw of the fireplace. He ducked down and looked up into the cavernous chimney. Reaching his hand up, he searched the dark flue. He stretched his fingers, sliding them through grime and cold embers along the damper ledge. He touched a smooth carved surface. With a tug he produced the ebony box. It was intact. "We need to get this to Simon."

A loud roar came from outside. Malcolm ran for the door and saw the square steeple of St. Mary disappear below the surrounding rooftops. Charlotte came up beside him and whined.

"Are we too late?" she asked, pushing her large head past Malcolm.

"No," he told her firmly. He took a step forward.

Charlotte grabbed the box from Malcolm's hands and jumped away to land in a crouch. Her wound spurted again from even that small exertion.

"You're still wounded," he protested.

"I'm faster than you." And she was gone, racing toward the collapsing house of God.

THE SKIN OF RA BURIED ASH IN A LAYER OF flashing linen. Simon and Kate fought to reach the necromancer, to do something, but a barrier of cloth whipped through the air. Time and again, the hardened linen slashed at them, raising welts and slicing skin. Kate had depleted her cache of vials. Meanwhile, Hogarth tended to Penny, who lay covered in blood from wicked gashes on her head and shoulder, barely conscious. Finally, the newly re-formed mummy of Ra sent its ruined tentacles out to grasp the skeleton of the poor church. It lifted itself above the sanctuary and began to crawl away.

"Where's it going?" Kate gasped, wiping dust from her eyes.

"I don't know," Simon said. "But if it ate Ash's magic, it may be even more unstoppable. I want you to get clear while I—"

"You cannot be serious starting that sentence," she replied with a flash of anger. "I will beat the self-sacrifice out of you if I must."

Simon raised his eyebrow and gasped out a weak laugh.

Suddenly a howl filled the church. Simon spied Charlotte as she leapt over the jagged wall around them, clamping the ebony box in her jaws. Hope flared inside Simon until the mummy suddenly stopped in its perch high above the ruin. Without shifting position, it struck out at the young werewolf. Charlotte bounded off crumbling walls, cracked marble, and smashed pews with glowing tentacles in pursuit. She pivoted and spun in a miraculous spectacle of agility, hurdling through coils of living, smoldering linen. The Skin of Ra gathered its mass and flung itself at her, tendrils snapping out and missing her by scant inches.

Then Charlotte favored her side and faltered. A tendril seized her left thigh and lifted her up. Charlotte took the box from her teeth with a clawed hand that was already transforming back to human. She flung the ebony case with the last of her unnatural strength. It sailed end over end through a grasping coil of linen into Kate's waiting hands.

She quickly studied the hieroglyphs on the box and began to recite loudly in ancient Egyptian. She was the only one with a decent chance at reading the spell properly.

At the sound of Kate's chanting voice, Charlotte let out a whoop of girlish delight before she was flung to the side. Hogarth caught the child in his massive arms, slamming against the pile of rock. He set her on her feet and slipped his tattered shirt off to cover the now-naked girl. Charlotte smiled broadly at him despite holding her side, which dripped with red blood.

The mummy shuddered as Kate's voice rang like singing crystal, carefully pronouncing each word. The air around St. Mary changed from damp London to rolling waves of desert heat. The linen flew toward Kate, smashing Simon aside. It wrapped around her. Simon struggled to his feet and dug his fingers into the linen as she continued reading, desperate to complete the spell. He fought to drag the cloth away from Kate's body but it was immovable. Yards of cloth swirled around her legs and torso and pinned her hands to the box. Then strips covered her mouth, cutting off her oration, as well as her breath. She struggled against it, but she was trapped. Her green eyes darted wildly to Simon. He tried to tear the charred fabric from her mouth and nose, but the cloth refused to yield. Suddenly Hogarth was beside him, fighting the linen as well, frenzied to save his mistress. Even his incredible strength was not enough to tear the skin of a god.

Simon then attempted to pull the box from Kate's hands, anything to make the linen release her, make it attack him instead. Again, he spoke aloud a runic phrase out of instinct, but without result. There was no way to extract the ebony case from her bound hands.

Her eyes bulged from lack of breath in her lungs. Then she stopped struggling and slumped.

Terror filled Simon and he yelled. There was only one chance to get the linen off Kate. He would give Ra what it wanted: limitless power. He ran across the church. Hogarth looked at him in astonishment, unable to comprehend why Simon would leave Kate to her death.

Simon leapt onto the shattered remnants of the altar. He raised a glittering object and repeated the word his mother had taught him, praying the device still worked. The gold key flared. The air above him swirled a vast hole in the fabric of space and the map of the world with its portals appeared. Somehow it had remained untouched by the linen, perhaps because it wasn't active.

The mummy froze. All the madness of its tendrils stopped. The linen released the limp Kate into Hogarth's arms. The Skin of Ra sped toward Simon like a slithering nest of serpents.

"Kate!" Simon shouted.

Hogarth tried to rouse Kate, slapping at her face. Simon was now at the center of the coiling linen. Tentacles held Simon fast while other tendrils of cloth stabbed deep into the portal. Several of the markers on the shimmering map suddenly winked out. Unearthly lightning crackled around them. Violent energy cascaded over Simon's flesh, searing him with its fiery touch. Limitless aether flowed around him, but he couldn't gather any of it. Instead, it passed over him to surge into the linen. The Skin of Ra grew, rising high above the jagged walls of the church. Simon's eyes began to roll up in his head as the tendril about his throat tightened.

A dark shape passed Hogarth and Kate in a blur. Malcolm vaulted wreckage and dove into the aether storm surrounding Simon. The Scotsman was immediately blown off his feet. He shook his head and fought back onto his knees. Tendrils of linen wavered near him but seemed to take relatively little interest given the feast of power it was enjoying.

The quivering map was losing its vigor and becoming translucent. More portal dots disappeared. Calcutta. New Orleans. Batavia.

Malcolm dragged himself, inch by inch, onto the altar, where Simon was suspended in a linen web. He climbed, staring into the slack face of Simon, then he turned away.

The map continued to vanish. City markers blinked away. Cairo. Paris. London. Warden Abbey. The map flickered as the linen drove several more tendrils into the faint swirl in space. It was a mere whisper of energy now. The last spot on the ghostly map was Hartley Hall. That dot started to vanish.

Malcolm reached out and clasped the hand in which Simon held the key. He felt cold metal. "Marthsyl!" he shouted.

The map spun and shrank to a spot in the air. Then it vanished.

The strips of linen that had been inserted into the portal were cut. The Skin of Ra shuddered as if in surprise. Then it shook itself with an explosion of pain that threw Malcolm and Simon against the walls with enough force to break bones. The mass of linen roiled in a cataclysm, slamming itself in throes of agony. Huge stones and deadly shafts of timber flew like cannon-balls.

Kate finally stirred, eyelids flickering as she heard Simon scream in pain. She staggered to her feet with the aid of Hogarth.

Simon rose on one arm, and shouted, "Finish it!"

Hogarth had found the box behind Kate, and she snatched it from his hands. Her desperate voice rang through the church as she uttered the final words of the spell. The box in her hands snapped open. The very air filled with sand. A howling wind swept across the Skin of Ra. The linen was trapped in the whirling storm and dragged back toward Kate. The body of Barnes slipped free of the cloth and fell heavily to the ground, nothing but a decayed husk. The linen flew into the ebony box in a seemingly endless trail. When the final yard of cloth slid inside, the lid shut and locked on its own, sealing the Skin of Ra inside once again. Silence yawned in the wrecked patch of London that had been a church.

Kate gasped once in the eerie silence. Hogarth took the box from her stiff grip. She ran for Simon, who staggered up in time to gather her in a weakened embrace.

"Good work," he said to her through hisses of pain. His left arm hung limp. "And you're right, watching someone you love die is a horrible thing. Never again for either of us."

Kate kissed him hard. He relished the feel of her in his arms. She was alive. That's what mattered. The terror that had gripped his heart when her breathing stopped was the worst he had ever experienced. He let his head rest against hers.

"I'm fine too," came a creaky brogue from a pile of rubble. Malcolm pushed himself free, trailing a stream of dust. "In case you were wondering. But just go about your business. Don't mind me."

Simon helped him up with a slap on the shoulder. He then turned to find the rest of the group. Hogarth and Charlotte were tending a badly beaten Penny. The engineer turned her head, blood dripping down her bruised face. She waved, then fell back in unconsciousness. They were all still alive although the blood and agony were plentiful. Malcolm tossed Charlotte his long coat, which she donned with a broad grin, wrapping herself up in its warmth.

Simon squeezed Kate hard with a grunt of pain, then

released her. They both looked down at the desiccated body of Barnes. It was a crumbling wreck now, with no animation. Simon prodded it with his foot and the jaw fell loose to the floor.

Kate asked, "What's become of Ash?"

"I don't know. Perhaps she managed to abandon Barnes's body in time, or perhaps the Skin of Ra ate her. Given her centuries of survival, we can safely assume she has slipped back into the shadows again."

"If she's alive, don't you think she'll come after us?"

Simon put his arm around her shoulder. "Who isn't coming after us?"

He felt something cold in the palm of his hand and looked down at the key. It felt different. He spoke the ancient word for miracle, but there was no response. The magic was gone.

The same could be said for himself. They were all alive. After such a battle, he should be laughing, enfolded in aether intoxication. There was only a hush from the realm of aether. He wanted to touch it, but it was not there. Not even a ghostly whisper of it.

Kate turned to Simon and he kept smiling although inside he was petrified.

Chapter 29

JANE SOMERSET SAT QUIETLY IN THE SMALL front parlor. The only sound was the click of her knitting needles. She paid little attention to the work; she had done it so much it required none. The mere activity, the constructive repetition, gave her solace. Creation of those little objects satisfied some need in Jane. It was as if she felt the warmth they would give a poor, cold soul.

Her father sat in a chair near her, turning the pages of the newspaper. He didn't truly read much of it, but the act of turning pages made him feel productive and knowledgeable. He was still a part of society if he sat with the news every day, even if he had no memory a few hours later of what he had just read.

The sound of the door knocker surprised Jane. She heard Mrs. Cummings pass by, heading for the door. The old clock read 9:00 in the evening. It was late for visitors.

Except perhaps Mr. MacFarlane.

Jane fussed with her frock to tidy the simple lace and puff the sleeves. She put her knitting aside. Then she snatched it up again. Best to look industrious rather than just staring off into space.

Mrs. Cummings appeared at the parlor door with a strange look on her face. She seemed both surprised and judgmental of Jane's frivolous new society of late-night guests. "You have visitors, Miss Jane."

"Visitors?" she stressed the plural. Jane glanced at her father, who seemed so focused on his mission flipping the paper that he had no time for interruptions. She again put down her yarn. "I'll see them in the hall to avoid bothering Father."

Jane endured another dose of Mrs. Cummings's wary gaze as she passed with a calm smile. As she turned from the parlor toward the front door, she received a shock. In the tiny foyer stood two men and a woman. Her eyes were immediately drawn to a large man in a long coat. He wasn't fat, simply massive. If Mr. MacFarlane was a sleek black warhorse, this man was a powerful draft horse. His hair was long and stark white and he wore a full beard. It was odd to see a man with a beard in this day and age, but he wore it naturally, as if he was a relic of an earlier era. The man's face was leathered dark, but his age was still indeterminable. He was like a mountain or a great tree, rather than a man.

The second visitor was a bit more normal, in a way, but more disturbing. His posture was less assured; he seemed to twitch even when still. His eyes were deep-set and his copper red hair was wild and unrestrained. Worn clothes draped on him, badly mismatched and fashionable a generation earlier at least. He had a look that Jane had seen many times, a man who felt begrudged by the world and could barely contain his outrage. That, or he was insane.

The woman wore a long cloak that covered her completely except for her head. She had a cold visage. She held herself aloof, as a noblewoman, but her peculiarity was more than that. She seemed to Jane to be more machine than person, built to observe rather than engage in the world around her. Her hair was silver although she was not elderly, and her eyes were ice blue and distant.

The woman visitor studied the house around her while both men regarded Jane as if they had heard of her and were trying to blend knowledge with truth.

The massive man bowed. "Miss Somerset, thank you for seeing me. I realize the hour is late."

Jane stopped several feet from the trio. She was fascinated by the older man and distressed by the others. "Do I know you?"

"You do not. I am a doctor of geology and divinity, originally from Rome. This is my colleague from Dublin, Mr. O'Malley, and my companion, the Baroness Conrad."

Jane nodded to the Irishman and gave a poor curtsy to the baroness. "I would ask you in, but my father is not well."

The white-haired doctor replied. "I will be brief, for now. I am forearmed with knowledge of you, Miss Somerset. I have taken the liberty of inquiring in the parish after you and your father."

Jane tilted her head in suspicion. "Have you indeed?"

He continued, "I am a man of science and have come here to offer you an opportunity that is both rare and precious."

"Yes?"

"All I spoke to in the parish claimed that you care deeply for others. You give of yourself totally. I am a man of means, Miss Somerset, yet I appreciate the work of those who feel suffering. I want to help you do that work in ways you never imagined possible." The man stretched out his thick hands, which looked as if they could crush rock. "I want to make a substantial subscription to your soup kitchen so that you may expand its reach far beyond its current ability."

"I thank you." Jane's heart began to beat at the thought of such a windfall. Certainly she had encountered men of charity who had come to faith late in life and needed to unburden themselves by giving to others. However, this white-haired man seemed different. He didn't have the aura of a gouty lord or sickening squire trying to pay his way into heaven. "Perhaps you should speak to the parish officials who manage the kitchen rather than to me."

"No. You are the one who matters. I admire you immensely. To that point, I intend to help you and your father so that you may do even more for those who need you. I know your family has fallen on difficult financial times, and the noble gentleman, your father, suffers from some mental ague. I will do all I can for him and, at the very least, I promise he will live in all the ease and comfort he deserves."

Jane tried to suppress the elation she felt at his words. "Why, sir, are you making such promises, if I may ask?"

He stared at her as if he would burst into insulted outrage that his largesse was being questioned. Instead, he clasped his hands together. "I have a vision, Miss Somerset. I want to bring the power of Heaven to change the face of this world. I want to bring the hand of God to Earth. But, as you know, the Earth must be properly prepared to accept such power. I need you to seed this land so that the will of God can be well and truly felt. I know how to make this happen, but I need you."

The thunder of his words rolled through Jane. Her knees grew weak and she had to take hold of the staircase banister. The doctor glowed like an Old Testament prophet. She recognized the fire of mission in the man. It was a fire she understood and respected.

Her other hand went to her gaping mouth. "I . . . I don't know what to say, sir."

The white-haired man's eyes sparked like a storm on the desert. "Please, call me Gaios."

Chapter 30

THE HOTSPUR CLUB WAS AN ESTABLISHMENT OF long repute in St. James. They served an excellent dinner and had many fine rooms for hire suitable for small or large engagements. A lovely warm fire crackled in the baroque hearth with white plaster ornamentation and a dark marble mantel. A large oval table was set with crystal and candles and a spray of festive winter foliage.

Simon parted the heavy brocade drapes for the twentieth time, searching for Kate's carriage. The steepled skyline of London showed dark against the night sky. He could see no wisps of magic, no streams of aether wandering across the city as if searching for something. Even after more than a month of looking at it, the world looked different without aether, so ordinary. He contemplated murmuring one of his ancient words, but he knew there would be no response from his body. His runic tattoos were gone.

Even more, the entire mystical world of London seemed to have grown quiet as winter grew old. It was difficult to say if the clash between Albion and Ra had exhausted the combatants or shattered their plans. Ash could've been destroyed. Gaios may have altered his scheme, whatever it was. Or perhaps the whole terrifying dream of a coming battle between Ash and Gaios had been merely an exaggeration. Simon only knew the silence of the supernatural had become deafening. On the nonmagical street below, he finally saw the Anstruther four-horse chaise approaching the front.

"This is a mistake," Malcolm said as he paced by the fire with a limp, hands clasped behind his back. He looked unusually dashing in white tie.

"Everything's a mistake with you." Simon turned from the window with a smile. He brushed lint from his black swallowtail coat, ignoring the tinge of pain from his healing collarbone. "Solving murders. Keeping werewolves. Is there anything you *do* like?"

"She's not ready for this. Neither of them. It's too dangerous."

Simon walked past the table, pausing to straighten a fork with a white-gloved hand. "We'll see."

A rustle of heavy silk from the corner came as Penny sighed in exasperation. She wore a long gown of exquisite sky blue with pearls sewn along the bodice. Her hair, which was typically tied up or tied down, glistened in fashionable ringlets. Most of the cuts on her face were healed, but she would have a few minor scars. Penny retrieved a lit cigar from the tray next to her and flicked off the ash. She put the cigar in her mouth, took a long drag, and blew smoke into the air. "Is this what gentlemen do when they go off by themselves? Bicker and wait for women?"

"You spent time in male society at Cambridge," Malcolm said to her. "You should know these things."

"They were all engineers. I had hoped gentlemen were more sophisticated." Penny lifted her feet onto a nearby chair and blew a perfect smoke ring into the air. "Oh well."

Malcolm eyed the engineer as she watched the delicate hoop of white haze drift into nothingness. It wasn't her enjoyment of a cigar that surprised him, but rather her comely nature in a gown. Before he could stop himself, Malcolm asked, "Do you enjoy poetry?"

She shrugged her bare shoulders. "Never thought much about it."

He pulled the small yellow book from his coat and tossed it to her. "Read this. You'll enjoy it."

Penny caught the book cleanly out of the air and flipped it open. She scanned a few lines. She looked up at Malcolm, with a grateful nod for his sharing the poetry of poor Eleanor with her. "Thank you. By the way, when can I read your poetry?"

"When I'm dead," the Scotsman droned.

"Something to look forward to." Simon pushed the drapery aside yet again.

Penny laughed and held up her empty wineglass, tilting it back and forth.

Malcolm brought the sherry decanter to her. "Nice shoes."

She crossed her leather boots. "Just pour."

Simon released the curtains and headed for the door. "I'm going down to help Kate."

Malcolm asked quickly, "Do you need help?"

"No, no. Relax. Smoke one of Penny's cigars while you wait."

Penny gave a crooked smile and drew a fresh cigar straight up out of her bodice. Malcolm stared at it with interest but waved a hand in polite refusal.

Simon swept down the stairs. They had rented the entire club for the evening. The reception hall held only the bare minimum of staff, whose discretion was paid for handsomely. These were the type who routinely kept the secrets of nobility.

A servant raced to attend Simon, calling for his cloak and hat. Simon waved him off and breezed into the frigid night in his dinner coat. His shoulder immediately began to throb. The Anstruther coach stood at the base of the portico, with footmen waiting. Hogarth saw Simon approaching and automatically opened the door so he could climb inside.

Charlotte grinned at Simon, gaping at his formal attire. "Mr. Simon! You look so handsome!"

"Thank you, *mademoiselle*. And your gown is stunning. The color suits you perfectly."

"I know! Miss Kate said it would."

Kate was in a flowing gown of deep crimson with a silver mantle over her strong, bare shoulders. Her stately appearance, however, was undone by the tension in her face. She sat next to Imogen, holding her sister's gloved hand.

"Ladies, I am to be your escort," Simon said. "I knew that if I didn't come, some other gentleman, overcome by your magnificence, would lure you to his party."

Charlotte giggled but looked with surprisingly adult dismay toward Kate, who laughed politely at Simon's glibness. Imogen simply stared down. She wore another mourning gown that had been altered to run a bit long, with a high collar and sleeves that extended to her wrists. However, there were accents of deep violet including long gloves, and her misshapen hand was hidden inside a fur muff that was on a silken cord around her neck. A hat with a long veil that prevented any view of her features covered her head.

Simon was disturbed when she pulled her tendril-fingered hand out of the muff and lifted the homunculus skull. She held it in her elegant silk-gloved hand and began to play it: *"My sister has a gold key that our father made. It's what you want. My sister has a gold key that our father made. It's what you want."*

Kate sighed. "Imogen, don't you want to come inside for dinner? The only people there are your friends. Simon. Malcolm. Penny. And Charlotte."

"My sister has a gold key that our father made. It's what you want. My sister has a gold key that our father made. It's what you want."

Simon sat back patiently next to Charlotte, letting Kate focus on her sister.

Kate's tone was warm and encouraging. "Are you worried about walking to the door? That people will stare at you? They might, but only because it is their nature to do so. You must overcome that. That is your challenge. If you don't, you allow the wrong people to win. You see that, don't you?"

The gears turned faster and the words of the skull sped up.

Charlotte added, "I'll be with you, Imogen. We can hold hands. Who cares what they think? I'd like to go in. Please? But I'll go back home if that's what you want."

The skull gradually grew silent, but Imogen continued to cradle it with her long, supple fingers.

"You have come so very far, my dear Imogen," Kate urged gently. "Everyone here who matters wants you with us for the celebration. You deserve to be here. You are a part of us. None here are perfect, but together we have overcome incredible odds time and again." Kate reached out and took the skull from her. Imogen tensed and her fingers reached out in shock.

"We are family, Imogen." Kate's voice was quiet but firm. She placed the skull on the seat across from her, next to Charlotte who stared at it wide-eyed. "You won't need that inside. Won't you come along? The others are waiting. Let's not disappoint them."

Imogen sat stone still, her hands clasping together tightly. A small shape appeared from the muff and her hedgehog waddled out onto her lap. It sat sniffing the air. She didn't appear to notice it.

"For me then," Kate said. "No matter how frightened

you are, do this for your sister. I want you to come inside. It's important to me. So I'm asking you, please, come with me. We won't stay long unless you wish it. But imagine if we have a grand time like when Father would take us out for Christmas dinner. Just us. Just family."

From inside the dark veil came a single gargled sound. "Yes."

Kate gasped and seized Imogen's arm. "You spoke! My God, Imogen, you spoke!" She turned to look at Simon, with tears already streaming down her cheeks.

Charlotte said, "I've never heard her talk. Did you hear her talk, Mr. Simon?"

Simon nodded and put a finger to his lips to silence Charlotte.

"Come, Imogen," Kate said with an unsteady voice, sliding toward the door. "Now we really have something to celebrate."

The door opened immediately. Kate moved out of the carriage and extended her arm back toward her sister. Simon sat quietly. Charlotte seemed eager enough to explode, but she stayed still.

The bustle of traffic roared in the street around them, and dozens of strolling Londoners glanced curiously at the livery coach. The horse's breath steamed into the cold night air.

Imogen herded the hedgehog back into her muff, then slowly raised her normal hand and placed it in Kate's palm. Kate drew her sister toward her. Imogen's black gown rustled as her hidden feet slid along the floor. When she reached the door, Kate held her hand tightly and took her other elbow since her strange hand was now buried in the muff. She held Imogen up as she stooped to put a tentative foot on the carriage step. The poor girl was shaking in fear.

"You're doing fine." Kate helped her sister take the first ungainly step. "We'll go as slowly as you need."

Simon went out and handed Charlotte down, offering his elbow for her tiny hand.

She squeezed it, and whispered, "Have you ever been to a party with a hedgehog?"

Simon pursed his lips in thought. "Once. But I was young and I had fewer options."

The girl laughed as Hogarth closed the carriage door behind them and gave a deep bow. "Miss Charlotte. Miss Imogen. Do have a delightful evening."

Simon and Charlotte followed Kate and Imogen as they walked up the portico and inside the Hotspur Club. Some of the servants stared, no doubt wondering about the shambling figure in the veil. Certainly it was possible that she was an elderly matron, but there was something odd about her. Simon quickly told the maître d' that they would not need to have cloaks and hats taken. Kate continued to push forward, speaking quietly to Imogen, assuring her that all was well. They reached the foot of the sweeping staircase. Imogen froze.

Simon patted Charlotte's hand and slipped out of her grip. He went forward and gently took Imogen's other arm. She turned her veiled face toward him and took a deep breath. She put her foot on the steps and they started up. Kate's face was strained with emotion. Her eyes glistened in the candlelight. Imogen gained strength as she went up, long gown trailing down the dark red carpeting.

When they made the top of the stairs, Kate reached out and the two sisters embraced. Simon put a comforting hand around Charlotte's shoulders to suppress her excited bouncing. The young girl then saw Malcolm standing in the open door to the dining room and she sprinted toward the Scotsman. "Mr. Malcolm!" She threw her arms around his waist and the hunter staggered, arms raised in shock, unsure how to react. Charlotte wrestled him back into the room, where Penny's laughter came bubbling out.

Kate walked Imogen to the door and let her sister enter alone to applause and shouts of her name. Then Kate turned back to Simon and clasped his face between her two hands.

"Thank you." She kissed him. "Thank you for suggesting this evening."

"Kate, this is hardly acceptable public behavior for a lady."

"For once in your life, shut up." She put a hand behind his neck and drew him close, kissing him again. Simon tightened his arms around her, tasting her for a long moment.

She slowly slid her hand down his cheek. "I never thought I'd see this. It's a miracle."

Simon grinned, and whispered, *"Marthsyl."*

Abruptly, there was a pulse of energy against Simon's chest, where the key hung near his heart.

If you loved *The Undying Legion,*
be sure not to miss the final book
in the thrilling Crown & Key trilogy:

THE CONQUERING DARK

by

Clay Griffith and Susan Griffith

Here's a special preview:

Chapter 1

THE MADMAN'S BOOTS RANG HEAVILY AS HE strode up the nave of Westminster Abbey. His embroidered attire was old-fashioned and unkempt, including ridiculously tasseled boots and lace cuffs. The fires of Hell and damnation drenched his hands in a shimmering hot blaze, causing dignitaries on the aisle to stand and rear back while those farther away stared.

From the walls behind the stunned assembly, statues of marble men stood stoic while stone angels mourned the intrusion. Passing tomb by tomb, the red-haired man marched down the stream of time. An overdressed guard rushed forward. The intruder set him ablaze with a wave of his hand, then pitilessly sidestepped the flailing soldier.

The stunned throngs began to move in a panic toward the doors. The intruder with the burning hands swept under the arch of the choir screen and looked on the theater of coronation. His feet muddied the black-and-white-diamond floor as a squad of guardsmen formed a solid line between the intruder and the royal family, who sat facing forward on a raised dais in the spiritual center of the church.

King William IV rose from his chair, resplendent in

an admiral's uniform, and turned with annoyance to view the disturbance. Beside him, the queen gained her feet as well, nervous and pale, contrasting against the white satin of her gown overlaid with a fine gold gauze. Her purple velvet train lined with white satin and a rich border of gold and ermine bunched around her legs as she twisted toward the line of soldiers standing with their backs to them.

King William motioned for the queen and the other grandees nearby to be removed from harm's way. More scarlet-breasted soldiers moved quickly to rush the dignitaries toward the north transept, where they found their way blocked by a woman.

She had shocking short white hair and wore trousers with high boots and a metallic corset over her midsection. Even more shocking than her mannish attire and hair was the fact that she had four arms made of strong rods and struts of brass and steel. Two of her hands held pistols like some mechanical horror of a highwayman. In a third, she brandished a thin walking stick like a country squire. Her free hand gestured threateningly at the approaching crowd. "I suggest you all remain in your places."

"What is the meaning of this?" King William's voice echoed through the hallowed halls of the Abbey, even above the sounds of fear and shuffling feet. "You want to stop my coronation? So be it! But spare the lives of my subjects."

The redheaded man in the nave laughed, eyes crazed and hair wild. The heat radiating from his hands could be felt as he sneered, showing he was missing a few teeth. "You're all guilty of the same sins as the rest of us. Why should we let anyone go?"

"Enough ranting, O'Malley." The white-haired woman pointed at the king with her walking stick. "You have something we want, Your Majesty. We intend to take it."

From the shrine of Edward the Confessor located behind the altar emerged a tall, languid gentleman dressed in the finest black silks, a fashionable top hat gracing his head. His sophisticated attire was hardly complemented by the strange bulky steel gauntlets that covered his hands and forearms. In his steel-sheathed right hand he worked a thin-bladed sword that gleamed wickedly in the candlelight. Where all others fell back, only Simon Archer came forward.

"I think not," was his calm reply.

One of the woman's pistols swung with the clicking sound of a geared arm to cover the newcomer. The other gun lifted directly at the king. Simon Archer leapt onto the dais, seizing the sovereign by the shoulders and pushing him down behind the throne. Two lead balls slammed into the chair, splintering it across Simon's back as he huddled over the king.

The sound of shots unleashed the panic anew. Hordes of people made for the closest doors, some shoving and pushing to save themselves, others shouting to allow the women to go first, struggling to assert a hint of civilization in the madness. Terrified crowds roared from the makeshift galleries in the north transept, swarming around the woman with the mechanical arms but fighting to keep their distance. She tossed her empty pistols aside and began to muscle her way through the panicked herd toward the dais.

"Baroness!" shouted the fiery lunatic, but turned as he heard the sound of weapons cocking behind him.

"That's right, lad. Face yer better," scolded a new voice, one laced with a thick brogue.

The wild eyes of the madman turned gleefully, pleased that someone had dared challenge him. His desire for violence was not going to be soothed quickly. "Who are you to say such? A pompous duke or lazy English lord?"

"A Scotsman!"

Laughter roared as loud as the flames around him as Ferghus O'Malley pointed a hand at the challenger dressed in a long frock coat striding up the nave toward him. "You're a dead man."

The Scotsman's black hair was pulled back from his widow's peak into a tight tail behind him. He sported a brace of four-barreled Lancaster pistols. Malcolm MacFarlane fired off two shots before he ducked below a bolt of fire that flared over his head. From his crouched position Malcolm shot again, and the shells shattered near the cackling Irishman's head before the flaming target leapt into the surging mob that was only trying to escape him. Malcolm cursed and fought into the crowd to close on the Irishman.

Assured that the gun-wielding Scotsman protected his flank, Simon Archer drew the confused King William onto his feet. "Apologies for manhandling you, Your Majesty, but please follow the lovely lady behind you. She will lead you and the queen to safety." Though it was phrased as a polite request, the timbre of his voice brooked no argument. These two attackers—Ferghus O'Malley and Baroness Conrad—were terrible threats with a legendary history of carnage and horror.

Simon didn't check to see if, in fact, the *lovely lady* was present; he knew she would be in the proper place. A tall regal woman with auburn hair was already busy herding bishops and earls and countesses under the shadows of the poet Chaucer in the south transept. She wore a full-length velvet cloak of royal blue trimmed with gold. Despite hurried gestures, her stature and grace depicted breeding and manners.

The king hesitated with fear in his expression. "My niece. I can't leave—"

Simon turned to the north transept where the king stared. Amidst the frantic mob being manhandled by the annoyed baroness, he noted the small shape of a desperate child nearly lost in the melee. No one paid the young girl any mind. Simon nodded sharply to the worried old man. "I'll see to her, on my word. You must go quickly, sir, before the baroness can reach you." Simon signaled toward the woman behind them. "Kate, take His Majesty, would you?"

The auburn-haired woman finished giving an archbishop a shove through the door, sending his high mitre flying, then she put two fingers to her lips and let loose a sharp whistle at the king. She jerked her head at the exit behind her and tossed back her elegant cloak to reveal a calf-length wool skirt and a linen blouse across which was draped a soldier's bandolier. In place of ammunition, the leather slots held numerous glass vials. From her belt, she pulled a length of metal some two feet long with a curved grip at one end. With a flick of a finger on an unseen switch, two prongs unfolded from one end. It was a strange crossbow. She came toward the king, impatient that he was barely shuffling in her direction.

King William regarded her suspiciously until his eyes widened in recognition. "My word. Katherine Anstruther." Then he started to turn away. "But I can't leave that poor girl."

Kate grabbed the king by the arm and yanked him to the exit. She spared only a brief glance at Simon before giving the king another more gentle shove out. "Simon Archer will fetch your niece. Now come on, a little faster would be better."

With the king safe, Simon spun to the baroness, watching the stark white of her hair as she came closer through the mob. Finally the last of the stumbling nobility cleared and the strange woman with four arms stood facing Simon twenty yards away. Something moved beside her. One of her metal hands was clamped around the lacy wrist of the small girl Simon had been after.

Princess Victoria, the niece of the king and queen and the heir to the realm.

The baroness lifted the girl, who was barely eleven years old, off the ground like a fresh-bagged quail. "The king left something important behind. Now stand aside or I'll kill her."

Simon kept his sword raised but froze in his tracks.

"Run her through!" the young princess shouted, grasping the baroness's goggles and wrenching them aside.

Simon gave only the barest thought to the bold attack of the little girl before he was on the baroness, the point of his sharp blade aimed at her heart. The half-mechanical woman flinched aside, sweeping up another arm to block the thrust. Gears and pistons in the arm clicked and a series of spinning blades ratcheted out along her forearm. Sparks flew and Simon leaned forward, forcing the deadly appendage back. Princess Victoria yelped in alarm and kicked at her captor, who finally tossed the troublesome princess aside. This freed all the baroness's limbs to meet Simon.

He fell back now, ducking under her arm with the whirring blades. He instantly returned to the attack. Although he weaved his sword with masterful precision, Simon lamented that he couldn't speak the power of aether into the blade. His skill allowed him to counter and riposte the swipes from the woman without fear if she had just the one weapon. However, all four of her arms struck at him. Simon almost smiled at the challenge as the steel fists came at him with incredible speed. He parried and ducked and whirled across the floor, trying to pull the baroness away from the winnowing crowd and the small girl, who came forward rather than retreating with the mob. The ring of steel meeting steel echoed through the church.

As he deflected one mechanical arm the bladed limb drove at him from the other side. Simon grabbed it and instinctively whispered a word of power. He was over-whelmed by her strength and the whirring blades surged inches from his face before he realized his idiocy. Only months ago he would have been able to fight back by summoning magic from the aether. With but a thought and a word, he would have had nearly limitless power at his command. No more.

His fingers curled tight and electrical current rippled over his knuckles, fed by a small power source inside his gauntlet. The heat inside the glove increased, but a shower of sparks brought the spinning blades to a whin-ing halt. The baroness screamed as the current coursed along the length of her metal arm and surged into her body. That shock should have dropped a draft horse, but she still moved forward with a face contorted by pain and bloody fury. Her mechanical body was clearly insulated.

One steel arm clamped around Simon's lower back and locked into place. Then he felt her walking stick pressed flat against his throat. She pressed down into him. He felt the merciless strength of the baroness driving into him, bending him over backward until he feared his spine would snap.

"Surrender!" Simon croaked with a ludicrous confi-dence he didn't feel.

The baroness smiled at him, enjoying the pain she brought and the flash of worry that crossed his features. She licked her lips with pleasure.

Simon reached up and clutched the walking stick with his metal gauntlet. He stared directly into her goggle eyes as he twisted his arm and snapped the stick. He was a bit surprised it was just a simple walking stick, a mere affectation. But the action caused the baroness to look at her shattered accouterment with both rage and confusion. The pressure against his backbone slackened slightly.

Simon took advantage of the brief delay in her murderous attack and immediately fell back, bringing her down with him. His legs jammed into her stomach and leveraged her into the air, stunned at the difficulty of such a feat without magic to fuel his strength. With a shriek of alarm, she made to grasp at him, but he gave her no opportunity, slamming her into the high altar. The impact rang throughout the church.

She took a deep breath, seemingly stunned by the unexpected resistance, and eyed Simon warily as she pressed a small device on her belt. There was an inhuman roar from the north transept. When it was echoed by a child's scream, Simon smashed his steel fist into the baroness's face. Her head slammed into marble and she slumped against the altar. He left her there and ran toward the scream.

Princess Victoria stood facing a massive manlike shape crowding the doorway of the north transept. The hulking thing dwarfed the girl like an Alp towering over a tiny chalet. The brute was huge and muscular, hunching forward and pounding the floor with bulging arms. Its head turned and a great toothy mouth opened in a snarl. Small sharp eyes peered angrily from under a heavy brow. It was a huge ape.

The monstrous gorilla shouldered its way through the small door, breaking the frame with sheer will and muscle as it fought to answer its mistress's call. Once inside, it rested its bulk on steel knuckles. Its spine was exposed and bristled with wires and metal rods, making it a literal silverback.

"Run, Your Highness!" Simon shouted as he raced toward her and the monster. The child backed away.

The great ape came at Simon like an avalanche, scattering chairs in its wake. The man leapt to the side and, as the beast's momentum took it past him, his arm fell like a piston on the back of its wired skull. His gauntlet crackled and arcs of electricity scurried like spiders from his hand to its metallic silver back. The ape crashed heavily to the stone floor in a heap, sparking and twitching.

Victoria had paused in her flight to stop at the edge of the choir to watch Simon's confrontation with the gorilla. She instinctively reached up to Simon, who gathered the young child into his arms on the run. He sprinted past the dais, sparing a glance at the baroness, who was beginning to struggle to her feet. Simon wanted to get the girl into trustworthy hands.

A column of blistering flame rose before them. Simon covered Victoria. The copper-headed Ferghus glared at them from the nave, his fiery hand feeding the flames that blocked their way.

"This line ends here!" Ferghus laughed. "If I can't have the king, I'll take the wee one."

"We're not done!" came Malcolm's ragged voice as he kicked his way free of a barricade of smoldering chairs beneath the burning choir screen. He aimed his heavy pistols.

Fire shot out of Ferghus's gesturing hand to form a barrier between him and the Scotsman. The bullets never reached him but melted into slag and went astray.

"Bloody hell!" Malcolm cursed.

"Malcolm, get out of the way!" shouted a woman's voice from the tiers of graceful arches above. A pert figure aimed a long tube at the Irishman amidst the flames.

Malcolm MacFarlane dove between the empty pews as the woman fired a canister. Ferghus flared again, renewing the wall of flame around him. The canister struck the barrier and exploded. The concussion blasted Ferghus off his feet.

Young Victoria looked up at Simon. "He breathes fire like a dragon."

With the princess still in his arms, Simon ran past the guttering fire column into the south transept. "Have no fear. We've slain many."

Victoria's eyes widened farther when Simon deposited her in front of a young girl not much older than the princess herself, slender and dressed in a simple white shift. The blond-haired girl was staring angrily into the church as if straining to join the fight herself. "Mr. Simon, the lady with the arms is up. Do you want me to—"

"I'll see to it, thank you, Charlotte." Simon coolly took up his sword and started toward the Kaliesque woman whose form wavered beyond the flames. She had seized hold of the legendary chair of King Edward. "That won't do." He nodded knowingly to himself and called back to Charlotte over his shoulder, "Take Princess Victoria to Kate."

Charlotte gasped at the princess and attempted a panicked curtsy. "Your Majesty!"

Victoria kept her eyes locked on Simon as he charged back into the fiery maw. "Who is he? Who are you all?"

Charlotte was already pulling the princess out the door, away from the blistering heat of the flames. "His name is Simon Archer. I'm Charlotte. We fight monsters."